Suspicion of Innocence

J.C. Berger

BLACK ROSE writing™

First printing

ISBN: 978-1-61296-338-9

PUBLISHED BY BLACK ROSE WRITING

www.blackrosewriting.com

Printed in the United States of America

Suspicion of Innocence is printed in Palatino Linotype

Suspicion of Innocence

CHAPTER ONE

At 2:32 the morning of December 31 Ed Cooper lay asleep beside his wife when his emergency pager cried out in the quiet darkness. Cooper struggled from bed, dressing quickly to fend off the chill. In another minute he was out the door.

He turned on his pickup truck's blue emergency flashers for the ride to the fire station. New snow brightened the landscape. It took him three minutes to drive to the station. He pulled on his boots and protective trousers as other volunteer firefighters rushed for their gear. Cooper sat between two men on the backbench of the fire engine cab as it sped to a house fire in an affluent area on the edge of exurbia with large estates bordered by the rolling hills of horse farms.

Flames shot from the roof as the engine and a tanker arrived. A ladder truck and a rescue vehicle stopped near the house. Firefighters scrambled with hoses while others connected lights to a portable generator. Cooper pulled on his air tank and facemask. He would be going into the building with his partner Mike Mansfield. After firefighters had knocked down the flames two teams entered the house. While one team searched the main floor, Cooper and Mansfield searched the second floor in a clockwise fashion. They peered into the first four bedrooms and two bathrooms. They found no one. Cooper walked toward the master bedroom. The door was slightly ajar. He kicked it open and swept his flashlight across the room. He stopped the beam at the bed. "Holy shit, Mike," he shouted, his voice muffled somewhat by his air mask. Cooper aimed his beam at the bed through a layer of smoke hovering just above the mattress. A woman, who he would later learn was Laura Morley, had been bound with neckties to the bed's four posts spread eagle – blonde, beautiful, naked and dead. Cooper shined his light on one of her hands, and noticed a large ruby ring encircled with diamonds. He flashed the beam on her other hand and saw a wedding band and large diamond engagement ring. He pulled out a knife and was about to slash the ties when he flashed his light on her face, and then moved it toward the pillow. "Christ, Mansfield, she's been shot in the head."

Cooper radioed the chief who sent up two firefighters to cordon off the bedroom. The electrical power hadn't been shut off and tiny shocks tingled Mansfield's and Cooper's feet as they walked across the main floor. They could detect the telltale signs of arson, where strips of carpet had been burned with gasoline. Outside, they spoke with the chief who directed them to the sheriff's department squad car in the driveway.

* * *

Later that morninging, Caitlin Schroeder lay in bed half asleep. Her radio alarm had awakened her just before eight o'clock. A news headline immediately caught her attention, and the announcer continued: ". . . State Police are calling it a brutal murder at the home of a prominent physician and his wife. Firefighters called to extinguish a blaze in exclusive Windsor Township early this morning discovered the woman's body. Detectives declined to identify the victim, but the house is owned by Dr. and Mrs. Martin Morley. . . ."

Caitlin bolted up in bed. Martin Morley was her client and she was preparing to file divorce papers for him the next week.

The radio station played part of an interview with Ed Cooper: ". . . We went into the master bedroom and found the victim on the bed." He paused to search for the right words. "She was tied to the four posts of the bed. My partner and I were going to loosen her, just in case she could be revived. That's when I saw that she had been shot."

Caitlin rose and walked to the kitchen. She pulled a notepad and pen from a drawer near the telephone and called the news director at the radio station. She had known him when she had served as an assistant district attorney nearly six years earlier. The news director let her talk with the reporter who had covered the fire at the scene.

"A firefighter told me she was naked, tied spread eagle and shot through the head," the reporter explained. "Police won't confirm it, though."

"What do the police think?" she asked.

"They're not talking much, but say it has the appearance of a robbery. But Ed Cooper, the firefighter I interviewed, said he saw expensive rings on her fingers, something a robber wouldn't leave behind."

"Was she raped?"

"Don't know yet. Cooper wasn't sure, but said he didn't notice any sign of a struggle."

After hanging up she called the State Police and talked with a Sgt. Harmon, telling him that she knew that Morley's children were in Colorado skiing and that Martin had gone on a skiing trip in the Northeast, but she wasn't sure where.

"Ms. Schroeder, do your client a favor," the officer said on the phone. "If you hear from him, have him call us immediately."

"I certainly will, Sergeant. And if he contacts you first, have him give me a call." She gave the detective her home phone number, her business number, and her cell phone number. She tried reaching Morley on his cell phone, but a connection wasn't possible. She then called several physicians Martin had been in practice with, only to leave messages with their telephone answering services.

As she made a pot of coffee, still in her flannel pajamas, she wondered what had really happened. The police had not been very forthcoming. She began to wonder how deeply the police suspected Martin Morley.

CHAPTER TWO

Four months before Laura Morley's murder, Caitlin Schroeder's professional life had teetered. Finances were tight and her practice was growing more slowly than she had expected. But that didn't diminish her sense of bravura. The morning after Labor Day, Caitlin strode into her office whipping a necktie in her right hand and carrying an oversized leather bag on her left shoulder. At forty-one, her gait was still sure and athletic.

"Maggie," she said to the receptionist, "where's Wanzer?"

"He asked not to be disturbed, Ms. Schroeder."

Caitlin smiled and moved toward Wanzer's office, necktie still snapping in time with her pace. His door was closed. She paused, she smiled, grabbed the knob and thrust the door open and announced, "Wanzer, I need help."

Startled, his head popped up from the brief he was reading. "Oh, Caitlin, come in." He smiled at her.

"How do you tie a necktie?" she asked as she waved it in front of her. "My son Michael starts seventh grade tomorrow. He has to wear a tie, and I don't know how to tie one."

Caitlin and Erik Wanzer shared an office with two other lawyers. They weren't partners, but shared the same office area and the same administrative assistant. They were independent attorneys bent on making their own fortunes in solo practice. The other two attorneys were quite successful at it, but Caitlin and Erik struggled.

"You still determined to send him to that private school?" Erik asked.

"I want him to be better educated than the rest of us." She could hardly afford the tuition, even with Michael's father paying half of it.

"Shouldn't be difficult ending up smarter than us." Erik shook his head. "What kind of knot?"

"A proper knot." Caitlin watched him rise from his chair and walk around his desk. His light brown hair, void of any gray, was slightly awry. His face had a certain charm that she admired.

"A four-in-hand, then," Erik said as he approached Caitlin. "It's not as symmetrical as a Windsor, but a lot classier." He adjusted the knot of his own tie for emphasis. He placed the tie around her neck. Erik was five-foot-ten, but Caitlin was a bit taller. Erik awkwardly tried to knot the necktie, trying to keep his wrists and hands away from her breasts. "You know, your. . . ," he stopped, unsure of what word to use. "I mean it kinda gives me a bad angle."

Caitlin laughed. "You mean my breasts are too big?" She watched Erik blush.

"I don't think they're particularly big."

"No, no. I mean, you're a little taller, so, anatomically I'm at a bad angle. Also, we need a mirror. I have to do this from behind, as if I were tying it on myself." Erik blushed again.

"Anatomically speaking, are my breasts too small?"

Erik's face flushed. "Oh, God, how'd I get into this. You look absolutely perfect. The French, you know, have a saying for breasts."

"What?"

"No, I'm not going to get into this. We have to study necktie tying, not French."

"Let's use the men's room."

They left for the restroom. He checked to make sure no one was inside. He asked her to take her shoes off then stood behind her with his arms over her shoulders. She stooped slightly. He tied the necktie for her. Moving to her front, Erik re-tied it twice then guided her hands through the motions. "Okay, Caitlin. Let's go back to my office. If you can tie it five times straight you'll be good enough to teach Michael."

On the way back they stopped at the coffee pot to fill their cups. In his office Caitlin quickly tied the tie five times. "Another mystery of manhood finally unveiled," she said and sat in the chair in front of Erik's desk.

"I wish it were that easy with women."

"Come to the doctor's with me this afternoon and you'll learn more than you care to."

"You sick?"

"Just the annual stuff." She brushed back a strand of hair.

"You are an unusual woman, Caitlin Schroeder."

"How so?"

"When I first met you, I would have sworn motherhood was the furthest thing from your mind. But it does consume you at times."

"Well, it was an error in judgment, getting pregnant, I mean. I didn't feel like going through an abortion. I thought I was getting old in my thirties at the time." She shrugged. "Besides, the father seemed like a decent guy, taller than me. And that's why I married him. I was pregnant, he was taller and I liked him. I hadn't planned on getting pregnant with him. Motherhood was just," and she paused briefly, "one of those sperm of the moment things."

Erik laughed in his cup, spilling a little coffee on his desk. "Is that why our relationship has been so platonic, because I'm shorter?" he asked while sopping coffee from his desk with a handkerchief.

"You're also three years younger. I don't want to rob the cradle for chrissake." This was a little game they played from time to time to keep their friendship from turning into something more dramatic.

"I've always found slightly older women more interesting, more appealing, a little sexier. Now, don't take that as condescending, Caitlin, even if it is." He leaned back in his chair and watched her laugh.

"What are you staring at?" she asked.

"Your smile. You have the nicest smile." He noticed a hint of a blush darken her cheeks.

"Condescension to compliment – you have a vast range today, Erik. You know what we have in common, though." She watched his eyebrow rise. "We're both broke. You can barely make child support on those two daughters, and I'm always searching for a buck." They had been friends for more than five years, since they started sharing office space.

"Well, not for long," Erik said.

"The big one come through, that product liability case?"

"Not yet." He rose. "Promise not to laugh?"

"At what?"

"I've got a government job lined up." He shoved his hands into his pockets and walked to the edge of his desk near her chair. "I'm going to Washington Monday for a final interview."

"What's the job?" She smiled, genuinely pleased for him.

He paused momentarily then turned away from her. "CIA."

"A damned spook?"

"No, no, legal affairs." He turned back to defend himself. "Nothing to do with terrorists, weapons of mass destruction, no drones or other evils."

Caitlin shook her head in feigned despair. "You're going to be a bureaucrat and I'm a mother. Now who'd have ever believed a thing like that?" She paused a moment. "But good for you, Erik. Just keep me posted." Caitlin glanced at her watch and suddenly sat up straight. "Jeez, I have to get to the courthouse. Two of my clients were picked up last night, wrongfully charged with drunk driving. Just common, hard working laborers celebrating Labor Day."

"Busy day?"

"Yeah, and two divorce hearings this afternoon," she said as she rose to leave.

"Pays the rent."

"What I need is a stable of wealthy clients. None of this nickel-dime junk. Something peaceful and lucrative for a change."

"You'd be bored in a month. You need that finely honed edge that worry and fear give you, Caitlin."

Fear wasn't on Caitlin's mind as she left her office building, but she shook her head at the prospect of driving to the courthouse. The Wednesday before Labor Day her car's transmission had developed a problem: she could no longer shift it into reverse. She had to park so she could leave by going forward. Caitlin only had the one car, a General Motors car they don't make any more. She couldn't afford to repair it at the moment; her resources were low and her credit cards had neared their limits.

The only time in her life when she didn't have to scrape for money was when she was married to Robert Brownell. When they moved to town eleven years earlier from Minneapolis he was general counsel for the largest bank in the region and she went to work as an assistant district attorney for the county.

The marriage ended in divorce six years later. He had become too boring, too corporate when he was promoted to vice president and general counsel of the bank's holding company. But worse, he had become too controlling. Several times he asked her to quit her job with the prosecutor's office and settle into a corporate spouse routine. "Trying those crimes seems so unseemly," he had explained. He suggested she volunteer legal services to worthy charities. They finally decided they just weren't right for each other. Her share of their settlement was enough to start her own practice. But she had been scraping ever since, scrounging for clients, fighting for every victory and penny. Caitlin loved it, sort of.

She loved it all right, except when little things went awry, such as not being able to drive her car in reverse. She sat in the car confounded by the problem. She lit a cigarette, inhaled deeply and blew out a long stream of smoke. She moved the shifting lever to the "R," but nothing happened. The automobile just would not move. She had tried it every time she had gotten into the car since it developed the problem nearly a week ago, and the results were always the same –

nothing happened, the car just sat there humming. Now she always looked for parking spots that allowed her to leave by going forward.

Her office, in a cluster of buildings designed especially for small businesses, was in the suburbs, but only seven miles from the courthouse. She spent most of the day at the courthouse working on the drunk driving and divorce cases. At four o'clock she drove to her doctor's office. The office was thickly carpeted and elegantly appointed. Even all of the magazines were current. There were sixteen physicians in the practice.

It was expensive to continue going to Martin M. Morley, despite her health care insurance, but he had been her physician for ten years, and she liked him. To help her insinuate herself better in the community he had arranged for her to become a trustee of Comfort House, a small nonprofit organization that aided battered women. She also had volunteered with him on fund raising events for Community General Hospital, where he was chief of staff for internal medicine.

After a few minutes of waiting, a nurse asked her to follow. When they approached the scale, Caitlin slipped off her shoes, set her large purse down and stepped up for the weigh-in. She stared straight at the wall. The nurse also measured her height.

"Okay, what's the damage?" Caitlin asked.

"One hundred eighty-one," the nurse replied.

"A hundred eighty-one? I don't weigh anywhere near that."

"No, no, that's your height in centimeters. You weigh only sixty-nine kilos."

"Please, give it to me in English."

"Your weight is one hundred fifty-two pounds and you're five-foot-eleven and three-eighths."

"Three-eighths?" Caitlin said. "That can't be. It's always one-quarter. I'm forty-one, you can't grow an eighth of an inch, especially at the end of the day. Your body compacts." She bent her knees slightly to demonstrate how the body shortens at day's end.

"I don't know, Ms. Schroeder, but that's what the measurer says. Want to try it again?"

Caitlin declined and they walked down the hallway to an examination room. Inside, the nurse took her temperature, pulse and blood pressure. The nurse left and Caitlin changed into an examination gown. She hung her clothes neatly on a wooden hanger. It was a dark blue wool suit. Her clothes were of good quality, not spectacular, but suitable for courtroom appearances and other works of her trade. For Caitlin fashion was not a priority.

She boosted herself onto the examination table, legs dangling over the end. In a few moments Dr. Morley knocked and entered. They shook hands and chatted some before Martin began the exam.

When the examination ended he helped her sit up. "You're fine Caitlin, not a thing wrong with you, except. . . ."

Caitlin shook her head knowing the lecture on smoking was about to begin.

"I do want you to quit smoking, though, and cut back on drinking. I'm an expert on the effects of alcohol, and it's rougher on women than on men. You combine smoking and alcohol and it's like begging for a very painful death."

"It's tough quitting smoking," Caitlin responded. "I probably should, though." She shrugged. "However, I don't drink that much."

"Every day?"

"No, and I never do more than a liter of gin in one sitting."

"I presume you're kidding." He laughed slightly and watched her nod and smile. "I'll make you a deal. I have a psychologist friend who's been very successful with hypnosis. I'll pay half his fee if you stay off cigarettes for at least a year."

"You losing too many patients?" She grinned.

"Well that's a way of looking at it, I suppose. If you quit smoking I keep you as a patient longer and make more money off you. But if you develop cancer or heart disease I have to turn you over to a specialist, a surgeon and then an undertaker." He was smiling. "Have you ever seen an embalming?"

"Just autopsies."

"That's right. You used to prosecute murder cases."

"All right, I'll try the hypnosis and cut back on booze."

Morley hesitated for a moment then said, "You're my last patient of the day. If you have some time, I'd like to talk to you about some legal needs of mine, but not here at the office."

"Want to do it over a drink?" She glanced at her watch. It was quarter after five.

"And after we just talked about drinking?" He smiled.

"One teeny martini isn't going to kill me."

"Probably not. Let's meet at the Country Club."

In the parking lot she noticed another car had parked directly in front of hers.

She slid into her car, lit a cigarette then put the car's shift lever in reverse. "Damn, damn, damn," she shouted as her car refused to move back. Martin then pulled out in his Mercedes, waving at her. She was grateful he didn't stop.

She shifted into neutral and slipped out, leaving the door open. Caitlin leaned her buttocks on the hood, kicked off her shoes and with both legs she pushed hard against the car in front of her until hers gradually moved backward. The car was on a slight incline and it rolled backwards far enough to give her room to slip out. As she returned to the car she could feel rivulets of sweat slowly roll down her back between her shoulder blades.

At the clubhouse, a rambling white wood building set back from the road, Caitlin parked her car far from the entrance where no one would block her. The Country Club straddled two counties, the more populous Adams County and rural

Johnson County. She had belonged to the club by virtue of her husband's membership. After the divorce she relinquished the privileges. She didn't mind. She didn't golf or play tennis, and she couldn't afford membership.

Morley was waiting for her at the entrance. They walked toward the bar. They took a seat next to a large window where they could see golfers teeing off for the first hole. A pair of golfers drove up in a cart. The golfers' knit shirts hugged bellies and chests burdened with fat. Caitlin looked at Martin. He was lean in a charcoal gray pinstripe suit. His light brown hair had begun to thin in the front, but it only made him more interesting to look at.

They passed a little time with idle chat and ordered their drinks, Martin asking for a Vouvray and Caitlin a martini with a twist of lemon. When the waiter brought the drinks she took a sip, winced and said politely, "I wanted a martini. A martini is made with gin, not vodka."

"You didn't say you wanted a gin martini," the waiter replied.

"That's because a martini is made with gin, otherwise I would have said a 'vodka' martini," she said, again politely.

The waiter left with the drink.

Martin was laughing.

"You can't let them get away with sloppy work," Caitlin explained and grinned.

The waiter returned with a new drink. She sniffed it and nodded approval.

"That's certainly an elegant looking drink," Martin remarked. "Reminds me of those old *Thin Man* movies."

"It's my special occasion drink, and I limit myself to one."

"Only one?"

"You know the old saw about martinis. 'Two aren't enough and three are too many.'"

Martin chuckled. "Tell that to my wife Laura, only she does vodka martinis." He paused a moment to watch Caitlin.

"What's the special occasion?" he finally asked.

"A new client." She offered what she thought was her most pleasant smile.

He smiled in return. "Indeed. I'd like to retain you as my attorney."

"Do you know the kind of law that I practice?" she asked.

"Oh, I've done my research. I remember your work as a prosecutor, all the stories in the paper, murderers and other vile types. Now you defend them, also a lot of drunk drivers, divorces, the seamy side of life. One of your colleagues, though, specializes in law for physicians. And you're also astute at contract law."

Caitlin smiled. "Have you been talking with Robert?" She watched Martin nod. He and her former husband were friends. "Robert taught one of my courses in contract law back in Minnesota," she continued. "He was teaching part time at night. I was going to law school part time and working full time at the newspaper. As a reward for the A he gave me for a final grade, I allowed him to buy me dinner."

"Well I trust his judgment on your capabilities as a lawyer." He folded his hands around his glass. "I want to sell my position in my practice. I want out. It's kind of a mid-life thing. I look in the mirror and see a rising hairline," his hand moved to the top of his forehead, "tired eyes and a sense of ennui taking hold."

"I suppose examining all sorts of bodies takes its toll," Caitlin replied.

"It's not the physical part. Once you put on the lab coat and the gloves, you've erected a barrier between yourself and the patient. There is no emotion. It becomes just a medical procedure, a step in a process. No." He shook his head. "It's later, when you look into their vapid eyes and see that your recommendations have not registered. It's just a long list of things like that. I'd like to get out. I guess I've made enough money. Perhaps I'll teach."

"Your practice does seem very lucrative, though."

"It is. I'll show you the books when we meet on this."

Caitlin nodded and reached into her bag for her calendar. They set a date for next week.

"There is one other thing." He paused briefly. "Divorce."

Caitlin's face was noncommittal. Divorce didn't surprise her. She knew Laura well enough to sense that being married to her was probably some form of hell.

"Divorce will cost me plenty, and I hate the idea of losing all that money. Oh, and money," he paused a moment, "that's one of my shortcomings, I like it too much."

Caitlin offered a bemused smile.

"Laura's father died about a year and a half ago," Morley continued. "And next month she stands to inherit about eight million. Do I get half, if we divorce after she receives the inheritance?"

Caitlin shook her head. "Off hand, I think you'd lose out on it."

"But she'll get half of what I've made?" His voice arched slightly.

"Under most circumstances she would. The assets you have accrued were done so jointly. We can go into the details at our meeting. And I'll write you a letter tomorrow letting you know what kind of information I will need for both the practice and the divorce."

Martin leaned back in his chair, sipped from his glass and said, "I could always wait until she dies, I suppose."

Caitlin raised an eyebrow and asked, "What do you mean?"

"She clearly has a death wish. Laura's an alcoholic, hides it from a lot of people, but not everybody, especially some of my colleagues. Martinis are her favorite drink." He pointed to Caitlin's glass. "Although, she is somewhat eclectic when it comes to alcohol." He shook his head. "And she's developed diabetes. She's forty-five. Too bad she doesn't smoke anymore." His lip curled ever so slightly. "But you can't time these things." He paused briefly. "Do you believe that self-destructive behavior is some sort of death wish that is ultimately rewarded?"

"Well, often that seems to be the result." Caitlin stared at his eyes then asked, "Do you think she'll make a scene?"

"Probably. She hates me and she loves to make scenes of any kind, depending on her mood. I suppose she has good reason to hate me."

"What do you mean?"

"Laura's not terribly bright, and I haven't exactly disguised my knowledge of that. Also," he paused slightly, "how can I say this?" He shifted in his chair. "Although I've been quite discreet, I've been able to find comfort elsewhere." Caitlin's smile disappeared, and Martin quickly added, "Don't worry, never with patients." He paused to tap her ringless finger, "I prefer married women."

She pulled her hand back and replied, "And I don't do it with clients either, and certainly not with married men."

"Well, good. We won't have that getting in the way of a solid professional relationship."

They talked for a few minutes, shifting away from business. She finished her drink. "I never explained my fees."

"Two hundred dollars an hour," Morley said. "At the big firms I'd pay double that, maybe more. And they'd at least double the time on the projects. That's another reason for selecting you." He sipped his wine slowly, looking at her over the rim of his glass. He put the glass down and added, "We never did discuss a retainer, did we?"

"We can do that at our meeting, but I think fifteen thousand would be a good starting point."

"Certainly." He pulled a blank check from his coat pocket. It was longer and wider than standard personal checks. From his breast pocket he retrieved a fountain pen, a large black Mont Blanc. She watched his hands as he wrote. His left hand lay flat on the table while he wrote with his right. His nails looked perfect. He wrote the check in jet black ink for fifteen thousand dollars, signed it and handed it to her.

Caitlin placed it in her bag. "I'll include a receipt with my letter."

"I think we're off to a good start," he said.

"These initial consultation meetings are always on the house," Caitlin said. She reached into her purse for her wallet.

The waiter brought the check to the table. She pulled out her last twenty-dollar bill.

"Would you note it on my account?" Martin asked the waiter. To Caitlin he explained, "You don't mind? It goes toward the monthly minimum I have to spend here."

They walked toward the exit. "You going to the black and white ball?" he asked, referring to the annual formal fund raising event for the hospital. It was always on the last Saturday of September. She had helped organize the gala, served on the committee, and had planned on attending the party. She needed *pro bono* work to keep her name before the public and to meet prospective clients. As they neared the parking lot he asked where her car was.

"By the fence, over there," she said waving in a distant general direction.

"Why so far away?"

"I like to walk. It's one of the ways I get exercise."

"Good, good. And see the hypnotist about quitting smoking."

"I promise. But one thing Martin," she paused. "If you knew all along that you would be quitting your practice, why did you offer me the deal on quitting smoking?"

"Some day some patient is successfully going to sue a physician for not emphasizing the dangers of tobacco and alcohol."

She shook her head with a bemused smile.

Caitlin started her car. It was 6:30 and she was anxious to get home. Her townhouse wasn't far from the country club in Adams County, while Martin's home was in an exclusive area in Johnson County. She turned the radio to a top forty rock music station and increased the volume. Banging her hands on the steering wheel to the beat of the music, Caitlin was happy, back in the money again. She stopped for a pizza on the way home, ordering what she called a "belly buster:" onions, peppers, sausage and pepperoni. She had just enough cash for the pizza.

She parked her car on the street, the front just inches from the driveway so she wouldn't have to drive in reverse to exit. With her big bag slung over her right shoulder she balanced the pizza on her left hip and bounded into the house announcing, "Hey, Michael, pizza tonight."

The twelve-year-old greeted his mother, and took the pizza, carrying it to the kitchen. She kissed him and rubbed his blond hair. "Mom, Dad's going to be here in ten minutes. He's going to teach me how to tie a tie."

"Oh, jeez." She pulled the necktie from her purse, saying, "Quick, in the bathroom, I'll teach you how to do this. It'll impress your father."

In front of a mirror she demonstrated the art of tying a necktie just as Erik Wanzer had taught her. Michael was wearing a t-shirt, and she said, "Go get a dress shirt on and tie it a few times for practice." She hoped her former husband wasn't bringing his wife Michelle with him. He wouldn't do a dumb thing like that, bringing the other reason for Robert and Caitlin's divorce.

Michael came back with a blue oxford cloth dress shirt with a button-down collar unbuttoned. She went through the routine again then helped him do it. Finally, he tied it three times in succession. They both faced the large mirror. Caitlin stooped and rested her cheek on the side of his face and said, "You look so handsome. You look so smart. I'm so proud of you." She squeezed him about the shoulders.

He pulled away slightly. "Why do I have to wear a tie?"

"School rules. Besides, you look like a million bucks. You make me feel good just looking at you." Michael's face reddened slightly. Just then the doorbell rang.

"It's your father. Keep your shirt and tie on."

She let Robert into the house, pleased to see him without Michelle. Caitlin and Robert were always quite cordial with each other, but their meetings were always an awkward moment for her. Kissing him on the cheek would be too familiar and shaking his hand too stiff. She just ushered him in. He was dressed in his banker's best – navy blue wool suit, conservatively cut, striped shirt and a dark red tie with little silver ducks on it. He was incredibly good looking, she thought. He carried a shirt, still in its Brooks Brothers wrapper, and a necktie.

"I thought Michael could use an extra shirt and tie," he said as they walked toward the kitchen. He declined the pizza she offered, saying he had to return to work. Then, standing stiffly, Robert asked his son, "How are you getting to school tomorrow?"

"Mom's taking me, if the car works."

"Just a little transmission problem," she said and shrugged.

"It won't go backward," Michael added. "It went out last week. I had to help Mom push it out of the driveway."

Robert looked at his ex-wife. A hint of disapproval registered in his eyes.

"The driveway slopes to the road." She laughed.

"You broke a heel," Michael replied.

"You need some money to get it fixed?" Robert asked and reached for a wallet in his inside breast pocket.

"No, no. The shoe's fine."

"I mean the car."

She could see that he was losing patience. "I've got plenty of money." She waived her hand. She saw Michael shaking his head in dismay. She hated any idea of taking money from Robert other than child support. "I'm taking the car to the shop tomorrow."

"Ah, Martin Morley must have come through."

"You know?" Now that angered her.

"Don't take this wrong," he began, "but a few days ago he

asked me about your legal skills. I didn't lie to him. I told him you were good, but more important, no one would work harder for him."

"Thanks." The word was hard to say.

"This is your chance to make the practice go, your first legitimate client, instead of all those drunk driving and child and spouse abuse cases." He folded his arms on his chest. "Why not corporate law, or a big firm? It would be very lucrative. I can make some arrangements."

Caitlin noticed Michael standing in the corner of the kitchen looking as if he wished he weren't there. She walked toward him. A small pile of straight pins from the new shirt lay on the counter next to him. He had tied his father's tie. She reached for the tie, felt the smooth silk, looked at her ex-husband and said, "I've always admired your taste, Robert. I wish I could have acquired some of that." She didn't want to talk about her practice. She detected a look of relief on Michael's face.

"You know, Caitlin, with a car like that, I'm surprised you don't have a cell phone. You can never tell when or where the car will break down."

"I have a cell phone." She picked up her purse, peered inside and fumbled around, finally extracting her cell phone. "See."

"Dad, she never uses it. It's hardly ever on."

"I use it to check for phone messages at the office when I'm at the courthouse."

Robert offered a wry smile. "What about Michael? He should have a cell phone, especially now that he's going to private school. Everyone will have one, just to check in with their mothers."

"Really, Robert, a seventh grader with a cell phone?"

Robert turned to his son. "Michael, may I buy you an I-phone?"

"Sure, Dad." He was excited with the prospect. "My friends have already taught me how to use one. I could teach mom."

Caitlin just shook her head, annoyed but in no position to argue.

When Robert left, Caitlin and Michael began eating their pizza. It had cooled, but they didn't care. Halfway through his first piece, Michael suddenly announced: "I don't think I can eat pizza anymore."

"Why?"

"Yellow dye number five. They put it in the cheese and it lowers your sperm count." He leaned back in his chair and set his slice on the plate and gave her a worldly look.

"Absolutely amazing, Michael. You're barely twelve years old. You don't even have sperm." Caitlin wanted to laugh but didn't.

"Some day."

"They don't put yellow dye in pizza cheese. Anyway, where did you hear this?"

"Friends." He examined his pizza. "The cheese looks kind of yellow tonight."

After they finished dinner Michael took the empty carton to a garbage can in the garage. While he was out, Caitlin opened the two pieces of mail, including one renewing her credit card.

Michael sat down at the table to finish his soda. He asked his mother why she hadn't accepted help from his father.

"I don't need it," she replied. "Would it ease your mind if I showed you a substantial check I received today as a retainer from a new client?" She pulled the check from her purse, and with her thumb over Morley's name, showed Michael the check, pointing to the fifteen thousand-dollar sum. "Are you impressed?" She watched him nod. "You should be. He's going to be a good client. I'll make honest money off him, no scuzzy, sleazy criminal stuff."

"You mean like armed robbery and murder?"

She shook her head in mock disbelief. "This will be more dignified."

"I like murder cases. I like reading your name in the

newspaper." Although most of her criminal work was as a court appointed defense counsel, it was not very interesting to the general public, but an occasional case made it into the newspapers and she was a hero at home. He was too young to remember news coverage of cases she had worked on as a prosecutor.

She tousled his hair. She pulled the new credit card and a letter from the envelope. Caitlin held up the card and said, "See, VISA loves me. They sent me my renewal card and this letter says, 'Ms. Schroeder, blah, blah, blah, after careful review we are increasing your maximum credit card limit by ten thousand dollars.' See, Michael, the bank loves me, VISA loves me and my clients love me. Anyway, I'll get the car fixed tomorrow. My timing was off, that's all. I like being precise and down to the last second. It's the German in me."

"What about the Irish half?"

"Well sometimes my Irish and German are in conflict. The result is the car breaks down before I'm ready."

CHAPTER THREE

On her way out to her car to leave for work in the morning Caitlin rubbed her thumb over the Army dog tag her much older brother had given her years ago. She kept the dog tag on her key ring. She didn't use it as a talisman, but touching it always conjured thoughts of her brother and family. She had never thought much about childhood while she was growing up. But later, as an adult, she figured it was a fairly good childhood. Her mother, Kathleen Malloy, was editor of a daily newspaper in a small city in the north woods of Minnesota. She kept her maiden name in business and took Klaus Schroeder's name for their personal life. Caitlin's father was a lawyer in practice by himself. Neither parent made a great deal of money, but they lived comfortably.

The summer before Caitlin began high school she started working at her mother's newspaper – minimum wage as a copy girl and janitor. Her first assignment was cleaning the rest rooms serving the newsroom on the second floor of the old Kasota stone building. As her mother handed her daughter the bathroom cleaning equipment her first day on the job she said, "You're going to develop a sense of independence. If you can clean urinals in the men's room of a newspaper, you can do anything."

During the school year she worked three hours every afternoon and four hours on Saturday morning. During her college summers she served as a reporter, an intern, covering everything from athletic events to zoning board meetings. After graduating, she quickly landed a job as a reporter with a newspaper in Minneapolis.

Her only brother had done the same, but Caitlin wasn't quite five when Sean died in Vietnam at the end of the war.

Before he had left for Vietnam he gave her one of his dog tags.

She played with the key ring as she sat in her car. She looked at the dog tag, which read "Schroeder, Sean S., US 19368879." The metal tag was only two inches long and a little more than an inch wide. There was a notch at one end. Sean had told her that when a soldier died in battle they put the tag between his upper and lower teeth and jammed the jaws together, wedging the notch between the teeth. She wondered if they had done that to him. Caitlin, saddened, cringed at the thought.

She rubbed the dog tag between her thumb and forefinger then inserted the key into the ignition. It had cost her a good piece of Martin Morley's retainer to repair the transmission.

Caitlin arrived at her office before eight o'clock, before anyone else. It was Monday morning, the last week in September. The sun shone brightly on leaves a few weeks shy of turning color. Just before nine o'clock while she worked on the Morley project, she could hear Erik talking cheerfully with Maggie and Allen Greene, the attorney who specialized in medical practices.

Erik knocked on her door and entered before she could invite him in. "Well Caitlin," he announced, "I brought a box of croissants, some jams and unsalted butter. . . *un petit déjeuner.*" Erik had lived in France, hiking the country for over a year before going to law school. He liked to toss a few French words at her now and then, since she had studied French in high school and college. Caitlin thought it a bit pretentious, but a little amusing, too.

"Is she a Francophile nut?" Caitlin asked Erik.

"Who?"

"The woman. I judge by the lightness of your step and the gaiety in your heart that you got laid over the weekend."

Erik's face turned red.

Caitlin smiled wickedly. "Ah, your face, it blushes so nicely, Erik. Clearly it was good for you. Was it good for her?"

"I didn't ask."

"You mean after your passions had reached their fevered pitch, and the thunder in your chest had subsided, you didn't roll over and whisper softly in her ear: 'How was it?'"

Erik dropped into one of the chairs in front of her desk. "You mean it shows?"

"I'm sure everyone's talking about it. They're probably all walking around nudging each other and saying, 'Erik finally got laid.'"

"Well it has been a while," he admitted.

"If it's any consolation, I've got you beat in duration of abstinence. In fact, the *Guinness Book of Records* called me the other day and said they wanted to use my name for the category of non-nun."

Erik laughed. He dunked his croissant in his coffee then bit into it, holding his hand under his chin to catch any drops that might fall.

"Dunking, that's so, so un-French," Caitlin said.

"Annoying, too, isn't it?" He grinned as he dunked it again.

"Well, yes. My father liked to take the heel of a loaf of rye bread Grandma would bring, and tear it into chunks and put them in a large mug of coffee and milk. Then he'd eat it. God, that was disgusting, especially if it drooled down his chin."

"Dunking is very American," Erik pointed out. "Ask any CIA agent worth his salt."

"Now tell me, where'd you meet her, this woman who had the strength and stamina to haul your ashes? What's her name, what's she do for a living? I hope not a lawyer. And how old is she?"

"Okay, I met her at a health club."

"I didn't know you started going to a health club."

"I started a year ago, and I've been a runner for years so I can eat more. I don't tell you everything I do, just my love life."

Caitlin rose from her chair, walked toward him and said, "Make a muscle." He did and she felt his biceps. "Very impressive." She returned to her chair and asked Erik to continue.

"Her name is Julie. She's an account executive with Crane Public Relations. And she's twenty-seven."

"I thought you like older women?" Caitlin teased.

"I do, but you won't have me. So I had to find someone young and gullible."

"I guess that's what I need to do. But I do have a date this Saturday."

"Oh?" Erik's eyebrow rose in curiosity.

"I'm not getting my hopes up. I had to ask him for the date and I had to buy the tickets."

"Doesn't sound very promising."

"It's not that bad, really. It's the hospital's black and white ball. You know, tuxes and white dresses. I had to buy two tickets because I'm on the damn committee. So that's why I asked him. Over the weekend I had to buy a formal looking dress. A very provocative one, I might add. It isn't easy, or cheap, to pretend being a prosperous attorney at law." She offered a sardonic smile. "This is setting me back a bundle and he probably doesn't even dance."

"Do you?"

"If I can lead."

"What's his name?"

"Ralph Dorrence."

Erik laughed. "He's got to be a heck of a lot older than you. Nobody born in this country and around your age or younger is named Ralph. How did you meet him?"

"He's a partner in an accounting firm, and we both serve on the Comfort House board."

"Well," Erik said, "if he's older than you and got married at an average age, then he's probably already put his children through college."

"I guess that's something to take comfort in." She shook her head in slight dismay. There had been a paucity of partners in

Caitlin's life since the divorce, not that she wasn't attracted to men, but running her practice and raising a child ate up a lot of time. Caitlin aggressively pursued men from time to time, but it took a lot of effort and often it was unimpressive in the end. She liked the three men she shared office quarters with. Two of them were married. And while she found Erik appealing, she didn't want to unbalance the office by becoming lovers. But there were moments she had a longing for Erik.

Caitlin twirled a pencil on her desk. "I look at this as kind of a business investment," she explained. "My client, Dr. Morley, will be there. And there are others I'm trying to lure as clients." She paused again for a moment to change direction. "Erik, I need some advice, professional advice. I have a hearing tomorrow before The Judge," she said, referring to rural Johnson County Judge L. Paddington Stone. He was notorious among women attorneys. Nearly every woman who had appeared before him had a war story of courtroom abuse. He often referred to female attorneys as "lawyerettes," or "bimbos of the bar." He sometimes called them "sweetie," or "cutie," making conducting business difficult.

"He called me 'honey' about a month ago," Caitlin told Erik. "I asked him to refrain from that. He looked contrite – petulant, pouting. I think it's time to play a little hardball with him."

"Don't. Not yet anyway. Save it for a better opportunity."

"Maybe you're right." She paused to light a cigarette, but realized she wasn't in her office and shook out the match. "This is no time to put up a fuss. The state's dropping charges against my client and I'm quitting smoking this afternoon."

Erik raised an eyebrow. "I'm sure the withdrawal will be pleasant for all of us."

About four o'clock she left for the hypnotist. In the car, she lit a cigarette, and inhaled deeply. She looked at her watch. She had thirty minutes, more than enough time. Caitlin took a circuitous route, chain-smoking along the way. When she arrived at the psychologist's office, which was in the same medical complex as Dr. Morley's, she carefully stored the remaining cigarettes in the glove compartment of her car – "Just in case the damned hypnosis doesn't take."

The psychologist, a young man with a sporadic facial twitch, told her that he had had great success using hypnosis, but only when the patient had a true desire to quit smoking.

Caitlin wondered how patients could be hypnotized while watching his twitch. She did agree with him, though, about wanting to quit smoking, but was uncertain it would work.

"After this, you'll still have withdrawal problems," he said. "Remember this is an addiction not a habit. So I advise exercise and lots of water and fruit juices. Lay off alcohol, coffee and tea for the first three weeks."

The hypnotist then droned, a long discussion on the positive aspects of why Caitlin wanted to be cigarette free. She couldn't find an argument against what he was saying, so she agreed with him. Eventually she slipped into a trance. She could discern what was going on, what he was saying, as if she were detached from the event and just observing. When he told her she would be in "deep, deep, sleep, deeper and deeper," she could hear herself snoring ever so slightly. Her out-of-body observer found that fairly amusing. Caitlin wasn't sure how long the process had lasted, but she wanted a cigarette as soon as she left the building. She decided, however, not to light up, and to give the hypnosis a chance to work.

CHAPTER FOUR

It was early afternoon, the last Saturday of September, and Martin Morley sat in a chair, his head tilted back over his hair stylist's washbasin. The stylist rinsed his hair then squeezed it with a towel. He escorted Martin to his station, and began to cut the doctor's hair. A plump but pretty young woman approached them, "Are we ready for our nails now, Dr. Morley?"

He said he was, and she set her equipment near his left hand and began the doctor's manicure. Martin had his hair trimmed, the gray touched up, and his nails manicured every other Saturday. It was a ritual that he enjoyed. It was important to Martin to appear prosperous and attractive. His appearance enhanced his practice and he practiced at his appearance.

Today for the trip to the barbershop – a salon dedicated to men – Martin wore tan slacks, brown tweed jacket with blue Oxford cloth shirt and dark brown silk tie with a geometric pattern of reds and yellows. He didn't believe in dressing down.

While Martin's hair had grayed somewhat, his barber was adept at maintaining it a light brown with just a hint of gray at the temples. As the manicurist buffed Martin's nails, the barber recommended a change in shampoos, suggesting something to give his hair "more body."

"Well, Hector, perhaps it's time to let my hair grow a little longer, maybe after the first of the year."

Hector – it was a name he chose for his business – looked quizzically at Martin. "Are you contemplating a lifestyle change, Doctor?"

"Perhaps you could call it that." Martin chuckled.

The manicurist finished his nails and wheeled a small table

with a vat of melted wax next to Martin's chair. Knowing the routine, he slowly dipped his left hand into the paraffin three times to coat it. She tied a clear plastic bag over the waxed hand and encased the bag with a white terry cloth mitten, then repeated the routine for the other hand.

When Hector finished cutting, he washed Martin's hair. Martin liked having his hair rinsed before and washed after the cutting. That kept cut hair from drifting underneath his t-shirt. At Hector's station the stylist brushed and blow dried the doctor's hair while the manicurist removed the mittens and wax, and massaged his hands.

"Are you going to the ball tonight?" Hector asked.

"How did you know?"

"A couple other physicians were in earlier and talked about it."

"It's a major fund raiser for the hospital," Martin explained.

"Community General is a very good hospital. My mother died there." Hector hesitated a moment. "I mean she didn't die because she went there, but that she was treated so kindly."

It was a good hospital, built in the 1960s with considerable help from Martin's late father-in-law, Sanford McDowell. His father-in-law had given considerably to the founding of the hospital and had chaired the fund-raising drive. McDowell had amassed a sizable fortune manufacturing medical products. McDowell. He had been very good at making money. But he also had wanted respect, and Community General was the way he believed he created that respect.

Martin – penurious and penny-pinching since childhood – left a two-dollar tip for the manicurist and four dollars for Hector. He knew that generosity was not one of his attributes. He opened his car door and slid onto the leather seat of the Mercedes. While careful with his money, he had no problems rewarding himself. Martin enjoyed the slight scent of leather still lingering in the car. It was a four-door sedan with every luxury. Martin loved the car, black and imposing. Martin enjoyed the trappings of success. Everything he owned was expensive. And that included Laura, but she was an expense he no longer wanted to endure.

He pulled into his driveway, pressing the button on the automatic garage door opener. The middle of the three garage doors rose. His wife's BMW convertible was on the left and a four-wheel drive, dark green Lincoln Navigator on the right. The house contained five bedrooms, a large study, a spacious kitchen with a double-sided fireplace that served the kitchen and the family room, several other rooms and a full basement with a well-stocked wine cellar and a large gaming room with a regulation billiard table. Martin didn't shoot pool. With both children now in college, the home seemed even larger. He figured he couldn't sell the house for what he thought it was worth. He had calculated his investment in the house and faithfully followed the Sunday newspaper's real estate section, but the housing market had been in a downward turmoil.

He spotted his wife sitting on a cushioned bench of the bay window in the passageway between the kitchen and dining room. She had curled her legs under her and rested a glass of white wine near her knee as she gazed out the window. Her face appeared wistful to Martin. She had been a controlled drinker, maintaining a steady state of glow from noon until bed with only occasional bouts with oblivion.

Martin had cautioned her about her drinking, but with no success. Once during a few moments of weakness – Laura had been drinking heavily for several days and was going through withdrawal – she agreed to treatment. Martin moved quickly, committing Laura to an exclusive institution – St. Alban's – fifty miles away. She was out in two weeks when they discovered she had smuggled vodka into her room.

Martin considered Laura a liability. At social gatherings she was often a loose canon rolling on a ship in a rocking sea. There was no telling whom she might insult, and sometimes, whom she might charm. Martin wanted out of the marriage, no daily reminders of Laura McDowell Morley. He shook his head as if to chase his thoughts away. He walked toward his wife. "You're looking very serene and very lovely," he said.

She turned her face and shoulders toward him, smiled softly and said, "You know, Martin, sometimes you can be so kind." She cocked her head slightly.

Martin leaned toward her and kissed her lightly on the cheek. He could detect mingling aromas of perfume and wine. He joined Laura on the ledge. "The bay window, the view and the light reflecting off your hair, it's as if an artist designed this."

"Well, I was the art director for this house," she replied. She always thought she could have been successful as an interior designer, or as an art director for an advertising agency.

"And a splendid job you did," Martin said.

Laura was an attractive woman. Although only five-foot-four, she had always seemed taller to Martin. She had begun to thicken a little, but her figure was full and still sensuous. Even Martin still found her sexually appealing at times, but he didn't like her anymore. Depending on his frame of mind he often hated her. But hate wasn't constant. And at the moment he rather liked her appearance, her disposition, and even his own.

"I'm looking forward to the party tonight," Laura said. "Daddy would be proud of his handiwork." Her voice softened to a little-girl tone and she seemed happy now.

"It's a very good hospital," Martin said. "Without his effort the hospital wouldn't exist." Martin wasn't sure if that were completely true, but it didn't matter. He suddenly found his wife appealing.

"I'll be getting Daddy's inheritance next month. What do you think I should do with the money?"

"Well, sixteen million dollars is a lot of money. You ought to hire an attorney." He rose, putting both hands in his pockets. "I just hired Caitlin Schroeder to handle some matters."

"Caitlin Schroeder?" She cocked her head.

"You know her. She's Robert Brownell's former wife," Martin explained. "I'm sure you remember Robert and Caitlin. He recommended her to me."

"Of course, I remember them. It's just that her maiden name threw me. She used to be that prosecutor in the news all the time. Now she defends criminals and drunk drivers." Laura shook her head as if Caitlin's career had taken a tragic dive.

"Robert swears she's excellent at contract law and other things. He's corporation counsel for Noreast Bancorporation and her ex-husband. What better recommendation?"

"I bet she's cheap, too," she replied with a smile bordering on the cruel. Laura often accused Martin of being cheap.

"Well, her rates are somewhat less than the big-name firms," Martin acknowledged and smiled. He was enjoying the little contest.

"What time is the party tonight?" Laura asked.

"Cocktails are at seven, dinner is at eight, Sam Johnson will say a few words for the Board of Trustees then there's dancing."

"What kind of band?"

"After dinner they'll have country and western music. The theme for the night is Texas Tux. They'll get a bunch of us up there in tuxes and cowboy hats doing a Texas two-step."

Laura giggled. "Sounds dreadful. *Passé*, too. I can't imagine you doing country dancing."

"You'd be surprised. I've been practicing around the office." He rose and imitated a two-step routine.

Laura laughed.

"I bought some fancy black dress cowboy boots and a black Stetson,' Martin added. "Wait 'till you see my outfit." He smiled.

"What should I wear? I had planned on my new beige gown.'

"Well, wear that. It's pretty on you. Besides, I bought some southwestern jewelry for both of us and a special black Mexican shawl for you that'll be perfect with that white evening gown." He had told her about the theme two months earlier and had mentioned it again just a couple of weeks ago.

"I sort of recall you talking about the cowboy theme. I thought you were kidding."

"Why don't you come up stairs and see what I bought? You might like it."

They went to their bedroom. He pulled several boxes from one of his dresser drawers. "I remembered a fine jewelry store when we were in Santa Fe for the opera a couple of years ago. Anyway, I went online and had them send me this stuff." He opened the boxes. For himself he had silver and turquoise studs and cuff links and an expensive string tie to substitute for his black bow tie. For her he had bought silver and turquoise bracelets, earrings and a barrette. These weren't the kinds of things he normally would buy, for he thought Southwestern fashions to be rather *déclassé*. But what he did buy was expensive and elegant.

Even Laura liked what he had bought. She quickly swept her hair back and inserted the large barrette. She looked in the mirror, checking both profiles. "You know, it's pretty nice," she said. "You amaze me sometimes, Martin."

He shrugged. "It ought to be pretty amusing, 500 Northeasterners pretending they're Southwesterners, cowboys in formal wear – studs and Stetsons."

"Oh, Daddy'd love that." She giggled slightly.

Martin shook his head. Daddy probably wouldn't have had any thought other than how much money the event would raise. Martin figured the dinner would net more than seventy-five thousand dollars. But all the pledges and donations would far exceed anything the dinner itself would earn. The hospital's foundation director was having a field day in a money factory.

Now, Daddy certainly would have understood that.

"What are your plans for this afternoon?" Laura asked.

"I thought I'd shower and shave, then take a snooze." He walked into the closet and undressed. He left for the adjoining bathroom in a terry cloth robe.

Despite the hair styling he had just received, he began rinsing his hair, squinting as the water streamed down his face. He saw the flesh colored form of his wife through the translucent shower door. She stepped in naked. "I thought you could use a little company."

She began washing his chest, rubbing soap over the hairs, creating a hefty lather. Then she slid her hand slowly to his stomach, then his penis. It had turned hard. "I like my men clean," she cooed as she began to soap his penis. "And when they're clean I like to do dirty things to them." She kissed him on the mouth.

He could taste a vestige of wine. He wondered why he was responding. He kissed her in return and washed her, lingering longingly on her vulva. Once out of the shower, they dried each other quickly then went to their bed where they continued making love. When they had finished, Laura dozed, snoring so faintly it almost wasn't a snore. They were both naked and uncovered. He rolled onto his left side facing her. He looked at her body, her breasts. He let his eyes drift to her pubic hair and her thighs. Clearly, he didn't hate her at the moment, but he wondered why they had made love. It was no longer a frequent practice.

He could never quite figure out why he married her. He wasn't in love, but he was in lust, as he used to tell himself. Besides, her father back then could provide all the impetus he needed to gain a successful practice. Martin squeezed his eyes shut then looked at Laura again.

A few faint stretch marks creased her lower abdomen, the battle scars of two births. Martin traced them lightly with the first three fingers of his right hand. A sense of affection engulfed him. He couldn't understand it.

He wondered about her health. He knew the consequences of years of drinking. There were so many organs affected by alcohol. He could chant the effects like a litany: high blood pressure, heart disease, digestive tract disease, immune system deficiency, prolonged bleeding. The list goes on.

He knew that women don't metabolize alcohol nearly as well as men do. She drinks like a man and will die like a man, only sooner. But when will Laura McDowell Morley die?

Not soon enough, Martin figured, suddenly remembering everything he disliked about Laura. If you wished someone dead, and made love with her, is that a type of necrophilia? He smiled inwardly at that notion then thought that she might live another year or maybe twenty-five years. There's no telling when one of those organs will give up. He rolled onto his back and pulled the sheet over their shoulders. She has all the conditions that mean she will die sooner than actuarial tables say. He remembered a biography of the writer Dorothy Parker, a heavy drinker who lived to be seventy-four. Laura probably doesn't have the strong organs of Parker. And she won't reform, so when will she die? Not soon enough. Martin Morley fell into a soft slumber.

Laura awoke before her husband. She quickly slipped on a brassiere and panties and pulled on a robe then left for the kitchen. She extracted a liter bottle of Stolichnaya vodka from a lower cabinet where she kept her daily supply of alcohol. There was also an unopened bottle of Chardonnay in the cabinet and another bottle in the refrigerator. When the wine bottle in the refrigerator would near empty, she would move the bottle from the cupboard to the refrigerator and bring up another bottle from the wine cellar that they had had built to Martin's exacting specifications. In the cupboard were also twelve-ounce bottles of club soda and quinine water. Scotch and other liquor nestled behind the mixers. She once explained to Martin, "I love my liquor larder laden," and laughed after tumbling over the tongue twister she had accidentally created.

She placed five ice cubes in an old fashion cocktail glass and poured vodka three-fourths of the way up. Then she added a smidgen of vermouth and dropped in an olive. She swirled the glass ever so gently, careful not to lose a drop. She lifted the glass to her mouth for a substantial swallow. She pulled it away, holding the glass at chest level. Laura rolled her eyes and purred softly. She offered the glass up in an imaginary toast to no one in particular.

She loved the taste of alcohol, especially the sharpness of the first swallow. And this was her first drink since waking from her nap. Even chilled, the drink created a warm glow. It was after four o'clock and she sipped slowly from her drink to spread her contentment evenly.

Laura moved about the kitchen tidying it. She continued sipping from her drink.

She thought about the sex with Martin. It was pretty good, she admitted. She made another toast, taking another swallow and then said aloud, "I done him good." She winked.

Suddenly she thought of Jim Crane, her lover. Was making love with Martin tantamount to infidelity to Jim? No! It was testimony to her love for Jim. Denying her husband sex could send a signal, perhaps alerting Martin, that she was having an affair. Besides, she mused, Jim would probably find this very erotic.

Laura knew this deception was nearing its end. It wouldn't be long and she would file for divorce then she and Jim would be free to marry.

She finished her drink and made another. This time she over poured the vodka and when she added the vermouth the drink reached the rim of the glass. She leaned forward and sipped from the lip of the glass as it sat on the counter.

Now she was suddenly angry about having made love with Martin. She knew that he had been unfaithful for many years. Laura, too, had had lovers – Jim was not her first, but he was the first she actually loved. She was certain that Martin had been the first to be unfaithful. She took a swallow from her drink and said, "Fucking bastard," adding a little fuel to her anger.

Laura took her drink and headed for their bedroom. Martin was in the shower again. She set the glass on a Stickley chest of drawers. It was an expensive piece of furniture. The bedroom had been furnished in Stickley furniture, not the early 20th century version of the arts and crafts movement, but expensive replications nonetheless.

Martin walked out of the bathroom with a towel wrapped around his hips.

"My, my, aren't we clean." Laura said. She lifted her glass for a short sip. "Had to take another shower just to wash me off?"

"What are you drinking?' Martin asked with a level tone.

"Vodka martini. Want one?"

"No thanks. I better hold off on the booze until this evening."

"You're no fun. Boring and predictable."

"A lot of physicians are."

"I like the kind who work hard and play hard." She walked toward the closet, slipping off her robe. She turned toward him, unfastened her brassier and cupped her breasts in her hands. "Maybe I'll find one tonight."

"It won't be me."

"That's because you can't get it up twice in a day."

"Not with you, anyway."

Laura suddenly ran toward him screaming, "You bastard." Her hands were up to scratch his face. He grabbed both of her wrists, and as she tried to knee him between his legs, he shifted his body so that her knee struck him mid-thigh. He was much stronger than Laura and quickly subdued her. He pushed her onto the bed. She resumed struggling, lifting her head, straining to bite his hand. She couldn't reach it.

"What the hell's the matter with you?"

"You sonofabitch," she screamed.

"Want me to call an ambulance?"

"I'll kill you. You think I'm some damn drunk like your father. You sonofabitch. I'm no alcoholic. You're just after Daddy's money." Her struggling weakened.

"I don't need your money. I make plenty of my own."

"That's all you're after is Daddy's money. I know it. You've been angling for it ever since his first heart attack. Maybe before that."

Martin placed a knee on one of her wrists and stroked her head softly with his free hand.

"Your Daddy wouldn't approve of this, Laura," he said softly. "He'd think you're overreacting. Besides, this party is for him tonight." He stroked her cheek. She quit struggling. He lessened his hold. She looked at him.

"We're announcing the new wing tonight, the one that will replace the current cardiology unit. All high tech, all modern. And it's all going to be in honor of your father. This was supposed to be a surprise. But they're going to name it after your father – the Sanford McDowell Cardiology Center. It'll be announced tonight."

Laura had begun to relax, to soften. She knew that the new cardiology section was going to be built, but had no idea that it would be named after her late father.

"Are you sure?" she asked.

"Of course." He pulled himself off her and set her free. The towel had fallen from his waist. He left thc bed, picked up the towel and re-wrapped it around his hips.

"Was this your idea?" Laura asked.

"Yes," he lied. The idea to name it after Sanford McDowell was really a consensus of everyone involved.

"That was very nice of you. But you're still not going to get any of my inheritance." Some of her former feistiness returned.

"Look, I don't want any of it. Change your will."

"I don't want to use our old lawyer." They had another attorney who had prepared wills and provided other services.

"Get a new attorney. I just hired one. She'll be at the party tonight. You can get recommendations from Caitlin."

"No way. I'll do it on my own." She paused for a moment. "What do I do when I get the check?" She rose from the bed as if suddenly discovering her nakedness. She pulled another robe from the closet and quickly put it on.

"Find a good banker," Martin advised. "Then hire an accountant, a money manager and a lawyer. It'll give you a great sense of independence."

CHAPTER FIVE

The Monday morning after the hospital fundraiser Caitlin walked into her office at a quickened pace, her large bag slung over her right shoulder, her attaché case in her left hand. Maggie, the administrative assistant, was already there, but Caitlin was the first of the attorneys to arrive. She settled behind her desk and within five minutes the telephone rang. It was a couple of minutes past eight o'clock.

The call was from the administrative assistant of William Thornton, an attorney representing the electric utility that Caitlin was suing on behalf of a client. Caitlin pulled the phone from her ear and fabricated a pained expression as the woman said, "Just a moment for Mr. William Thornton." Caitlin returned the phone to her ear to hear him ask, "Can we meet over lunch today at the club?"

"Which club?" She knew which one it was.

"The Centurion."

It was formerly a private men's club, but several years ago, two women accountants successfully forced the issue, and the board of directors on an eight to seven vote allowed women as full members. Just the year before that, the club had finally allowed women to enter the club's dining room – if accompanied by a member – through the main door. Previously, they had to enter by the back door if a member was waiting for them inside.

Caitlin hated the place. Aside from the ancient sexism, she just didn't like all the classism that the Centurion Club stood for. Although she could forgive many things, the Centurion's food wasn't very good, and that was truly unforgivable. But, she accepted Thornton's invitation. Perhaps a settlement was in the offing, she thought. The utility could afford to settle well for it was going to lose the case anyway, she figured.

Thornton's firm – Durstin Barton Bidwell – with 140 lawyers was the largest in the city. She didn't like the firm. It used to be

Durstin, Barton, & Bidwell, but "they took the damn commas and the ampersand out. What the hell's a Durstin Barton Bidwell?" she had asked her friend Erik Wanzer. She also disliked the firm because it was the largest, the snootiest, the wealthiest and the most powerful.

Shortly after she ended the telephone conversation with Thornton, Erik popped his head through the doorway. "You have a hell of a wicked grin on your face, Caitlin."

"I'm counting my golden eggs before they're laid," she said, then explained the lunch meeting and the possibility of a settlement. "It's probably the usual initial offer in anticipation of a counter, so they can make a more serious push before deciding it isn't worth the agony of defeat at trial followed by an embarrassing story in the papers," she said. Caitlin knew it was too soon to expect a settlement, although she was confident the suit would be settled before trial.

"Could be," Erik said. "But you still look pretty chipper." He paused for a moment then said, "You had that date with Ralphie. Well, come on, fair's fair. Did you finally get lucky?"

"Let's just say that the gossip columnists might write that we're 'an item.'"

"That's all you can say about the first man that you've had in how many months?"

"He asked me to be discreet." She offered a demure smile.

"Really?"

She walked toward Erik and felt the biceps of his right arm. "You seem pretty strong today. That health club is doing wonders. Would you help me move my desk so the window will be over my left shoulder?"

"Caitlin, this is the third time this week. The other day you wanted the window over your right shoulder."

"Nicotine withdrawal. It's driving me nuts. Nothing looks right in this damn room."

Erik shook his head and helped her rearrange the furniture.

* * *

A few days later in anticipation of her meeting with Martin Morley, Caitlin dressed in her best suit, a deep navy blue with a faint pin stripe. She wore a white, silk blouse open slightly at the throat. Her earrings were small and gold. She wanted to look professional and successful, and attractive.

"You have a case before the Supreme Court?" Erik asked.

"What do you mean?"

"Looks like a high court suit to me. Very lovely, *très distinguée*."

She smiled her thanks and explained, "My new client. He's coming here today."

"Ah, the Good Doctor." A slight, barely discernable edge crept into his voice. He stood straight with his legs slightly apart.

Erik then started to move toward the door, but Caitlin stopped him by asking, "Before you go would you do me a favor?"

"Sure."

"My furniture, one more time?"

Erik slapped his head and said, "Addicts, damn drug addicts," and began laughing.

"I'd like to put it all back the way it was before I quit smoking. You know, the sofa over there." She pointed to a wall near a set of bookshelves. "And I want the desk so I can see out the window. I need more light. And a view."

"A view? It's just a parking lot," he said and gestured toward the window.

"And a sidewalk. I want to see who's coming and going. Erik, I swear, this will be the last time. All the nicotine has been flushed from my system now. See, I don't even have the shakes anymore." She held her hand out steady.

Erik shook his head and said, "*Madame, à votre service*." He bowed slightly and swept his arm toward the furniture to be moved.

Caitlin had enough client work to keep her busy until Martin's four o'clock appointment. She spent the hour before his arrival reviewing notes she had taken regarding some research and a discussion she had had with one of the attorneys she shared the office with – Allen Greene. He had agreed to assist her on the sale of Martin's share of the partnership.

Martin arrived a few minutes before four o'clock. Erik was in the reception area talking with Maggie. He looked up when Martin entered, "Ah, Dr. Morley." He offered his hand. "I'm Erik Wanzer, an associate of Ms. Schroeder's." They talked for five minutes then Maggie ushered Martin into Caitlin's office.

'You don't like him, do you?" Maggie said as she returned to her station.

"I barely know him." Erik shrugged his left shoulder as if Maggie's comment were ridiculous.

"Yeah, but it shows."

"You're reading this wrong, Maggie. Besides, I'm the counselor."

"Only in matters of law and French cuisine."

Wanzer shook his head and walked away.

When Martin entered Caitlin's office, she rose and they shook hands. "No waiting for an appointment with you," Martin said with a smile. "You're much better than we doctors."

Martin settled into the chair in front of Caitlin's desk. He set his slender briefcase on his lap. "First, I'd like to give you all of the material you asked for. At least I think I have it all." He withdrew several documents and reports from his briefcase.

Caitlin put on reading glasses that had been resting on her desk.

"Are those new?" Martin asked. Caitlin looked up. "The glasses?"

"I've had them a couple of weeks."

"Presbyopia."

"Pardon me," she said and set the documents down.

"That's what happens to your eyes when middle age sets in. Presbyopia generally starts in the early forties."

"Nice word, presbyopia."

"It's from the Greek for 'old eye.'" He smiled as he watched her wince, and then he resumed, "When people start needing glasses to read or view anything up close, about age forty or so, they begin to realize their mortality. It's the beginning of middle age." There was a little merriment in his eyes. "It's the first organ they can see deteriorate."

"That's pretty amusing, seeing your eyes go. I suppose all of my organs are deteriorating."

"Certainly. The maximum heart rate for most drops about a beat per minute every year. All of the organs diminish in one way or another. Well, I shouldn't lecture."

"Not exactly a comforting thought, is it?"

"Just look at it as part of life's progression. We are all meant to die sooner or later. But anyway, your glasses are very becoming. They have a nice effect on your smile."

Caitlin thought she was blushing slightly at the compliment and muttered, "Let's get back to your legal concerns."

Allen Greene arrived and Caitlin introduced him. Allen named some of the physicians he worked with and described the legal services he had provided then returned to his office.

"Allen seems very competent and works with some pretty important practices in town," Martin said when Caitlin's colleague left.

"He's made a specialty of this. It's a nice niche that won't go away for a long time."

"Well, that's another of the reasons I'm getting out. I don't want the increasing hassle," Martin said. "Hell, it's too much of a hassle now."

"Allen will provide us with a written assessment and a fair value of your partnership. We do need an independent accountant to review it, also."

"Why can't we use my practice's accounting firm? It'd save a lot of money."

"For the same reason you're not using their attorney. They don't represent you."

"Who would you get? I really don't want a big accounting firm. They'd just eat up too much capital. How about that friend of yours, the one I met at the hospital ball, Ralph?"

"I'm a little reluctant – "

Martin waved his hand. "Don't worry about that. I have no problem using someone you're dating."

Caitlin smiled at the euphemism. "When the time comes to select an accountant, I'll give you three firms to consider, with a synopsis on each, and I'll add Ralph's as a fourth. His firm is good at this sort of thing, and I guess I'd be remiss not to include it." Caitlin then asked Martin if he had a deadline for completing the sale.

"I don't want to be hasty, but I'd like to accomplish it before the first of the year."

"Have you discussed this with any of your partners?"

"You're the only person I've told. I haven't hinted to anyone, not even my wife. I want out and I want out quickly and quietly." He hesitated a moment then continued, "Frankly, I'm tired of examining people who refuse to take care of themselves. I suppose there's more to it than that." He paused again, watching Caitlin's unreadable straight face. "I got into medicine because I was smart enough. My father was an alcoholic, an assembly worker for General Motors. My mother a waitress. Neither were particularly bright. I lucked out. Some recessive genes from eons ago just popped out. Think of all those millions of little sperm cells squirming up the uterus, each one trying valiantly to make it to the fallopian tubes in search of a nice, plump juicy ovum, and one of these dinky sperm has half my genetic makeup and it swims to the ovum that has the rest of my picture." He crossed his legs. "Considering my parents and their forebears, it is rather miraculous that I turned out the way I did." He chuckled a moment then continued, "I chose medicine because I could do it and I could get the loans to do it. And in the end it would pay well. There was no great love for humanity compelling me. Is this shocking?"

"Not at all. I suppose that's why most people choose a career. They can do it and they have an interest in it."

"I do have an interest in medicine, but it's academic, and the practice of medicine has become mechanical for me."

"Shall we discuss the divorce now?"

He nodded, uncrossed his legs then leaned forward slightly.

"You filled out the questionnaire that I sent you," Caitlin said, "so we can dispense with the mundane details. When do you want to file?"

"In January. That'll be about ten weeks after Laura receives her inheritance."

"Could you elaborate?"

"Her share of her father's estate is roughly sixteen million dollars. It's been in probate for a year and a half because of some sibling squabbling over charitable donations. The hospital took a big chunk. The disbursement is in two weeks."

Caitlin put her hands together, only the fingertips touching. "You can't realistically expect to receive any of the inheritance if you file ten weeks after she receives it."

"I figured that."

"But it may serve to diminish alimony."

"That's what I was hoping for. Our net worth is considerable, I suppose. I want as much of it as possible. I've waited a long time for this."

"What do you mean?" Caitlin asked, arching an eyebrow.

"I'd have divorced her five, six years ago, but it would have been too costly. Her father had heart disease, and I knew he was going to die within a few years and that Laura would inherit a sizable sum. So I waited. He lingered for three and probate has dallied for nearly two more. I wait no more. With

Laura's drinking and diabetes we can expect an early demise, but I don't want to wait for that either. I want out in January."

"We certainly can do that." She paused for a moment then said, "The other day you mentioned that you have had affairs over the years."

He nodded and smiled.

"Is Laura likely to accuse you of adultery? Employ delaying tactics?"

"Probably. If provoked she'd do anything to break me or make life as miserable as possible." He paused for a moment then continued, "But you know, she hasn't been exactly pure, either."

"Is she currently having a liaison?" Caitlin asked.

"I'm pretty sure she is," he replied smiling at her choice of words.

"Are you having an affair at this time?"

"Not at the moment."

"Good. I hope it stays that way until after we file." Caitlin made note on her legal pad. "If you'd like, I could hire a detective to obtain some proof of Laura's infidelity. I recommend it. This could serve you well if she tries to bring adultery accusations against you, or make the whole process more difficult."

"Oh, I like that idea. Do you have a good detective?"

"I've been using her off and on for five years. She's very good."

"Let's do it. Laura's nuts enough to make this messy, prolong it forever. Let me tell you what happened Saturday." Martin explained how he had come home in the afternoon and Laura had joined him in the shower and they made love then less than two hours later she attacked him. "After that she was fine the rest of the night. She's like the nursery rhyme of the girl with the curl in the middle of her forehead." He twirled an imaginary curl over his brow. "At one time I suppose I did love her. We met at the hospital where I was a resident. She was a volunteer. Eros intervened. She was just so extraordinarily sexy to me back then, and interesting. I don't know why, but she was. We had long walks on the hospital grounds and made love in hospital storage rooms when we were moved, which was often." He smiled at the recollection.

After Martin left, Caitlin transcribed her notes onto her computer. When she finished she sat back in her chair, staring at the screen. Dr. Martin Morley was certainly interesting. Caitlin had found his story of making love with his wife titillating. She wondered if he had recounted the episode just to arouse her curiosity. Caitlin wasn't sure what to make of him. To her there was something just a little frightening about him, but also strangely attractive.

CHAPTER SIX

In the early afternoon on the fifteenth of October, Laura Morley left the office of the executor of her father's estate with an envelope containing a check for more than sixteen million dollars. It had been a cold meeting with the lawyers, her two sisters and brother and their spouses, all unhappy with the outcome, all thinking they had deserved more – except Laura. She had come without Martin and viewed the whole scene as the opening of a new life for her.

She drove to her bank to deposit the check in her savings account, an account she held jointly with Martin. The teller suggested she talk with a bank officer since the deposit was such a large sum. Laura smiled. The wine she had during lunch had that effect on her. She met for a short time with a bank officer, a vice president, who explained a wide variety of options. She explained that she wanted to set the money aside until she could hire a financial advisor. The money was placed in existing accounts, including one that offered more interest. They were all joint accounts, but she would change all that after hiring an advisor.

She returned home, and about four o'clock decided to make herself a vodka martini. She measured the ingredients with great care – precisely four ounces of Stolichnaya vodka and exactly one half-ounce of Cinzanno dry vermouth poured into a small pitcher of six ice cubes. Laura liked to say Stolichnaya with what she thought was a Russian accent, and pronounce vodka as *vood-ka*. She swirled the liquid around in the pitcher to chill. Then she strained the drink into a long-stemmed cocktail glass. She added three olives stuffed with anchovies. Laura lifted the glass to her nose, sniffed it and then put it to her lips for a small swallow. Her eyes lit up and she purred, "Ummm, this is the best day ever."

She didn't drink martinis straight up very often. Usually she preferred them on the rocks, but this was a special occasion. And what could be more special than sixteen million six hundred seventy-six thousand ninety-three dollars and fourteen cents? She was now a totally independent woman. She would no longer have to rely on Martin. She would, of course, have to set up some sort of special account for herself, talk to a lawyer about a divorce, find a financial advisor, an accountant, and then she'd have to figure out what it was exactly that she wanted to do with her life. She definitely needed to talk to another lawyer about her will. She had to knock Martin out of her current will and leave all her money to their two children. But all in due course, of course. She took another, slightly larger swallow from her glass. It was a delicious martini. She rolled her eyes in total pleasure.

The telephone rang. It was another vice president from the bank. He wanted to know if Laura would like to meet with him to discuss her funds further. "I want to hire a personal financial manager," Laura said. "When I do that I'll be getting back to you." She figured the bank was interested in retaining her as a client.

She drank only the one martini before Martin arrived. They had planned on dinner at the club. She told him of the settlement, and explained what she was going to do with the money once she hired an attorney and accountant. He handed her a list of lawyers and financial managers. She folded the paper neatly and placed it in a filing slot in a walnut secretary in a small room that she used as her office. The office, just off the dining room, was where she liked to drink a little port after dinner and just think. She kept personal items there, mementoes and photos of her parents and her son and daughter. Her mother had died of complications resulting from diabetes ten years earlier, and her father had died of heart disease. She never concerned herself with any genetic correlation, although, Martin certainly had cautioned her many times. For a long time she had hated just about anything Martin told her. "Anyway," she said to him whenever he made mention of it, "we all have to die sometime. We might as well enjoy life while we can." And if she were drinking at the moment, she would raise her glass to underscore her comment.

One thing led to another – one little postponement after another – and a month slipped by without her contacting someone to advise her. She thoroughly enjoyed basking in the feeling of independence she had just knowing she possessed all of that money. It wasn't as though it were stuffed under the mattress. It was in the bank gaining interest. In fact, she reasoned, it was probably making more sitting in the bank than she was actually spending. And she was spending only Martin's money that he earned. That thought drew a wicked smile.

One evening when she was alone with a bottle of port in her office she calculated her financial situation. She set the port glass on the upper left corner of the desk, pulled out a pad of blank paper and a calculator. She wrote down the amount she had deposited. She tried to recall what the interest was that she was receiving. Probably, she tried to recall, averaging three and a half percent. She thought that was what it was. Then Laura tried to remember what the rates were nationally. She thought they were lower. A lot lower. But, she wrote down three and a half percent and divided it by twelve with her calculator. It came out to .002916666. She multiplied that by the money she had and came up with 48,637.49. That was the amount of money she figured she was earning a month, a lot more than what Martin took home from his practice. Of course his money was after taxes and other deductions, and certainly didn't include any funds from their various investments. But it pleased her nonetheless. If it were only 1 percent interest then her income would be only a third of $48,638.59, she thought. That's still a heck of a lot of money, Laura figured.

These were serene times for Laura. She wasn't fighting with

Martin. In fact, Martin had been unusually solicitous. She couldn't understand it. There were times these past few weeks that she felt toward him as she had when they first were married. She was pregnant at the time and loved him very much. Ah, those were lovely days, she remembered. He was in residency, working long hours. He'd come home late, crawl into bed with her, cuddle up and rub his hand over her belly swollen with their daughter Cathy.

A tear came to Laura's eye as she recalled those tender times. She sat in the armchair of her small office, lifted the glass of port. Laura took a light sip and set the glass down, centering it perfectly on an old watermark on an expensive end table. She rubbed her eyes. She knew she had to do something about this marriage, the money, too. But, might as well wait until after the first of the year, January, yes, January. Start afresh. I'll interview some financial advisors. Find a lawyer. God, I've got to talk with Jim. He'll know what I should do.

Thoughts of Jim Crane brought a smile to her face. There was something absolutely delicious in having an illicit affair, especially with someone you love. It was such a fine concoction of bad and good, sin and pleasure, lust and love. God, this is wonderful.

CHAPTER SEVEN

Anita Zombrowska, squat and square, paced the floor of Caitlin's office, puffing a cigarette. "So you quit smoking," she said. "Does my smoking bother you?"

"No," Caitlin lied. "I just pity your addiction. Of course, your lungs – putrefaction surely must have set in by now." Caitlin shook her head in mock disgust.

Anita forced a cough, tapping her chest. "Yeah, like my bank account. You can't fix my lungs, but maybe you can fix my bank account."

"That's why I asked you here. I need some proof of infidelity."

Anita rubbed her hands together, a gleeful look on her face. "Oh, that's my favorite." She had worked for Caitlin off and on for the past five years, ever since Caitlin represented Anita in her divorce. Anita described her ex-husband as a "sleazy lawyer specializing in divorce and personal injury cases, an ambulance chaser of the lowest order." Her nickname for him was "The Sonofabitch." She had learned her detective trade working for him. But since her divorce she had branched out. She had changed her name back to her maiden name and then put an *a* at the end instead of the *i*. She declared that this made it singular and feminine in Polish. Her business consisted of her, an administrative assistant and part time help from her daughter. A-Z Investigations was a good little business.

Anita sat down in the chair facing Caitlin across the desk. The private investigator was wearing baggy green sweat pants and sweat shirt and white running shoes. Short, scruffy blonde hair framed her face. She had been pretty at one time, but put on weight about ten years ago and lost some of her allure. "It's better to be short, fat and dumpy," she explained once to

Caitlin. "That way men don't hit on me. . . unless it's the end of the evening, they're alone and totally drunk."

Anita crossed her arms under her breasts, resting them on her abdomen. "So, who's the poor sucker, the fellow I get to screw for screwing?" She unfolded her arms and twisted her hand as if turning a knife into someone.

"It's a woman this time. Laura Morley, wife of Dr. Martin Morley." She handed Anita a photograph of Laura and Martin and a manila folder with a paper providing some details. "Now, you don't have to get a picture of him actually putting it into her. A little hand-holding, or kissing, or walking into a motel room together will do. We also need complete secrecy."

"Piece of cake."

"Her husband has a meeting in Palm Beach, which Laura declined to visit with him. Her husband figures she wants to be with her boyfriend, Jim Crane."

"Declined, hell, she just wants to recline with Jimbo. You know these craven housewives. And a doc's wife at that. Do you think it's good sex?" Anita snorted.

"You're a piece of work," Caitlin said shaking her head.

"You starting to get more men for divorce cases?"

"Yes."

"Word's getting around that you do a hell of a job for a woman. Men aren't that dumb. They figure you know the enemy."

Caitlin laughed. "Perhaps."

"When do I get started on this, Caitlin?"

Caitlin knew when, but looked at her calendar anyway. "It's the last Thursday of October, next weekend when the doctor leaves for Palm Beach. He's certain she'll be seeing her man then. She'll be driving her husband to the airport before noon. I'll call you with the time, and you can pick them up as they leave home."

Anita Zombrowska pulled a ballpoint pen from her purse. It was a gray Papermate retractable ballpoint pen with a black plastic clicker and shirt pocket clip. She clicked the pen and began writing on the inside cover of the manila folder Caitlin had given her. The ink was black. She stared intently at the first page in the folder. Although her face was no longer pretty, her eyes still contained considerable merriment – right at the outside corners where smile lines had deepened. It was an appealing appearance.

She resumed writing. Caitlin wasn't sure what Anita was writing.

When Anita finished she looked up, retracted the tip of her ball point as though it were an exclamation, then asked, "When you going to have a big case for me instead of this Peeping Tom stuff?"

* * *

When Martin Morley landed in West Palm Beach and checked into his hotel in nearby Palm Beach, the first thing he did was call Caitlin. "I thought the detective was going to be on the case this weekend?"

"She is," Caitlin replied.

"I didn't see anyone."

"That's the way it's supposed to work, Martin."

He paused for a moment. "I guess you're right. What does she look like?"

"She's forty-eight, blonde, short and stout – strong stout, not corpulent looking. Dresses like a middle class housewife shopping at the supermarket. Drives a late model, gray Subaru station wagon. You couldn't pick her out if you knew her."

Martin laughed. "I don't know why I was so concerned. I kept looking for a detective and couldn't see one."

"Martin, relax. Enjoy the conference. We'll take care of this end. By the way, what conference are you attending?"

"Oh, it's a seminar on practice enhancement."

"You mean sales and marketing?"

"Yeah, but we don't like those words. They're anathema to physicians."

"If you're quitting the practice, why are you attending?"

"I was committed to this conference nine months ago, before I made my decision to sell. Anyway, I'm with Philip Wain and his wife, and another colleague. Phil's one of our surgeons and I figure this might be a good time to let him know of my plans."

"That sounds reasonable. But, play it a little close to the vest, if you can."

CHAPTER EIGHT

When Laura Morley had dropped her husband off at the airport, Anita Zombrowska waited in her car behind and across from Laura's BMW on the one-way road that looped around the airport parking lots and in front of the terminal. Anita lit a cigarette, a Virginia Slims menthol. She looked at the package and nearly muttered, "You aren't what you smoke." She laughed and wondered what kind of quiet, dull life Laura led.

Laura stepped out of the car to see her husband off. She closed the trunk with a remote control device after Martin removed his case. They talked for a few moments. Laura put her hand on Martin's shoulder and pulled him to her. Anita watched her kiss him passionately for several seconds and figured Laura was probably feeling guilty for what she's about to do. Anita snickered at the notion.

They stopped kissing. Martin left and Laura returned to her car and drove off. Anita followed from a safe distance. Laura drove downtown and down a parking ramp beneath an office building. Anita knew it was the office building where Jim Crane's public relations agency was located. The detective parked in a delivery zone on the street, turned on her car's emergency flashers, and grabbed two magnetized signs. Outside the car she quickly stuck a magnetized sign on each of the front doors: A-Z Rapid Delivery. Carrying a large manila envelope and a clipboard, she dashed inside the building and waited at the bank of elevators. When one coming up from the parking area opened she saw Laura alone inside the cabin. Two people entered and she followed. She saw that Laura had pressed the button for the eighth floor. Knowing that Crane Public Relations was on the eighth floor, Anita exited at the third and took the stairs to the basement.

In the basement she talked to the parking attendant in his office near the elevator bank. "I'm just moving into the building," she said and opened her running jacket to show a sweatshirt, as though that would explain her visit. "I'll probably rent parking. How does it work?"

"Five hundred dollars a month. We give you a reserved slot." He motioned to the wall with a board of hooks, numbers and keys. She spotted Crane's name on the panel, parking area number thirty-seven.

"Mind if I look around?"

"Suit yourself, ma'am."

She found Crane's car, a dark brown Cadillac, and quickly jotted down the license number. Anita didn't think Laura and Jimbo would be long in the building. She was right. Five minutes after she returned to her car, Crane drove up the ramp and turned in the direction opposite the way Anita's car faced. Watching in the rear view mirror she waited until Crane had driven nearly a block, then Anita made a U-turn and followed. It was an easy follow. They were heading east toward one of the older suburbs, not an elegant section, but home to a lot of restaurants. There was one restaurant called the White House located in a rather secluded area. Anita suspected that was where they were going. They turned onto a wooded drive to the restaurant. Anita went to a gas station and changed clothes in the rest room. She was now wearing a dress and blue blazer. She drove to the restaurant, found Crane's car and parked about a hundred feet from it.

Just inside the building, Anita waited for her eyes to adjust to the lower level of light. She spotted Crane and Laura sitting at a table by a long bank of windows that overlooked a fairway of a golf course. The setting appeared very romantic. There were glasses of wine on the table, a partially filled bottle. Their elbows rested on the table and Crane clasped Laura's hands in his. It looked like something out of a movie, Anita thought. It would have made a great photograph to demonstrate Laura's infidelity. Anita took a seat at the bar near the couple. She knew the bartender, who brought her what she usually drank on the job – tonic and extra lime juice, no alcohol. The first sip always puckered her mouth. Anita could see Crane and Laura via the mirror of the back-bar. Her view was obstructed partially by the necks of liquor bottles stationed on a lower ledge in front of the mirror.

The lovers ordered food, then a second bottle of wine when the soup arrived. Anita couldn't catch everything the lovers said, but did hear Crane ask, "Do you think your. . . suspects."

". . . Too caught up. . . own world. He's. . . cheating on. . . for years. . . ."

"Do you think we're cheating?" Crane asked.

"No. . . we're not. . . . Besides," she paused to touch his cheek lightly, "I love you. . . ."

Crane's hair was white, making him appear older than he was. His face was nice looking with a reddish cast. He was thin and about five or six inches taller than Laura. Anita guessed he was in his early fifties. She kind of liked him, poor dupe.

The lovers seemed to be talking softer now and Anita could barely hear any words. Still looking in the mirror, she saw Laura hand a long white envelope to Crane. Anita thought she heard the word "money," but she wasn't certain. Crane peeked inside the envelope, then slipped it into an inside suit coat pocket, took her hand and kissed her fingertips. Anita wrote a few words on a slip of paper. Their voices rose slightly, loud enough for Anita to hear as she had when she first arrived. They talked about going back to his condominium for a while. Laura giggled. Anita was sure they were talking about making love. "You're such an animal," Laura said in a husky, breathy voice.

Anita thought she heard Crane respond, "You bring out the beast in me." Anita smiled, confident they would go back to his place. She slid fifteen dollars on the bar toward the bartender and left. She went back to the gas station and changed into her sweat suit, running pants and jacket.

Crane's home was in a relatively new condominium complex, just a few years old. His unit, close to a small wooded area, was fairly secluded. Anita scouted the area then returned to her car. She had brought a camera with a telephoto lens and another one with infrared equipment, just in case she had to do some night work. But she figured she could finish the job before dusk. It was a little after two o'clock.

The Cadillac pulled up to the parking spot near Crane's door. He slid out of the car and walked around to Laura's side and held the door open. They kissed as soon as she rose. Anita shot. Laura put her hand on Crane's crotch and rubbed it. Anita shot some more. They walked, he with his arm around her. Anita shot again. At the door they kissed long enough for Anita to get off three more shots. They went inside.

Anita figured she had enough, but decided to head for the wooded area in the back and wait until sunset, just in case there would be a better opportunity. The temperature was near 70 degrees and the sun shone in the clear sky. It didn't shine on Anita sitting in her dark gray running suit in the cool woods. The leaves were off the trees, but there was plenty of brush to keep her from the lovers' view.

She didn't have to wait long for her opportunity. Crane and Laura walked onto his secluded deck. Anita looked through her telephoto lens. They had champagne flutes in their hands. The breeze seemed to carry their voices toward the woods, and Anita could hear most of their conversation.

"Why the champagne, Jim?"

"I just wanted to make a salute to you, enhance our anticipation." He toasted her.

"I'm so enhanced already. I don't want to wait any longer." She unfastened the button on her skirt.

Anita rolled her eyes.

Crane moved closer to Laura. He set his champagne glass on the deck's rail and slowly began unbuttoning her blouse. She started to work on his shirt, ripping off two buttons. "Wait Laura. Let me undress you first."

He undressed her slowly. She moaned and squirmed when he pulled her panties and hose down. To her nude form he offered a salute with his glass and finished the champagne.

"Now, Jim, now, now!"

He handed her the champagne and began to undress.

Both naked they kissed wildly.

He ran his hand between her legs.

She dropped her glass. "Damn."

They tip-toed cautiously around the broken glass then hurried into the condominium. A slight breeze rippled a curtain at the door they hadn't quite closed.

Anita's last shot was of their bare backs going into his home.

When Anita returned to her office, she called Caitlin. It was well after five in the afternoon, but she figured Caitlin was still at work. "I've got enough to prove infidelity. I mean, you'll have to be the judge. I have some kissing and hand-holding. Stuff like that. And a few other things. It should be enough. I'm going to print them tonight. Want me to bring prints and a disc over tomorrow?"

"Yeah. Can you bring them to my house?"

CHAPTER NINE

Later in the early evening Jim and Laura lay in his king sized bed on their backs, both naked and holding hands. "Are you watching us in the mirror, Jim?" she asked.

"Yes, and now I know why I had the laser eye surgery. Before, without my glasses, I wouldn't be able to see us. I wouldn't be able to appreciate the pure erotic pleasure of the moment." He released her hand and turned to his side facing her. He delicately ran his finger over her right cheek just below her eye. "All of this pleasure is enhanced by my love for you."

"Oh, and I love you, too, so much."

They held each other. He moved his hand to her back and drew his fingertips along the vertebrae from her shoulders down to the small of her back. They pulled apart slightly.

"Let's get serious for a moment, Jim."

"I am. I am serious about you."

"No, I'm talking about the money, the five hundred thousand dollars I'm lending you. I'll have the other half for you before the end of the year. I don't want to do it in a one-lump sum. I mean, I just don't want Martin, that bastard, to get suspicious. If he asks, I'm just going to say I made an investment. I'll tell him I'm buying some annuities from a friend."

"Well, it is an investment. We can make you a silent partner in the company – "

"I don't like to be silent, silly." She pressed a finger over his mouth. "I like to speak my mind."

"We can make it a loan. Or, we can make you a partner in my company, which would then be *our* company."

"Oh, I don't know anything about PR. I'm not even sure what it is. Are you what they call a spinmeister?"

"I suppose that's part of it."

"Let's just make it a simple loan. No interest, no nothing."

"I'll have some papers drawn up and we'll sign them. And with interest, or the IRS will claim it's a gift. We don't want the IRS to clamp down on you and declare this loan a gift and make you pay taxes on it."

"That would be awful. How much would I have to pay?"

"I'm not sure, but with state and federal taxes and the bracket you're in, I'd guess it would be quite a bit, near fifty percent. I don't know what the gift tax rate is, though."

"Half?" her voice rang with incredulity.

"That's why we have to make this a loan. I'm going to have papers drawn up later. I'll use my business as collateral."

"No need for that."

"You want it to be a signature loan?"

"Sure," she replied not quite sure what a signature loan was.

He paused a moment, then said, "I've made some changes at the office. I cut two higher ranking account people and next week I'm cutting three from the backroom, people who don't have billable hours." He looked at her, then explained, "They don't work on accounts and can't bill for their services. Bookkeepers, computer types, that sort of thing."

"Aren't you afraid you'll look like you're not doing well?"

"No clients or prospective clients ever see anyone in the back shop. Just as well, too. But, that's why I'm not cutting any more from the front end, the people who deal with clients. I need the critical mass to give the impression of success. I've got a couple of young people who are very promising and a lot less expensive than the veterans. We're back on the road to success."

"Oh, you are a success, Jim. You couldn't help it when the economy soured. The war in Iraq just going on and on. And we're still in Afghanistan. The mortgage crisis. The price of gas. I mean, who'd have thought that would happen?" She widened her eyes in disbelief.

"Don't worry, things are getting better, the economy is beginning to improve. Nothing is bad forever." He caressed her softly.

"I'm not worried. I have a lot of money. I want to share it with you." She moved closer to him, nestling in his arms. "When this is all over and I divorce Martin, why don't you sell your business and go on a long, long cruise with me?"

CHAPTER TEN

Anita arrived at Caitlin's home the next day at mid-morning. She was wearing a bright red sweat suit and white running shoes with pink laces. She carried a large envelope.

"Where's your son?"

"At a friend's house. Why?"

"Just thought I'd ask. Didn't want him coming in here asking about the pictures, embarrassing stuff, you know."

"I thought nothing embarrasses you, Anita." Caitlin smiled.

Anita shrugged. "Just didn't want to explain the fucking photos to him."

"As in intercourse?"

"Not actual coitus, just prelude stuff," Anita said. "Or, as they say in the women's magazines – foreplay. I guess you could call it that." She laid out eight- by ten-inch glossies on the dining room table, all of the shots she had taken up to the episode on the deck.

"I guess those will do," Caitlin said. She seemed a little disappointed. "Too bad they didn't register at a motel. But the kisses and handholding are enough in court these days. And that is her hand on his crotch."

"These sex things are all so damn seedy," Anita said.

"Well, sure they are."

"Usually it's the men who are creeps, but I kind of liked this Crane guy – Jimbo. Who's the bad guy in this case: Jimbo, Laura or the client, or another woman? Or, is everyone bad?"

Caitlin shrugged.

"Want to see the other pictures?"

"You have more?"

Anita pulled two computer discs and the rest of the photos out and spread them across the tabletop. She described what happened on the deck. "It was pretty erotic. I'm glad I was working the camera or I might have had an orgasm."

"Really?"

"Naw, I've seen better." She placed all of the pictures in a neat pile and handed them to Caitlin with the envelope and discs. "I have copies of the discs," she said then added, "That Jimbo, though, sure is hung well."

Caitlin laughed. "I thought you didn't notice such things."

"I'm a private investigator and paid to be observant."

"Sounds more like you're a *privates* investigator," Caitlin responded.

Anita snorted. "Beats the hell out of a real job."

Caitlin shook her head. "Yeah, well give me your bill Monday and I'll pay you right away."

"That's what I like about you Caitlin, you're prompt with the money."

"It's not always easy."

"Hey, I know what it's like workin' on your own; no one to watch out for you but yourself. It ain't like workin' for the government."

They talked a while longer then Anita laughed. "I forgot to tell you, but some of it's in my report, I think she may be paying Jimbo for sex."

"What do you mean?"

"I saw her hand him an envelope. I think she said something about money, but I'm not positive. I mean, I wouldn't tell your client she gave him money since I didn't actually see a check or clearly hear the *M* word. But you might want to keep that in the back of your mind."

"She has plenty of her own money. Maybe it was something else, though."

CHAPTER ELEVEN

Martin sat on a chair at a table by the pool of his hotel in Palm Beach. The afternoon sun warmed him. He wore swimming trunks, a short-sleeved shirt and a white brimmed hat. He was barefoot. His deck shoes lay under his chair. Martin curled his toes and gazed across the pool toward the ocean, the surf rolling in gently. He was trying to relax, but having a difficult time. The meetings he had planned to attend would be interesting even though they weren't very relevant anymore. There was a cocktail reception that evening. On Friday there would be a full day of lectures, and Saturday morning's session would be followed by a luau.

Philip Wain, the surgeon, and another one of their partners, approached Martin. "Have you seen Angela?" Philip asked. Angela was Philip's wife of three years.

Martin shook his head and said he hadn't. He didn't like his partner – too brash, too coarse, too aggressive, too much the surgeon, and a high-ego thoracic surgeon at that.

"Angela plans to come to the pool, so when you see her tell her I've gone to an acquaintance's office to discuss a new procedure he's been working on. We'll be back in two hours, plenty of time for the reception."

Philip left with the other partner and Martin sat back in his chair again. Philip wasn't aware that Martin disliked him, for Martin could be very diplomatic. But Martin did like Angela. She was astonishingly beautiful. Philip divorced his wife of eighteen years and married Angela, sixteen years his junior. She had owned a successful modeling agency, but sold it to her partner when she married Philip. Recently, however, she had opened a new agency, a small boutique that didn't require constant attention.

Martin was aware that Philip possessed a great appetite for women and wasn't a man who liked to suppress his appetite. And there was always a bout of braggadocio after one of Philip's conquests. What Martin wanted to do was have sex with Angela and then make sure Philip found out about it. That would be his parting shot upon selling his share of the practice.

Martin much preferred married women. It gave him a sense of conquest without having to worry too much about the aftereffects. No long-term commitments. There was something absolutely delicious about taking another man's wife, and Angela would be the perfect candidate.

As his mind dwelled on Angela she walked toward him from behind, wearing a short robe that covered her swimsuit, but not her thighs. "My, Martin, you are looking pensive."

"Oh, hi, Angela." He stood up, slightly startled by her. "Philip was here and then left to visit a fellow surgeon, something about a new procedure. He'll be back before the reception."

"They probably want to discuss a new twist on ventricular assist, or some such nonsense." She took off her robe, revealing a black swimsuit cut high on the thighs. "You like?" She turned.

"New suit?" He remained aloof, as though he weren't interested in her.

"No. I meant how it looks on me, or me in it." She smiled a bit of a pout.

She was clearly flirting, and it gave Martin a pleasant feeling, almost of anticipation. "Why Angela, you surprise me. You're always spectacular looking. I would think you couldn't possibly have any self doubt."

She laughed, her dark hair blowing gently in the breeze. She sat in a chair next to him. "You know, you're the first man I've known who hasn't made a pass at me, or at least hinted at it.

Does Laura keep you on a very tight leash?"

"Hardly. Actually, I'm waiting for you to make the pass."

"Maybe you'll get your chance." She touched his upper arm.

"You're certainly a beautiful woman, Angela. But don't let it get in the way. I find you far more interesting than beautiful."

They ordered drinks without alcohol from a waiter. "Daytime drinking is such bad form and alcohol ruins the skin," Angela said, "especially in this sun." She touched her face. "You never know when I might have to make a real living again."

"You and Philip aren't having a spat, are you?"

"Oh, no. He adores me."

"A little adoration goes a long way." Martin pulled at his right ear slightly.

"Are you happily married, Martin?"

"Of course not."

"Yes, that's what I figured." Angela smiled as though she were confirming all the office gossip that her husband had been bringing home.

"You're very perceptive," Martin remarked. "That's one of the things that's interesting about you."

"What else?" She crossed her legs at the thighs and sat a little straighter, more attentive.

"You've run your own business, started up another one. There's a brain between those pretty ears." He watched her touch an ear. "I'd like to know how you think, what you think."

"Now you're making a pass." She smiled.

"No."

"You mean I don't appeal to you?" She raised an eyebrow. "You aren't gay, are you? That would be an incredible waste."

Martin smiled. "You certainly appeal to me, but I'm waiting for you to make the pass."

"Why?"

"It would be far more erotic."

She leaned back and uncrossed her legs. "Perhaps I will."

CHAPTER TWELVE

Martin arrived at Caitlin's office early on the afternoon following his return from Palm Beach. Caitlin was anxious to see him. She had paced the floor, going over the things she needed to discuss. There was nothing monumental, but she wanted to rehearse. With her hands clasped behind her, she liked to pace and think things through just as Klaus, her father, did. And she walked back and forth, sometimes circling her desk and chair. She stopped, folded her arms in front of her and stared at her door as if in anticipation. Maggie knocked, poked her head in and announced Martin's arrival.

Caitlin greeted him as he entered, shaking his hand. He seated himself in the chair across from his attorney. She looked across the desk at him and said softly, "Well, Martin, we have sufficient proof of Laura's infidelity."

"Good. That should give us the edge just in case she wants to put up a stink."

She described Anita Zombrowska's report as she handed him a copy. "This isn't the kind of thing you should take home or leave in your office, Martin. I suggest you leave it with me. Also," she paused and pulled out a number of photographs, "we have photos of her holding hands and kissing Jim Crane." She handed those photos to him.

He looked at each then raised his head and said, "Is this enough?"

"Yes. But we also have some more revealing shots."

"May I see them?"

"Of course. But I want to caution you that they are indelicate." She handed him the other photographs, wondering what his reaction would be.

He looked at each, his face impassive as though he were

examining an x-ray for a second opinion. When he finished, he returned them to Caitlin and smiled. "Well that should take care of any counterattack Laura might launch." He paused then asked, "Are you concerned about invasion of privacy, Caitlin?"

"No. It was out on the deck. It's as I said, indelicate."

"Kind of like blackmail, isn't it?" he said.

"That's a felony. What we've done is unquestionably within the law." She pulled the report closer to her. "Inside the report, our investigator says she saw Laura hand Jim Crane an envelope. We have no idea what was inside."

"Probably payment for his services." He chuckled. "I've given everything considerable thought." He changed the subject. "I'm determined to dissolve the partnership before year-end and file for divorce the first week in January. I told Philip Wain – he's one of the partners I went to Palm Beach with. I told him I'd be making a proposal soon."

"What was his reaction?"

"Hard to describe. I think he thought I was nuts, but at the same time I detected a sense of relief, or maybe envy." Martin shook his head.

"Well, we're on schedule with your partnership matter," Caitlin said. "And we can file the divorce papers the first Monday after New Year's. You received my letter and Allen Greene's report?" She stopped while he nodded. "We're going into our conference room in a moment to meet with Allen and the accountant." Caitlin was still seeing Ralph, but Martin had insisted on using Ralph's accounting firm.

After the meeting Martin wrote a check to cover expenses incurred and to take care of professional fees Caitlin anticipated through the filing in January. When Martin left, she wrote checks for Allen, Ralph and Anita. It gave her a great sense of relief and comfort. Her financial condition had begun to improve.

Erik entered her office at five o'clock. "God, you look happy. The Good Doctor write another check?"

"Why do you call him the Good Doctor?"

"Just a turn of phrase, a hackneyed one at that."

"It sounds like you don't like him," Caitlin said.

Erik paused for a moment. "I suppose I don't, but that's irrelevant. He's your client, not mine. Anyway, you don't have to like someone to represent him. I mean, we've both counseled creeps. Remember that disgusting rapist you got off the hook with just misdemeanor sexual assault. He was beyond creep."

"But he was innocent of rape. Besides, you can't compare Martin with him."

"No, no. I'm not saying they're kindred spirits. I'm just saying I don't like Dr. Morley. It's a gut feeling."

"Well, I like Martin. I've known him for years." She felt a little guilty defending Martin before Erik.

"Look, Caitlin, we're friends, but we don't have to like all of each other's friends, too. I mean, I kind of like Ralphie, but you clearly don't like my Cutie Pie, as you so fondly call her." The four of them had gone to dinner and a play together one Saturday.

Caitlin laughed and shook her head. "Erik, Julie's just a kid and not worthy of you." She was also a little jealous, she admitted to herself. She thought that a bit odd.

"I've lowered my standards in recent months," Erik explained. "Just for libido maintenance purposes."

On Caitlin's way home she stopped for pizza, soda and beer. At home she found Michael in his room finishing his homework. She kissed him on the head.

"I smell pizza," he said.

"You bet."

They sat at the kitchen table. He poured a Coke and she poured a beer. She took a long swallow of beer. It tasted absolutely delicious. The pizza was deep dish with the works. "Michael, I will eat your anchovies," she announced and began moving them from one half of the pizza to the other.

"They're disgusting, Mom."

She picked one up with her forefinger and thumb, tilted her head back, and dropped it into her mouth. "Oh, that's delicious.

Some day, Michael, your taste buds will mature and you, too, will like anchovies. You're genetically disposed toward it."

"Dad doesn't like anchovies. I have his genes, too."

"I won't hold that against you. I'll just eat your anchovies, then." She plucked another from the pizza and plopped it into her mouth. Michael grimaced.

"Why are we partying?" he asked.

"Our finances are looking up. I think we're going to buy a new car."

"Really?" He watched his mother nod. "Can we afford it?"

She shrugged indifferently.

"I worry about money," Michael admitted in a serious tone. "Is there such a thing as the poor house?"

"Not any more. Years ago they used to put people in jail if they didn't pay their bills. They called it debtors' prison."

Michael took a slice of pizza. "How could they make any money to pay their bills if they were in prison?"

"I don't know what ever happened to them, but we have a much better system now." Caitlin took a bite of pizza. A string of cheese fell on her chin. She pulled it off and put it in her mouth. "Well, I think we can afford a new car and have a little ballast."

"What's ballast?"

Caitlin shook her head. "They used to put a load of bricks in the bottoms of ships to keep them steady in the water so they wouldn't tip over." She held her hand up vertically and tipped it back and forth as though it were a ship bobbing. "And on land the rocks – called ballast – were put along railroad tracks to support the rails and ties so trains could ride over them without toppling over. It just means a balancing factor, which is a good thing for us."

"How do you know so much?"

"Jeez, you're inquisitive tonight." She smiled. Caitlin relished the camaraderie with her son. "I've been around for forty-one years, Michael. My mind's like old fly paper with a lot of useless things sticking to it."

"What's fly paper?" he asked and laughed.

"Sticky glue paper they hang in barns to catch flies and other disgusting bugs."

He screwed up his face at the picture she described. "One more question, Mom. What kind of car are we getting?"

"I don't know," she smiled, just happy to be there with her son. "A cheap Jeep, maybe – something that can go both forward and backward – so we can go camping in the mountains and cross-country skiing in the dead of winter." Michael's eyes lit up. She knew he had always liked the idea of having a Jeep. "Maybe we'll get a Jaguar or a Cadillac," she joked.

"I'd rather have a Jeep," Michael replied. "Or, what about one of those Korean SUVs. They're a lot cheaper."

"You mean a karate car?" she asked.

"What do you mean?"

"You know, it sounds like the noise they make during a karate match." She lifted her hand and as she made a downward chop, she shouted, "Hyundai!"

Michael laughed.

Caitlin finished the last of her pizza and washed it down with the remainder of her beer. "Look, Michael," she said as she pushed her plate away from her, "things may have been tight financially from time to time, but I've slowly built up the practice. And, while we're not on Easy Street, we are filling a lot of potholes and heading toward the comfort zone." She just wanted to make him feel better. She realized that she'd never live in the comfort zone.

"Mom, where is Easy Street?" he asked with a bit of a smirk.

"Wise guy." She faked a cuff to the back of his head.

In a day or two she knew she would have an entirely new set of worries every bit as aggressive as the old worries and that Easy Street would never be closer than down a few tough blocks.

CHAPTER THIRTEEN

The day of the annual office Christmas party Martin's partners decided to turn it into a farewell celebration. They had recently reached agreement and signed the contract.

Laura refused to attend the party. "I'm just not going. I can't understand why you're quitting." Her voice rose with each sentence. "You didn't even discuss it with me. I was the last person to learn. It's such an embarrassment. Frankly, Martin, I'm mortified." Then she screamed, "I hate you," and walked across the expansive kitchen to fetch her drink.

"You didn't seem interested." He purposely had decided to tell her last. She would have just gotten in the way and blabbered too freely.

"Well, Martin, just what in the hell do you plan to do when this is over?" Laura's voice settled somewhat.

"I'm not sure. Teach maybe."

"Teach? All you want to do is fuck coeds."

"Now Laura, really, children don't appeal to me."

"Not even your own."

"That's absurd."

"Then, you want to fuck the professors' wives."

"If you're worried about money, we have plenty." He never understood why she couldn't string together a full train of logical thought.

"You're not touching Daddy's money," she screamed.

"I don't want any of it," he said in a quiet, even voice, which seemed to anger her more.

"You're just dying to get your hands on it. I've contacted an accountant. We're going to set up a special account after the first of the year. Then I'm getting a divorce."

"Oh, well, maybe I should seek some of that money, you know, equal distribution of the assets. I'll be unemployed at first, so I could get alimony." He laughed, amused by the notion. Martin knew Laura would have a few drinks on the thought of him getting alimony from her.

"You son of a bitch." She threw her empty martini glass at him. It missed by a couple of feet and crashed on the kitchen's ceramic floor.

Martin, in a dark conservative suit and a necktie with reindeer and a bright red Santa Claus on it, swept up the broken glass, stooping to search for scattered shards. He didn't walk barefoot in the kitchen even though the ceramic floor was heated, but he knew that Laura sometimes did. He didn't care if she bled to death from the shards; he just didn't want a mess. He liked things neat.

Martin actually was glad Laura wasn't going to the party. He really didn't want her around. Why spoil another evening. He always had more fun without her.

The party was at his country club. He had been mildly surprised at how readily his colleagues had accepted his decision to leave the practice. His own portion was quite lucrative and the specialists particularly benefited from his referrals. Of course, he planned to stay on for six months to wind down his own practice, transferring his patients to the other internists, and providing counsel to the practice. He would be reimbursed for his consultation services, but no longer a member of the practice. He wasn't sure exactly what he was going to do with his life now that the die was cast. Once he was rid of Laura he could do just about anything.

He was the last to arrive at the party. There was a round of applause as he entered the room. Everyone except Sonja, the office manager, was drinking. She was a tall, overweight blonde, the first to greet him. She gave him a crushing hug. "Dr. Morley, I'm going to miss you," she said while releasing him.

"Well," he laughed, "I'm not exactly leaving tomorrow. I'll still be around for the next few months."

A few moments later Philip Wain came over and shook Martin's hand, pulling him aside. "You know, Martin, your leaving us is a godsend."

A waitress came by with a tray of champagne. Martin took one, smiling his thanks. "Why's that?" Martin knew the answer.

"Our dwindling patient base. It's not too bad now, you know, but it won't be long. The HMOs are killing us, eating us alive. Who knows what this mismanaged health care will continue to do, but it won't be anything good. And it'll be even worse with government inspired health care." Philip moved a little closer to Martin. "The HMOs want you, all the primary care physicians, to cram in more patients per hour. Tell me, Martin, how much shit can you put in a ten-pound bag?"

Martin laughed, "Twelve pounds, I suspect." He shook his head to commiserate. They had had versions of this discussion many times at partnership meetings, hospital physician lounges, cocktail parties, wherever doctors congregated. He knew the litany of complaints. He sipped his champagne and frowned at its taste of mediocrity.

"You know, Martin, medicine isn't what it used to be. If I had it to do over again, I wouldn't. I'd find something else."

"Investment banker?" Martin asked with a short laugh.

"Hell, man, anything would be better than what this is going to be, even the way the stock market's been going – "

"How about lawyer? Would you rather be a lawyer? You could specialize in malpractice, suing physicians."

Wain's face registered disgust briefly. "Speaking of lawyers, I like your new attorney, that Schroeder woman." He nudged

Martin lightly in the arm with the hand that held his wine glass. "What's it like to fuck a six-foot lawyer?" He laughed loudly from his barrel chest.

Martin smiled. "Frankly, I'd like to find out."

"You mean to tell me you haven't bedded her yet?" His tone was disbelieving. By Martin's accounting Philip Wain had gone to bed with what the surgeon would have described as every 'fuckable nurse' at Community General Hospital.

"Who's Martin going to bed with?" Angela asked from behind.

Philip jumped ever so slightly. "I was teasing Martin about his lawyer. She's a tall looker."

"Philip, dear, Martin's a married man. He wouldn't do a thing like that." Angela offered a look of feigned surprise.

"It was just man talk, Angela."

"That's one of the problems with men. It's all they have on their minds."

"Not me," said Martin. "I'm rather pure. I've been reading the Good Book lately."

The three of them laughed.

"Oh, there's Simon," Philip said. He motioned his head toward an oncologist partner. "I need to talk to him for a few minutes. Can I leave you two alone for awhile?" He looked at Martin then his wife, "Angela, will you entertain Martin? It's his last Christmas party with us."

Angela shook her head. Little gold earrings, miniature Christmas ornaments, shimmered with the movement of her head. She wore a simple red dress scooped at the neck. Simple designs accentuated her beauty. Her eyes were large and blue. With the contrast of her dark hair her eyes sparkled like ice shimmering in the light.

"So you're bailing out of the practice?" she asked.

"It's hardly a sinking ship, although I might be a rat."

"I didn't mean it that way."

"I know you didn't." Martin stopped to wipe moisture from

his glass with his forefinger. "Frankly, I'm tired of being a physician," he resumed. "I'm sick of sick people, all people."

"Well thanks," Angela pouted slightly as if offended.

"Not you, Angela, certainly not you."

"I didn't think so." She shifted her body, the left shoulder rising a little. She smiled.

"What are you and Philip doing for the holidays?"

"He's going to Scottsdale to visit his folks through New Year's, play golf, that sort of thing. Taking his sons with him. I hate Arizona. Dries my skin. It's no place for a model. I'm going to Baltimore to see my mother. And you?"

"I'll be around here for Christmas then I'm off skiing at a lodge not too far from here."

"Sounds like fun. You taking Laura?"

"No, she doesn't want to go. I'm going alone." That wasn't true. He had a woman he planned to take with him, but he didn't want to tell Angela that.

"Sounds lonely." She reached out and touched his hand, the one holding his drink. "I bet you can find someone there to talk with. I bet you're rather adept at that." She smiled wickedly.

"Perhaps," he chuckled.

"I like skiing. Why aren't you going to Colorado?"

"Too many loose ends to wrap up here."

"When are you leaving?" She moved a little closer to him.

"After Christmas – the twenty-ninth."

She ran her finger over his knuckles on the hand holding the glass. "I'm thinking of returning from Baltimore then. Want someone to ski with?" She looked up into his eyes.

"Are you making a pass?"

"I bet you don't fumble." She smiled, light from the chandelier glinting in her eyes.

"When should I pick you up?"

"Five o'clock at my office." Angela moved a little closer to Martin. "Are you good?"

"I'm a fair skier."

"I meant," she paused, slapping him lightly on the wrist, "are you entertaining?"

"I work very hard at it. And I take pleasure in my work, great pleasure."

"I bet you do." Her voice turned huskier.

"I couldn't invent a better way to end the year than being with you." He meant that, and he sensed that she caught his conviction.

They talked a little while longer. Martin described the cabin they would be staying in, complete with an attendant to stoke the fireplace every morning before guests arose. The owners of the lodge had blended the old with the new – stone fireplace, pine walls, down comforter, a whirlpool bath large enough for two.

Now Martin had to devise an excuse for Karen, the woman he had originally planned to take skiing. Karen, while pretty, wasn't very refined, and he really didn't like the name – Karen. He was sure he'd be bored in short order. Karen was the wife of one of the members of the country club. Martin had lured her – it wasn't difficult – into going with him to the resort. She and her husband were about to embark on a messy divorce. Martin had recommended Caitlin as a good divorce lawyer for Karen.

Now there was the opportunity with Angela. She surely was a tantalizing conquest. Making love with Angela while the husband golfed, oh, what a delicious thought, and her name, what a marvelous name. The evil and sensuous nature of it all delighted Martin.

CHAPTER FOURTEEN

Caitlin appreciated Martin's recommendation that Karen retain her for the divorce. She had already received two other clients from Martin. They were all divorces. "Divorce is nice money, if you can ignore the emotions," she told Erik Wanzer, who was sitting across from her in her office.

Erik shook his head and said, "I'm glad I'm getting out of this. Government work is so much more civilized."

"The CIA? Bunch of damn spooks, dirty tricks, overthrowing legitimate governments. They couldn't even find weapons of mass destruction." She shook her head in feigned disgust.

"I won't be involved in any of that." He dropped his voice to a more business-like tone and said, "My job will be like a corporate attorney."

"Now that sounds really exciting." Caitlin enjoyed teasing Erik and knew that he particularly liked it. "You don't even belong to a political party. How'd you wrangle this CIA job?"

"It's my total objectivity that interested them."

"I know you lean to the left, politically."

"But nobody else knows that."

"You amaze me, you spy. You," she paused, "you bureaucrat."

Erik feigned a hurt look. "Well, I'm still going to maintain a vestige of my practice here, you know. I won't be looking for new business, just winding down of the old. There are still a couple of interesting cases and a few divorces. I never really did like doing divorce."

"Divorce can be fun," she countered cavalierly.

"Yeah, don't we both know that already." He was smiling.

"You having your daughters for Christmas?" she asked.

"Yes, but not for New Year's Eve. And you?"

"Like you, Michael this year is spending Christmas with me and New Year's week with his dad. We alternate every year." She took a sip from her coffee cup. It was late in the day and she needed a little jolt of caffeine. Setting the cup down, she asked, "You and Cutie Pie going to do it up royally for New Year's?" Then in staccato fashion said, "Some exotic motel, heart-shaped bed, a dining-dancing package – *prix fixe* – including domestic champagne and confetti for the stroke of midnight?" She smiled mischievously, her eyes gleaming.

"You sure are a wicked woman, Caitlin Schroeder. Why do I put up with this?"

"I don't know," she replied, suddenly somber.

"I'm certainly going to miss your company come January second."

"Thanks, Erik. A girl needs a friend." She hadn't thought until now about the vacuum his departure would create.

Erik cast his eyes downward, seemingly embarrassed. Then he picked his head up, "I don't have a date for New Year's. If you want to know the whole truth, Julie and I broke up several weeks ago."

"Ha," Caitlin slapped her hand on her desk, "I knew it. Those young twenty-something women – wicked, wanton and wild. They'll do it every time to you lonely middle-aged men. All they want to do is screw, screw, screw. And then they just leave you spent in the dust."

"I'm not middle aged," Erik protested, laughing.

"The hell you aren't. You're going to be forty in two months, so actuarially you are forty, and forty is middle aged. I know, damn it, I'm already there. I'll be forty-two a few months later. I know middle age my friend, intimately." She leaned back in her chair and ran a finger over the light creases that slightly accented the corner of her eye.

"Julie and I split up several weeks ago. I think she found an older man in her office. Besides, I couldn't stand talking with her. We were on entirely different planes." He leaned back in his chair and clasped his hands behind his head. "Soooo, I'm celibate again."

"She went for an older man? Older than you or just 'older?'"

Erik shrugged.

"Well, I'm sure it was great for a while. You were bouncing around here like an eighteen-year-old." She picked up a pencil and doodled with it a bit. "If it's any consolation, Ralphie and I split up, too. I was going to break it off," she pointed the pencil at Erik, "and you know what he did? He beat me to the punch and broke it off before I could. It was just two Saturdays ago. He never had it so good, the slime ball. You know what it was?" She watched Erik shake his head. "I think I was too good in bed for him."

Erik, laughing, asked, "Want to do New Year's together – nothing romantic – just eat, drink and laugh?"

"Okay. We don't want to go out someplace, do we?"

"Nah, that's for amateurs," Erik said. "How about my place. I'll cook."

"No, my place. You can spend the night in Michael's empty room."

"Alright, but on one condition. I've heard your culinary horror stories. I'll cook."

"It's a deal. Beats the hell out of Chinese."

"I'll pick out the wine, too."

"You don't have to get belligerent about this. I'll do the other stuff, make the drinks, buy hors d'oeuvres. I'll pick up Pernod and an Edith Piaf disc." Caitlin was elated, although she didn't want to show it. Last New Year's she spent with Michael and the year before she was dreadfully alone. "Shall we dress for the evening, Erik?"

"*Mais certainement.*"

CHAPTER FIFTEEN

It was six in the morning four days after Christmas. Light snow had begun to fall. Martin poured himself a cup of coffee. He had been awake for an hour. Martin had been an early riser since childhood when he took over a morning newspaper route. He was in the kitchen this early winter morning, though, waiting for his daughter and son, whom he had offered to drive to the airport for their ski trip to Colorado.

He shook his head in bewilderment. Just a generation ago he would never have imagined taking a ski trip on Christmas break. He was born poor, or at least it was his vision of poor. His father worked in an automobile factory, which should have provided enough money for a middle class upbringing, but he drank a large portion of his income, eventually dying of cancer of the liver. His mother was a waitress who earned a fair amount in tips. But raising four children devoured a lot of wherewithal.

Martin's parents embarrassed him. His father wasn't a mean drunk, just an alcoholic who managed mostly to keep out of trouble. As a youngster, Martin disliked having friends to the house, particularly when his mother was leaving for work or returning from her waitress job. He shuddered remembering the sight of food stains on her uniform when she came home from the restaurant.

Martin excelled in school. He couldn't help it. While his brother and two sisters struggled to break even, he was an A student through high school, and graduated *summa cum laude* from college. He did study ferociously, though, for he instinctively knew education was his only salvation.

"Dr. Morley, are you ready for rounds?" his daughter Cathy asked as she burst full of energy into the kitchen. She wore her blonde hair short and was pretty in a youthful exuberant way. Martin was pleased that she hadn't inherited her mother's disposition or her intellect. He enjoyed his relationship with his daughter, but his relationship with his son was often strained.

"I'll stop by the hospital after I drop you and Carlton off at the airport," he said.

On the drive to the airport with his daughter and son the conversation began aimlessly then shifted to Laura. "Dad, is something wrong with Mom?" Cathy asked.

"I think so."

"It isn't serious is it? She seems so, I don't know."

"She's drinking more," Carlton offered. He was more solemn than his sister. A narrow, long nose sharpened his face in a way that annoyed Martin.

"That's the problem," their father added. "I'm afraid she's an alcoholic."

Cathy nodded. She was in her first year of medical school at Cornell in New York City.

"If she doesn't stop, she'll die," Carlton, a senior at Colgate, added. He liked getting to the point quickly.

"I talked her into a treatment center a couple of years ago while both of you were away at school. It didn't work. After a week she smuggled a bottle of vodka into her room." Martin later found out that one of the aides at the treatment center had a prosperous side business of supplying liquor to patients willing to pay thirty dollars for a pint of cheap vodka. "They caught her and expelled her." Martin shook his head.

"Dad, I'm sorry for both of you." Cathy put her hand on her father's arm. Carlton sat in the back seat of the Lincoln Navigator eyes downcast.

"I'm at the end with your mother," Martin said.

"What do you mean?" Carlton asked.

"I don't want to spoil your trip, but I'm going to file for divorce in two weeks."

Cathy shuddered slightly. Martin rubbed the top of the dashboard with his gloved hand as though dust were there.

"What was Mom's reaction," Cathy asked.

"I haven't told her yet. I didn't want to ruin the holidays for her. I'll tell her after the first."

Cathy nodded.

"I think it's best," Carlton remarked. "I mean Mom's been making everyone's life miserable for several years. I dread coming home." He paused for a moment then added, "I don't know why you stayed around all these years. Maybe you were just waiting for Mom to kick off from all of her drinking."

"Carlton, you can apologize when you get back from Colorado," Martin said in measured tones. "Think it over while you're there."

"Jesus, Carlton, you're such an ass sometimes." Cathy paused and decided to adjust the subject a little. "I wish it didn't have to be. I wish Mom were the way she used to be."

"She's always been an alcoholic," Martin said. "It's just that it didn't become pronounced until five or six years ago. In fact, I wasn't aware until then. I'll spare you guys the lecture on alcohol." He paused for a moment. "You both drink, don't you?"

They nodded. He caught Carlton's face in the rear view mirror. "Drinking is fine," Martin offered. "Just don't emulate your mother."

They laughed nervously, even though Martin hadn't intended his remark to be humorous.

"When are you moving out of the house?" Carlton asked.

"After the first. I've leased an apartment." Neither he nor Laura had told them about selling the practice. He planned to save that for another time.

"I suppose the house will end up being sold," Cathy said.

"Yeah, it's too big anyway," Carlton added.

Martin dropped them off at the airport, kissed Cathy on the cheek then hugged Carlton as if forgiving him.

He watched them carry their bags and skis into the airport. Martin drove off slowly, heading to the hospital to check on three patients. One went in with chest pains two days before Christmas. Another was a kidney stone on Christmas Day. And the third was an old woman about to die. She had been his patient for fifteen years.

He saw the two men first. Both would be out of the hospital by the next day. The chest pain appeared to be gall bladder problems. He spent more time than usual with Mrs. Miller, though. Her daughter was with her. She also was a patient of Martin's.

"They want to do an operation on me, Dr. Morley. Why?" the old woman asked.

"The jaundice, your liver. I have to talk with the surgeon about it."

"I'm eighty-six and going to die anyway," she said.

"Now, Mom," the daughter said. She inched closer to her mother's side.

"You don't have to be operated on, Mrs. Miller," Martin said. He reached for her hand. "That decision is up to you and your family." He genuinely liked the old woman and was sorry to know that her remaining weeks would probably be spent in pain and fear.

"I'm dying, why operate," she stated. She seemed content with the inevitability.

"From the day we are born we're meant to die," Martin said softly. "But the human spirit wants us to forestall that date as long as possible." He held her hand. "That's what it's all about." He rubbed the thin translucent skin on the back of her hand. "Why don't we bring in the specialists. We can all talk about this. And then you can make an informed decision."

They had the meeting a little later in the morning. The

surgeon and specialist recommended surgery. Martin sided with Mrs. Miller, arguing that the operation might prolong her life, but he didn't think it would be for long and that there was a strong prospect of pain.

The daughter tried talking her into the surgery: "Mom, don't give up hope."

When the specialist strongly recommended the operation, Martin pulled himself out of the discussion. Mrs. Miller finally relented, too weak to argue.

Martin walked off knowing what would happen: she'd be in pain, she'd be in intensive care for two or three weeks, she'd be on a ventilator so her lungs could keep transmitting oxygen to the blood stream, her eyes would dart between bouts of drug suppressed pain, drifting in and out of consciousness, she'd be too weak to talk much, her kidneys would eventually fail and she'd die. Martin had seen it all before. He shook his head, wondering what went on in the minds of patients as they lie slowly dying, knowing they're dying.

On the way out he stopped at the nurse's station, looked at the nursing supervisor and said, "I suppose it's a way to make money."

"Pardon me, Doctor."

She was quite pretty and he gave her a large smile. "I was just thinking about the futility of medicine, but it's an honest way to earn a buck."

She laughed. "Very honest, Dr. Morley."

He wondered what she looked like without her clothes on. It was just a stray sexual notion running through his head. He shook his head as if to dispel the thought. "I'll see you next week, Ms. Adams." He walked off, glanced over his shoulder and saw her bending over the desk to reach for a telephone. He liked the view.

Martin ate lunch at a small café in a village near where he lived. He had a bowl of soup and read *The Wall Street Journal*. When he returned home he packed his suitcase and took another shower. He always washed between patients, and showered after rounds or a day at the office. While he was dressing, Laura walked into the bedroom. "You sure you don't want to come along, Laura?" he asked. "You used to like skiing. Nice lodge there, too."

"No, I'm sick of skiing. I don't like it anymore. Besides, Western Alps Ski Resort?" She wrinkled her nose in disdain. "It's kind of low rent."

"Well, it's not Aspen or St. Moritz." Martin shrugged. "What are you going to do while I'm gone?"

"Oh, I don't know, relax maybe."

Martin pulled on a sweater, a thick ribbed, navy blue sweater with a crew neck. He laced a pair of over-the-ankle boots, expensive French hiking boots. "Oh, I thought you'd be seeing Jim Crane while I'm gone," he said, not looking at her directly, but catching her startled face out of the corner of his eye.

"Oh? Who's he?" Laura asked, sitting on the edge of the bed.

"Your lover."

"I'm sorry, I don't have a lover."

"That's not what my agent says."

"Your agent?"

"A private investigator I hired. The detective has been ferreting out the truth for me. Ferret. What a nice choice of words. It aptly describes you and Jim Crane."

She leaped from the bed and with hands on her hips shouted, "I don't know a Jim Crane and I don't have a lover."

"Sure you do. He's the owner of Crane Public Relations, the hotshot PR firm I've read about. Pretty well hung, too, judging by the pictures I saw of you and him on his deck." He watched fear and anger overpower Laura's face.

"You son of a bitch," she growled slowly.

He picked up his case and headed toward the door. "I'll call you from time to time to see if you're having a good time. I'll have my private investigator keep an eye on you, or can you be trusted to stay home and not go out and fuck big Jim? This stuff's going to look bad for you when we file for divorce. Maybe the court will give me some of your inheritance."

He left the room, Laura following. In the garage he put both downhill and cross-country skis on the rack atop the large Lincoln Navigator. Laura said nothing, arms folded across her middle. Her face glowered in the dim light of the garage.

As he entered the car, he punched the button of the garage door opener, lowered his window, and said, "I do hope you behave yourself, Laura. It's going to be very messy in court when I'm finished." He closed the car door and started the engine. He drove out and hit the button again just after passing under the garage door. He smiled.

CHAPTER SIXTEEN

To kill some time before meeting Angela, Martin drove to a shopping mall the afternoon of December twenty-nine. The mall was packed with people returning gifts and looking for bargains. For some reason he couldn't fathom he was enjoying the press of humanity. It had been a long time since he could afford such leisure. He had spent all of his life working very hard. As a youngster, in addition to his paper route, he mowed lawns and shoveled sidewalks for money that he kept hidden from parents and siblings. When he started college on a scholarship he worked part time as a dishwasher and busboy. After his first year of college he obtained a summer job as a railroad right of way maintenance worker. He kept that summer job throughout college. It paid well and allowed him to dress and act more like his fellow students.

About 4:30 he headed toward Angela's office in an old restored downtown building. She had let the receptionist off early. Angela greeted Martin as he entered. "You're very punctual," she said, smiling. She was wearing black stretch pants with stirrups, a red cashmere sweater with a delicate gold chain around her neck. Her earrings matched her chain. She kissed him briefly on the cheek, just a brush of the lips against his skin. He barely felt it.

Martin carried both of her suitcases. She carried her skis. At his car she inquired about the "skinny skis" next to his downhill skis.

"Cross-country skiing. I thought we'd try that, too."

"You mentioned something about it earlier. I didn't know the skis were so different, though. But I bought a cute outfit, wool knickers and stockings."

"Exactly what you're supposed to wear. We can rent skis and boots for you at the lodge. We'll have a marvelous time."

Martin drove north with Angela. Snow was still falling softly, but now a couple of inches lay fresh on the ground. About a mile out of the city he suddenly said, "Son of a gun," and slapped his hand lightly on the steering wheel. He pulled over.

"What's wrong? You forget something?" she asked, her eyes darting with curiosity.

"Yes." He turned the emergency flashers of the car on, pulled off his gloves, unfastened his seat belt, turned and faced Angela. "You know," he said, "we're embarking on what's going to be a great and momentous occasion. We're about to become lovers, and we've never even kissed." He moved toward her, his face only a couple of inches away, staring at her eyes, her mouth, and then he kissed her. It was a slow, easy kiss that built in intensity. He pulled back, kissed her face, kissed her eyes and kissed her mouth again with great desire. As a driver passed them Martin honked his horn and waved, still kissing Angela. Finally they stopped. He pulled a big fuzzy mitten off her hand and kissed her fingertips and her palm.

He turned in his seat, refastened his seat belt and resumed driving.

"You don't need your stethoscope to hear my heart pounding," Angela said. She leaned back in her seat, pulled the lever that made the backrest recline and said, "Now, that was a kiss. Is there more to come?"

"Yes, yes."

Angela returned the seat to its upright position.

"I thought we'd have dinner first. A little wine, a little food."

"I'll be crazy by dessert."

"We'll take dessert back at the cabin."

"The cabin – that could be our main course."

Martin laughed softly. "I'm sure it will be."

They drove for ten minutes without saying anything, each wallowing in their own delicious, sensuous thoughts. Finally, Martin said, "I forgot to tell you, Angela, but you look absolutely beautiful. You take such nice thoughtful care in looking good. I'd like to think you did it for me."

"Well, I did. But I thought – I remember what you said back in Palm Beach – that you liked me for my intellect, not my beauty." She was smiling.

"Absolutely, but I'd have to be some kind of stupid not to appreciate your beauty, too."

She squirmed ever so slightly in her seat.

"But you know, Angela, I find you far more interesting than beautiful. And interesting is far more arousing than beauty."

"So, what's interesting in a woman?"

"It's difficult to pinpoint. The way you hold your head erect, the chin, the eyes, the way you talk. What you say and how you say it. The words you choose. I like your laugh. It's deep and throaty. Your sense of humor, your intelligence; it all adds up to a very intriguing woman. And that's arousing."

"Aren't you building this up a little too much? You might be disappointed."

He looked at her, shook his head, and said, "I bet my expectations are surpassed."

She rubbed his shoulder and kissed it. "I've really been looking forward to this. It's all I've been thinking about for the past week. It was nice to see my mother and brothers, but Baltimore was an absolute bore. I've never been so glad to return as I was this morning. Maybe it's the expectation that you were talking about, the anticipation."

They arrived at the resort about seven o'clock. Martin drove directly to Cabin Fourteen where they would be staying. Martin had arranged everything: logs were burning, started by a cabin fireplace attendant. Martin suggested Laura freshen up while he went to the lodge to check in.

"You won't put my name on the ledger will you? I wouldn't want Philip to find out."

"No, no. Everything is very discreet here. As far as they're concerned I'm here alone."

Angela smiled.

When he returned, her clothes were unpacked and hanging in the closet. There was a little room left for what he had brought. He unpacked his bag. Martin had brought a Harris tweed jacket and wore it over a light sweater for dinner. She had taken off her sweater, put on an off-white silk blouse and a coral colored sweater vest.

They dined for two hours and talked of things they probably would never remember. They talked of their spouses and how disappointing they were. She asked why he didn't leave Laura. He said he was filing for divorce in January. And he asked her why she didn't leave Philip. She said she needed the security, her business wasn't what it had been, and frankly, she enjoyed the luxury. She figured Philip was not to be trusted around other women. There were just too many telltale signs of Philip straying. (Martin knew it was true, but decided to say nothing.) Angela said she had been faithful. (Martin doubted that was true, but didn't care.) Philip, overbearing at times, had turned into a bore, both in bed and out. Martin said Laura had become an incredible drunk. He also said she had been unfaithful many times and was currently having a torrid affair. Angela could understand Martin's situation. She asked if she were just another conquest. He said he had never gone to bed with a woman who hadn't planned it. Angela smiled. He admitted he was a very willing victim, though. She laughed a borderline giggle. They laughed a lot. They ordered dessert. Martin carried it back to the cabin. She accused him in an amusing way of being literal. He said it would taste good later after love making, perhaps with a little champagne. He had brought a half case of expensive champagne.

In the cabin they attended to details: Angela removed her make-up; Martin hung up their coats and put the chocolate cheese cake in the little refrigerator, then he took it out, thinking it would taste better at room temperature; he stoked the fire and added another log; there was a little sink and mirror outside the bathroom and he used it to brush his teeth, wash his hands and set up his toiletries; even though he had just brushed his teeth, he ate the chocolate mint that rested on top of the pillow; he took off his shoes and padded around barefoot; he unwrapped Angela's chocolate mint and asked if he could eat it, putting it into his mouth as she came out of the bathroom, before she could say "yes"; she offered a slight moue and giggled.

"Did you really remove your make-up?" Martin asked. "I can't tell the difference."

She began to unbutton his shirt. "I want to undress you." He didn't resist.

When he was naked, she began kissing his chest, licking his nipples, running her hands over his scrotum and hard, hard penis. He began to undress her. And in bed they made love. And, indeed, they surpassed their expectations. After lovemaking, they ate the cheesecake and drank a bottle of champagne, and made love again. Martin slept as he hadn't slept in many years, a hard sleep, but he awoke shortly before seven.

They skied the next day until a little past noon. Angela, while a good skier, wasn't quite of Martin's caliber. He was considerably more graceful on the slopes. They lunched at the lodge, putting away a large amount of food. Martin easily talked Angela into trying cross-country skiing in the afternoon. There were 40 miles of public ski trails beginning just 200 yards from the lodge. Martin gave her a demonstration on how cross-country skiing worked. He told her she wouldn't have any difficulty since she could already downhill ski and had skated in her youth. Angela was rather athletic.

Martin brought along a backpack with water, a Thermos of coffee, and cookies from the lodge. They were out for two hours. At a lean-to they drank the coffee, dunking the cookies. The temperature was eight degrees above zero but with hardly any wind. It seemed much warmer than it was. They skied back to their cabin where the fire roared in the fireplace that an unknown attendant had stoked. The sky had darkened. It was only a few days past the winter solstice.

In the cabin, Angela planned to take a shower before dinner. Wearing only a robe she sat on the bed, her back resting on the headboard and her legs stretched out, and said she wanted to call Philip in Arizona before taking a shower. She used her cell phone to place the call. Martin sat next to her, gently massaging an ankle and calf.

"Oh, hi, Philip. I'm at the airport in Baltimore. . . . Mother's fine. . . . I miss you, too." Martin began kissing her leg on the inside, slowly working his way up. "Of course I miss you, especially in bed. . . . I'm having a delightful tingling feeling right now. Imagine that, in an airport. . . . You are the best ever, Philip. You know that." Martin had pulled back her robe and began kissing her near her neatly trimmed pubic hair. "God, I wish you were here right now. We've never done it in an airport." She giggled. Martin ran his finger over her clitoris. She moaned ever so slightly. "Philip I can hardly wait for you to get home. Do you still love me? Am I still the most...? Yes, love, see you then." She hung up and pulled Martin up to her face, "You are deliciously wicked." She kissed him passionately.

He kissed one of her breasts, gently licking the nipple, feeling it stiffen on his tongue

"Do you want to make love now, or wait until after dinner?" she asked. Martin was wearing his cross-country skiing knickers and a turtleneck still sweaty from skiing.

He ran his tongue down to her navel. "God, I love the taste of your skin," he said. He pulled himself up and added, "I suppose we could wait until after dinner."

While Angela showered, Martin called Laura. "Just thought I'd find out how you're doing," he said with a solicitous tone. "I'll be home New Year's Day. Now, don't do anything that'll get you into trouble. My detective is out there waiting for you and Jim to do your thing."

"You sonofabitch," she shouted, forcing Martin to pull the phone from his ear.

"And lay off the booze," Martin added. A wicked smile crossed his face.

Laura slammed the phone onto the receiver with a loud crack and Martin winced as he again pulled the phone from his ear.

Dinner with Angela lasted past nine o'clock. When they returned to the cabin, Martin tossed another log on the fire. He pulled a spare quilt from the closet and spread it over the floor before the fireplace screen. He opened a bottle of champagne and poured two glasses while Angela changed. She returned wearing only a gossamer gown. "After a day of woolens, I wanted something a little more delicate and feminine," she announced and turned a quick pirouette.

"Verrrry nice," Martin replied, his eyes glinting at her gown. He offered her a glass of wine. They toasted each other. The fire blazed and the cabin was quite warm. Sitting by the fire, they talked and finished the champagne. Martin poured another glass and they took a short sip and set their glasses down. They began to kiss. Soon they were both naked. She was on her back letting Martin play. He kissed her on her mouth and face. He reached for his wine glass and rubbed her nipples with the cool base. A little champagne spilled onto her breast and he licked it.

He spilled a little more above her navel and licked that away. He worked his way down with his wine and mouth to her vulva.

When they finished, Martin lifted Angela up and carried her to the bed. He crawled beside her. "That was incredible," she murmured. "I've never been fucked like that before." And with a marvelously contented smile she rolled over and fell asleep. Martin lay beside her. In ten minutes, when her breathing deepened, he arose and turned off the lights and pulled the quilt away from the fire screen as an added caution against an errant spark.

CHAPTER SEVENTEEN

Laura Morley began worrying about her husband the moment Martin left for his ski trip. She poured herself a glass of wine. That asshole hired a detective to spy on me, she thought as she took her first swallow. It was late afternoon and this was just her first drink of the day. She wished Jim were with her, but he was out of town visiting family. He had planned to return the day before New Year's Eve. It's just until tomorrow, she agonized. She missed him.

Laura finished her wine and made herself a martini. She needed something with a little more bite. She pushed her glass against her refrigerator's ice dispenser then filled it with vodka and a drop of vermouth. The olive jar was empty. She swore. Laura proceeded to get drunk, drinking slowly until nearly midnight. Before going to bed, she retrieved a bottle of aspirin from her bathroom's medicine cabinet. She vaguely recalled Martin having told her – several times – that taking aspirin after drinking increases bleeding in the stomach. "Fucker," she mumbled and took four.

The next day, December 30, Laura awoke without a recognizable hangover. But later in the morning she could feel the after effects of having drunk too much. Jim called about mid afternoon. She was relieved to hear him and, explaining about the private investigator, asked him to come over. "Make sure no one follows you," she cautioned.

When he arrived, he smiled broadly, hugged her, kissed her on the cheek and the mouth and announced, "Not a soul on the road. No one followed me."

Laura took his hand and walked him to the kitchen. Jim had

been in the house before, but had never had a tour, although they once made love on the floor of the family room atop an oriental carpet. As Laura guided him through the house he seemed impressed, looking about as though it were a showplace. He asked questions about each of the rooms and their furnishings. The house was sumptuous, decorated by a professional, although Laura liked to claim it was her own scheme. Crane stared at the richness of the furnishings. "Very impressive," he said. "I admire your work, Laura. It's your soul shining through."

"I don't think any room came in under twenty-five thousand dollars," she said with great glee.

In Martin's office, Crane asked, "Should I leave him a message on his computer? Maybe say, 'Dear Asshole, Laura Morley is the greatest lover. She loves me and I love her.'"

Laura laughed nervously as they headed toward the kitchen. She then recounted what Martin had told her before he had left.

"He's a real bona fide sonofabitch, isn't he?" Crane said.

She offered to make him a drink. He looked at his watch, raised his face, smiled

broadly again, and announced in quick succession: "Well, it's after five, the sun is past the yardarm. Scotch, a little ice, a little water. Want me to make it?"

"Please, I'm just too nervous." Laura handed him a bottle of Scotch and placed two glasses on the counter. She retrieved the ice. Jim made a Scotch for both of them – Laura's tastes in liquor were eclectic – carefully handing the drink to her with a cocktail napkin.

"I'm so worried. I know he's after my money." She paused. "Oh," she said, slapping herself lightly aside the head, "I almost forgot." She went to her office off the dining room and brought back an envelope. She pulled out a cashier's check for two hundred and fifty thousand dollars.

Jim accepted it, thanked her and returned it to its envelope. Before putting it into his sport coat pocket he pulled out folded sheets of paper. "We're both going to sign these. There are two copies. It's a promissory note."

Laura took it, put on her reading glasses and read part of it. "Jim, we don't have to do this. I trust you to pay it back." She handed it to him.

He refused it. "Too many relationships end over money. It has a subtle but insidious effect." He explained that he couldn't have asked for a better deal – three percent simple interest, payable over ten years. "It's just as if it were a gift." She had given him another two hundred fifty thousand dollar check a couple of months earlier, and the note covered the full five hundred thousand dollars. They both signed two copies of the document. She was about to put hers in her office when she turned and said, "You keep it, Jim. I'm just afraid Martin will find it before he and I separate. This way it will be safe and so will I."

"Okay, if that's what you want." He shrugged and shook his head, commiserating with her worrisome distraction. "I'll put the papers in my safe at home." He said he would place the check in his bank's night depository on the way home. "This is going to be the salvation of my business," he said, wiping the condensation from his Scotch glass with the cocktail napkin. He set the drink down and kissed her. "Thank you very much. But mostly, thank you for believing in me." He inserted the loan papers in his coat pocket next to the check.

"I'll always believe in you, Jim. You're my salvation, my reason for being. But I worry so much about Martin taking my money and squandering my life."

They kissed for a long time, until the phone rang. It was Martin calling from the mountains. Her face paled as she heard his voice. She swore loudly into the telephone and a few moments later slammed the phone.

"I take it that was Martin," Jim said shaking his head.

"The son-of-a-bitch." She took a large swallow of whiskey. She recounted the phone conversation.

"Tell you what," Jim said. "Next week, I'll take you to my lawyer. I'll call him tomorrow, first thing in the morning. I'll make an appointment for you to see him. I'll drive you there, but I want you to see him alone. You can file for divorce and he'll advise you on what to do with your money. We can take care of everything. Martin's not invincible. With your money you can hire the best of lawyers to stop whatever he's planning."

She went to him, rubbing her hand gently on the side of his face. "You're so good to me. Your thinking is so reasonable." Her eyes welled tears.

"I love you, Laura. I've never met anyone like you. You've been unloved and unappreciated for too long." He kissed her on the mouth then rubbed his cheek against the side of her face. "In some ways I'm glad Martin turned into such a bastard."

She looked at him curiously.

"If he hadn't, we wouldn't be in love. There would be no reason for my existence in your heart."

She daubed her eyes with a tissue. "Oh, how sweet and tender, Jim." She kissed him lightly on the lips. She knew Jim loved her.

"Want to go out to dinner tonight?" Jim asked, excited with the possibility. "We could come back here and make love, leave markings on Martin's side of the bed."

Laura laughed then said, "I'm afraid he might return tonight, or the private investigator might follow. Why don't you go home and I'll call you about eleven. If he hasn't returned, come over and devastate me. Just do something wildly erotic, wicked and wonderful. It'll help me get my problems off my mind." She rubbed his penis through his trousers. She could feel it harden quickly. Jim eagerly agreed with the plan. They talked a while longer and then he left.

Laura was suddenly hungry. There was half of a large pizza in the refrigerator that Cathy and Carlton hadn't finished. She pulled it out and warmed it in the microwave oven. The Scotch and Jim's visit had loosened the hangover's grip. She had two beers with the pizza. The last swallow was the best.

She now felt in a port mood. She rummaged through the liquor cabinet looking for Martin's expensive port. She uncorked it and took the bottle and a glass to the family room. Laura inserted a movie video into the cassette player. It was a video Cathy and Carlton had forgotten to return to the rental store. She didn't look at the title to see what it was. She took a couple of aspirin laced with a soporific and downed them with a glass of port. She watched the movie and drank. The movie was a romantic comedy, but she began to cry halfway through it. She cried for five minutes, until she took down a whole glass of port. It was a small glass. Laura finished the port, small glassful by small glassful. At half past eleven o'clock the night of December 30, she was too sleepy to remember to call Jim, and went to bed.

CHAPTER EIGHTEEN

A few hours later, at nearly two in the morning of December thirty-one, a lone car with its lights off drove down Lonepath Lane and turned onto the Morley driveway. A man in black tight running pants and shirt, with a black ski mask pulled over his face, exited from the car. The night was cloudy and dark. He entered through the garage side door. Laura, too sleepy to remember, had not locked the doors or turned on the alarm system. He entered undetected.

Inside, he quickly checked all of the rooms. Laura slept soundly in the master bedroom. The man found silverware in the dining room, three thousand one hundred dollars cash in Martin's office, one hundred thirteen dollars cash in Laura's purse. He also set the computer aside by the door where he had entered and placed the silver there, too. He was extremely quiet, opening drawers softly, never closing them.

He went upstairs to the master bedroom. He removed jewelry from Laura's jewelry box, and a few things from Martin's dresser top box. He took a handful of ties from the tie rack and began to bind Laura's hands and feet to the bedposts. She awoke slowly, groggily, squirming slightly as he fastened the last knot.

"Oh, Jim, you've come anyway," she said, her speech a little thick.

A soft nightlight from the bathroom cast a faint glow onto the bed. But the figure all in black was indistinguishable. "I'm glad you came back. Are you going to devastate me?" she cooed. He ripped her nightgown down the front of her. She gasped with delight. He drew a cold gun barrel up and down her torso and over her nipples. She moaned with mounting passion, her hips moving rhythmically. He placed the barrel into her mouth and she sucked at it. Pulling it out, he ran it down to her vulva and rubbed her clitoris with the tip of the barrel. She moaned. "Oh, Jim, this is the best." The man placed the gun in his left hand, pulled the glove off his right hand and began to play with her clitoris. As she became more and more aroused, he was more vigorous in his rubbing. "I'm going to come, Jim, I'm going to come. Take me the rest of the way, please." And she moaned.

Just as she was well into her orgasm the man shot her through the temple.

He replaced the glove, returned the pistol to that hand and picked up the sack of jewelry and fled the room. The gunshot would go undetected, but he moved quickly. He stashed everything in the car and pulled out a two-gallon can of gasoline, tossing the cap and nozzle to the side of the driveway. He ran through the first floor of the house pouring fuel on the carpet then splashed gasoline on the wood paneled walls of the family room and on the staircase.

He left the house and tossed the gas can towards the woods. He started his car and then returned to the house to set it on fire. He turned his car lights on a mile past the house. The man escaped unnoticed.

CHAPTER NINETEEN

On December thirty-one Caitlin's train of thought kept switching from the radio news of Laura Morley's death to the evening she would be sharing with Erik. Caitlin had become excited about New Year's Eve. She put fresh sheets on her son's bed, figuring Erik would need to sleep there. He probably shouldn't drive home on New Year's Eve. It would be a hell of a situation if she had to defend him in a drunk driving case just before he goes to work for the CIA.

She wondered whether he was going to try to make love with her. She didn't think so, but if he did, why not? She didn't know what her problem was, perhaps just loneliness, a certain emptiness.

Deep in the recesses of her bedroom closet, Caitlin retrieved an old cocktail dress, black and décolleté with gold sequins that bordered the V that dipped to her bosom. She had bought it ten years earlier after she had finally lost the weight that she had gained bearing Michael. It was for a special occasion with her former husband. She wondered if she could still get into it. She had grown a dress size since then. She tried it on and it still fit, although snug. But it was precisely at this moment, the morning of December thirty-one, that she came to a great and new understanding of herself: I'm never ever going to be that skinny again. She shook her head, not sure if that realization were relief or despair.

Caitlin knew what Erik was making for dinner, so she was able to buy wine with some confidence. At a French bakery she picked up a *gâteau de Noël* that she had ordered earlier. Erik had told her about the bakery some months ago. He was a marvelous food informant.

At the supermarket she gathered fixings for the next day's breakfast. There was a jar of *Bonne Maman* brand preserves; a loaf of unsliced bread that she could cut for thick pieces of toast; a little Brie cheese; a dozen eggs; mushrooms; and scallions. Now she had the ingredients for the one thing she was really good at in the kitchen: the omelet. Caitlin owned two omelet pans. She had bought them several years before she had married, thinking it was nice to have two omelet pans for when a man spent the night. She might have read that in a woman's magazine, but she couldn't remember. Caitlin also selected caviar and a tin of *pâté de foie gras* and gathered an armful of odds and ends. The ritual of preparing to entertain a man pleased her.

At her home Caitlin called the State Police again to find out if anything new had developed on Martin's whereabouts, or the murder of his wife. She learned nothing. Authorities seemed cooperative, but in the dark. She watched the local evening news, flicking the remote control from station to station, not wanting to miss anything. The story wasn't much different than the radio reports from the morning, just more detail on the Morleys. One of the reports ended with, "But where's Dr. Morley?" She shook her head knowing that he now was a prime suspect in the minds of everyone – especially the police.

Caitlin spent a long time on her make-up, trying for the perfect effect. She looked at her face in the mirror with a critical but prejudiced eye. She saw every delicate, faint crevice as a crevasse. She ended up taking the makeup off, slathering on cold cream in disappointment. This had never happened before. After the second attempt, which really wasn't much different from the first, she felt slightly satisfied. She never thought she was pretty, just decent looking, good enough to get by. But tonight, she wanted to look her best. She wasn't sure why and shook her head at the mirror.

Although her legs – especially in a short skirt – looked best when she wore high heels, she decided on a pair of flats, not wanting to tower over Erik, or stumble. When she was a student at the University of Minnesota a friend from New York once remarked that she walked "like a Minnesota farm girl in her first pair of heels." Caitlin had been self-conscious ever since.

Erik arrived at the door wearing a tuxedo and carrying a brown grocery bag in each arm. Caitlin grabbed one of the bags as she greeted him. They carried them to the kitchen. "I have to go back for the rest of the stuff," he said. He returned from his car with two loaves of French bread, a large cast iron frying pan and a sack of kitchen utensils.

He set everything on the counter in her kitchen, turned on the oven, looked at Caitlin and said, *"Tu es trop belle pour moi."*

"Really?"

"C'est vrais." He shook his head. "I've got to cut this French stuff out."

"Why? Do you talk this way to all the women?"

Erik laughed. "I tried it on Cutie Pie, but she didn't understand or find it particularly amusing."

"Does anybody study languages anymore?"

"Not even English," Erik replied.

"I guess America has become the land of the illiterati," Caitlin said.

Erik gave her a despairing shake of the head. He looked at her for a few moments. "Anyone else coming tonight?"

"Just the two of us."

"Then I'm really flattered. You dressed just for me. You are ravishing."

She put a trio of fingers at the V of her neckline wanting to believe everything he said. "Erik, you look very handsome in that tux. You're wearing a vest instead of a cummerbund. I think that's very elegant." Her former husband had told her once that the cummerbund was a recent affectation, that a vest was the classic accouterment to a tuxedo.

Caitlin opened a bottle of white wine that she had been chilling and poured a glass for each of them. She toasted Erik on his new job and new career, and admitted she was going to miss his good company. She set the hors d'oeuvres on the kitchen table.

"I love *pâté*," Erik said as he slathered a thick slab on a slice of French bread. He took a bite and savored the flavor. "I don't know why I'm such a Francophile. I was only there a year and half." He lifted his glass of wine, "Well, to you my good friend. My only regret about going to Washington is leaving you." He took a swallow of wine to wash down the remnants of *pâté* and bread.

Caitlin looked at the toe of her right shoe, lifted her head and said, "What about your daughters?"

"That's all set. I get them for six weeks in the summer and all major school breaks. And I'll be here from time to time as I wind up some old cases. It'll be nice for everyone." He scrubbed two baking potatoes, poked a fork into them several times, slathered them with olive oil and placed them in the oven.

"I love baked potatoes," Caitlin said. "They're my favorite."

"These are going to be twice baked."

"That's even better, twice as good."

Caitlin left to put some music on her player. When she returned she said she had bought a disc of old Edith Piaf hits that she would play after dinner.

"She always conjures up thoughts of Camus, Sartre and deep existentialism," Erik said.

"Smoking Gauloise, drinking Pernod in some dark café and muttering," Caitlin said, switching to a thick French accent and pausing to make believe she was smoking a cigarette, 'Hell is," she paused, "other people.'"

Erik laughed, "Sartre may have been right," then took off his jacket and put on a white cotton apron. He removed his cufflinks and rolled up his shirt sleeves. He unwrapped the butcher's paper from the meat and sprinkled some cracked pepper on both sides, pressing it with the heel of his hand.

"Steak *au poivre?"* Caitlin asked, marveling at his deftness in the kitchen.

"Not exactly, but close. I'm also going to make a little *sauce dijonaise,* a simplified variation."

While he worked, they talked and ate *pâté* and caviar, drinking a little wine. They talked some about Laura Morley's murder.

"I don't know who in the hell did it, but I bet Martin's a definite suspect in the eyes of the police."

"Do you think he did it?" Erik asked.

"I doubt it."

"Is he capable of it?"

"I don't know. I guess just about anybody is capable of murder, the right provocation and everything. But well thought out pre-meditated murder is another matter, however. Maybe it was a robbery, but the cops are awfully anxious to talk with Martin." To change the subject Caitlin asked, "Need a *sou chef?"*

He put her to work peeling shallots and garlic. Then she opened a can of anchovies for him, washing her hands when she finished.

In a large salad bowl he mashed garlic and an anchovy together with a little white pepper. He squeezed the juice of a pair of lemon halves into the bowl and added olive oil. He coddled an egg and added that. "It's my version of a Caesar salad," he explained. He lifted Caitlin's hand and smelled her fingertips. "Ah, soap, garlic and anchovy." He grabbed one of the squeezed lemon halves and at the sink rubbed it on her fingers. He put her hands under running water and rubbed them. "Now the smell should be gone," he said as he dried her hands.

"How did you learn your way around the kitchen?" she asked.

"So many mistakes, so many moments of culinary mediocrity."

Caitlin laughed. "Well, what about the lemons?"

"I saw it in a movie. Remember Louis Malle's *Atlantic City* with Burt Lancaster and Susan Sarandon? She worked at an oyster bar and would come home smelling like a fishmonger. Burt Lancaster was an old man with a strong sense of libido, and a voyeur. He watched from his apartment through her window as she cleaned up after work. She was nude from the waist up, and was using lemon wedges to remove the odor. It was kind of erotic in a dirty old man sort of way, and I remembered the technique."

"That's absolutely amazing," Caitlin said, laughing. "So the best way to train or teach a man is through sex or food."

"Preferably both. At least that's how I like to be trained."

"I like to think women are a lot more refined than men."

"But the primordial urges drive us all. We're being a lot more refined tonight, of course." Erik took a sip of wine. "And isn't talking about sex – or, our intercourse about intercourse – on a more ethereal plane than actually doing it?"

"I suppose there is some validity to that, especially since we both struck out again in the relationship game." Caitlin found Erik vastly amusing. He was particularly interesting to her this evening. Clearly the kitchen was his best platform.

He continued preparing the meal, cleaning and tearing lettuce, drying it and returning it to her refrigerator. Then he pulled the potatoes out of the oven. He sliced long strips of peel off the lengths of the potatoes. He scooped the white flesh into a bowl and added butter, salt and a little milk. He began to beat it with an electric mixer.

"My mother always made lumpy mashed potatoes," Caitlin said as she watched. "She claimed the lumps told you it was homemade."

"These have to be smooth, though, because I have more stuff to add." He then put in some grated Parmesan cheese, a little sour cream and fresh-chopped chives. He mixed and stuffed it back into the potato shells.

After he returned the potatoes to the oven, he salted the fleshy sides of the two tops that remained and slathered on a bit of butter. He handed one to Caitlin and he ate the other.

"Gee, Erik," she said, the melting butter oozing onto her fingertips and down the palm of her hand, "have you ever thought of opening a restaurant?"

"I do very small groups. Cooking for more than six or eight becomes work." A little butter drooled down his chin. He swiped at it, licked his fingers, and grinned.

Caitlin went to the dining room to light the candles. "I like the candles to get a head start," she explained. She also opened a bottle of red wine.

They talked for a half hour, continuing to discuss the Laura Morley murder then switching to their careers. Erik told her he greatly admired her, was a little envious because she was able to make a go of solo practice, while he wasn't.

She said it was only because she was a woman. She receives child support, while he has to pay it. "That's probably the deciding factor," she added. Caitlin didn't know if that were true, but it seemed the right thing to say at the moment.

Erik placed his cast iron pan on a burner and turned the heat on high. When the pan had heated sufficiently, he put the thick steaks in. He cooked them without oil for several minutes on each side. When they were finished he covered them on a serving plate and created his sauce with a little wine, chopped shallots, Dijon mustard and cream. He added the juices that had settled on the warming plate.

Caitlin tossed and served the salad while he placed the steaks in shallow pools of sauce on the plates. She started the coffee pot. And he rolled down his sleeves, replaced the cufflinks and exchanged the apron for his jacket.

With her first bite Caitlin declared, "Erik, I think I've gone to heaven. This is superb."

They ate and talked and laughed and drank the bottle of wine. She served the chocolate Christmas log and a rich French (of course) roast coffee, and small cognacs. Caitlin put on the Edith Piaf music.

"Pretty melancholy stuff, isn't it?" Caitlin said.

"But a good way to end a year." He saluted her with the brandy snifter. "I'm going to miss you, Caitlin."

"And I'll miss you." She already did.

The Piaf disc ended shortly before midnight. "I've got a bottle of champagne chilling in the refrigerator. Would you like to pop it at the stroke of midnight, Erik?"

He fetched the bottle and she put on some soft jazz, melancholy saxophone. Holding the cork, Erik screwed the bottle loose just as Caitlin declared it the New Year. It didn't gush, but a steamy essence rose from the bottle's top. He poured the wine. They toasted. And then they kissed, hesitantly, with reluctance. When they parted, Caitlin blinked her eyes to brush aside a slight haze that had formed.

"Want to dance, Caitlin?" Erik asked and took her in his arms. She kicked off her shoes. He was a nice dancer and it felt good to be in his arms. She didn't know what to do. They danced through three songs then glided to the table where the champagne glasses were.

They talked for a half hour longer then Caitlin asked if he'd like to stay in Michael's bed. He said he thought it would be the wise thing to do. They parted at the bedroom doorway with a brief kiss. In her own bedroom she sat on the edge of the bed for a few minutes wondering why she hadn't been aggressive.

The next morning she concocted the omelet of the century. He stayed for two hours after breakfast. He assembled all of the equipment he had brought and took it out to the car. On the way back in he handed Caitlin her newspaper stuffed in an orange plastic wrapper. They slowly said their goodbyes. He was leaving the next day for Washington. They stood at the doorway. He brushed back some strands of her hair that had fallen over her eyebrow.

"You know, Erik, I think we could have made love last night."

"It would have killed me, Caitlin, to become your lover just two nights before moving to Washington. I wouldn't have been able to handle it." He kissed her gently, turned and left.

She waved a slow goodbye and walked back to the kitchen, tapping the newspaper on her thigh. She poured a cup of coffee, sat at the kitchen table and opened the paper. The banner headline announced: "Prominent Physician's Wife Found Murdered in Home."

She blinked her eyes, realizing it was time to get back to business, and read: "Laura Morley, wife of prominent internist Dr. Martin Morley, was found nude, bound and shot to death in her burning home in the affluent suburb of Windsor."

Caitlin set the paper down before continuing and wondered: where in the hell are you, Martin? Probably with some damn woman. She shook her head.

CHAPTER TWENTY

On January 1 Martin awoke well past seven o'clock. He could see the digital clock from the bed. He and Angela had danced until one at the ski lodge's party. They fell asleep as soon as they went to bed, but awoke a few hours later to make love. Martin clasped his hands behind his head and stared at the ceiling. This is the latest he had slept since... then he shook his head and smiled. He figured that Angela would probably sleep another two hours. It annoyed him ever so slightly when the woman he was with didn't awaken on his schedule. He turned his head to look at her. A bit of her back was exposed. He admired it for a few moments then pulled the down comforter over her shoulders. It wasn't really cold since the phantom fireplace tender had arrived quietly and mysteriously before Martin awoke.

Martin lay in bed for a half hour before arising. He was naked. He went to the sink, brushed his teeth and shaved. When he finished, a husky voice from the bed said, "You look cold standing there without clothes. Why don't you come back here and let me warm you up."

He returned, sliding beneath the covers and into her warm embrace. They made love again. Angela was a marvelous lover. Maybe she was the best.

"Too bad we have to go back," she whispered in his ear.

"I'm never going back, not in my dreams, anyway."

"We have to," she licked a little perspiration that had formed at the diaphragm of his chest, "find a way to keep meeting like this."

They showered together. After packing they left the ski resort in search of a restaurant. By the time they finished breakfast and drove the remaining hour and a half, it was a little past noon. Martin drove Angela to her office building where he transferred her luggage and skis to her car. They kissed goodbye and agreed to talk in several days.

Neither had read a newspaper or listened to news since arriving at the resort.

He headed home wondering what was in store for him there. Driving slowly along Lonepath Lane he admired the winter scenery. At his driveway he saw two Johnson County Sheriff's Department squad cars blocking the entrance. He pulled over and walked to the closest squad car.

"Hi, deputy, I'm Dr. Martin Morley. I live here. Is something wrong?"

A sergeant in another car exited and walked quickly to Martin. "I'm sorry, Doctor, but your home was burned and I'm afraid that your," he stammered slightly, "wife has died."

Martin stood stiffly, grimacing, and asked, "Did she burn to death?" He shuddered and watched the deputy shake his head. "Smoke inhalation?" Martin asked.

"I really can't tell you much. Do you think you're capable of following me to the State Police Post Headquarters in Enola, or would you rather ride with me?"

Martin said he could drive. He coughed lightly into his gloved hand. He removed the glove and rubbed his eyes as though he were trying to loosen some emotion that was gripping him. "May I go up and look around?"

"Not until the crime lab is finished. They're coming back again tomorrow for one more look. State Police are handling this investigation."

"Where is Laura?"

"At the medical examiner's in Williamsville."

Martin followed the squad car to the State Trooper Post in Enola. The post served a four-county area. The uniformed troopers were used mostly for highway patrol for Interstate and U.S. highways. The Criminal Investigation Division, however, handled serious crimes that the more rural counties' sheriffs' departments weren't equipped to investigate.

The Post Headquarters was a two-story, yellow brick building set back fifty yards from two-lane U.S. 16 that ran through Enola, a village of about two thousand residents. Martin had been through the village a number of times while on his way to other places.

He parked his car in an area marked for visitors and waited for the sergeant to lead him inside. They entered the front door, stopping briefly at the front desk. The walls were painted beige. Past two swinging gates and behind the front desk photographs of the governor, the president of the United States, and the commandant of the State Troopers hung on the wall. State and U.S. flags flanked the photographs. Fifteen feet behind the desk in a radio room with a large glass window sat a uniformed dispatcher. Along one of the side walls stood a five-foot high bank of gray steel filing cabinets extending the length of the wall. There were also three gray steel desks behind the front desk. No one sat at them, although there was a computer screen, keyboard, mouse, phone and baskets of forms on each desk.

The sergeant who had escorted Martin asked the doctor to follow him. Martin obliged, saying nothing. They went through the swinging gates and behind the front desk to a doorway on the right that led down a short hall to a small windowless office with no name on it. The sergeant opened the door for the doctor. Inside were five men. Only one was in uniform, a captain who looked about forty-five. All were taking sips of coffee as Martin entered.

The man in uniform set his cup down, shook hands with Martin and introduced himself as Capt. John Krebbs, the shift commander this New Year's Day. He explained that he was sorry that they had to meet under such circumstances. He introduced Lt. Nelson Warren, who seemed to Martin to be in his late forties; Sgt. Willie Clemens, who was the only black detective and appeared to be about fifty; Sgt. Harley Harmon, about thirty-eight; and Detective-Investigator William Steinert, who appeared to be in his early thirties. They were with the Criminal Investigation Department.

Each of the men shook hands with Dr. Morley and offered their condolences.

"Can someone tell me what happened?" Martin asked in a steady, calm voice.

"Yes, but why don't we go to the conference room," the captain said. Everyone followed the captain to a larger room that had a rectangular wooden table and eight chairs. A video camera on a tripod rested in a corner. It was turned off. There were no windows to the outside. They sat down, the captain at the head.

"Doctor," Capt. Krebbs began, "a little before three o'clock yesterday morning the Town of Osceola Volunteer Fire Department responded to a call at your residence. They found the place pretty well engulfed in flames, but were able to knock it down fast. The Johnson County Sheriff's Department was at the scene. Upon investigation by fire fighters they discovered Mrs. Morley in her bedroom." The captain paused, lowered his head a little, then lifted it and continued, "This is a little gruesome, but since you're a doctor you've probably seen much worse. Mrs. Morley was tied to the bedposts, spread eagle, naked and shot once through the head with a .38 caliber bullet. We recovered the bullet from the mattress."

"Was she," Martin hesitated a moment, "abused in any way?"

"We don't think so. The medical examiner hasn't finished his examination yet, but it looks like she wasn't beaten or raped. I'm not with the CID unit, our Criminal Investigation Department," the captain continued. "Lt. Warren is in charge. Sergeants Clemens and Harmon are veteran detectives, who've worked many homicides. And Detective/Investigator Steinert is our best materials evidence man, maybe the best in the state."

Steinert smiled softly, lowering his eyes slightly. Martin suspected he was trying to look modest, but actually loved the compliment. Martin took an instant dislike to the investigator. "Do you have any idea what the motive was?" Martin asked, directing his question to the lieutenant.

"It may have been robbery," the lieutenant said. "We need to go through the house with you, but it'll be dark pretty soon. We'd like to go through with you tomorrow morning." The lieutenant watched Martin nod in agreement. "Meanwhile, we have some questions we need to ask you."

"Go ahead, I want to help."

"First, we'd like to know where you were and why it took so long for you to contact us." The lieutenant had a yellow legal tablet in front of him and was holding an inexpensive ballpoint pen, the black plastic cap on the table.

"I was at Western Alps Ski Resort," Martin said. "I had been there for three nights. I haven't read a newspaper and there was no television in the room. Until I pulled up to our driveway I had no idea anything had happened."

"And your children?" Sgt. Clemens asked.

"Cathy and Carlton are skiing in Colorado."

"You must like skiing an awful lot to go up to Western Alps alone," Steinert said.

Martin looked at him for a few seconds then said: "I wasn't alone."

"Who were you with?"

"You act as though I'm a suspect."

"Of course you are," Steinert said and looked at Sgt. Harmon.

"Everyone who knew Mrs. Morley is a suspect," Sgt. Harmon explained calmly. "We have a temporary motive of robbery, but that may not have been the motive at all."

"Well, look. I was with a woman for the past three days. I don't want to tell you who she is. She's married and I like her very much and don't want to cause her any unnecessary grief." No emotion registered on anyone's face and Martin's voice remained steady. "Look," he paused, "it's not any deep, dark secret, but Laura and I were not getting along. She was an alcoholic and I bet if the medical examiner checks her blood, he'll find alcohol in significant volume. Also, I was about to file for divorce next week. I've already made a deposit and first month's rent on an apartment downtown. If you suspect something other than robbery, I suggest you check out a Jim

Crane of Crane Public Relations. He and my wife were lovers. I have no reason to suspect Mr. Crane, however. But he should be just as suspect as I am."

All of the detectives were writing on pads of paper or notebooks. "We'll certainly check into Mr. Crane," the lieutenant, finally, said as his eyes rose from his tablet.

"Who's your lawyer for the divorce?" Steinert asked.

"Caitlin Schroeder."

"She's been calling since yesterday," Capt. Krebbs said.

"Oh?" Martin raised an eyebrow.

"She said she'd be home all day if you need her."

"Doctor," the lieutenant said in a calming voice. "No one is accusing you of anything. We're just at the beginning of our investigation."

"In other words you have no leads, no anything other than a burned house and my dead wife."

"That's right," the lieutenant acknowledged. "As you can see, we do need your cooperation."

"I'm certainly willing to help," Martin responded in earnest.

"We'd like to meet you at your house tomorrow morning at eight," Sgt. Harmon said. "We expect the fire marshal will have made a conclusion from his investigation by then."

Martin agreed to be there. They talked for an hour. He told them he usually kept a sizeable amount of cash in the house, about three thousand dollars. He said he would have to check his records to be sure how much he had.

"That seems like an awful lot of money," Sgt. Clemens said.

"I grew up poor. The cash gives me a sense of security."

Night was fast approaching and the lieutenant suggested they quit and give the doctor a chance to gather his thoughts. Martin told them he would get a room at the Sheraton Downtown and stay there until he could get a few pieces of furniture delivered to his new apartment.

"Before you check in, Dr. Morley, I'd like you to go with Capt. Krebbs to the Williamsville Regional Medical Center to make a positive identification of the deceased. Are you up to it?"

Martin nodded.

The four criminal investigators continued to sit at the conference table when Martin left with Capt. Krebbs. "What do you think?" Sgt. Harmon asked.

"He's certainly a suspect," Lt. Warren said.

"But he's probably got proof of being at the lodge."

"It's less than a two-hour drive from here," the lieutenant said.

"What about the woman?" Sgt. Clemens asked.

"I bet she didn't stay awake all night begging for more from that cocksucker," Steinert interjected.

They laughed.

Steinert pushed his coffee cup aside. "There's something about our doctor that just doesn't register. Did you watch his face. It was so unemotional."

"Well, he is a doctor, trained to control himself," the lieutenant replied.

"He's just too cool and collected," Steinert continued. "I bet he did it. He's slime." He tossed his pencil on the table.

"Let's not jump to conclusions, guys," the lieutenant said. "Let's just gather our evidence in a cool methodical way. The DA will be in here tomorrow afternoon. What have you got so far for physical evidence?" He looked at Steinert.

"We found the gas can that was used," Steinert said. "I found it this morning about 10 feet from the side of the driveway, not far from the garage. It was obscured by shrubs. Unusual, though. It was metal, not like all the plastic ones they sell now."

"How do you know it was the gas can that was used?" Clemens asked.

"It was open. It was clean. No snow on it. No dirt. No rust. It still smelled heavily of gasoline. And we found the nozzle next to the driveway. It was inverted." Steinert paused and demonstrated with his hands as he said, “Know what I mean? The nozzle was pointed down so that when you screw the cap onto the can, the nozzle is directed into the can.”

“Any prints?” Clemens asked.

“I haven’t finished," Steinert said. “You'd expect something, at least fingerprints from the store where it was bought. I'm not giving up. I’ve gotta check the inside of the handle, yet.”

The lieutenant turned to Sgt. Harmon and said, “When we meet the doctor at the house tomorrow, let's try to get samples of his prints. Can you handle that Harmy?”

“Sure," Harmon said. He paused for a moment. “I think Steinert's right, I bet the good doctor did it. I mean, the ski resort never told him. He never saw nothing on TV or heard nothing on the radio for two days? And then he comes home. Surprise! Shit, man.”

“They were probably doing something more than just waiting for the news on TV," Steinert said.

They all laughed again.

“It's too early, guys, to form an opinion," Warren said. “Shit, if the DA heard us talking like this we'd all end up back on highway patrol.”

“Hell, it doesn't even look like a normal robbery," Harmon said. “A real killer and robber, one after money and valuables, would have cut her fingers off to get those rings. Those rings are worth a lot.” He shook his head. “It doesn't make sense.”

“Let's just do good work," the lieutenant cautioned. “I suspect this is going to be a case that gets one hell of a lot of publicity. In fact it already has.”

CHAPTER TWENTY-ONE

At six o'clock Angela turned on the television. The evening news led with Martin's return, but no video of the doctor. Angela sat there dumbfounded. This is awful. Someone kills Laura while I'm fucking her husband. She shook her head with a sense of incredulity.

Finally she got up, thought about calling Martin, but didn't. Instead she called Philip in Arizona. "Dear, terrible news," she said then recounted what she had seen on the television. She didn't have a newspaper. "I just turned on the TV for the first time since yesterday," she explained. "The television reported that the police said Martin was in Western Alps Ski Resort when Laura was murdered."

"Probably with some bimbo," Philip said.

Angela smiled. "Why are you always so critical of Martin?"

"Christ," Philip continued, almost laughing, "Martin hated his wife. He's probably thrilled thinking this'll save him a bundle on divorce, alimony, property settlement, and lawyer fees. But that might not be so bad if he's buffin' that six-foot lawyer of his."

"Are you crazy, Philip? Laura's been murdered. Martin's marriage might have been on the rocks, but murder?" She shuddered.

"I don't mean he did it. I mean he's probably not disappointed that she's dead."

"I don't think he's quite that callous, Philip."

"I suppose not." He paused briefly. "Did you miss me?"

"It's been almost two week – "

"...Since you've been laid really well," he finished her sentence for her.

"Well, I do miss that." She gave herself a delicious smile at the irony.

"I'll be home in two days. We'll make up for lost time." Philip, of course, couldn't see his wife's smile suddenly turn to a pained wince.

A few minutes after she hung up, Martin called. He explained what had happened and added, "State Police wanted to know where I was. I didn't tell them about you."

"Well, they can't possibly suspect you, Martin." Suddenly Angela became very fearful, worried that she'd be dragged into this mess.

"They told me everybody who knew her is a suspect. They don't have a clue who did it."

"Television news reported it was robbery," Angela said.

"I guess you never know about these things."

"I know you didn't do it," she giggled slightly, "but do keep me out of it, please. I couldn't withstand the public scrutiny and Philip's reaction."

"Don't worry, Angela. I promise I won't drag you into this."

After the call, Angela paced the room trying to figure out what she would do if Martin decided to use her as an alibi. Deny it and Martin could be charged with murder. Admit it and her marriage would be over. She knew this was an awful dilemma. Maybe, just maybe, Martin would not implicate her.

CHAPTER TWENTY-TWO

Martin met his children at the airport late the night they returned from Aspen. They looked worn out from three days of partying. Cathy talked about the ski trip as they walked through the parking ramp toward the Lincoln Navigator. They had just set their luggage down outside the car when Martin told them of their mother's death. "There's no good place or time to tell you this, but your mother has died." He watched their faces suddenly turn into anguish. "She was murdered the other night." He then provided the details, the three of them standing in the concrete cavern of cars, his voice clear, but hollow sounding, reverberating off the surrounding cement. Cathy cried and Carlton bumped his head softly on a concrete pillar in the parking ramp. Martin had expected them to react more calmly, more rationally. Perhaps it was the violent nature of Laura's death that bothered them, rather than the death itself. He drove them to the hotel where he had a suite.

The next morning at seven o'clock, he called Caitlin at her home. He provided her with the information that he had then added, "I'd like to stop by your office after I meet with police at my house, or what's left of the house," he said. Caitlin concurred. She offered to accompany him to the house. "Undoubtedly, you're a suspect," she explained. But Martin demurred with a hint of arrogance.

Martin asked Cathy and Carlton to accompany him to the remains of their home. "You might find something salvageable that means a lot to you," he explained. They agreed to go along, shuddering at the thought of being at the scene of their mother's gruesome death. "I just don't want to go into your bedroom," Carlton insisted.

They remained quiet for most of the drive. Carlton finally

broke the silence: "I suppose, since you were filing for divorce, that this doesn't bother you very much."

"That's not true," Martin replied. He struggled not to admonish Carlton. "I may have wanted out of the marriage, but I didn't wish your mother harm. On the contrary, I really wanted her to do well. Perhaps without me she might have had a renaissance."

Carlton crossed his arms over his chest, and leaned his shoulder into the corner of the back seat and door. His position kept his face out of alignment with the rear view mirror. "I didn't mean you wanted her dead," he said as an offering of apology.

"I didn't think you meant that, just that you thought it wouldn't bother me as much as it affects you. And that's true. Laura was your mother, no matter my differences with her."

The car dropped into silence once again. Five minutes passed and Carlton said, "Well, I loved Mom."

"I did, too," Cathy added.

"I'm glad you both said that. It makes me feel a lot better," their father said.

"Why were you skiing alone?" Carlton suddenly asked.

"I wasn't alone. I was with a friend."

"Oh, who?" Cathy asked.

"It's not important," Martin replied.

Again it turned silent in the car. Their mother was murdered, their home torched and now they learned that their father was involved in what they figured was some sordid affair.

At their house a squad car again was parked in front of the driveway. The sheriff's deputy moved the car aside and pulled back the yellow police ribbon that cordoned the driveway's entrance. Martin drove to the house. All three of them expected the house to be a heap of rubble, but most of it was still standing, though clearly ruined. The garage was intact, although the doors were open. Neither of the cars appeared damaged. Much of the roof at the opposite end of the house was gone. Two unmarked police cars were parked in front of the garage. Martin joined them.

Lt. Warren and Sgt. Harmon sat in one car. Sgt. Clemens was behind the wheel in the other with Det. Steinert next to him. They slid out as Martin's dark green Lincoln Navigator pulled up.

Martin introduced his children to each of the State Police investigators. They toured the house. It smelled strongly, acrid and burnt.

"I'd like to go through the house, room by room, and do an inventory of what's missing," Sgt. Harmon said.

In the kitchen Martin saw the Scotch bottle with a fourth of the whiskey still in it. "It looks like she was drinking Scotch, which is not her usual drink."

"Two people," Harmon said. "There were two glasses with the remnants of Scotch with her fingerprints on only one of them. It seems peculiar that there would be two glasses next to each other, both of them drunk from, but with prints on only one glass." Harmon looked at Steinert.

Steinert pointed to a crinkled cocktail napkin. "Perhaps that's the answer." He picked it up at the corner. "The creases make it look like it was holding a drink. See the circle where the glass had set? Perhaps that's why there are no fingerprints on that glass."

Steinert paused for a moment then continued, "As you'd expect, we found different sets of fingerprints all over the house. I'd like to get a copy of yours and your children's so we don't waste a lot of effort trying to lift everything we see."

"It's fine with me." Martin looked at his son and daughter. They agreed.

"After we're done with the inventory, I'd like to take our important papers with me. Do you mind?" Martin asked.

His desk drawer was open in his office in the house. He looked inside and announced that the cash was missing. "It wasn't a very safe place," he admitted, "but we do have an alarm system. I suppose it didn't go off."

"It wasn't set."

"Laura hated it," Martin recalled. "She kept setting it off accidentally. The alarm people always call when it goes off and they ask for a code word. One time – I wasn't here – she set it off and couldn't remember the code. Three squad cars were in the yard in a matter of minutes." He chuckled and shook his head.

In the master bedroom he saw that blood had stained the bedding. His children did not accompany him to the room. He stared at the bed for a minute then turned to where Laura kept her jewelry. "Well, it appears to be all gone. I have an inventory of all her jewelry in my office downstairs, the expensive things that I'm aware of, and my own stuff, of course."

The clothes were ruined by smoke. Other than some artwork and china, nothing seemed salvageable. Even the automobiles reeked. "Can I come back tomorrow with an insurance adjuster and some people to help me with the stuff that can be saved?" Martin asked.

"Certainly," Lt. Warren replied, "if Det. Steinert has completed his work."

"I better be done by then," Steinert said. "There's a snow storm coming."

Martin returned to his office on the first floor of the home and gathered the papers he needed. Police had already removed financial statements. His computer was stolen, but he had always backed up his data on discs, which he had stored in both his practice office and his safe deposit box. In Laura's office on the inside of her secretary, near the right hinge of the door, which also served as a writing table when opened, was a key on a slip of paper on which she had written "Hera." The Greek goddess's name was the code word for their safe deposit box. Before they had married, Martin had told Laura that she reminded him of Homer's description of the queen of the gods, the goddess of women and marriage – "Hera of the white arms," he had told her. He wondered if he was a romantic at the time, or if he had said it because he thought it seemed romantic. But she did have lovely arms. Martin picked up the key and slipped it into his pocket.

"Everything smells so bad," Cathy remarked as they drove to Enola to provide the police with their fingerprints.

"Do we have to go back tomorrow?" Carlton asked.

"I could use some help."

"I suppose, but I'm really going to hate it," he said, yet Carlton agreed to return.

Back at their hotel in the early afternoon, Martin called his insurance agent and made an appointment to review the damage then he called a funeral director. He told his children he had an appointment with his attorney that afternoon, and left with a half hour to spare.

Martin stopped at the bank to check the deposit box. Inside were all of the documents he had stored including the will and absent bank data and even the statements Laura had placed there. He gave the statements a quick cursory examination. Martin failed to notice the missing two hundred fifty thousand dollars from October. The December withdrawal had not yet appeared on a statement. The accounts with her inheritance were joint accounts with Martin. It brought a warm smile.

Later at Caitlin's office he gave her a quick summation of his assets.

"You're a very wealthy man now," she said.

"I wasn't bad off before this. Everything had been moved to low risk investments before the market started to crumble. I never moved them back to anything more lucrative. I'm glad I didn't after the 2008 implosion. Who knows what'll happen in the market next? I suppose it's time for things to go up again." He smiled. "But now with her money and the life insurance, and the sale of the practice, and everything else I better hire one heck of a sharp financial wizard." He shook his head as if he couldn't believe it.

"Have the investigators become more curious about you as a suspect?" she asked. "It's a logical thought progression on their part, especially after viewing your financial statements. If I were still a prosecutor you would be my prime suspect at this point."

"Fortunately for me, you're on my side." He then recounted what had happened. "I think having me as a suspect is an easy way out for them," he acknowledged. He cited his alibi. "Of course, Western Alps is only a two-hour drive from here, but I was with someone."

"Who?"

"I don't want her brought into this unless they decide I'm their boy."

Caitlin nodded and explained the confidentiality between counselor and client.

"It was Angela Wain, wife of Dr. Philip Wain. You know him, one of my former partners."

Caitlin's face remained passive, but what a wicked man, she thought. "If they want to interview you again, I would like to go along. It would be wise to have me there."

"I don't think it's necessary, at least not at this point. It might be misconstrued as some sort of admission of something. I'd like them to direct their attention to finding the killer and leaving me alone."

"We certainly don't want them to get a notion about you. I would like to be present, though. It would serve you best if I were there," she insisted.

Martin declined, smiling and saying, "Only if I have something to worry about. I really think I can take care of myself on this matter." His tone was adamant.

"Okay, Martin, but be careful of what you say and how you say it. If they begin to go beyond what looks like routine questions, don't hesitate to ask for me. It's your right. Insist on it. Their questions may sound routine, but you never know what kind of conclusion they're trying to reach. You'll need a professional outsider to filter it and protect you."

CHAPTER TWENTY-THREE

While Martin was meeting with Caitlin, Jim Crane stood at his office window overlooking downtown trying to decide how to handle matters with the police. He was distraught about Laura's death, but more worried about himself. Clearly, he's a suspect, he figured. I'm her lover. Her husband and children are out of town and she's dead. Martin is sure to blab about the detective he had hired to spy on us. Jesus Christ, what the hell kind of shit have I got myself into now?

He called his attorney. "I've got a problem," he told his attorney, Gregg Wallace. "First, I made an appointment with you for next week. Well, I have to cancel it. My friend is dead." He then explained the circumstances, but said nothing about the money Laura had given him.

"I can't see why they would have a motive, but if they bring you in for an interview, then you better call me," Wallace advised. "Otherwise, just answer their routine questions. You are innocent, aren't you?"

"Of course, of course, I am. I was bringing Laura in to meet you to start divorce proceedings for her." They talked for a while longer then Crane concluded his business.

He went to his desk and logged onto his bank account via computer. He punched the *enter* button hard a couple of times. "Christ, this fucker's slow today," he snarled at the screen. Finally, his account popped onto the screen. The bank showed the deposit of the two hundred fifty thousand dollars from Laura. He breathed a sigh of relief.

His administrative assistant knocked on the door and entered. "Jim, I thought you'd be interested in the mail," she said. "There are four checks."

"Great. I guess my paychecks won't bounce after all." He

saw her startled look. "I was just kidding, Gail."

"I knew things were slow, but I didn't think they were that slow."

"Not to worry. Our balance sheet's okay, but we do need more accounts. In fact, I want you to set up a staff meeting for Monday. Everyone from account executive on up."

"In the e-memo, how shall I describe the meeting?" she asked.

"A sales exhortation."

"Really?"

"A wrap-up of last year and prognostication for the remaining fifty-one weeks of this year. I do want to exhort them on new business and expanding activity with existing clients. Also, I want to discuss – but don't put this in the memo, or even mention it to anyone – turning this into a real firm, a partnership." He watched her arch her eyebrows.

Jim finished talking with his assistant and she left the room. He turned back to his screen. He really didn't want to lose total control of his agency, which he had built from scratch, but letting employees buy into the firm was as good a plan as any to salvage his business. Having a stake in the business might inspire them to do more and better. He would carry the loan from Laura on his business books as a loan from him. The company could pay him back. Christ, I'm really in business now. Making the company employee-owned was a prospect he had toyed with before. He should have done it before the economy imploded, he realized. But this will work now. I can sell my share in two years when the economy has recovered and I'm out of here. I'll be fifty-eight and ready to fuckin' retire.

Jim had stashed the loan papers he and Laura had signed in his personal safe deposit box. Absolutely no one knew about that money, although Martin would be sure to find out, Jim had figured. I'll just consider it a gift from Laura. After all, that's what it really was. And Martin can pay the goddamn gift tax. He leaned back in his high-backed leather chair, clasped his hands behind his head and smiled. Serve the son-of-a-bitch right.

Jim had been fraught with anxiety ever since waking up New Year's Eve day. He hadn't slept well and news on the radio exacerbated his nervousness. He listened to the intensity of the news reporter when he said state police were looking for Dr. Morley. Wouldn't that be something if they arrested Martin, Jim had thought at the time. Serve the bastard right.

He began plotting how he would handle the money Laura had given him. The papers they had signed had never been filed with anyone. He had the only copies. But his biggest concern of the moment was the police investigation. Maybe I'll get lucky.

Jim Crane was a lot calmer now than he was New Year's Day.

CHAPTER TWENTY-FOUR

Laura Morley's funeral was held a week later at a fairly small Episcopal chapel in the village near the home where Martin and his wife had lived. The priest provided a touching eulogy of "a woman who had a zest for living and a zealous commitment to helping the less fortunate." Martin wondered where he obtained his information. Then he recalled that Laura had served on a church committee called Human Development that provided resources for various organizations that helped the poor, the homeless, battered wives and others in need. She used to make sandwiches once a month for a shelter for the homeless. And she delivered meals, turkeys, hams and other things to poor folks on holidays. He recalled her descriptions of where she had visited. She had seemed genuinely interested in their plight.

Suddenly he realized he didn't know much about Laura after all, especially over the past eight years. I guess I was too wrapped up in my own life to know what was going on with hers, he thought.

Martin had expected only a small turnout for the funeral, but friends packed the chapel to standing room. Laura's two sisters, brother and their spouses were also there. He had not spent much time with her family, other than her late father. Actually, he had rather liked her father. They had a lot in common. But Martin did not particularly like Laura's sisters and brother. Laura, however, had remained fairly close with her siblings, even during the squabbling over their father's estate.

Also attending the services were other family members of Laura's – aunts, uncles and cousins who Martin had not seen in several years. Most of them lived out of the area, a situation that he much appreciated.

The news media were on scene in force. It was a slow news period. For the eight days since the murder there had been daily media coverage. Martin had expected their interest to subside as the investigation continued. He found the media attention annoying, but knew there was nothing he could do. His face had become recognizable to many. He felt strange about everything. He couldn't be a grieving husband, not when everyone knew his marriage had been doomed, that he was about to file for divorce. And he couldn't act happy or content. He figured his best response was none. Be noncommittal, he told himself.

Everyone from Martin's former practice, including Philip and Angela, were in the chapel. Caitlin arrived fifteen minutes before services were to begin. Walking up the nave she couldn't remember what side to sit on, or even if there was a side on which she should sit. At weddings you sit on the left if you're a friend of the bride. Is there a rule for funerals? Probably not, she thought. She sat on the right. When she saw Martin, their eyes made brief contact and she nodded ever so slightly.

Jim Crane arrived. He tried to be inconspicuous, but his white hair stood out in the darkness of the chapel. He knew no one, as he had expected. He wouldn't be able to pay his condolences. Laura was lying in state in an open coffin before the altar. He wanted to look, but controlled his urge. He just sat in the pew remembering the good times with Laura.

Martin didn't see Jim Crane at the back of the chapel. Sgt. Clemens, the black detective, also was there along with the State Patrol's post commander. Clemens was one of only six black faces at the funeral. It surprised Martin that there were even that many.

The chapel walls were dark stone, and the room dimly lit, giving it a medieval look. What little daylight filtered through the stained glass windows seemed to be eaten by the sea of dark clothing the mourners wore.

At the cemetery, everyone huddled about the grave. It was

cold, near zero. The priest read from the Bible, but Martin couldn't hear him. All he could think of were scenes of burials in movies – especially westerns – where mourners would toss in flowers or mementoes once the casket was lowered while *Rock of Ages* played in the background. He wondered if for Laura he should toss in a bottle of vodka and a handful of olives, then shook his head to return to reality. He was no longer sure what reality was, what he should think, or how he should think.

The return ride in the funeral home limousine with his children was solemn, somber. No words passed.

CHAPTER TWENTY-FIVE

Toward the end of the first full week of the New Year, detectives seemed to be at a standstill in their investigation. Several days after the funeral they asked Martin to meet with them for routine questions. Martin agreed, but telephoned Caitlin just before leaving for Enola. She was out and he declined to explain to Maggie, the administrative assistant, why he was calling Caitlin. Despite Caitlin's warnings, he thought her presence unnecessary.

The same detectives who met him when he returned from skiing were in the conference room, but Anthony Wollman, the Johnson County District Attorney, had now joined them.

"Frankly, we're at a bit of a dead end right now," Lt. Warren admitted to Martin. "We're not turning up anything. We need your help."

"Glad to, Lieutenant," Martin smiled as he sat in the chair they directed him to. He looked up to see the video camera on a tripod aimed at him like a gun. He was taken aback, but kept his presence.

"Do you mind if we turn on the TV camera?" the lieutenant asked. "That way we don't have to worry about misreading our notes. Of course, if it makes you uncomfortable."

"That's all right," Martin said. "Turn it on."

Detective Steinert turned it on, and Warren asked, "Doctor, would you state your name, the date, and time?"

Martin responded, glancing at his Blanc Pain watch.

"Doctor," the District Attorney said, "if you say anything incriminating we'll use it against you in court. You have the right to remain silent. And you have the right to an attorney."

"I thought this was supposed to be routine."

"It is," Wollman said. "But we are required to tell you these things. That makes it routine. Also, it's for your own protection. We're not being accusatory, either." Wollman shifted in his seat. "Now this may sound bad and I don't mean to insult you, but if you can't afford to hire an attorney, one will be appointed for you."

Martin laughed. "I can certainly afford an attorney. I'm a rather prosperous physician, an internist. In fact, I have an attorney."

"Would you like us to call her for you?" Wollman asked.

"You know who she is?"

"Of course, Caitlin Schroeder," Wollman replied. "She's excellent. Want me to call?"

"No, I don't need an attorney for this."

Wollman shook his head. "She's going to be dismayed if you don't call her."

In turn Martin shook his head, smiling, "I really don't think it's necessary."

Everyone smiled. "We know your position in Johnson and Adams counties where you practice," Lt. Warren said. "We know that you have a very good attorney, but we have to give you these Miranda warnings. You must have heard them many times on television."

Martin shook his head. "I don't watch much television, just a little public TV or news programs now and then. That's all."

"Doctors are very busy professionals," Sgt. Harmon conceded.

"Basically, Doctor," Wollman said, "you have the right to remain silent, not talk to us, and you have the right to be represented by an attorney. These are your constitutional rights."

"Well, I have nothing to hide."

"First," Lt. Warren asked, "I'm wondering if you could identify these?" He shook three rings from a small brown envelope into his palm.

Martin took them, smiled and said, "They're Laura's." He

held the wedding band up and added, "Those are her initials and our wedding date engraved on the inside." He returned the rings to the lieutenant. "You find them at a pawn shop?"

"None of what was stolen is turning up in pawn shops, on the street, or otherwise," Lt. Warren said. "These rings were left on your wife's fingers. Rather peculiar, we think. The crime doesn't fit anything that's ever happened around here, not even in Adams County. Whoever did it made off with a lot of jewelry, silverware, and of course, the cash, but left these valuable rings. And nothing that was taken is turning up. And there's no talk on the street."

"Maybe he left those rings because there wasn't time to take them off," Martin offered. "Laura's fingers sometimes plumped up after drinking. Or, maybe it was an out-of-state man."

"Unlikely," the lieutenant responded. "How would he have known where to go or who to rob? We think it may have been someone who knew Mrs. Morley, or was from the neighborhood." The lieutenant shook his head. "You know, Dr. Morley, there hasn't been any crime in that area in years. The sheriff's department hasn't even made a call there, other than false alarms from home security systems."

Martin chuckled, remembering false alarms deputies had responded to when his wife couldn't remember the security code. "That's a pretty law-abiding neighborhood," Martin acknowledged.

"Nobody really needs the money. But maybe some teenagers are using drugs or looking for strange thrills."

"Perhaps you or your wife had an enemy," the lieutenant said. "Maybe the husband of the woman you took skiing."

"Oh," Martin shook his head as if trying to better grasp what they were saying. "I doubt he would have suspected that his wife and I were having an affair. Besides, he was out of state and this was the first time she and I had done anything. I mean, I had never given him any reason to suspect anything."

They began to interview him about Laura. They talked for nearly fifteen minutes then Det. Steinert asked Martin why he was seeking a divorce.

"Frankly, she was an alcoholic. I had her committed once, but it didn't take. I was at the end of my patience. We were both having affairs. It was awful and it was over. The marriage, that is. The papers were to be filed this week by my attorney. She's actually my divorce lawyer. I didn't suddenly just hire Ms. Schroeder for criminal defense."

"We know," Wollman said. "She's an excellent attorney, and I have a high regard for her. Again, would you like her here? I can call her now. We do consider you a suspect."

"I really don't need an attorney for this."

"Suit yourself," Steinert said.

Martin noticed Steinert's faint smile curl slightly at the corner of his mouth. Steinert smiled frequently, but no smile lines appeared at his eyes. Martin decided at this point that he did not trust the investigator.

Except for Angela's name, Martin provided details of the skiing trip. "We arrived on the twenty-ninth of December, at night, about seven o'clock. The next morning we arose early. We down-hill skied until around noon, had lunch and cross-country skied until nearly nightfall. Then we went to dinner."

"What time did you get back from dinner?" Sgt. Harmon asked.

"It must have been about nine o'clock. I'm not exactly sure." Martin squirmed ever so slightly. He saw Lt. Warren slip Steinert a note. He wondered what was on it.

"And then what did you do?" Steinert asked.

"We made love. Is that what you wanted to hear? Or do you want more intimate, lurid details?" He really detested Steinert.

Ignoring the question, Steinert asked, "Who was the woman?"

"Do I have to tell you? I'd rather not."

Steinert shifted his body in his chair, appearing as though he had moved closer, and said, "You don't have to tell us. But it would look like you're trying to hide something if you don't."

"I promised her I wouldn't drag her into this," Martin countered.

"What's her name?" Harmon asked.

"Do I have to?"

"We're not going to plaster it all over town," Harmon continued. "What's her name?"

"Jesus," Martin exclaimed.

"All we want is her name to verify what you say," Wollman added. "What's her name?"

"This is not fair."

"Nor is your wife's death," Harmon responded.

Martin shook his head.

"Maybe you're making it up, having an affair at Western Alps," Steinert added.

"Perhaps it's a fantasy of yours. Or, perhaps you killed your wife."

Martin shook his head again. He looked at the other detectives. They all stared at him, even Wollman, anticipating a name. "Okay, it was Angela Wain."

"Who's she?" Steinert asked.

"She runs a small modeling agency back in the city, called Wain's Women."

"Is it legitimate?" Steinert asked.

"It's not a whore house if that's what you're implying," Martin's voice rose and sounded testy, but he quickly calmed himself and said, "Her husband, Dr. Philip Wain, is a former partner of mine. It may seem pretty awful to you, but that's the way these things happen some times."

"Former partner?"

"Yes, I sold my practice just before the New Year. Ms. Schroeder handled that for me."

They went into some detail on the sale of the practice. They wanted to know why he sold out, what he planned to do. After what seemed like interminable questions on the sale, Sgt. Clemens changed the subject to Laura's life insurance. "How much life insurance did you hold on your wife?" he asked.

Martin turned his head to Clemens. It was the first question the sergeant had asked. "I haven't received it yet," Martin said. "It seems the insurance investigator hasn't finished his investigation. They said I'd likely get it in two weeks."

"How much is it?"

"One and a half million dollars."

"That's a lot of money." Clemens shook his head as though it were difficult to grasp the meaning of that much money.

"Yes it is," Martin replied. "I've got a policy for two million on myself. We've had these policies for several years."

"Yes, we know," Clemens replied.

The interview continued until the videotape cassette was used up. Sgt. Harmon replaced it with a fresh cassette. They resumed the interview.

"Dr. Morley, what kind of gas cans do you own?" Steinert suddenly asked.

"Those big five-gallon plastic cans," Martin replied, holding his hands wide apart to demonstrate the size of the cans. "One has diesel for my Mercedes and the other gasoline."

"You don't own a two-gallon metal can?" Steinert asked.

"No, no. They're ugly. I think they're unsafe, too. Spark from the metal." Martin shook his head to underscore his disdain.

The detectives carried on with the interview. In all it lasted a little under four hours. Except for the insistence on naming Angela, Martin thought it went fairly well. He had thought earlier, before the interview, that he might have to implicate Angela. The overall interrogation by the detectives seemed superfluous, though. He wasn't even sure, now that it was over, why they call it an interrogation. It was more of an interview. Martin had grown weary with the seemingly stupid, innocuous questions, repeated over and over as though he were stupid enough to give different versions. He wondered how police were ever able to catch criminals and gain convictions. Juries, on the other hand, must be dumber than cops, he figured.

As Martin was preparing to leave, Wollman, the District Attorney, said, "We'll let you know if anything breaks on this." He shook hands with Martin.

The four investigators and the prosecutor retrieved some coffee from another room after Martin left, and returned to the conference room.

Wollman looked pleased. "What do you think?" he asked, looking at Warren.

"My heart tells me Dr. Morley did it," the lieutenant said.

"Why?" Wollman asked.

"He hated her, wanted to be rid of her and likes money," the lieutenant said.

"He's slime," Steinert added.

"That's pretty subjective," Wollman snapped.

"It won't hold up in court," Steinert admitted with a slight chuckle then added, "but it's good enough reason to investigate it from that angle. Expensive rings were left on her fingers, no sign of a struggle, the killer knew where to go for the money and jewelry, and then set the place on fire to throw us off."

Sgt. Clemens rose. "I don't know," he said. "I mean the doctor may not be the kind of man you could learn to love, but that doesn't mean he did it. I'd like to keep an open mind."

"Trouble with you, Willie," Sgt. Harmon pointed a finger at Clemens, "is you're too rigid. If Morley didn't do it, we'll find out and shift gears. Besides, who in the hell else could have done it?"

"Mrs. Morley's lover," Clemens replied.

"He's certainly a prime possibility," Wollman conceded, "but I tend to think that Dr. Morley is a very good suspect at this point. We do need to interview Mrs. Morley's lover, too. We're a little too focused on Dr. Morley. There are problems with him. We can't, for instance, place him at the scene. I'm going to need a hell of a lot more evidence. I mean, we only have a hint at a motive – he didn't like his wife. Hell, there's got to be a lot of guys out there who hate their wives and could use the insurance money."

Everyone laughed at that.

"This is going to take some good police work," Wollman continued. "There was a price sticker on the gas can. See if you can locate where it was bought, and by whom. It looks brand new. You guys know the routine. And jeez, more work on motive."

A few of them groaned a little, knowing that their next few weeks were going to be filled with boring legwork.

Lt. Warren cleared his throat. "I want you, Willie, to interview that Crane guy and Angela Wain."

Harmon slapped his hand on the table. "Why you giving Willie all the good sex stuff?"

"What do you mean?" the lieutenant asked.

"He gets to interview the lovers of the Doc and the Doc's wife. What do I get?"

"You may research newspaper stories on Dr. and Mrs. Morley. A little library time will calm you some, Harmy." The lieutenant smiled.

Harmon snapped his pencil in half.

"And find out where that gas can was bought," the lieutenant added.

"What about me?" Steinert asked.

"I want you to concentrate on hard evidence that might put the doctor at the scene. Know what I mean? Then help Harmy find where the gas can was purchased.

"And Willie," Lt. Warren turned to the sergeant, "I want you also to check out the lodge. Talk with the folks up there and see if they recall this Angela woman. Try to get a picture of Ms. Wain to take around at the lodge. Interview everyone. I'll talk to friends of the deceased and her husband, his former partners, too."

Wollman rose and said, "I want this real clean. Morley's too prominent to fool around with. If he did it and we don't have good, solid evidence, there's no way we can win in court. And do me a favor?"

Their heads rose slightly, and they all looked at him quizzically.

"I want slow, methodical police work, no stone unturned. If you start to doubt our Morley theory, let me know immediately and we'll shift gears, as Harmon says. I don't want to waste time on Morley if we don't get consistent support for our theory."

CHAPTER TWENTY-SIX

Sgt. Willie Clemens had made an appointment with Angela Wain for the late morning. Knowing she was a model, he had dressed in his best suit, a dark brown with a light gray stripe. He wore highly polished brown shoes. His shirt was white and starched with a dark red silk tie with silver polka dots. It wasn't the clothing he regularly wore to work. This was the same outfit Willie called his "Sunday-go-to-meetin' clothes." He carried his gun in a holster under his suit coat over his right hip. Willie was tall and good looking. He knew he was good looking, and just as he entered her business door he wondered if he was good looking enough to be a model.

"I'm Sgt. Clemens," he said to the receptionist, displaying his police identification. "Mrs. Wain is expecting me."

He entered Angela's office, extending his right hand to shake hers. She smiled. He was amazed at how beautiful she was. She invited him to sit. Willie accepted and took out his notebook and pen.

"How may I help you?" Angela asked.

"I mentioned on the phone that I was investigating the Laura Morley murder. I understand that you knew both Mrs. Morley and her husband, Dr. Martin Morley."

"Dr. Morley worked with my husband, Dr. Philip Wain, the thoracic surgeon. And I knew both Laura and Martin quite well socially."

"I have to ask you a delicate question, Mrs. Wain." He felt his face darken.

"Well, shoot." Angela laughed. "You're a policeman and probably carry a gun. So maybe I shouldn't have said 'Shoot.'" She smiled.

Willie laughed slightly. He seemed self-conscious. "Well, Mrs. Wain, we talked with Dr. Morley and asked him about being out of town when his wife was killed. He said he was at the Western Alps Ski Resort with you for three nights." Willie was clearly uncomfortable.

Angela laughed. "Men." She shook her head. "Sergeant, Dr. Morley's a nice man, I suppose, but when it comes to women, he's a little bit nuts. He's been a little overt. Know what I mean?" She watched the sergeant nod. "He has made pointed sexual propositions over the past year. More than mere innuendo. I think of me running off with him was wishful thinking on his part." She smiled knowingly.

Sgt. Clemens smiled. "He claims he was with you."

"Nope," she shook her head. "I've been here in town since a few days after Christmas. My husband was in Arizona with his mother for the holidays. Dr. Morley, of course, knew I would be alone." Angela looked at her watch. "It's just about noon, Sergeant. Want to join me for lunch? We can talk about it some more."

"No, thank you, Mrs. Wain. I have another appointment."

"Look, you have to eat lunch. It'll just be down stairs in the café." She stood up quickly and walked toward Willie, putting a hand on his shoulder, smiling beautifully. "Come on, Sergeant, I won't get you in trouble with your wife. It's all in the line of duty."

Sgt. Clemens relented, smiling a bit awkwardly. He picked up several copies of her brochure as they walked out. It was a quick lunch, for Willie had a one o'clock appointment with James Crane. Angela asked him questions about his wife and children. She said he was a very handsome man and wondered whether he photographed well. "I don't want to hurt your feelings, Sergeant." She touched his hand lightly with the fingertips of her right hand. "But there is a demand for older men as models. Guys in their forties."

Willie smiled, not knowing what to make of this. "How much demand can there be for a fifty-one-year-old black man?"

"You're fifty-one? I never would have believed it." She shook her head in amazement. "But to answer your question, Willie, it's diversity. Companies want to show ethnic diversity. Tell you what." She tapped his hand again. "I've got a shoot coming up in two weeks that might be just right for you. Why don't you show up? We'll try it out. It's for the cover of a company's annual report to shareholders. If it doesn't work, that's life. But we pay one hundred fifty dollars an hour with a four-hour minimum guarantee. Interested?"

"Yeah, I'm interested." He nodded, wondering if he was being duped.

"I'll call you tomorrow, Sergeant, with the details. Just because my agency is Wain's Women, doesn't mean we aren't equal opportunity employers." Angela paused a moment and added, "We hire men, too." She laughed at that, her throaty, husky laugh.

Sgt. Clemens left wondering whether he, indeed, had been duped. When he arrived at Jim Crane's business the receptionist was on the telephone. Willie took the time to look around the lobby. He thought it quite attractive in a subdued way, very relaxing looking. He liked the silver rendering of the company name behind the front desk – Crane Public Relations. He wasn't exactly sure what public relations was, but figured it was something like advertising. The receptionist interrupted his thoughts then. He told her he had an appointment with Jim Crane. She called, announced his presence and quickly showed him to Jim's office.

As Willie walked in Crane stepped through a doorway next to his desk, wiping his hands with a white cloth towel. "Having a private bathroom in your office is one of the perqs that comes with having your name on the door," Crane said, smiling. He tossed the towel through the doorway to the bathroom and then shook Willie's hand. He motioned toward a leather chair in front of his desk.

Willie took the seat, sinking to a level just a couple inches below Crane's. "As I mentioned on the phone, Mr. Crane, we're investigating Laura Morley's murder. We're not so sure robbery was the motive as the media reports. Dr. Morley says you were his wife's lover."

Crane chuckled. "He really is a son-of-a-bitch."

"What do you mean?" Willie asked.

Crane leaned back in his chair, clasping his hands behind his head. "The day before Laura died. That was the 30th. I came back from out of town and talked with her." His look was somber.

"At her house?" Sgt. Clemens asked

"No, over the phone. She was a nervous wreck. Apparently, before Martin left on his ski trip, he told her he had hired a detective to follow her. "The detective took some photos of us in rather compromising poses. I don't know. I haven't seen the photos." He sat up straight, bringing his hands to the desktop. "That's what Laura told me. Then about five o'clock she told me that he had just called her. He warned her not to spend the night with me. She was really shook up. She said she slammed the phone on him. Probably broke his ear drum." Crane chuckled. His voice turned more serious as he said, "It wasn't that I was afraid to go over there, with or without a private detective following. You could say I was alarmed though. Laura was certainly afraid. She was planning to divorce him and it worried her that he had had a detective spying on us."

Sgt. Clemens leaned back in his chair and asked, "You haven't seen Mrs. Morley since before Christmas?"

"That's right. I spent the night at home on December 30, when I returned from visiting some of my relatives in Pittsburgh for Christmas. Laura and I had planned to celebrate New Year's at my country club. She said she'd call me later in the evening to see if I might like to make a clandestine visit. She never called. Maybe I should have just gone over there."

"We might have two people dead then. You and Mrs. Morley," Sgt. Clemens said. He waited a moment to let what he had said sink in. He watched Jim slowly shake his head. "Mr. Crane, have you ever been to Mrs. Morley's house?"

"Yes, twice. The last time was just before Christmas." He paused and cocked his head. "You know, if you're trying to match fingerprints, I'll certainly let you take mine. I was in the family room and the kitchen. You might find them around the wet bar in the family room."

"If we run across any we don't recognize, we'll take you up on that. Meanwhile, can you tell me what you did the night of December 30th?"

"Well, I stayed up and waited for her to call. I went out to bring a pizza home and picked up a movie at the video store. I ate the pizza and drank a couple of beers. I went to bed about midnight. I'm afraid I don't have any better alibi than that. Look, Sergeant, if you think I had anything to do with this, I didn't kill Laura. I had no reason, no motive. I loved her. We had been talking about getting married." He paused, looking as though he were about to cry.

Willie reached for a handkerchief, but Crane quickly regained his composure and motioned to the sergeant to put the handkerchief away. "I thought I was tougher."

"That's okay, sir. There's nothing wrong with showing a little emotion in a situation like this." Willie waited for a moment then asked, "Do you think her husband could have killed her?"

Crane, who was staring at his desk top, looked up and said, "I don't know. I suppose so. They sure hated each other." He rubbed his chin for a moment then resumed, "You know, she ran into a lot of money recently. About sixteen million dollars in inheritance from her late father. That's a hell of a lot of money, but I doubt Martin would kill for that."

"Perhaps jealousy, though. You were her lover. And you said he had a detective take compromising pictures of you and

Mrs. Morley."

"Are you suggesting that he killed his wife and is trying to frame me?"

"That's a possibility," Willie responded.

"I sure as hell hope not. I hope you bear that in mind during your investigation. They hated each other. Pinning it on me would sure be a lousy reward to me for giving her the one thing she needed and craved."

"What's that," Willie asked.

"Love, unquestioned love."

Willie paused for a moment then asked, "Mr. Crane, I feel a little stupid, but what exactly is public relations?"

A broad smile suddenly formed on Crane's face. "Other than my sister, you're the first person to ask me that. And most people don't know what it is, although they like to make believe they do. I guess they're just too embarrassed to ask."

"I hear a lot of things about good PR and bad PR, but I'm not sure what PR is."

"Friendly persuasion, Sergeant, friendly, planned persuasion." Crane seemed rejuvenated. "You use communications tools: TV, newspapers, the Internet, Facebook, Twitter, other forms of communication to persuade people to your way of thinking, whether it's politics, philosophy or underarm deodorant. Makes no difference. You know, it's like your Highway Patrol. You want people to wear seatbelts. Over a period of time you have a lot of newspaper stories and television features on the very positive aspects of wearing seatbelts. You have contests. Give speeches. Work with kids. Next thing you know, more people are wearing seat belts because they heard the message and saw the light."

Willie nodded understandingly. "That's a good way of explaining it, Mr. Crane."

* * *

Back at post headquarters Sgt. Clemens met with the other detectives in Lt. Warren's office. Willie handed over the brochures he had picked up at Angela's office and pointed to the stunning photographs of her.

"She's some choice piece," Harmon said. "You get this and I get a dog of a librarian with wire rimmed glasses."

Willie laughed. He recounted his meeting with Angela. "And then she bought me lunch and offered me a try-out as a model."

"But you're so goddamn ugly," Harmon said.

"Yeah, but she likes me." Willie tapped his chest.

"Shit." Harmon shook his head.

"I think she spent the time with Dr. Morley," Clemens suddenly became serious. "That's a gut reaction. There's no other reason to befriend me. What's this beautiful white woman doing inviting a black cop to lunch then offering him a modeling job? I'm pretty, but not that pretty."

Everyone laughed, including Clemens. Willie then discussed his meeting with Crane. "I don't think Crane was involved, but I wouldn't rule it out, either, and I'm not so sure the doctor did it," he said finally. "But I still have to go to the ski resort and check the people there."

"Well my research shows a motive," Harmon announced.

"What's that?" Lt. Warren asked.

"Money. Greed. Good old stand-byes."

"Explain," Warren said.

"A small newspaper story back in October explained the distribution of the estate of Sanford McDowell. His daughter, Laura Morley, received sixteen million dollars. Divorced, the good doctor gets none of that, and has to split half of his assets with his wife. With his wife dead, the good doctor gets it all. I haven't got the complete tally, but I think with the insurance, inheritance, house and everything, it's going to be twenty million dollars, probably more. I have no idea what his investment portfolio looks like."

"That inheritance," Clemens interjected, "is another reason why Crane probably didn't kill her. He knew she had the inheritance and he would be sharing in her wealth, her inheritance, once they were married."

* * *

The following morning Sgt. Clemens visited the ski resort. The resort's manager could not recall whether Dr. Morley was with someone. "Often we have singles coming up looking for a partner," the manager said. "In fact, we have a pretty good reputation for that. Discretion, too. No one was with Dr. Morley when he checked in at the desk, or when he checked out. I handled his arrival and departure."

The *maître d'hôtel* also didn't recognize the photos of Dr. Morley or Angela. Sgt. Clemens began to waver on his initial belief that Dr. Morley didn't do it.

* * *

The next day, the second day of a January thaw, Melanie Williams walked along Lonepath Lane with her five-year-old son Joshua for a mid-day stroll. A half-mile from the Morley driveway, Joshua spotted something in the ditch. He started toward it. His mother pulled him back. "Don't go in there, Josh," she cautioned.

"Looks like a gun, Mom," he said.

Indeed it did. She stepped into the snow-covered ditch and bent over the gun, then climbed back onto the road. The snow had melted just enough to expose most of the weapon. She quickly reached into her coat pocket to retrieve a cell phone to call police.

Later, ballistics tests demonstrated that it was, indeed, the murder weapon.

CHAPTER TWENTY-SEVEN

Michael Brownell, Caitlin's son, was thrilled the Friday evening they drove to the automobile dealer to trade in the old car for their new one – an inexpensive Kia sport utility vehicle. "All we have to do, Michael, is avoid having an accident on the way to the dealership so we can get what they offered us for this heap."

Caitlin had feigned difficulty in deciding what automobile to buy, and had asked her son to help make the decision. It was down to the Kia and a Chevrolet sedan. "In this country, Michael, they judge a person by what she drives. Am I an SUV or a Chevie?"

"An SUV. They'll think you're an adventurer," he advised.

"Then let's get one that's British racing green," she said laughing.

Excitement about the new car started to build the week before they picked it up. By the following Friday morning she thought he was going off the deep end. He had trouble tying his necktie and forgot to take his lunch to school. She dropped it off for him on her way to work.

The office, meanwhile, wasn't as much fun without Erik. A new lawyer had joined their group, picking up the lag in the rent.

Erik, who disdained e-mails for their impersonal look, had begun handwriting letters to Caitlin. He promised to write every two weeks or so. And she wrote to him. It was soothing therapy for a Sunday afternoon. Although, they did switch to e-mails for more urgent matters.

The Sunday after picking up her car, however, she drove Michael around town, looking for snowy streets to test the four-wheel drive, but the thaw had eliminated that possibility.

Back at home she started going through her newspapers. At four o'clock Martin called: "Caitlin, I'm at the State Police Post Headquarters in Enola. They've arrested me for Laura's murder."

"Damn," she said. "What happened?"

"State Police came to my apartment this afternoon, showed me a warrant, arrested me, handcuffed me, and stuffed me into the back of a squad car." He sounded distraught.

"Martin, try to calm down. I'll be there in less than an hour."

She explained to Michael what had happened and that she would call Mrs. Riley, a next-door neighbor to look after him.

"Mom, I don't need a babysitter. I'm twelve years old."

"I just want her to stop by a couple of times to look in on you. She's not going to sit here and feed you baby food." She called Mrs. Riley, a seventy-year-old widow who Caitlin often called on to watch out for her son. Mrs. Riley usually checked on Michael when he returned from school.

Caitlin quickly dressed in a tweed jacket and plain wool skirt, pulled her hair back with a couple of clips – no time for make-up – threw essentials into her large leather bag, bade Michael goodbye, promised to return in four hours, and headed to her garage. She jotted down the mileage. Damn bookkeeping, she muttered and backed out.

They're a bunch of sons-of-bitches, she thought. Damn cops arrest him on a Sunday so he has to spend at least one night in jail. They know he could make bond on a weekday. Her mind shifted to a faster pace, trying to recall what Martin had told her and what he possibly could have told investigators. She slammed her hand on top of the steering wheel. She knew she should have insisted on going along with him for the police interviews. What the hell kind of counselor am I?

She began to wonder whether Martin did kill his wife. There's certainly enough circumstantial evidence to give the police and DA cause to suspect him. What the hell! They're trumping everything up because it's the easy way out. They can't find the real killer, so they arrest the husband. Too damn easy.

Caitlin parked at Post Headquarters, glanced in the mirror on the back of her sun visor and acknowledged that she wasn't looking her best.

She waited at the front desk until the sergeant called for Anthony Wollman, the District Attorney. "Caitlin, good to see you." Wollman had a large smile on his face as he offered his hand to her. They had opposed each other in Johnson County courtrooms on a few occasions, and Caitlin also knew him from when she was chief assistant prosecutor in Adams County. He was an average looking man of average height wearing a blue blazer with a red and white striped shirt with no tie. He may have been average looking, but Caitlin had always liked his eyes.

"Why have you arrested my client, Dr. Martin Morley?" she asked after shaking hands.

"He killed his wife, and we can prove it." His voice was matter of fact. His face disclosed nothing.

"Why did you wait until Sunday to arrest him? Just so he could spend some time in jail before posting bail?"

"Caitlin, we obtained the warrant Thursday morning. He wasn't home when we went to arrest him, and we had a judge waiting for us. We had police keeping an eye on his place. He turned up late this morning."

"Sorry." She shook her head and wished she could quit jumping to conclusions. "I'd like to see my client. Where's he going to spend the night?"

"Johnson County Jail. Oops," he said. Pointing behind her over her shoulder, he added, "Here come the media." A newspaper reporter and photographer walked through the headquarters' front door, quickly followed by a television crew.

"Did you call the media, Anthony?"

"No, no. One of the television reporters called the shift commander who let it slip. By the time you talk with your client, this place will be packed with those vultures."

"I used to be one."

"What?"

"A vulture, a reporter in Minneapolis. Actually, we were more like crows working on road kill. But they're going to eat this case alive. You're not going to get a conviction on this. Now let me see the warrant."

Wollman took her back to an empty office and gave her a copy of the warrant.

"Anthony?" she asked, looking above her reading glasses.

"Why don't you call me Tony, like everyone else?"

"Anthony is your name and I like to call you Anthony. Besides, if we're on the telephone and I say 'Anthony,' you're assured it's me and not a pretender." He smiled and Caitlin asked, "Now, may I see my client?"

He directed her to another room. Martin was sitting on a wooden chair, his hands shackled in front of him. A uniformed trooper stood nearby. The trooper left at Wollman's direction and the District Attorney soon followed.

Caitlin sat on a wooden chair facing Martin across the small table. Martin lifted his cuffed hands from his lap and placed them on the table. He appeared calm.

"Are you all right, Martin?"

"I'm okay now. Can you get me out of here?"

"I reviewed the warrant and I'm afraid it is in order," Caitlin said. "The arrest is legal. We can get you out of jail, when they set bail, but unfortunately that won't be until tomorrow. You're going to have to spend at least one night in the Johnson County Jail."

"Why?" he asked, his eyes and voice registering shock and incredulity.

"You have to be arraigned before a judge and they can't do that until tomorrow morning at nine. They will certainly ask for a substantial bond; I'll ask that you be let out on your own recognizance. The judge will probably set bond rather high at first."

"Why?"

"This isn't fraud or breaking-and-entering, this is first-degree, premeditated murder. If the state had reinstated the death penalty last year, you would be facing a Gurney and a sharp needle if convicted."

Martin winced.

"They want to put you away for life, Martin. And they're salivating over this."

"What do you mean?"

"You're a doctor, you're prominent, you're rich, and we're in a poor county in Upper Appalachia."

"Why are you being so negative, Caitlin?"

"I want to make it perfectly clear to you what you are facing – life in prison, no parole. You have to fully comprehend the gravity of this. My first important question to you is, did you kill your wife? Or, are you in any way responsible for her death?"

They were looking each other square in the face. "I did not kill Laura," Martin responded. "What I told you a couple of weeks ago is exactly what happened."

She didn't quite believe him. That was her first reaction and it annoyed her. Caitlin swiped at a strand of hair that had begun to tickle her brow. "I'm developing a suspicion, Martin, that you may be innocent."

"Suspicion?" He seemed exasperated. "I swear this is impossible. I am innocent."

She threw her hands up and declared, "All right, I believe you." She leaned back in her chair. "Here's what's going to happen, the procedures." She leaned forward. "You'll be arraigned tomorrow. Bond will be set. I'll need power of attorney to obtain the funds from your accounts. I'll bring the documents with me. I'll need the keys to your apartment, or wherever you keep your stuff, your account data. You probably won't be out of here until late tomorrow afternoon at the earliest."

"I thought you'd be able to work some magic and get me out of here tonight." He suddenly looked despondent.

She put her hand on his shoulder and said softly, "I'm saving the magic for later when we'll really need it, Martin. Meanwhile, if it's any consolation," she pulled her hand back, "they once busted a well-liked Catholic bishop in Minnesota for drunk driving and he spent the night in jail." She smiled in a commiserating sort of way. "After they set bond, they have to set a date for a preliminary hearing within fourteen days. We have the right to waive that. It's a hearing to determine whether there is probable cause to have you stand trial. It's pretty cut and dried. But it's our opportunity to find out a lot of the evidence the state has. Then we can plan our defense, our strategy for the trial."

"Won't the case be thrown out at the preliminary hearing?"

"It could happen, but it's unlikely." She shifted in her seat and continued, "I'll stop by a drug store and get you some toiletries. I want you looking decent tomorrow. I know the head jailer. He'll make sure you're safe and treated well."

The gravity of the situation did not escape Martin now.

"Martin, what about your children? Do Cathy and Carlton know you've been arrested?"

He shook his head. "No. They were out when the police arrived."

"I'll stop by your place and let them know." She dreaded the prospect, but saw no out.

Martin's head hung down for a moment. As he lifted his head, Caitlin thought he looked very old. "I have to go out and meet the press, Martin. They're here in droves. Face it, your name is going to be smeared for the next few months until a jury finds you not guilty." She rose and patted him comfortingly on the shoulder.

When she left the room, she headed for the main room of the post headquarters. The media were facing the front desk –

four television crews, three radio reporters and three print reporters, plus photographers. She was sure there would be more at the arraignment.

Caitlin walked toward Wollman who was talking with a captain in the State Patrol. "They're really chomping at the bit, aren't they?" she observed.

Wollman turned. "I thought they were vultures. Now they're horses. You're mixing metaphors, Caitlin."

"They're some kind of animals."

"Are we treating your client well enough?"

"No. He should be free. He didn't do it."

"Come on Caitlin, we would never have arrested him if we didn't have a case. There's no sloppy police work on this one. The State Police are too good, too thorough, too professional to allow any screw-ups."

"Time for me to leave," she changed the subject.

"Are you going to talk to the media?"

"I'll make a statement. Will you do me one favor, though?"

"What's that?"

"Take him out through the downstairs garage so he doesn't have to run the media gauntlet." She smiled wearily. Wollman nodded in agreement and Caitlin walked off, letting herself past the small wooden swinging gates that separated the lobby from the back offices. Reporters were calling her name. She stopped, looked up at one of the women with a television camera operator next to her and said, "Yes?" as though she were mildly surprised to see any media interest in her.

"Care to make a statement regarding the arrest of Dr. Morley?" the reporter asked.

"Sure," Caitlin said. All of the cameras were aimed at her, poised for a sound bite. With her shoulders back squarely, she waited a moment, then said, "Dr. Martin Morley is innocent." She stopped, smiled and pressed her way through the crowd. The pleas from reporters for more comments engulfed her. She waved her hand. "Sorry, I have work to do. Talk to you tomorrow after arraignment." Once outside she hurried to her car and took off for the county seat, Williamsville, about fifteen miles away.

Caitlin didn't want to go back to town to Martin's apartment and rummage around for toiletries in front of his daughter and son. She stopped at a Wal-Mart store on the way to the jail and purchased a razor with a couple of cartridges, some shaving cream, a small bar of soap, toothbrush, toothpaste, and comb. She wondered what kind of toiletries Martin used at home. Expensive things, she thought. She went to the store's newsstand and selected several magazines. She then headed toward the men's department and chose a white shirt and a blue sweater. They were inexpensive and definitely not of the quality that Martin was accustomed to, but they would be good enough for an arraignment.

Now Caitlin began to think that perhaps Martin really wasn't guilty. The forlorn look when she told him he would spend the night in jail had raised a sympathetic feeling in her. She knew she had to be more objective about this. She fingered the buttons through the plastic wrapper of the shirt.

The Johnson County Courthouse was a five-story, aged red sandstone building. The basement housed the Sheriff's Department. The jail was on the top floor and used for short-term sentences and for prisoners waiting for pending court appearances and trials. She parked her car and walked down a ramp to the entrance of the Sheriff's Department. A blue and white squad car was parked on the ramp in front of the door. Inside she greeted the desk sergeant and asked, "Is Herschel in?" If she were lucky the head jailer would be in.

"Yes ma'am." He directed her to a phone that went directly to the jail.

She called to let him know she was coming up. Caitlin knew Herschel from having interviewed a number of inmates over the years.

The elevator took Caitlin to the fifth floor, dropping her off in a small waiting area. Herschel peeked at her through a small, thick plate window, unlocked the door and let Caitlin enter. He was an inch shorter than Caitlin, wore navy blue polyester pants and a white, short sleeve shirt. His necktie had a thick Windsor style knot, and the bottom point of the tie rested at the center of his substantial belly. The thick lenses of his glasses enlarged his eyes. He smiled widely as he opened the door for Caitlin.

"It's good to see you again, Caitlin. Want some coffee?" He took her to the galley just a short distance from his desk near the elevator. A guard was in the kitchen pouring coffee from a large, commercial sized stainless steel vat. He drew a cup for Caitlin and handed her a ceramic mug that advertised a hardware store chain.

Herschel and Caitlin stood in the kitchen doorway. "What do you need, Caitlin?"

"One of my clients, Dr. Martin Morley, is being brought in in a few minutes. He's accused of killing his wife. I believe he didn't do it."

Herschel shook his head in understanding and rubbed his thick, curly graying hair.

"I brought a little bag of toiletries and stuff. He'll be arraigned tomorrow. Will you see to it that he gets it?" She handed him the bag. "I put a shirt and sweater in there, too. Tell him that I said he had to wear it for court tomorrow."

Herschel took everything out, setting the items on a counter and examined each carefully. He removed the disposable razor from its packaging. Caitlin unwrapped the shirt and pulled out the straight pins.

"I'll make sure he leaves here clean shaved and neat, Caitlin."

"Thanks, Herschel." Herschel was his last name. Nobody ever called him by his first name. Most people didn't know it was Herb.

As she continued to drink her coffee, the elevator arrived. Herschel peered through the plate glass and said, "It's your client, Caitlin." Then he opened the door. One uniformed State Trooper, a sheriff's deputy and two detectives from the Post Headquarters escorted Martin, his wrists cuffed behind him, into the jail. Martin's head was down, but he looked up as they walked into the jail and saw Caitlin. He smiled weakly.

Caitlin tried to give him a reassuring smile. As Martin passed her, Herschel opened the door to the main jail area. The sound of steel barred gates reverberated coldly. Martin glanced once over his shoulder as the doors clanked behind him and he disappeared from Caitlin's sight. She shook her head. It was such a sad sight: Martin, once proud and arrogant, now being hauled off in handcuffs to a cold, forboding cell. She wondered what he was thinking about. Then she began to feel guilty again for not having been at his side when State Police had interrogated him.

She set her coffee mug down, stood up and placed her hands on her hips and paced the small area. Fifteen minutes passed before Herschel returned. "We're not going to keep him in the holding tank, Caitlin. I put him in a private cell."

"Thank you, Herschel. May I talk to him in the morning before arraignment?"

"If you get here by seven-thirty and make it quick."

"Okay, that's good. I'll see you then. I'll bring doughnuts for your jailkeepers. Thanks for everything."

"I won't be here, but I'll leave word. Good to see you again, Caitlin." He escorted her to the elevator.

On the drive to Martin's apartment, she pondered his situation, wondering what kind of evidence the state had. The drive went rather quickly as she thought of all the reasons why Martin could not have killed his wife. At Martin's apartment she rang the buzzer.

Carlton greeted her at the doorway, unaware of the purpose of Caitlin's mission and unsure who she was. "Did you say Caitlin Schroeder?" he asked.

"Yes. I'm your father's attorney. May I come in?"

Carlton ushered her in looking unsure.

Cathy walked into the room and asked, "What's up." She looked at Caitlin's face. "Has something happened to Dad?"

The three of them were standing just a few feet inside the doorway. "I'm afraid your father has been arrested and charged with the murder of your mother."

Cathy gasped. Carlton, eyes down, muttered, "Figures."

"What do you mean?" Caitlin asked.

"I mean, I've been reading the papers, watching TV news. Who else would police suspect? I mean it's so easy for them."

"I'll take that as belief in your father's innocence," Caitlin replied. "Look, I've been a chief assistant prosecutor and have tried homicide cases. Believe me, we'll get a verdict of not guilty." She watched their looks of belief. "Your father, however," she continued, "has to spend the night in jail, pending his arraignment. I expect to have him out by late tomorrow."

"Poor Dad," Cathy responded. "This has got to be terrible for him."

"I saw him just a little while ago. He's holding up well. He's a strong man. I'll see him early tomorrow. I know the head jailor and he'll make sure your father is treated well."

They talked a while longer then Caitlin left. She arrived home a few minutes before eight o'clock. Michael and Mrs. Riley were at the computer playing games. Michael turned toward his mother as she entered. "I saw you on television, Mom. You were great."

"I hardly said anything."

“It's the way you said it. You were standing so straight and you said,” lowering his voice to sound authoritative, “'Dr. Martin Morley is innocent.'"

Caitlin laughed and tousled his hair. “It's good to have a fan club. Tell me, did Dr. Morley appear on the news?”

“They just showed a photograph of him with a video of a squad car driving away in the night, and said he was being taken to the Johnson County Jail.”

CHAPTER TWENTY-EIGHT

Caitlin's caution to Martin about the seriousness of the situation haunted him during his night in jail. He paced the small cell until ten o'clock when jailers lowered the lighting. It was too dark to read the magazines Caitlin had brought. He wondered whether he should find another attorney. No, he thought. No one would devote the time and effort that Caitlin would. And she's a seasoned veteran of criminal cases. Hell, she has both prosecuted and defended all kinds of awful criminals. He paced another hour, reaffirming his commitment to Caitlin, but he was deeply worried.

He slept from midnight until five o'clock. He woke up uncertain where he was, then suddenly remembered. He shuddered, not from the dank air, but from the seriousness of his predicament. None of the prisoners had talked to him during the night. He was alone, desparately alone.

Martin was lying on his bed, on its thin mattress. In the darkness he couldn't see into the cell that faced his, but heard a noise, a rhythmic ticking. It kept on for a while. The ticking became a little louder and the rhythm picked up and then there was a grunt, a groan, a low moan and the sound of someone rolling over in the steel-frame bed. The sonofabitch is jacking off, Martin realized. He shuddered. The jail was silent now, except for the occasional extraneous creak of an old building. A few dim lights faintly illuminated the hallway, but at six o'clock all of the lights turned on. He heard groans and complaints and other noises of prisoners awakening, like an orchestra of bad musicians struggling to tune their ill instruments.

Martin had a sink in his cell with only cold water and a toilet without a seat. He urinated and flushed. Then he washed, shaved and dressed in the shirt and sweater Caitlin had purchased. At six-thirty he sat on the edge of the bed, hands clasped in his lap, worried, feeling his life unraveling rapidly.

At six forty-five, a trusty wheeled a stainless steel cart down the cellblock walkway. There were steel trays with breakfast on the cart. The trusty prisoner put Martin's tray on a little open entry window. Martin took it from him. The tray's five compartments held an eight-ounce carton of milk, two scrambled eggs, two slices of bacon, two pieces of buttered toast and a dollop of canned fruit. Coffee was served in a hard plastic cup. A spoon was the only utensil. Martin ate slowly. The food wasn't particularly good, but he ate it anyway, even the greasy bacon, which he normally would have rejected. Although he was worried and nervous, he took some small comfort in the food.

***

Caitlin arrived at the jail at seven o'clock. Herschel's assistant let her in. He gave Caitlin coffee. She handed him a box, saying, "I promised Herschel doughnuts for the guards." He thanked her with a smile. She exchanged idle talk with the jailer as she sipped her coffee. In a few minutes he picked up his phone and requested Dr. Morley be brought forward.

Martin arrived with a guard. He was clearly relieved to see Caitlin, for she represented salvation. They talked with the bars separating them. "I guess I got you up pretty early," Martin apologized.

"It's okay. You have a decent night given the circumstances?"

"They treated me well enough."

"I just want to tell you what to expect this morning. They're going to take you in chains – handcuffs and leg irons – about eight-thirty, down two floors to one of the courtrooms. The media will be there. Just keep your head high, don't smile, no expression, and don't shuffle, even with the leg irons."

"Why is this important?"

"I don't want you looking furtive, guilty or cocky. We have to pick a jury from everyone out there in television land. In court, answer the judge's questions about your name and so forth. Say 'Yes, Your Honor', and 'No, Your Honor.' When he asks you how you plead, say, 'I stand mute.' and I'll enter a plea of not guilty." They talked a little longer then Caitlin left.

Across the street from the courthouse was a McDonald's restaurant, sunlight brightening its small golden arches. She went there and ordered a carton of milk and a cup of coffee. She read the newspapers, the headlines flashing across the tops of the front pages announcing Martin's arrest. The stories weren't particularly spectacular, but the layout was. One lede read, "State Police arrested Dr. Martin Morley Sunday for the brutal murder of his wife Laura, capping several weeks of intensive investigation.

"Mrs. Morley's nude body was found bound early Dec. thirty-one in her charred home on Lonepath Lane in the affluent community of Windsor in Johnson County. She had been shot through the head. Her husband, a prominent and prosperous physician to the wealthy, is charged with first degree murder and arson. . . ."

Caitlin continued examining the newspaper: there were photos of the burned house, head and shoulders pictures of Laura and Martin from newspaper archives; and shots of the two of them from five years ago. They had been a beautiful couple.

Caitlin knew the media would home in on "prominent and prosperous" in an "affluent" neighborhood, and "physician to the wealthy." She didn't like it. It set a negative attitude in the minds of most readers. But, it was as she had expected.

She went back to the courthouse. While she waited for Martin a former client approached her. Caitlin talked to the woman for a few minutes. Deputies then brought Martin down the hallway, and Caitlin joined the entourage. The media were there, television cameras silently recording everything. Martin held his head high, looking straight ahead as deputies led him to the courtroom. They sat on a back bench, Caitlin next to him, deputies standing on either side of them. It was Monday morning and the courtroom was filled with the Monday Morning Wash: all of the people arrested for petty crimes, drunk driving, battery, disorderly conduct, and a few minor felonies in addition to Dr. Morley.

They began making their appearances before County Court Judge William Appleton. Some pleaded guilty on the spot and were fined or given short jail terms, based on the recommendation of the prosecutor, an assistant to Anthony Wollman. Others pleaded not guilty. Trial dates and small bonds were set. The court recessed briefly before hearing Martin's case.

Martin and Caitlin continued to sit on the back bench with the two deputies. "This is awful," Martin said in a lowered voice.

"What do you mean?"

"These people. The courtroom's full of some disgusting looking people."

Caitlin shook her head. "Martin, you've been living in a vacuum. This is reality. This is a poor county. These people are rural, they're poorly educated, and most look unhealthy. See that fat woman up there?" Caitlin pointed to an obese woman in gray sweat pants and sweatshirt. "I talked to her a few minutes before you got here. She's trying to get her husband out of jail. I represented her once on child neglect." Caitlin shook her head. "On Saturday night her husband was arrested for drunk driving. She wants him back so he can go to work, so they can make enough money to sustain themselves and their children in their trailer home. Their trailer home is surrounded by defunct refrigerators and washers, the skeletons of cannibalized cars, and other remains of fifteen years of living in desperation. Do you get the picture, Martin?"

"God, that's bleak."

"Martin, it is bleak out there. Lonepath Lane is an anomaly in this county."

Court resumed. Martin was the last to appear before the judge. He followed the directions that Caitlin had given him earlier. The judge set a date for a preliminary hearing. On the matter of bail, Wollman asked the judge to set bond at two million dollars.

Caitlin rose sharply.

Martin looked aghast.

"Your honor, two million dollars is both punitive and absurd," she said. "Dr. Morley has been an upstanding resident of Johnson County and a practicing physician in Adams County for more than twenty years. He's given back to the communities. He was chairman of the board of trustees of the Comfort House, a home for battered women and their children. He's actively involved in a number of civic-minded efforts. This man has spent a career of giving. I request the court release Dr. Morley on his own recognizance."

As Caitlin settled in her chair, Wollman rose quickly. "Now, that's absurd, your honor. We know Dr. Morley has more than sixteen million dollars in liquid assets, he's sold his position in his partnership and has given every indication that he is not going to be here." He pointed angrily at Martin with a sheaf of papers. "We're talking about an evil man who has plotted every step of the brutal murder of his wife. Both she and her late father were pillars of our society."

The judge slapped his gavel. "Enough counselor, Dr. Morley hasn't been convicted. Have you any other comments, Ms. Schroeder?"

"I didn't expect such histrionics from Mr. Wollman. But, Dr.

Morley isn't about to run. He has two children in college. One is in her first year of medical school. Dr. Morley is devoted to his responsibilities. Were he going to run, he would have collected his money long ago. He would have taken his money and run. I ask the court to exercise some restraint."

"This court will set bond at seven hundred fifty thousand. We can revisit this again, if need be, after the preliminary hearing." He slapped his gavel and added, "This court's adjourned."

Caitlin huddled with Martin. "Thank God you were able to get that bond down," he said.

Sitting at the defense counsel table, they made arrangements for Caitlin to secure the bond. "I have a bail bondsman, a couple of them, but one that I particularly like," she told him. "You'll only have to raise ten percent."

She had brought papers for him to sign, giving her access to his money. Martin had been keeping most of his money in fairly liquid accounts. He gave her the names and locations of appropriate account documents. It took Caitlin most of the day to round up the money, but Martin was released just before five o'clock. Caitlin drove him to his apartment. On the way, she said, "I want you to think all of this through in its entirety. Then let's have a long talk. How about Wednesday at two o'clock?"

"That's great, I should make it back from returning Cathy to school in New York by then. I think my flight arrives at one."

Caitlin dropped him off at his apartment. On her way home she wondered what kind of evidence the authorities had. She was certain they wouldn't have proceeded with just a basket of circumstantial evidence.

CHAPTER TWENTY-NINE

Assuming the state could present enough evidence at the preliminary examination to have Martin bound over for trial, Caitlin's next concern was how to conduct the trial in a county other than Johnson. There was a time when physicians were held in great esteem, but not anymore. She knew the prosecution, using thick lurid colors, would paint a picture of a rich internist, physician to the wealthy, powerful and prominent. And they would surely portray him as a philanderer. If it goes to trial she was certain she would never find a jury of his peers, just a jury of rural poor reluctant to believe a rich man.

The hearing had been scheduled for the beginning of February, but she had it postponed until March 2. Her meeting with Martin offered no new insight into the case. The story was the same as he had given her earlier in the month.

She decided to talk to Western Alps Ski Resort. The resort had a record of him having stayed there, but there was no double occupancy rate and no one could remember if anyone was with him. She showed employees a photo of Angela, but nobody recognized her. A desk clerk, unable to identify her, explained: "Most of the women who come here are good looking." Caitlin drew the same kind of response that Sgt. Willie Clemens had – no one recalled Angela.

She telephoned Angela Wain at her office, but Angela denied having been with Martin. "This is just what I told the police," she said. "I think Martin has a testosterone problem that's clouding reality. You know, he's a notorious womanizer. I think he can't deal with rejection."

Clearly, the preliminary hearing would end up a discovery procedure for the defense, learning some of the evidence of the prosecution. The authorities had to have more of a case than a motive of greed and the ability to commit the crime. Caitlin was perplexed. What kind of hard evidence could they possibly have that she doesn't know about?

On the day of the hearing, Caitlin sat in the courtroom with Martin at the defense table. There were about fifty spectators packing the small room. The court assigned the media to the vacant jury box. A tall, thin-faced man in a charcoal gray wool suit with light pinstripes and vest, who didn't dress at all like the reporters, joined the media.

The courtroom hadn't been redecorated – other than the white paint above the dark oak wainscoting – since the courthouse was built. The benches for judge, jury and spectators were all a medium oak, well worn. State and U.S. flags drooped from staffs on either side of the judge's bench. It was a small but imposing room. Caitlin had appeared in the courtroom before on several occasions, and, of course, had appeared before Judge William Appleton.

The morning was eaten away by Wollman's witnesses who had to establish a crime, the time and all of the minutiae needed to make his case. The medical examiner established the cause of death. The fire chief testified on the fire. Ed Cooper, the volunteer firefighter who discovered Laura Morley's remains, described what he saw when he and his partner had entered the master bedroom. And his partner corroborated his testimony. The state fire marshal declared the fire arson and that gasoline was the accelerant. These were the witnesses that the defense would have trouble refuting. Detectives testified on their specialties. The woman who spotted the gun also testified. The state ballistics expert identified it as the murder weapon, a .38 caliber revolver. He said it was not registered to anyone in the state and apparently hadn't been fired in the commission of any other crimes.

Caitlin kept most of her cross-examination brief.

In the afternoon Wollman began to establish a motive. Detectives testified that Martin admitted that the marriage was failing. Caitlin moved that the testimony be stricken and that any information gathered from Martin during the interview that detectives recorded on video be inadmissible. She didn't think she had much of a chance, but Judge Appleton took it under advisement.

Other witnesses and evidence indicated Martin had sold his medical practice, that Laura had recently received sixteen million dollars in inheritance and that Martin was the sole beneficiary of a one and a half million-dollar life insurance policy on Laura.

Caitlin was beginning to wonder if the state had much of a case beyond circumstantial evidence. She began to feel a little better about her position.

The state's final witness was Detective Investigator Steinert. Wollman asked if any fingerprints were found on the pistol.

"We found a partial print on the trigger guard." Wollman brought out a blow-up of a partial fingerprint. Steinert identified it. A blowup of a print of Martin was set next to it. With a pointer Steinert explained the similarities between the two prints.

Caitlin felt relieved, thinking that a partial fingerprint might be enough to bring her client to trial, but not enough to put him behind bars. But was that his fingerprint? Maybe Martin isn't as innocent as he has proclaimed.

Steinert then testified that they had found the gasoline can believed that carried the fuel that was used to ignite the house. "It was fresh, no rust, no corrosion, nothing to indicate that it had been there more than a day." Wollman brought out a photograph of a gasoline can in the snow. Steinert identified it as the can he had photographed the morning of their investigation, the morning of the fire. Wollman introduced the gasoline can, a red two-gallon metal container. The metal handle had been cut and pried back.

Caitlin put on her reading glasses. She and Martin examined it and handed it back to Wollman. Martin whispered in Caitlin's ear that he had never seen the can before. The can was tagged as evidence.

She removed her glasses, rubbed her eyes lightly with her fingertips and waited for Wollman to resume. It was four o'clock. Steinert testified that he had found two five-gallon fuel cans in the garage. Both were plastic. One contained gasoline and the other held diesel fuel. "We thoroughly examined the metal can for fingerprints. We detected no prints at first. Nothing turned up, as though the can had been wiped clean. Then we found the pistol and the partial print." Steinert paused for some dramatic effect. "Then it suddenly hit me." He gestured with his right hand toward Wollman. "If you're going to dump gasoline, the print may be on the inside of the gas can handle. We carefully pried it back and detected two clear fingerprints."

At this point Wollman introduced more fingerprint photos, placing them on the easel. With his pointer, Steinert described how the prints matched the two middle fingers of Dr. Morley's right hand.

Caitlin's face registered no emotion. She glanced at Martin. He turned his palms up, shrugged and looked totally desperate. He tried whispering to her, but she waved him off.

Wollman and Steinert continued with their questions and answers. Finally, the prosecutor rested the state's case.

Caitlin cross-examined Steinert extensively, trying to determine the thoroughness of his work. After twenty minutes she decided not to pursue the issue further. She could have prolonged the hearing, but declined to recall any witnesses.

Wollman requested the court have Dr. Morley stand trial for first-degree murder.

Judge Appleton ruled in favor of the prosecution and ordered Martin Morley bound over for trial, and that bond be continued at seven hundred fifty thousand dollars. Caitlin put up no objections.

When the judge left for his chambers the media surrounded the prosecution table, except for the tall, well-dressed man in pinstripes. He left the courtroom, sliding out with only Caitlin noticing. Print reporters gathered around Wollman. Caitlin heard one of the television reporters ask Steinert if she could interview him in the hallway. "Your testimony was certainly very damning," she said. Steinert puffed up a bit, smiled and agreed to the interview. Caitlin knew Martin would take a beating on television this night, both newscasts on all stations, and a drubbing in the morning newspapers.

She had driven Martin to the hearing and would drive him back to the city. They pulled out of the courthouse parking lot. Caitlin was angry, but restrained herself. Martin was morose.

About two slow silent and agonizing miles outside of town, Caitlin pulled into a wayside park. She told Martin she wanted to talk with him. They got out of the car and walked to a picnic table. She wiped a couple of inches of snow with a gloved hand from the tabletop for herself and Martin. They sat down facing the road, resting their feet on the long wooden, snow-covered plank attached to the picnic table. She put her hands on her knees and tapped them a few times. "Martin, did you lie to me about not killing Laura?"

"No, I did not kill her."

"Tell me then what the hell happened? How your fingerprints ended up on that gas can?"

"I don't know. I didn't kill her. I've never seen that gas can. There can't be any fingerprints of mine on that can." He, too, was facing the road, shoulders in an even line with Caitlin's. He turned toward her, their knees nearly touching, "It is absolutely impossible for my fingerprints to have been on that gas can." He stopped for a moment and looking straight into Caitlin's eyes, he clenched his fist and added: "Absolutely impossible."

He said it with such conviction and such passion that she tended to believe him, renourishing her earlier suspicion of innocence. "Martin, how did they get those prints?"

"Steinert lied," he snorted.

"He's a cop. A state trooper. Who's going to believe that he lied?"

"Caitlin, I tell you, he's fabricating that evidence. It happens all the time somewhere in this country, cops adjusting evidence to suit their premise. Why don't you talk to him. You'll see. He's a liar. Did you see how he was in court? So self involved. So cock sure of himself. And they think he's the best in the business. I bet he's screwed other people, too. This man is evil." Martin shuddered as though some sort of evil gris-gris were lurking in the gray skies.

Caitlin took a deep breath then forcefully exhaled it. "Martin, I've been a skeptic all of my life. It's difficult to change, but for some unaccountable reason, I believe your theory. I'll do some legwork on this. Meanwhile, can we suggest that you owned that can?"

"They have it on video tape that I owned only five-gallon plastic cans." He stopped for a moment. "Those cannot be my prints on that metal can, Caitlin." He shook his head. "Do whatever it takes. Put your detective on this. I don't care what it costs. I don't want to go to prison, especially for something I didn't do."

"I'm trying to keep the video tape from being entered as evidence during the trial," she offered. "But it may not work."

"Caitlin, you're just going to have to find a way to prove they fabricated those prints. Imagine, the gas can looks brand new and they find only my prints on it. Nothing else. Not even a store clerk's print." He paused a moment, then resumed, "If I had killed Laura I would have worn gloves. There are surgical gloves everywhere in the house. Besides, it would have been so much easier to use a drug, to have doctored her diabetes medication. I can think of a dozen drugs off hand. Now, the police with only a handful of circumstantial evidence are falsifying fingerprints. Hell, the kids and I gave police our fingerprints to use in conjunction with their investigation."

"Jesus." She pulled her lower lip slightly. "I've got to get to work on this." She looked at him then said, "Just out of curiosity. Where were you when they wanted to arrest you?"

He laughed slightly. "I was at Karen's house."

"Karen Phalen, my client?"

"Yeah, but I knew her first. Remember, I recommended Karen to you."

"Jesus, Martin," Caitlin shook her head again.

CHAPTER THIRTY

Anthony Wollman rose graciously as Caitlin entered his office in Williamsville. He occupied a second-floor corner of the courthouse. Caitlin enjoyed visiting the elegant old building. It inspired a sense of timelessness. The world may be moving on, but some things tended to stay the same – at least for a while anyway.

She liked Wollman. She felt he was an honest man trying to do an honest job. It's just that he was clearly wrong about Morley.

"Caitlin, how can I help you?"

"The Martin Morley case."

"You want to plea bargain? I'm afraid not. This is cold-blooded, pre-meditated, first-degree murder. I guess no case is air-tight, but this one, I assure you, is hermetically sealed."

Caitlin knew he was exaggerating, but that was his job, to exude confidence. "Anthony, he didn't do it." She smiled softly, exuding her own sense of controlled confidence.

"Caitlin, you amaze me. We have motives – overpowering greed and hatred – and we can put him at the scene with his prints on the gas can used to destroy his house. It's pretty cut and dried, Caitlin."

"Fingerprints, Anthony. That's why I'm here."

"What do you mean?"

"How did you get fingerprints? I believe my client didn't do it, so the only thing I can assume is that those fingerprints were planted, fabricated."

"Absolutely preposterous! Caitlin." Wollman rose, shaking his head. "Are you accusing the State Police of falsifying evidence? Come on."

In a conciliatory tone she replied, "They're human with a

vast array of frailties, like anyone else. Evidence tampering is not an uncommon occurrence these days, or any day."

"Have you gone off the deep end?" Wollman asked.

"I believe my client. He never saw that gas can. They've only had plastic gas cans at their home for a number of years. Five-gallon ones."

"Clients lie," Wollman suggested.

"Yes, but Martin Morley, until just recently, had been my personal physician – for years. We were social acquaintances and served on various boards and committees together. My former husband and he are friends. I've come to trust Dr. Morley."

Wollman twirled a long, yellow, number two lead pencil in his hands. "Everyone has multiple personalities, Caitlin. You're different with me, say, than you are with your colleagues back at the office. If I may quote Emerson, 'There is an optical illusion about every person we meet.' We all present different faces at different times to different people. You're only seeing just one facet of Dr. Morley, I'm afraid. The facet you're not seeing is the cold-blooded killer. I'm not talking about a man who killed during a moment of extreme anger, a crime of passion, say, but a man who plotted his wife's death for several months." Pointing a finger at her he added, "And carried it out with cruel, cold, calculated precision."

"Anthony, is that your opening statement or closing argument?" She watched him shake his head. "In the entire world of possibilities, Anthony, I suppose your theory is just that, a possibility. But my client's not guilty and I'd like to know how the heck you got those fingerprints?"

Wollman shook his head again. "I guess I have to admire your tenacity, Caitlin, but Det. Steinert is considered one of the best in the state. He's provided the crucial link in solving a number of crimes for us, and also in Iroquois, Bellingham and other counties. I mean, he's good." Wollman leaned back in his chair and smiled.

"Of course, Anthony, there is the possibility that the real killer placed those prints at the scene."

He shook his head, no smile.

They talked for a while then Caitlin left and headed for Enola and State Police Post Headquarters. At the front desk, the sergeant recognized her. She asked for Steinert. "He'll be back in a couple of minutes Ms. Schroeder. Let me get Sgt. Clemens for you instead. He's the only one back there now."

Sgt. Clemens came out. He ushered her back to the investigative bureau, brought her a cup of coffee and asked how he could help her.

"I'm not going to ask you any questions about the Martin Morley case," she replied with a smile.

"Thank you, Ms. Schroeder."

"Please call me Caitlin."

"Then call me Willie."

"Well now – outside the courtroom, anyway – we're friends." She offered her hand and they shook. "I really came to talk to Det. Steinert."

"That's who everybody wants to talk to."

"What do you mean?"

"He's popular with the press, if you saw all that news coverage. Today he's speaking at the Kiwanis Club. Tomorrow it's with school children. He's popular with everyone."

"Why's that?"

"He solves crimes. He has more," Willie thought for a moment, "charisma."

Caitlin smiled, not sure how to respond. "What did he do, take one of those Dale Carnegie courses on How to Win Friends and Influence People?"

Willie laughed and slapped his knee lightly with his right hand. "As a matter of fact, he did. The first few months while he was taking that course, he was unbearable. And the first year afterward he was just full of himself." He slapped his hands together lightly. "He's still full of himself."

Caitlin watched Willie's hands for a moment – long, slender fingers, strong looking, but slender.

"He never forgets a name now," Willie said. "I have to take notes on everything. Maybe I ought to take that Dale Carnegie course. I'd like to make lieutenant before I retire."

"When's that?"

"I want to retire in two years."

Just then Steinert, approaching Caitlin from behind, said, "Ms. Schroeder, how are you?"

Caitlin rose and turned. She shook hands with Steinert. His grasp felt a little soft as though he were afraid to squeeze firmly, afraid that he might hurt her, or maybe it was his way of exerting a sense of power over her.

"Hope you haven't been talking to Sgt. Clemens about the Dr. Morley case." He winked.

"No, actually we were talking about you," Caitlin said, offering a smile.

"Oh, yeah, really?" His face seemed to brighten.

"I saw the news coverage after the preliminary. You handle the media very well."

"Thank you. They let me work with the media a lot here because of my training."

"Oh, what's that?" She saw Sgt. Clemens' hand cover a smile.

"Dale Carnegie course. I took it a few years ago, out of my own pocket. I thought it would be good for career advancement. Want to come over by my desk and talk?" He motioned his head toward his desk a few feet a way.

"Sure," she noticed Willie shake his head slightly. She turned to him, offered her hand and said, "Thanks for your help, Willie."

He smiled back.

At his desk, Steinert said, "I like working with the media."

"I used to be a reporter," Caitlin said.

"Oh, where? Around here?"

"No, in Minneapolis. I covered police for a couple of years, a lot of general assignment, and then I worked on the copy desk while I went to law school nights."

"Nothing like education," Steinert said. "I just finished my bachelor's degree."

"You ever think about going to law school?"

"No, not really. Maybe the federal government, FBI, CIA, Treasury, too."

She nodded thoughtfully.

"Here, let me show you something." He pulled out a large scrap book and opened it. "I keep all the clippings of me." He turned a few pages to show her.

"Very impressive," Caitlin said. She scanned the headlines and the ledes of various stories. She looked at the book for several minutes. She closed it and said, "Everyone says you're very good at digging up that hidden evidence."

"I don't think it's necessarily hidden, just not in the obvious places. Or sometimes it's so obvious you can't see it. The old forest for the trees thing."

Caitlin nodded.

"I have a video cassette with a lot of television coverage of me. My Significant Other tapes them for me."

"You're not married?"

"No wife, no kids. Although, I really like kids. And some day I'll probably have a pair of my own. Later this week I'm speaking at an elementary school. Kids are the solution to society's ills."

Caitlin agreed. They talked for a while longer then she said she had to leave.

As soon as she entered her car she jotted down several of the cases she had read about in the scrapbook. Driving back, she was wondering what to make of William Steinert. She didn't like him. "God, if he gets a federal government job, I hope it's the CIA and not the FBI."

CHAPTER THIRTY-ONE

As winter dissipated, Caitlin began to re-energize. She met with Martin, saying they soon would be setting a trial date. They had been assigned Judge Harold Wilson as the trial judge. Caitlin explained that that was a good sign. He was a better judge than L. Paddington Stone, the only other judge who could hear the trial in Johnson County. But she did want the trial moved to another county. "You just won't get a good jury in Johnson County," she told Martin. But he failed to understand why a noted physician would not garner respect.

"The trial probably won't be until this summer," she said. "In the meantime, what are you going to do?"

"Everything is so undecided. They don't want me back at the practice to ease the transition of my departure because of the publicity. They think I'm guilty."

"Did you ever think of doing some work gratis?"

He shook his head and asked, "What did you have in mind?"

"There are clinics I could set you up with for poor people. Rural poor, inner city poor, Indian reservation. You name it, it's here in this state. There are a lot of people who could use your help. And," she leaned back in her swivel chair, "it wouldn't look bad when we ask for a reduction in bond."

Martin thought about it for a moment. "Actually, I wouldn't mind. I need something to do. Rural poor sounds good to me."

"Since you're standing trial for murder, it may not be easy to place you," she cautioned. "But you're innocent until proven guilty."

Within two days Martin was assigned to a clinic not far from Enola, in a small town in the northeast corner of Johnson

County. The office was a large trailer, a converted mobile home. Not knowing what to expect, he brought some of his own equipment. He had his expensive Littmann cardiology stethoscope – top of the line – and other diagnostic equipment – ophthalmoscope and otoscope. But he also brought a halogen examination light and an electronic diagnostic device for measuring middle ear infection. Martin thought he would wait until his first day was over before bringing any more equipment. Over the years he had collected quite a number of diagnostic instruments, never throwing any away. They had been in storage at his former office. And if the clinic needed more equipment he could bring more of his own or cajole his former partners into lending, or even giving what was needed. They would relish a tax write-off for something they no longer used or needed.

He pulled up to the trailer, the Johnson County Mobile Clinic, at 7:30 Monday morning. There was a dented, partially rusted, large blue and white Chevrolet Blazer parked next to it. It looked like it could go through and over anything, and probably had. Martin knocked on the trailer door.

"Come on in," a powerful female voice bellowed.

A squarish woman with short-cropped blonde hair sat behind what served as a reception desk. She rose. He figured she was about five-foot-six, built like a fireplug.

"Hi, I'm Pat Nordstrom. I run this place." She offered her hand.

Martin shook it. "I'm Dr. Martin Morley."

"This isn't the country club crowd we deal with here. You don't need a suit."

"I'll take it off and put on a lab jacket."

"This is Monday. You know what we get on Mondays?"

"What?"

"A lot of battered women, their pre-school children. Nothing glamorous about this job, Doctor. It'll just wear you down."

"You don't seem worn out."

"I'm too tough." She didn't smile.

"May I call you Pat?" Martin asked.

"If I can call you Martin."

"That's my name."

She brought him a cup of coffee and refilled her mug. "The other two nurses who work here know about your situation, the murder charge, but they're willing to work with you. We talked it over. With a trial coming up, we all figure you'll be on your best behavior. Besides, we need a doc." She finally smiled, more of a menacing grin.

He smiled politely, unable to devise a better response.

The day turned out to be long and arduous. As Nordstrom had said, most of Martin's patients were young mothers and their children. There were also some elderly men and women. The mothers, though, were poor, uneducated, and overweight. They all seemed to be breeding children in their own image and likeness. Most of the adults were smokers. He cautioned each of them to stop smoking, talking to eyes that registered nothing.

At the end of the day, after the last patient, he asked Pat about the smoking.

"It's the only pleasure they get, that and a few cans of beer, and the hors d'oeuvre of preference – tortilla chips and nacho cheese," she explained. "By the way, they call them Mexican chips here."

Martin shook his head. "What a waste of humanity."

"It's actually worse than you think."

Martin figured it was going to be a long spring and summer before trial. He promised to work three days a week at the clinic. It turned out to be good therapy. The dread of going to the clinic helped to keep his mind off the more serious concern about the trial. As time wore on he thought less and less about his legal problems. They didn't seem as terrible and as pressing as they had been in the beginning. Moments of shear panic, though, did pierce his armor from time to time. They occurred at strange times, during an examination of a patient, or coffee with the nurses, or lunch alone at a café in the town as he shifted from one story in his newspaper to the next. But he learned to live with it and life was not as dreary as he had thought it would be. In fact, he enjoyed working with Pat and the other nurses. They shared an interesting cynical camaraderie.

CHAPTER THIRTY-TWO

Two weeks after Martin had started his volunteer medical assignment Caitlin and Wollman were scheduled for court to set a trial date. They appeared in the judge's chambers. Instead of Judge Wilson, Judge L. Paddington Stone was assigned to them.

"I thought Judge Wilson was the trial judge," Caitlin said, keeping her tone untinged.

"Sorry to disappoint you, Honey, but Judge Wilson had a heart attack two days ago, and I'm the only one left who can handle this," Stone explained. He was in his shirtsleeves. A bow tie he had been wearing was untied and dangling at the collar of his white shirt.

Caitlin nodded. She thought she could detect the faint essence of a martini on his breath. It was two-thirty in the afternoon. "Well your honor, it'll be a privilege to have you try this case."

"Why, thank you Dear."

Wollman sat quietly and impassively.

They set the trial for the first Monday in August. "We're going to need that time to prepare our defense, Your Honor," Caitlin said. "But in the spirit of a speedy trial, I wouldn't like it to go beyond that."

"Is there anything else you want to bring up at this point?" the judge asked.

"I'd like to talk about a reduction in bond. It's what we had arranged with Judge Wilson before his illness. Dr. Morley is outside and we'd be glad to appear before you in court."

The judge had his administrative assistant call the bailiff, clerk and court reporter. All appeared in the courtroom. The judge had his black robe on, the pink and blue bow tie now tied.

Caitlin asked that the bond be rescinded and Dr. Morley placed on his own recognizance. Wollman again argued his same points as before.

"Your Honor," Caitlin returned, "Dr. Morley, while currently unemployed, is volunteering free medical services to the indigent in Johnson County. He's not about to jump bail. He's looking forward to a trial that will vindicate him, not to a life as a hounded fugitive."

The judge rubbed his chin for a moment then said, "Well, Darling, I think bond is in order, but I agree that seven hundred fifty thousand dollars is exorbitant. This court will lower Dr. Martin Morley's bond from seven hundred fifty thousand dollars to four hundred thousand dollars." He winked at Caitlin.

Wollman was about to object, but the judge raised his hand and motioned the prosecutor to sit down. Stone turned to Caitlin and said, "Well, Honey, I hope your client realizes what a fine, attorney you are. He should appreciate your good work."

"Thank you, Your Honor."

The judge dismissed the court.

Outside in the hallway, Martin said he could understand why Caitlin didn't want the trial in Johnson County, especially with Stone as judge. "How can he get away with talking to you like that?"

"I could have brought it to his attention, but he might have upped your bail. I once just charged at him without a plan and got knocked on my seat."

The next day Caitlin, looking for advice, called Erik at the CIA and said, "Frankly, I don't want Judge Stone as the trial judge. I won't be treated fairly and as a result, my client won't receive a fair trial."

"You know most of the women attorneys who've appeared before him," Erik said. "Why don't you give them a call, find out what sexist gauntlets they've had to run, and document it.

Ammo for your cannon."

For the next two weeks she did her research, and she began to develop a plan to have the trial moved out of Johnson County.

On April two, the day before an appearance before Judge Stone on a motion to have him step down and move the trial to Adams County, an assignment editor from Channel 10 called Caitlin. She knew the media would be calling her, trying to find out what would happen, whether it would be worth sending a television crew to Williamsville.

"Tom, I can't tell you what I'm going to do, or what's going to happen. But back when I was a newspaper reporter those many years ago, I would have planned to be there. Judge Stone likes the attention and permits the camera. The defendant will be there. I guess you'll have to exercise some keen news judgment on this one."

She ended up with calls from all of the television assignment editors. She said the same thing to each of them. Print reporters didn't call her, but she knew they would be there. She explained to Martin what her plan was. "Will it work?" he asked as they sat at the defense table, waiting for the judge to arrive. It wasn't quite one-thirty.

"Either it will work, or the judge will treat us with a lot more respect from now on." She had planned the venture well and was convinced intellectually that they could pull it off, but she was on edge. She wasn't sure what would happen to her case, but she was convinced it would make a great news story. She shook her head, bewildered by her chutzpa and knowing she was tottering on the brink of contempt of court.

The bailiff asked the court to rise then announced the arrival of the Honorable L. Paddington Stone, and declared the court in session. Caitlin rose and pulled her shoulders back. The judge sat with his dark red paisley bow tie and white shirt collar peeking above the yoke of his black robe. He rapped his gavel and said, "In the matter of the state versus Dr. Martin

Morley and the motion before this court that the court's presiding judge step down and the trial be removed to Adams County, I would call on the defense counsel to state her case. You want to come up here Cate?"

Caitlin rose. "Your Honor, for the record, my name is Caitlin Schroeder. That's Caitlin, not Cate. It's spelled C-A-I-T-L-I-N."

"We know your name, Honey. There's no need to get so uppity. This is a small-town, friendly court."

"Your Honor, Honey is a romantic term of endearment, or it means bee spit. Which definition are you using?"

Stone slapped his gavel, "Ms. Schroeder, I could hold you in contempt of this court. Now proceed with this matter." He looked up and saw the reporters taking notes and the camera running. He looked back at Caitlin and suddenly understood.

"Your Honor, over the past three years, this court has consistently produced a clear message of disdain for female attorneys appearing before this bench. I am prepared to file transcripts from appearances by ten different female attorneys who have appeared in this court. All of the transcripts demonstrate this court's cavalier disregard and disrespect for the professional standing of the women as officers of the court. Clearly, my client cannot receive a fair trial before this court. . . ."

Caitlin finished her argument and waited for the judge's reaction. There was a pause that lasted sixty seconds. It seemed like sixty minutes. Finally, the judge asked if the state had any comments on whether the judge should step down and the trial be moved to Adams County.

Wollman rose as Caitlin sat. "Your Honor, the state has no objection to this court trying this case," Wollman said. "We have found the judges in Johnson County to be fair, considerate and professional. And we see no need to remove the trial to another county. In fact, we prefer it be held in Johnson County where the crime was committed and the defendant resided."

After Wollman sat, the judge said he would take defense

counsel's motion under advisement. "A decision will be forthcoming on Friday." He rapped his gavel to adjourn court.

All rose at the bailiff's direction.

Martin was grinning. Reporters rushed Caitlin. She gave a brief statement: "The treatment female attorneys have received in this court has been a grave concern of mine, and my concern becomes exacerbated the closer we get to trial for Dr. Morley. Without the proper respect from the bench, we cannot receive a fair trial in Johnson County."

"Are you going to file a grievance with the State Court Administrator?" one of the reporters asked.

"I've filed what I'm going to file. I'm only interested in making sure my client, Dr. Morley, receives a fair trial."

She answered several more questions and then offered to take phone calls on it from reporters when she returned to her office.

After the media left, Caitlin cleared her files and papers from the defense table, not saying anything to Martin, who just sat there smiling. Wollman came over and said, "Don't you think you were a little rough on the judge?"

"Rough," she said slowly. "Rough? And what has he been to me and my female colleagues all these years?"

"He does get a little loose-tongued after a couple of martinis," Wollman admitted.

"Antoninus, Antoninus, in vino veritas." She shook her head and added, "I have to go now. Martin, are you ready?" She turned, and over her shoulder added, "I'll see you, Anthony, when we get a new judge and set a trial date in Adams County."

Just as she was about to leave, the bailiff approached Caitlin and told her Judge Stone would like to see her in his chambers. She asked Martin to wait, and followed the bailiff to the judge's office. Inside, Stone sat behind his large walnut desk, leaning back in his dark red leather, high-backed chair. His robe was off, his bow tie tied, and shirt cuffs and plackets buttoned. He motioned for Caitlin to sit down. Finally, he asked softly, “Why?”

“The courtroom and the proceedings are too serious for this kind of demeanor," she replied. “As a result, my client cannot receive a fair trial. It's really that simple, your Honor.”

“Are you sure," the judge spoke slowly, “that you're not being vindictive?”

“I am angry with the way I've been treated by you," Caitlin admitted. “But my primary concern is my client.” She paused and considered her next statement carefully. “It may seem complex, Your Honor, but it really isn't. When I am subjected to ridicule, or perceived as being treated that way, jurors, my client and prospective clients no longer take me seriously; their respect diminishes. My clients will suffer, and my career as well.” Caitlin stopped, waiting for the judge to say something. She noticed a photograph on a corner of the judge's desk near her. From her angle she could discern him and his wife, and four children. They were all dressed in their finest. The youngest stood in front of the judge. She was about 14 and had Down's syndrome. The judge's hand rested on her shoulder.

“Ms. Schroeder, if I step down, what kind of impact do you think it will have on our professional relationship in future cases before this court?”

“We'll be respectful of each other, Your Honor.” Suddenly she felt a little sad for the judge. “Judge Stone, this is not a personal issue. It doesn't matter who tries this case, as long as it isn't in this county. I'm convinced Dr. Morley will not get a fair trial here whether you're the presiding judge or not.” She didn't know what else to say. She looked at the family photograph again and lifted her head slightly to look at the judge.

“Yes, that's my family.” He sighed.

"I only have one child. Sometimes I wish I had had more. I have a picture of my son and me on my desk. You have a very lovely family.

He smiled with weary eyes.

In two days, Judge Stone stepped down from the case and directed the trial be conducted in Adams County. He had conferred with the senior judge of Adams County and the State Court Administrator. With Stone's colleague in the hospital, there were no other qualified trial judges in the county.

CHAPTER THIRTY-THREE

Despite her nurtured cynicism, Caitlin had now convinced herself of Morley's innocence. Granted, he was a bit of a lout with women, but that didn't make him guilty of first-degree murder. He was also rather arrogant. But he is brilliant. There's nothing more pitiful than arrogant men who aren't all that bright.

The more she thought about Steinert's fingerprint discoveries, the more she came to believe that he had fabricated evidence. If Morley is innocent, how else could the fingerprints have turned up on the gas can? And in only that one spot? And a partial print on the trigger guard? It just didn't make sense.

She bought a metal gas can at an old gas station. It was similar to the one submitted as evidence. She went through the motions of tossing gasoline from the can. She had others try it, visiting acquaintances in her office building. There was no absolute way people held the can, although right handed people tended to hold the hand with their left hand with their right hand at the bottom.

Why would he have taken a glove off, other than to strike a match? And that would have been done after pouring the gasoline. In all likelihood, Martin, of all people, would have worn surgical gloves. No trouble for a doctor to strike a match with surgical gloves. And, if Martin had done it, and wore no gloves, then he would have left other fingerprints. Wiping them off would have been too time-consuming, especially after a gunshot and a house set ablaze. Why were there no other prints on the can? She went over the scenario dozens of times and couldn't come up with a logical conclusion, other than that

Martin's prints were planted. Maybe the real killer planted them. But how? And who? Then maybe it was all just wishful thinking on her part. She shook her head in exasperation.

Steinert had demonstrated the same kind of miracle evidence-gathering in a variety of criminal cases over the past five years. The stories in his scrapbook revealed that. But it wasn't enough for Caitlin. She called a friend at the *Daily News*, Lacey Larson, who was a writer in the features section of the newspaper.

"Caitlin," Lacey said after picking up the phone, "that was a hell of a job you did on Judge Stone."

"Oh, he'll still be re-elected next November," Caitlin said, "but at least he's off my back for a while. One good thing about all of this is that I've gotten a few new clients. Two of them are sexual harassment cases. They're going to be a couple of good cases, and probably good stories down the line. But that's not what I'm calling you about. I need a favor."

"What's that?" Lacey asked with just a hint of reticence.

"Let's have lunch."

They met at noon at a downtown vegetarian restaurant on a street that contained the back entrances of stores and office buildings. "I quit eating meat," Lacey tried to explain her reason for a vegetarian diet, "not because I love cows and pigs all that much. But I'm just trying to avoid a gallstone operation my doctor has hinted may be imminent."

Caitlin shook her head in commiseration. "It's tough getting old. I'm wearing reading glasses now. But some things don't change. Here I am just turned forty-two and there was a pimple on my face this morning." She pointed to a reddish bump on her chin. "I'm damn near thirty years past puberty and still getting pimples."

"I have this to look forward to?" Lacey was thirty-eight.

"Maybe the pimples will stop with menopause," Caitlin said, shaking her head in dismay. They both laughed.

The restaurant was dimly lit. It was a converted tavern. The ornate bar and back bar now served fruit juices and other nonalcoholic elixirs. The young man behind the bar sported delicate earrings in both ears and wore a T-shirt that advertised a ten-kilometer run for an AIDS halfway house. Their waitress was dressed in black slacks and black blouse buttoned to the throat. Lacey described the attire as "alternative quasi-chic."

What the restaurant lacked in traditional elegance, it made up for in its kitchen. The food, to Caitlin's surprise, was excellent. She had a creamed pumpkin soup with potatoes and a pasta dish with olives and a considerable amount of garlic.

Caitlin filled Lacey in on the Martin Morley case, no more than was necessary, though. She didn't explain her belief that Steinert was lying about the fingerprints. "I need to do a fair amount of research over the last five years on a Det. William Steinert. They're all news clippings from your paper. Trouble is, your research service won't let me use your computer. They'll give me the dates stories appeared then I have to go look them up on microfilm at the public library."

"Oh, hell," Lacey said. "I'll run it off for you. Jeez, I thought you were looking for some kind of news coverage." Lacey, wearing a dark, frumpy suit that needed pressing, brushed her brown hair back with her hand. "Those two sexual harassment suits, any of them a story?"

"Maybe in a couple of months when we file. I can set it up for you, if you'd like that."

"I'd have to see what it is first, but I'm dying to get off features and back to hard news."

"One of them involves a high profile company in town. If that works the way I expect it will, it'll be a big story. When it's ready to break, I can make sure it's yours."

"That would be great, Caitlin."

Caitlin thought Lacey a good reporter even though she had been sidelined on the features section for the past two years.

The next day Lacey dropped by Caitlin's office with a stack of computer printouts. "I didn't think there would be so many stories," Lacey said. Most of the stories had appeared in regional editions of her newspaper. “What are you going to do with this?”

“Read them and find out why this guy is such a hot shot.”

“Aren't they all?”

“Who?”

“Men.”

They laughed.

As soon as Lacey left, Caitlin delved into the stories. She found ten that particularly interested her. In each of them Steinert was responsible for solving crimes through his deftness as a fingerprint expert. Two of the stories took place in Johnson County, while the others were in three other rural counties that were part of the State Patrol district that the Post Headquarters in Enola covered. There were five homicides, and the rest were robberies and burglaries.

She set up appointments with the attorneys who had represented the defendants in each of the cases.

In Piedmont, a city of about 20,000, she met with a young attorney, barely thirty years old. He was in practice with an older brother – Patterson and Patterson. Patterson, the younger, said he vividly recalled the case that Caitlin brought to his attention. “It was my first murder case. My only murder case. I was appointed by the court. The kid had no money. I had handled a number of criminal cases, so I wasn't exactly a novice.

“The case still bothers me. This kid, Paul, a high school drop out. Frankly, he wasn't too smart, an IQ quite a few points below average. Not retarded, though. I thought he was a harmless boy.” He gave Caitlin a brief overview of the case. “If it wouldn't have been for the fingerprints, we'd have won. Sometimes I think if I had been a little more astute, we could have gotten something less than life.”

In several of the cases defendants plea-bargained, although their bargaining powers were limited because of fingerprints

Steinert had uncovered. In every case the fingerprints put the defendant at the scene of the crime when no other evidence or witness could.

Although it was risky, Caitlin decided to talk with two of the prosecutors involved. She didn't want to talk with Wollman, and the fourth prosecutor was no longer living in the area. Caitlin would handle her with a phone call later.

Both prosecutors she talked with spoke highly of Steinert and all of the investigators with the Enola post. "He's the best I've ever seen," one of them said. "It's amazing how he's able to do what he does. The whole bunch is great. Their work is so clean and precise. We get a lot of pleadings and plea bargains. Very little goes to trial when the State Patrol's Criminal Investigation Division is on the job. Our conviction record is phenomenal. I don't want to sound like I'm insulting the city police or sheriff's department, but the state guys are real pros."

When Caitlin finished her investigation of the cases she had selected, she had this picture: In every one, no physical evidence linked the suspect to the scene of the crime until several days later when state investigators were able to come up with fingerprints. But that was all she had. And to most people, she feared, it was all entirely plausible. But her suspicion that State Police were fabricating evidence festered.

Caitlin drove to the Enola Post Headquarters after setting up an appointment with the chief of investigations there – Capt. Alfred Quincy. He wasn't available when she arrived, but Sgt. Willie Clemens invited her back to the investigators' area. They stood around his desk drinking coffee and making small talk. Steinert came by and said hello.

"I've been checking around," Caitlin said, "and you really are very good at finding that telltale piece of evidence."

"Well Ms. Schroeder, we don't let the bad guys go free here. That's our unwritten motto." His smile annoyed her. She wondered if she were reading everything the wrong way. Was she so anxious for acquittal that she had begun to believe anything to back up her position?

Willie, Caitlin noticed, was shaking his head. He sat down at his desk and pulled out a sheaf of papers. Steinert leaned toward Caitlin's ear and whispered, "I'm being interviewed by the CIA next week. It won't be long and I'll be in the big time."

"Congratulations," Caitlin whispered back. "You'll be of great service to the country."

Steinert saw Capt. Quincy approaching and whispered to her, "Don't tell the captain. I haven't broken the bad news to him yet."

"I won't say a word."

Capt. Quincy arrived and invited her into his office. He was six-feet-six with shoulders nearly as broad as the doorway Caitlin followed him through. He was in his shirtsleeves rolled a few inches above his wrists. A small pistol nested in a holster toward the back of his right side. It was attached to the belt of his civilian trousers.

He motioned for her to take a seat, and he sat down as well. "Ms. Schroeder, I understand you've been investigating us," he stated in a matter of fact tone.

"What do you mean?" Caitlin asked, suspecting the prosecutors had called him.

"Anthony Wollman called, as did prosecutors in two other counties in our jurisdiction, saying that you are questioning our ethical standards."

"As you know, Captain, I am defense counsel for Dr. Martin Morley, and I find it highly suspect that you have so many criminal cases in which you miraculously discover fingerprints or other evidence conclusively linking your suspect to the crime."

"Are you accusing us of tampering with evidence, Ms. Schroeder?"

"It's not an accusation, Captain. I just find it suspicious and I aim to find out if my suspicions are correct."

"Ms. Schroeder, why don't you simply defend your client?

Don't go after old, cold cases that have run their course. In fact," his voice lowered, "I would encourage you not to stick your nose where it doesn't belong." He pointed at her nose.

"Are you trying to intimidate me, Captain," she asked sharply.

Quincy arose quickly, both hands on his hips, one next to the gun and said, "I'm not *trying* to intimidate you, Ms. Schroeder." He paused to smile condescendingly, and said, "I just like my investigators to be able to do their jobs without a lot of outside interference, especially the kind that is unwarranted, uninvited and unnecessary. Do you understand me?"

Caitlin rose and said with a forced smile, "In that case, Captain, I'll just continue with my business. Thank you." She turned and walked out ramrod straight.

In her car, with both hands at the top of her steering wheel she rested her forehead on the backs of her hands. She felt entirely intimidated.

CHAPTER THIRTY-FOUR

Caitlin wrote to Erik, using his personal e-mail address, asking him to find out if Steinert had been interviewed for a job with the CIA. "I'm convinced," she wrote, "that Steinert is a sonofabitch who has fabricated evidence over the past five years. And he may be an inveterate liar. My problem is, I can't prove any of it. Maybe I'm wrong. Maybe I've been hoodwinked by Martin. Damnit, if Martin *is* innocent, then the cops *are* lying.

"It's easier defending someone you know is guilty than defending someone you believe is innocent. Give me a guilty client any time, there's less toll on your soul."

He replied right away and said he'd look into it, but it may take awhile. Ten days later Erik skipped the handwritten letters and e-mailed her:

I've given up being a Francophile nut. There is an Indian couple living on the floor below me. They're from somewhere in the interior of India. Every night there is an incredible aroma of intermingling exotic spices.

Please consider: cardamom pods, green cardamom, black mustard seeds, curry leaves, toasted cumin seeds, garlic, ah, lovely garlic with its pungent, passionate disposition toward the palate. I finally gave up. I took a course in Indian cuisine. Of course, I now serve beer instead of wine.

And, oh yes, your friend, William Steinert, has been interviewed by my agency a couple of times, including the usual polygraph examination. I know nothing more, but will keep my eyes on the ground and my ears peeled, or something like that. I'll let you know as soon as I can learn more. It may take a while.

Caitlin quickly e-mailed Erik saying, "Please, please, be more vigilant and not so cavalier about this. I need help, any information you can give me. Did he flunk his lie detector test? What was the reaction of his interviewers? Anything."

Erik dashed off a response saying only: "Will do." It made her smile. She missed him. The few times he was in town he stopped by the office to see her, but spent most of his time with his daughters.

It was late May and Caitlin was becoming more nervous about her defense of Martin. She called him in for a conference. He arrived the next day, dapper and happy. "So what's up, Caitlin?" he asked, just a little too cheerful to suit her.

"Martin, we still face serious problems. Let's go over everything from the beginning." She slid a yellow legal tablet in front of her and placed her pencil on top of it. She motioned for him to begin.

Martin recounted everything. When he finished she asked, "Now, I want you to think about minutiae. Even things that don't seem to have any relation to your problem."

"Relations! Public relations!" Martin snapped his fingers. I went over the bank accounts the other day, the ones where Laura had placed her inheritance when she received it last fall. I have since transferred all of it to accounts that are fairly liquid but bearing more interest. I did that a few days after I was arrested. Anyway, I finally got around to checking on the old account files a few weeks ago. She had withdrawn two hundred fifty thousand dollars in October and the same amount again on December twenty-ninth. Nestled in her files were two check stubs from the bank. The checks were drafted to James Crane, her lover." He sat back and smiled.

"Martin," Caitlin exclaimed with a hint of exasperation in her voice, "Why didn't you tell me this sooner? To defend you properly, I need every bit of ammunition I can get. Right now about all I'm doing is sweeping up dust."

"Are things that desperate?" Martin asked, suddenly

alarmed.

"I'm treating it that way to assure your freedom, Martin. So, I need every bit of help from you that you can muster." She shook her head wondering why he hadn't told her about the money that had gone to Laura's lover. "I mean, this is really revelatory and relevant." She paused then asked, "Is there any documentation on the money?"

"Nothing other than those checks and the bank statements," he replied. He thought a moment, then asked, "If it is a gift, who pays the gift tax?"

"The giver. You were still married at the time and filing joint tax returns. It looks like you're the giver. Better check with your accountant. Tax is not an area of my expertise."

Martin's jaw dropped. "Jesus," he swore, "that's going to cost me a bundle. And I'll probably have to file an amended form and then pay some sort of penalty."

Three days later Caitlin had an appointment with Jim Crane. She stood in front of his office door: Crane Public Relations. "CPR," she thought, a lot of companies need CPR. She smiled, shaking her head as she opened the door. Inside, a receptionist behind a high counter greeted her. Large silver colored letters spelled out the company name. It was rather attractive to Caitlin. She liked the combination of stainless steel and the dark mauve of the wall behind the receptionist. She introduced herself to the receptionist. After a brief phone conversation between the receptionist and Crane, he entered the area and shook hands with Caitlin, saying, "I'm Jim Crane, Ms. Schroeder, let's go back to my office and see what I can do for you."

Caitlin followed him. He had a corner office that gave him half a room full of windows. She sat in the leather chair in front of his desk, sinking a few inches lower than she preferred. He sat behind his desk in a firmer looking leather swivel chair. "How may I help you, Ms. Schroeder?"

"As I mentioned on the phone, Mr. Crane, I represent Dr.

Martin Morley in his defense against the charge of murdering his wife. I understand that you were friends with Mrs. Morley."

"Yes, we knew each other."

"Let me get to the point. You and Mrs. Morley were lovers."

Crane didn't say anything, not a muscle moved in his face.

"Mr. Crane, last fall Dr. Morley retained me to prepare divorce proceedings for him. And in so doing, we hired a private investigator who captured on film scenes of you and Mrs. Morley that indicate you and she were having a sexual relationship."

"All right, we were having a love affair." He slowly twirled an expensive ballpoint pen point down on a note pad. "I loved her. And she loved me. He's such a bastard."

"She must have loved you very much."

"Yes – " He stopped abruptly. "What do you mean?"

"She gave you a two hundred and fifty thousand dollar bank check in October and again on December twenty-nine."

Crane rubbed both his hands through his thinning white hair. He smiled wanly.

"We have a bank record of two, two hundred fifty thousand-dollar checks made out to you," she added.

He clasped his hands on his desktop. "Yes, she did give me some money."

Caitlin leaned back for a moment, then leaned toward him and said, "Give?"

Crane fidgeted momentarily. "Yes, it was a gift."

"It wasn't a loan?"

"No. It was a gift."

"For what? Your services?"

"Laura wasn't seeking public relations services from me."

"Let's quit being coy, Mr. Crane. Why did Laura Morley give you five hundred thousand dollars last year?"

"We were in love. We had planned on getting married. Laura didn't know that her husband was about to file for divorce. She had planned on using my attorney for the divorce.

That was the plan, anyway. In fact, I had set up an appointment with my attorney. You can check with him, Gregg Wallace. Anyway, I needed the money as a stopgap in my business. She gave me the money."

"Why?"

"We were in love. She was a very trusting soul. She trusted me and I loved her. It's as simple as that."

Caitlin was shaking her head. "Why don't you tell me what happened the evening of December thirtieth?"

He related the same story he had told Sgt. Clemens. "You don't believe me, do you?" he finally said. "You think I killed her? I already have five hundred thousand dollars from her. Why would I kill her? We were lovers. You have the pictures and, apparently, an eyewitness. There are dozens of people who knew we were in love, including my mother." He stopped, shook his head and lowered his eyes. When he looked up tears appeared. "I truly did love Laura. She had been so unloved for so long." He pulled a handkerchief from his pocket and dabbed at his tears.

"You'll be getting a summons as a witness for the defense, Mr. Crane." Caitlin rose to leave and added, "You might save a few of those tears for the witness stand."

CHAPTER THIRTY-FIVE

The next day Martin brought a copy of his bill from Western Alps Ski Resort to Caitlin's office. Caitlin noticed that the bill indicated a phone call being placed at five-thirty-two p.m., December thirty, to his residential phone. She also saw that his dining bills were too high for a single person. He certainly wasn't alone for at least part of that night.

As she took the expressway downtown to a meeting with Angela Wain, a State Trooper pulled her over. He walked to her window, his hand on his holstered gun. She lowered her window and said, "Yes, Trooper?"

"Your license please."

She fished in her large purse, found her wallet and retrieved the driver's license. "Why did you pull me over?" she asked as she handed it to him.

"In a moment Ma'am." The trooper went back to his squad car for several minutes. He returned, handed her the license and said, "Ms. Schroeder you were exceeding the speed limit."

"Trooper, I set cruise control at a little over fifty-five miles per hour. Do you mean to tell me you're stopping cars for going fifty-eight miles an hour in a fifty-five speed zone?"

"Ma'am, I clocked you at sixty-two miles an hour."

"Seven over the limit?"

"Yes, Ma'am."

"For Christ's sake."

"No need to be abusive, Ma'am, and take the Lord's name in vain." He shifted his body weight from the right foot to the left. "Because it was only seven miles an hour over the limit, I've only written you a warning ticket, just a reminder."

"Thanks, Trooper." She took the warning ticket, folded it neatly and placed it in her purse. As the trooper headed back to his squad car, she took off. She hadn't shut off her engine and just out of curiosity she pressed the resume button on her cruise control. The Kia accelerated and leveled off at the halfway point between fifty-five and sixty miles an hour on her odometer. She had been accustomed to exceeding the speed limit, but since getting the car she had been using cruise control, usually setting it around five miles an hour over the limit. She wondered if they were purposely trying to harass her.

She arrived at Angela's office a half hour late, but the receptionist ushered her in after a brief call to Angela. Caitlin figured Angela would be attractive, but she didn't expect quite the beauty that was sitting behind the mahogany desk.

They swapped a few pleasantries then Caitlin said, "I am defense counsel for Dr. Martin Morley. As you know, Dr. Morley will go on trial in two months for the murder of his wife. Dr. Morley said he spent three days and nights with you at Western Alps Ski Resort – the nights of December twenty-nine, thirty, and thirty-one."

"Ms. Schroeder, as I had mentioned on the phone to you some time ago, he's lying. I don't know if you noticed, but Dr. Morley has a problem with the truth. He's been wanting to go to bed with me for the past three years, from the day he met me, when I married his partner, Philip Wain. For three years he's been making these offensive suggestions. He's constantly on the make, if you know what I mean. It's been most annoying. But this is an outright lie, saying we're lovers. That's carrying this thing, this dementia, too far."

"Are you denying what he claims?"

"I certainly am."

"If I called you on the witness stand, would you stick with that story, knowing that perjury is a felony?"

"On a stack of Bibles, Ms. Schroeder." She shook her head as though she couldn't believe this was happening and that Caitlin could be so gullible about Martin. "I would never go to bed with him. I cherish my marriage too much, and I truly love my husband." Angela sat back in her chair and pressed the finger tips of both hands together. "There are a lot of men like Martin out there, as you probably very well know. He fashions himself a great lover, but really?" She laughed and turned her palms up.

Despite the earlier denial over the telephone, Caitlin hadn't expected Angela to deny it again. With the possibility of being called as a witness at trial, Angela certainly was aware of what perjury would mean. Caitlin was confounded by it. She cut the meeting short after a couple of more questions and headed back to her office. Either Angela or Martin was lying. But why would Martin lie about that -- unless, of course, he had been lying about other things as well.

At the end of the day Martin stopped by her office. "How did it go with Angela?" he asked, a bit of a smirk on his face.

"She denied being with you," Caitlin said in a matter-of-fact tone.

"What?" He sounded as though he couldn't believe it. "Why would she deny a thing like that? We had a great time."

"Martin, it's simply your word against hers, and we cannot put you on the witness stand. And if we put Angela on the stand, she denies everything. So all we have is a woman who says she didn't go to Western Alps Ski Resort with you and no one who remembers seeing her there." Caitlin stopped to let her point sink in, then resumed, "Perhaps Angela is concerned about her husband finding out."

"Philip?" Martin raised an eyebrow. "He could be a bastard about this, I suppose. But hell, he's screwed every operating room nurse worth looking at. He goes to one of those operating room nurses conventions and he's just like a kid trapped overnight in a candy factory. Really, he's quite immature about women." Martin shook his head as though he couldn't believe his former partner's behavior.

Caitlin was shaking her head, too. "Sounds like a

testosterone overload to me – all of you." She tapped her fingers on the desk for a moment then asked, "Did you and Angela make love in Western Alps those three days?"

"Caitlin, don't you believe me? I can give you details about our love making, things only a lover could possibly know."

"You can spare the intimate, procedural details. Just tell me what happened."

He recounted the trip and the stay in the cabin. He started to laugh. "You know there was one thing that happened. It was our second evening there. After we had downhill and cross-country skied all day, Angela was in a robe. That's all she had on. She sat on the bed and called her husband. She was pretending she was calling from the Baltimore airport. He was talking about sex to her. I started playing with her. You know what I mean?" He saw Caitlin nod, and continued, "So, while I was playing with her clitoris, he was making sexual remarks on the phone, she was kind of moaning saying how aroused she was getting in the phone booth, and could hardly wait until he came home." Martin stopped. Noticing that Caitlin wasn't smiling, he added, "I guess you had to be there to appreciate that."

"I suppose so," Caitlin said, although she did, to her chagrin, find herself somewhat amused by the story. "Where was her husband?"

"She called him at his mother's home in Scottsdale, Arizona."

"I didn't notice that on your hotel bill."

"She used her cell phone."

"Ah," Caitlin said. "We have something now. We could subpoena the phone information, pinpoint the date, time and place called and from where it was made." She rubbed her hands. "We can force Angela to testify on your behalf. I think I'll save this, though, for a time a little closer to trial."

"What are you going to do?"

"Eventually?" Caitlin smiled. "Convince her to tell the

truth. Just for added assurance I'm going to send our private investigator to the ski resort to find someone who saw you together. Somebody has to remember."

Martin smiled broadly. "It's sure going to hit the fan when Philip finds out."

"Does that worry you?"

"It interests me," he said, raising his eyebrows.

Caitlin rose from her chair and walked toward her bookshelf. "Martin, this is only one aspect of your defense. Will Angela testify that you were with her all night?"

"Of course. We were inseparable. Like this." He entwined the first two fingers of his right hand. "We skied all day and made love all night."

"Well, that's good, but we still have the matter of the fingerprints, Martin."

"You're just going to have to prove that they made that up. I tell you, Caitlin, those prints are absolutely impossible."

"The Enola Post has developed a reputation for making miracle, last-minute evidence discoveries," she acknowledged.

"Well, this is one of them. Did they ever check out Jim Crane's prints? He had a motive. Money. Five hundred thousand dollars is a lot of money."

"People have killed for a lot less than that, Martin." She shook her head remembering the cases she had prosecuted that involved death over just a handful of dollars.

"Have I disappointed you, Caitlin, my story of being with Angela, the other woman? I suppose I am a scoundrel that way." He proffered his best bad-boy look.

Caitlin had moved back to her desk. "Well, you did warn me that you had a reputation as a philanderer." She found it kind of interesting, and just for the briefest of moments wondered what it would be like to make love with Martin Morley.

"Yes, I did," Martin said. "It's a personality flaw."

"And Angela was a challenge?"

"Let's just say it was a hell of an adventure."

When Martin left her office, Caitlin called Anita for assistance. A half hour later Anita came in for photos of Angela and Martin. Caitlin handed her the Wain's Women brochure and a glossy of Martin.

"Some looker," Anita whistled. "I can see why the hell he killed his wife for her."

"He didn't kill her, Anita."

"Sorry, just a reflex."

CHAPTER THIRTY-SIX

Anita Zombrowska arrived at Western Alps Ski Resort the next morning. Except for caretakers, it was closed until mid-June when the warm weather trade would arrive for hiking, canoeing, swimming and tennis. Two vans from a contractor were parked in the driveway where carpenters were taking a coffee break. She found one of the caretakers. Anita was disappointed that there was no regular staff to interview. The caretaker gave her a brochure. She read it. "What's this about someone lighting the fireplace before you awake?" Anita asked.

"One of the young fellas from town comes in, puts a log on the fire, stirs it up while the guests are asleep – about four or five in the morning. The boys keep the fire going all day long, too, so it's nice and cozy when they come back from skiing."

Anita was able to obtain a name and address of one of the men who performed this job for the resort. It was the only name – Pete Rant – the caretaker could remember. "If this fella can't help you, the manager will be back later this afternoon."

Anita drove to the house in town where Rant lived. It was divided into small apartments. There were four rusted mailboxes without names outside the front door. The building was in need of paint, and a short length of slat was missing from the porch floor near the door. Anita talked to one of the residents who suggested she look for Pete at a bar on Main Street.

She walked the few blocks to the bar and at a small table in the tavern she found Pete Rant eating a bowl of chili and drinking a beer. She walked up to the table with the only young man in the place and said, "Mind if I join you?"

He looked up, a slightly pocked face with a few withering pimples, then looked back down at his chili and said, "Leave me alone." Pete crumbled two saltine crackers on top of his chili then stirred it.

Anita tossed her private investigator identification on the table. He picked it up with a soiled right hand. "You really one of them detectives?" His face suddenly lit up.

"Yeah," she sat next to him. "Can I buy you a beer?"

He nodded and returned her identification. He appeared to Anita to be in his mid-twenties. A waitress arrived and Anita ordered two beers.

"You carry a gun?" he asked.

"Sometimes."

"What kind?"

"A nine-millimeter, semi-automatic."

He grinned. "Cool, man."

"My name's Anita Zombrowska." She offered her hand.

He shook it and said, "I'm Pete Rant."

"I understand you work at Western Alps during ski season," she said as she handed him her business card.

"They in trouble over there?" he asked.

"No. But I've got a client accused of murdering his wife. He claims he was up at the ski resort," she offered a salacious grin, "making love with another woman."

"A murder case. You gonna find out who really done it?"

"I gotta get him off the hook first."

"How can I help?"

"A few people remember seeing him there, but nobody recalls the woman he says he was with. You go to most of the cabins and light the fires. I wonder if you might have seen them."

He leaned back in his chair, taking a large swallow from the beer that the waitress had just brought. "What's in it for me?"

"You'll be reimbursed for your expenses at the trial: transportation there; a couple nights in the city; and, hotel room, travel, food, that sort of thing. We'll take good care of you. But," she pointed her finger at him, "you gotta tell the truth. You can't say that she's the woman if you're not absolutely certain, 'cuz the prosecutor will kill you at the trial. No perjury, understand? Besides, perjury's a felony. And that means hard time."

"Okay."

Anita pulled out a picture of Martin, "They were here December twenty-nine and checked out January one," and handed it to Pete.

He looked at it for sixty seconds then said, "Looks familiar, but I ain't certain. A lot of them rich men look alike."

She handed him the brochure with Angela's picture. One look and he said with a lascivious grin, "Oh, yeah, that's her."

"What do you mean?" Anita asked.

"Cabin Fourteen. I'd recognize her better with her clothes off. I mean she's some good lookin' piece and she sure likes to fuck. I went to start up their fire about five o'clock one of those mornings, the first one." He lit a cigarette for himself with a Zippo lighter then offered Anita one. She took it. It was a Marlboro. He lit it for her. He inhaled deeply on his and continued, "They really don't need them fireplaces. It's plenty warm inside. But what the hell, I get paid to do this and everyone always leaves the fireman a nice tip. I make good money." He inhaled deeply on his cigarette again. "Anyway, they were both in bed, buck naked, on their backs, sleeping. She had her hand on his cock."

"What'd you do?"

"I rekindled the fire and got the hell out of there." He took another swallow of beer, finishing the glass. "Tell you, though. I had a hard on all day long."

"You sure it was her?" Anita asked.

Pete laughed. "You don't forget a woman that looks like that. Besides, I saw her more than once." He licked his lips and ran the back of his hand over his mouth.

Anita ordered another round of beer. "Well, what else did you see?"

"Nothin' much the next day. I mean they were in bed with the covers pulled up. So, all I saw was her face. Pretty face. How come the rich guys get all the good lookin' women?"

"Cuz, the assholes are rich," she said. "My ex – The Sonofabitch – wasn't rich and look what he got." She laughed and Pete laughed, too. They were comrades now.

"Well," he took another swallow of beer, "I saw 'em again, the next day after that, early New Year's Day morning. I was at the cabin and the side window, there's a curtain. It was pulled back a crack. One of the lights was on." Pete Rant squinted at Anita. "Does everything have to come out in court? I mean, I was kinda peeping."

"Can't blame you for peeking, but maybe it won't have to come out."

"Well, I peeked through the corner of the window. I can get fired for this. Anyway, they were fuckin'. She was standin', bent over, holdin' onto the footboard, and he was gettin' her from behind. I watched the whole thing. I watched 'em come and everything. I never seen it in real life before. I mean seein', it's not the same as when you're doin' it yourself. Know what I mean? She was very happy. Her face and the way she looked that night is permanent in my brain, like a tatoo." He grinned and pulled up his sleeve to show the tattoo on his right arm. "I lit some other fires, then came back and lit theirs after they had gone back to bed. They left me a nice forty-dollar tip, too. Best tips are from those that get laid."

They talked a while then Anita obtained his cell phone number.

Late in the afternoon Anita arrived at Caitlin's office. She recounted Rant's story.

"You sure he's positive on the identification?"

"Yeah, he looked at Angela's picture and the first thing he said was 'Cabin Fourteen.'"

Caitlin quickly pulled the file with the copy of Martin's checkout receipt. She read it, looked up at Anita and smiled broadly, "Cabin Fourteen."

Caitlin then explained the problem with the fingerprints. She said she absolutely believed Martin was telling the truth, therefore, somebody is tampering with evidence. Anita shook her head. "I mean it's possible, but. . ." and shook her head again.

"Just do me a favor. Nose around a little. Discretely. Maybe you have some friends in the Johnson County Sheriff's Department. You know, some interdepartmental jealousy or rivalry, anything somebody might be willing to share."

"Okay. I'm yours for the money."

Caitlin shook her head. "It sure is a luxury to be able to retain you."

Anita folded her arms on her chest and smiled.

CHAPTER THIRTY-SEVEN

Caitlin dug deeper into suspicious cases of the Criminal Investigation Division of the Enola Post. But all she could find was continuing nourishment for her suspicions. There was nothing that would stand up in court. The trial was just a few weeks away and she figured she was no closer to a solution than she was back in May.

She decided on one last trip to the Enola Post to talk with Steinert. She knew she could ill afford the time for a trip to Enola, especially if she returned empty handed. "My dance card is full," she had e-mailed Erik. Publicity from the Morley case had opened floodgates and she received more criminal cases. Then, Caitlin gave the story on the sexual harassment suit to Lacey as she had promised. It was fair game to the media once it was filed in court, but she tipped Lacey off when that would occur and made it easy for the reporter to gather information for her story. Caitlin filed the suit late in the afternoon, meaning Lacey's story would run in the morning edition, easily beating television reporters. The case involved the largest bank in the region, the flagship of her former husband's holding company, Noreast Bancorporation. The thought that he would probably take a lot of ribbing from colleagues amused her. When that story broke she was inundated with phone calls from women who believed they had been harassed or discriminated against in their work places. Several became clients, and her workload thickened.

As she headed toward Enola, rain began to fall. About halfway there she caught the flashing lights of a State Patrol car in her rearview mirror. This was the third time she had been stopped. The trooper, wearing an orange slicker and wide-brimmed hat with a clear plastic cover, approached her. "Going a little fast, weren't we Miss?"

"I had my cruise control set at exactly fifty-five miles an hour," she responded.

"I'm going to write you up for driving too fast for conditions. This rain is coming down too hard for a speed of fifty-five. May I have your license, Ms. Schroeder?"

"How did you know my name?"

He hesitated a moment. "I've seen you at Post Headquarters and your picture has been on television and in the newspapers a lot lately."

It was true about the publicity, but she knew he was lying. Caitlin fished out her wallet from deep in her purse, pulled out the driver's license and handed it to him.

While the trooper was in the squad car she wondered whether going to Post Headquarters was such a good idea after all. They certainly wouldn't be very receptive.

The Trooper returned to Caitlin's window and announced, "I've had a change of heart, Ms. Schroeder. I decided not to write you up. Would you do me a favor, though, and drive a little slower in weather like this? Hydroplaning, you know." He held his hand out flat and moved it as if it were gliding over a sheet of water. "You don't want that happening."

She thanked him and he walked back to his car.

At Post Headquarters she asked to speak with Lt. Warren. He came to the front desk and escorted her to his office. "Well, Ms. Schroeder, what brings you out on a day like this?" He seemed pleasant.

"The Dr. Morley case, as usual. I was curious why you hadn't investigated James Crane."

"Oh, we did. And it's pretty obvious: We don't think he murdered Mrs. Morley."

"They were lovers."

"Yes, and that's one of the reasons why Dr. Morley killed

her. Crane told us that your private eye had taken compromising photos of Mrs. Morley and Mr. Crane. She was found stripped naked, tied spread-eagle. As a result, we think Dr. Morley was being vindictive, which was among the motives that were brought out at the preliminary."

"Did you check out Crane's fingerprints?"

"He wasn't a suspect, although we did interview him. It was at the suggestion of Dr. Morley. I think the doctor was trying to toss in a, what do you call it? A red heron."

"A red herring, Lieutenant. The fish, not the bird that eats the fish."

He snorted and said, "Whatever. We think he was trying to take us off his trail."

Caitlin didn't bring up the five hundred thousand dollars Laura had given Crane. Apparently the police knew nothing about the money – another weapon in her arsenal. She asked the lieutenant a few more questions then said she had finished.

"Can you find your way out on your own?" the lieutenant asked. "I've got to make a couple of phone calls."

"Sure." She offered her hand, but he turned to his phone.

On the way out she stopped at Willie Clemens's desk. "How's it going, Willie?"

"Not bad, Caitlin. Just putting bad guys in prison. Your client going to go free?"

"I sure hope so, but it's a tough row to hoe. I still can't figure out how you guys get those obscure fingerprints."

"Me either," he muttered under his breath, but not so softly that Caitlin couldn't hear.

She decided not to pursue it at this point. Too risky, she figured, as she looked over each of her shoulders. She said goodbye to Willie and headed toward the exit just as Steinert walked out of the crime laboratory wiping his hands with a paper towel. He stopped and smiled a nice cocky grin. "Ms. Schroeder, you still trying to figure out how we work our magic?" He crumbled the towel and tossed it into a wastebasket next to Sgt. Clemens's desk.

"Well, I confess, you guys sure have me stumped."

"I'll let you in on a little secret. It's not magic. It's just plain, solid police work. Dogged persistence."

It was as smug a look as Caitlin could ever recall. "I certainly wish my clients would choose to be arrested by police who weren't quite so thorough," she told him.

Steinert laughed, then leaned toward her and whispered, "Keep this under your hat, but it looks like I'll be on board with the CIA in a couple months. They like my style."

"I bet they do," she said and then bade him goodbye. She shook her head as she walked out. If the CIA likes dirty tricks, they're certainly going to like Steinert.

She drove back to her office through rain. Troopers didn't stop her this time. First thing on her return, before hanging up her raincoat, she called Erik at the CIA. "Can you dig around a little deeper and find out if this William Steinert has been offered a job with your CIA? Trial is three weeks away and I'm getting desperate."

Erik paused and then asked, "Do you remember Cutie Pie – Julie?"

"The child who hauled your ashes? How could I forget? What does she have to do with this murder case?"

"She works for Crane Public Relations. She's an account executive. She had told me she had fallen for an older man at the office. And Crane is the only 'older man' there. Maybe he needed to get rid of Mrs. Morley."

"Oh, my God, Erik! Why didn't you tell me this sooner?"

"You mentioned Crane a few weeks ago in a letter, but I didn't put it all together until just now." They were still swapping handwritten letters as well as e-mails.

"I'm sorry. I don't mean to sound unappreciative. I'm just too caught up in this case."

The next day just before noon, Anita stopped at Caitlin's office. She lit a cigarette, blew out the match and put it on top of Caitlin's computer. “Sorry, but you're not very hospitable to smokers. No ashtrays. You should treat us better. We're an endangered species.” She paused to chortle over her joke. “Anyway, you were right about the fingerprints, according to my source. I mean he won't testify. In fact, you probably wouldn’t want to use him.”

“What kind of credibility does he have?”

“Zilch. He was kicked off the sheriff's department. But he swears Steinert and some of the boys are fixing prints to get convictions of people they think are guilty.” Anita shook her head. “And to think at first I thought the Doc had done it. But that proves my point, I'm *damn near* right all the time.”

When Anita left Caitlin called Julie at Crane Public Relations and asked her to come to her office for a discussion. She explained that she was defending a man in a murder trial and needed to talk with her. Julie stopped by about four p.m.

Caitlin and Julie shook hands and walked back to her office. Caitlin closed the door and directed her to a chair in front of her desk. She could see why Erik had fallen for her – twenty -eight, perky and pretty. They passed a few a moments with idle talk then Caitlin explained her situation in the defense of Martin. “I’m convinced that Martin is innocent and that leaves me with only one other suspect – Jim Crane, your boss.” She watched Julie’s surprised reaction. “Mr. Crane,” Caitlin resumed, “had told me that he was having an affair with Laura Morley. But my understanding is that he was also having an affair with you.”

Julie closed her eyes and shook her head. “Does all this have to come out at the trial? It could cost me my job.”

“It will cost you your job if Mr. Crane did kill her, although the murderer could very well have been someone else.”

Julie shuddered. “It’s hard to believe that I may be sleeping with a killer.”

“I’m not accusing him. I’m just trying to get to the truth so Dr. Morley doesn’t have to spend the rest of his life in prison for a crime he didn't commit. Why don't you tell me what happened."

Julie drew a deep breath and explained that she and Jim had begun their affair in early December. She knew he was also involved with Laura. "He told me and he also promised that he would proactively try to break it off." She shook her head again. "I knew this was wrong from the very beginning. I just can't go to bed with him anymore. What should I do?"

"Find another job. Distance yourself. I know the executive vice president of another PR agency. I'll put you in touch with her. She'll give you a call in a few days. I may need your testimony at the trial, however."

* * *

Two weeks before trial Caitlin made another appointment with Angela. Angela was reluctant to meet with her, but Caitlin insisted, saying, "We're going to subpoena you, Ms. Wain. I suggest you hear me out before we put you on the witness stand and you perjure yourself." That caught Angela's attention. Caitlin also didn't want Angela to appear hostile on the stand.

At Angela's office the mahogany desk again separated them. "Dr. Morley insists that the two of you spent three nights at Western Alps Ski Resort," Caitlin said. "He described very vividly what happened the late afternoon, early evening of December thirty. The man who lit your fireplace every morning will identify you. I might add that it will be in an embarrassing manner. He saw you making love and has a descriptive way about him. You also made a phone call to your husband at his mother's home in Scottsdale, Arizona." She gave an abbreviated version of what transpired and then said, "I'm about to subpoena the data from your cell phone company. So you can see that I'm here to save you from a prison term for committing perjury on the witness stand."

Angela leaned back in her chair, shook her head, sighed deeply and said, "Shit, that son-of-a-bitch. I hate him. This is going to ruin my marriage." She glanced at her nails on her right hand then looked up at Caitlin.

"Maybe not," Caitlin said. "I need a little more information. On the night of December 30, your second night there, tell me what happened."

Angela acquiesced: "We got there the night before, made love a couple of times and again in the morning. We skied all morning and cross-country skied all afternoon on the 30th. We returned to our cabin about four-thirty. I showered, came out and called my husband as you noted. I think Martin called his wife, although I didn't listen in. Then we had dinner, came back and started to make love on a quilt by the fireplace. We finished in bed, totally exhausted. I mean we had been outdoors skiing all day, ate a huge meal, drank a little wine. We slept like logs. Woke up the next morning and made love again. One thing about Martin, he is insatiable."

"What time did you wake up?"

"I'm not sure, seven or eight. He woke me, doing something erotic."

"Why didn't you tell me this before? Martin could end up in prison without your testimony."

"Oh, I figured you'd be able to get him off. I don't know how I'm going to explain this to Philip. He's been very good to me, and I do love him."

"I'm sure you can figure out a way," Caitlin said.

"Are you and Martin lovers?"

"No."

"Well, when it's all over. He's not a bad guy, in bed that is." She smiled.

Caitlin raised an eyebrow. Martin, she realized, certainly is a curiosity. She returned Angela's smile. "I don't think he's my type," Caitlin replied. But she admitted to herself that he had raised her prurient interests at times.

* * *

In the waning hours of daylight Erik telephoned. “Caitlin," he told her, “I've talked with our recruiters. They have been interviewing William Steinert. He's been through two interviews and undergone a couple of polygraphs. But nobody knows any more than that. The main guy who did the interview is in California on a recruiting tour. He's supposed to be back at the end of next week. What do you expect to learn from our recruiters?”

“I don't know, maybe something from the polygraph. I'm sure they'd ask him about his career. Of course, you guys are always looking for spooky creeps. Steinert's right up your alley.”

“It's not done that way anymore.”

“Well, when he returns, will you talk to him and let me know? I haven't got one credible witness on the tampering.”

As they hung up, her doorbell rang. Michael answered the door, closing it after a few moments and returned to the kitchen. “Mom, there's some big guy at the door.”

Caitlin moved quickly to the front door and peered through the peephole. It was Capt. Quincy. She opened the door. “Captain, you frightened my son.”

“Did I? He didn't let me introduce myself.”

“Would you like to come in?”

“No, Ms. Schroeder. I see that you subpoenaed several attorneys who have represented convicted felons in cases my men have investigated.”

“Yes.”

“Do you think that this is a wise idea?”

“Yes. It's your job to convince the jury beyond a reasonable doubt that Dr. Morley killed his wife. It's my job to demonstrate reasonable doubt.”

“I don't want to see these cases reopened like old wounds. I don't want my men falsely accused, just so you can win a case. This could destroy our unit's effectiveness.”

“My intention, Captain, is to have the jury reach a verdict of 'Not Guilty.'"

"Just be careful," he paused, "if you know what I mean, Ms. Schroeder." He turned sharply and walked away.

Caitlin shuddered and walked inside. She found Michael and asked him what the captain said at the door.

"He just said, 'Is your mother in?'"

"He didn't try to say he was a captain with the State Police?"

"No. But he sure looked scary."

"A big man. Just do me a favor from now on. Don't talk to strangers."

"Mom, I know better than that. I'm not a kid anymore." He stood as straight as he could and Caitlin saw that Michael would be a tall man.

She hugged him and kissed him. "I just worry about you. You're my only child and I'm too old to have any more babies."

"Aw, come on, Mom." He pulled away, but not too far.

* * *

The following evening Caitlin planned to meet Michael at the ballpark where he played baseball in a program the school district sponsored. The game was scheduled for six p.m. and would end around eight or eight-thirty. She and Michael had planned to go out for a victory pizza, or a loser pizza, whatever happened.

A new client, Jill Horowitz who was filing suit against her employer, was expected at Caitlin's office at five p.m. But she called and said she would be late. Jill didn't arrive until ten minutes to six. And she lingered longer than Caitlin had expected. At seven o'clock Caitlin left her office. It was raining. Suddenly she realized the league had probably canceled the baseball game and the star left fielder would be sitting in the dugout waiting for his mother. She stepped on the gas then eased up, fearing that the State Police were just around the bend. Maybe the coach gave Michael a ride home. After all, the coach had given him a ride to the ballpark. But knowing Michael, he'd be waiting at the ballpark for his mother, just tossing a ball into his glove, making a better pocket. "Thwack, thwack," she imagined the sound of the ball hitting the worn leather.

She arrived at the park, a diamond and an infield rimmed past the baseline by a chain link fence with dugouts on the first and third base lines. Rain glistened on the worn planks of the small stands of bleachers next to the dugouts. She parked the car. No other cars were there. Wearing a raincoat but no hat or umbrella, she looked around, head high, standing on her toes even though she didn't need to, looking for her son. She couldn't spot him. She walked to each of the dugouts, peering inside. No Michael. Caitlin called his name a few times, put her fingers in her mouth and blew a shrill whistle. No Michael. She panicked.

She ran toward her car. It was still raining. The heel of her right shoe stuck in the mud and she ran out of it, hopping and finally putting her stocking foot in the mud to keep her balance. She sank to her ankle and said, "Oh, shit." She took a deep breath, but it didn't still the fear. She retrieved her shoe, put it back on her muddy foot and returned to her car. She was wet and angry and afraid. She fumbled through her purse looking for her cell phone. Once she did find it, it took her another minute – it felt like an eternity – to turn it on and locate Michael's phone number. She called, but all she got was his voicemail: "This is Michael Schroeder Brownell, please leave a message and I'll get back to you." She waited for a beep then asked, "Where are you." She was afraid it sounded desperate, but she was desperate.

She started the car and drove off hastily. At her home she pulled into the garage and quickly jumped out of the car, only to see Mrs. Riley standing in the doorway to the house.

"Hi, Caitlin. I checked on Michael when I saw him come home a little early." She always kept an eye out for the boy as part of an arrangement she had with Caitlin.

"What would I do without you, Betsy?"

"Quit your practice and go on welfare." Mrs. Riley laughed. They hugged each other and then Mrs. Riley left through the garage door.

Michael knew his mother was home, but was sitting at the kitchen table quietly reading the sports page of the morning newspaper.

"Jeez, Michael, where were you?"

"Hi, Mom. They called the game on account of rain. A nice police detective gave me a ride home."

"Holy crap, Michael, I've asked you a thousand times not to take rides from strangers."

"Mom, he's a policeman with the Adams County Sheriff's Department. I play with his son, Jeffrey McBride. Remember? We're on the same team. You know Jeffrey's father from back when you were a prosecutor."

"But your cell phone, you didn't answer your cell phone."

"It's upstairs. I'm home. I can always use the house phone." He cocked his head.

Caitlin tried to calm herself. She sat at the table, pulled a section of the paper toward her, took her muddy shoes off and set them on the newspaper. "Look, Michael, things are kind of hectic right now. I'm worried."

"I can tell."

"I don't think my worries are unreasonable. I want to see if your father can take you for the next few weeks, until the trial is over. Would you mind?"

He could see that she was serious and replied with enthusiasm, "It might be fun." He stood and looked at her muddy shoes and then at the foot with the mud on her hose. "How'd you get so dirty, Mom?"

She explained. He walked over to the kitchen counter and pulled off three sections of paper towel from the roll and handed it to her. She wiped her foot and he took her shoes to the sink where he began to clean them for her.

She started to laugh.

"What's so funny?" Michael asked.

"How many kids out there clean their mothers' muddy

shoes? It's supposed to be the other way around, Michael." Light tears formed in her eyes.

Caitlin called Robert, her former husband, and explained her situation. "I'd feel a lot better if you took Michael until the trial is over."

"Are you in danger?"

"It's mostly in my head," she replied.

"Michael and I could have an interesting time. I'm going with the C.E.O. and C.F.O. on a financial analyst tour, you know, meetings in New York, Boston, Baltimore, San Francisco, even Minneapolis. Think Michael would like to see a little of the country?"

"That would be great, Robert. What about your chief executive and chief financial officers?"

"They're bringing their wives. Michelle is coming along, too. I'll just bring my son as well. I'll pick him up tomorrow night."

After hanging up Caitlin turned to Michael. "Do you get along with your Dad's wife, Michelle?"

"Sure. She's okay."

CHAPTER THIRTY-EIGHT

The evening after Robert picked Michael up Caitlin attended a meeting of the Comfort House Board of Trustees. It didn't break up until nine-thirty. It was a three-hour meeting that shouldn't have lasted more than sixty minutes. But everyone went off on tangents. It reminded her of covering town zoning board meetings when she worked for her mother's small town newspaper.

The Comfort House, unmarked and poorly illuminated by street lights, was located in a deteriorating neighborhood. She had parked her car across the street in a small lot behind a darkened church. Clouds hid the quarter-moon as a light mist fell. The streetlight was out. She could almost touch the darkness. Caitlin with her large bag slung over her shoulder walked with her usual long, purposeful gait, but as she approached the parking lot, she slowed, thinking that something was amiss. She shook her head and continued to her car. Another car had parked a little too close to hers and she had to move sideways toward her door. She had the key in her hand and unlocked the door. It wouldn't open far enough for her to slide in. As she started to scoot back between the cars to go to the other side, a deep voice said, "Ms. Schroeder."

She froze. Stuck between the two cars, she couldn't even run if she had to. The rush of fear eased its grip slightly, and she said loudly, "This is Caitlin Schroeder. Who are you?"

"It's Sgt. Willie Clemens, Caitlin."

"Just a second." Caitlin felt the relief. She worked her way back, trying unsuccessfully not to brush her clothes against either of the cars. She walked toward two other cars parked about fifteen feet way. Willie stepped out. "Willie, I'm certainly going to go to heaven."

"Why do you say that?"

"Because you just scared the hell right out of me."

"I'm sorry, Caitlin."

"I didn't have a heart attack, so I must be in good health. What can I do for you?" She dusted the front of her skirt where it had brushed against her car, but a large smudge still soiled the back of her skirt where it had swiped the car next to hers.

"I need to talk to you about Dr. Morley."

"Better not do it here. People are going to be coming out of the Comfort House soon."

"There's an all night breakfast place on the near south side called Sarah's. Blacks and whites hang out there. We won't be conspicuous. It's at Fifth and Commercial."

They went to their respective cars, Caitlin wondering what she would learn.

Sarah's was in a single story, well worn, wood building. A sign outside said, "Breakfast ANYtime." The line below in smaller lettering said, "Ribs, Chops, Chicken, Barbecue." Inside, the dining room was nearly empty of patrons, but crowded with chrome-plated tables with Formica tops and chrome plated chairs upholstered in turquoise and gray plastic that had frayed at the corners. A long counter faced twelve stools where three patrons sat. There were only two tables with customers at them. Willie was one of them in the far corner. She went to him and sat in a chair on his left.

"Have you had breakfast yet?" Willie asked.

She laughed and said, "No."

"You can have something else if you want."

"Breakfast is fine." She looked at the menu. A waitress came over, a large black woman in a blue uniform with a smudge of egg yolk on her pocket where she kept the order book. "You first, Willie, I'm still looking," Caitlin said. She had never been in the restaurant before, although she had heard that it catered to musicians when the clubs and bars closed in the early morning.

Willie ordered a stack of pancakes and sausage. The waitress looked at Caitlin. "I'll have home fries with two eggs over easy served on top of the potatoes." Caitlin paused, looked at Willie and returned to the menu. "And a fried smoked pork chop, a large glass of whole milk, a cup of coffee, and two slices of whole wheat toast with no butter." Then, as a note of explanation to Willie, added, "I haven't eaten since noon."

The waitress left and Willie said, "All that high fat, high cholesterol food and you ask for toast without butter?" He was laughing.

"Willie, you have to draw the line somewhere. And I choose to draw it with the toast. Two pats of butter would put me over the line – a run for a midnight bicarbonate."

"I don't know why I'm laughing, because I've got some serious matters weighing on me." The waitress brought the coffee and Willie waited for her to leave before continuing. He took a deep breath. "You're on the right track, Caitlin, about the fingerprints." He stopped and looked at her face for a moment.

"Willie, that's a damn courageous thing to say."

"It's not courage, Caitlin. It's self-preservation. Sooner or later they're all going to get caught – they're too damn cocky and full of themselves – and I'll be sucked down the drain with them, like water in a bathtub – dirt and all. I haven't been part of this, but it'll be guilt by association." He took a sip of coffee and swiped his lips with the first knuckle of his left hand. "I've suspected something for a few years now, but I don't have any proof," Willie continued. "All I have is an overheard discussion, a lot of winks and grins when I ask how they found certain evidence, and one time I heard Lt. Warren say, 'They're fuckin' guilty, just put 'em at the scene.' That's the mentality: we know they're guilty. Those are the kinds of things I've overheard. And, there are just too many cases where Steinert comes up with fingerprints at the last minute."

"Why haven't you been part of this?"

Just then the waitress brought their orders. When she left, Caitlin attacked her plate and Willie resumed: "I'm the only black detective at the Enola Post. They don't really trust me. I haven't been in Enola as long as they have, and theirs is a little club." He dabbed a piece of toast into the egg yolk then ate the toast's moist yellow corner. "I certainly wasn't the first black in the State Patrol. But I was among the first groups to go through the academy when things started to really open up. It's pretty well integrated now. Any racism is pretty subtle and that goes for both sides of the coin. A few years ago, however, I made a ruckus about no blacks being promoted very high. As sergeant then, I was the highest. They transferred me to Enola. My wife explained it to me. She said, 'Enola's just *alone* spelled backwards.'" Willie laughed. "I'm still alone."

"Are you willing to testify about the fingerprints at Dr. Morley's trial?"

"Yes, but I have no concrete evidence, no proof. All I have is what I've heard and observed. It's what you lawyers call hearsay evidence. I couldn't prove anything in the Dr. Morley case or any of the others. But believe me, it's crooked there. Not everyone, but enough of them. They need a full investigation by some independent investigators." He shook his head as though he couldn't quite believe how all of this could have happened.

"It would be nice if you had proof. But your testimony will certainly help. I'm interested in establishing doubt in the minds of the jury. After your testimony this may just do it."

They discussed Willie's charges for forty-five minutes. He agreed to meet with her at her office at 6 a.m. Friday. That would give him a little more than an hour to talk with her and still be able to make it to Enola in time for work.

Finally, Caitlin asked him why he was doing this.

Willie pulled a wallet from his hip pocket and removed a photograph of his four grown children. He pointed to one of his two daughters and said, "She just graduated from divinity school. All my life I preached to my kids about integrity and honesty and being able to live with yourself. I'm a hypocrite for not doing something sooner."

"You shouldn't be too tough on yourself, Willie. Life's tough enough and it's going to get a lot tougher."

"It don't matter none. What's two more years alone in Enola?" He laughed again.

"Of course," Caitlin said, "I'm not going to tell anyone about our conversation, not even the client. I'm going to save your testimony until the end. So I hope you don't tell anyone."

"Not even my wife until the day I'm supposed to testify."

"By the way," she rotated her coffee mug, "are either of us in danger?"

"I don't think so. But they been harassing you, pulling you over for speeding and stuff."

She shook her head vigorously and told him about Capt. Quincy at her door.

"He's mean, but not stupid. I don't know if he's involved in all this or not. But he's in charge of all the investigators. Lt. Warren could be as high as it goes. Just be cool. They probably think you're weak and intimidated easily."

They talked for a while longer and then left for their homes. At hers, Caitlin spent two hours writing about the meeting with Sgt. Willie Clemens. Turning off the computer and rubbing her eyes, she suddenly wondered whether Willie was a decoy. Get him on the stand and he denies everything.

CHAPTER THIRTY-NINE

The trial began the first Monday of August. Caitlin was nervous. She didn't show it, but inside she was as fearful as she had ever been. Her strategy was to portray Dr. Morley as an upstanding member of the community, a physician who took the Hippocratic oath to save lives, not to destroy them, and then press the issue of reasonable doubt. She was aware that the prosecution could blow holes in her fingerprint theory. Even Sgt. Clemens's testimony would be weak, but it would have an impact on the jury, she reasoned.

Caitlin figured they would spend about two days picking a jury and that the trial would last two weeks, maybe three.

The trouble with solo practice was that there was no one she could confer with, no one to bounce ideas off, and that worried her. Her colleagues at the office weren't practiced criminal lawyers. Two of the three men did some trial work, but none of them had ever tried a murder case. Erik would have been a good resource, but she couldn't talk to him over the telephone; she was now afraid that the State Police might have tapped her phone line or found a way to listen in on cell phone calls. She deduced, though, that the state police in Enola didn’t have the technological wherewithal to tap into her e-mail. But she opened a new e-mail address just to be sure. She e-mailed Erik a lengthy letter that explained her strategy. He replied immediately with a critique and some suggestions.

Caitlin and Martin met Sunday the day before the trial to go over last minute details. And they met again for a half hour before entering the courtroom the morning of the trial. She went over her plans again with him, but declined to discuss Sgt. Clemens. “Martin, I'm confident we can gain acquittal," she said with guarded enthusiasm.

“I've had faith in you from the very beginning,” Martin said. “I haven't wavered.” He smiled and then added, “Well, just once I wavered. When I was in jail. But it was night and they wouldn't let me make another phone call.” They both laughed nervously.

“You certainly are a calm, controlled man, Martin Morley.”

“Part charade. Sometimes I wake up in the middle of the night with a tremendous gripping fear. Or during the day while examining the poor in Johnson County, I would suddenly start thinking of life in prison, being raped by other prisoners, whatever horrible thought was available at the moment.”

“That surprises me Martin.” She touched his arm lightly to offer some reassurance.

Caitlin had asked Anita Zombrowska to join her at the defense table during the trial. “I need an extra pair of hands and legs and a good mind," Caitlin explained to the private investigator, “and you know your way around the courtroom better than most lawyers.”

Martin wore a blue suit, a shirt with a banker's stripe and a red and blue striped tie. Caitlin wore her basic grays, saving her best sincere blue for summation. And Anita, who usually dressed for chasing muggers, wore a simple dress and navy blue blazer. This was the first time Caitlin had seen Anita in heels.

Judge Michael Grossman presided. Caitlin had practiced before him both as a defense counsel and years earlier as a prosecutor. She admired him, figuring he was one of the best trial judges in the state and rarely reversed.

The courtroom was filled with spectators and media. Caitlin noticed that sitting in the middle of the audience on the prosecution side of the courtroom was the tall blond stranger with the thin face that she had seen during the preliminary examination. Again he was dressed in conservative business clothes: a lightweight wool, medium gray, pinstripe suit. He and Martin were the best dressed men in the courtroom. Caitlin leaned toward Anita and whispered, asking her to find out who the man was.

"I've seen him before," Anita whispered back. "He's a private investigator like me. Name's Scott Seager. Wait'll first recess and I'll get more info for you."

During the first recess Anita left the courtroom. A few minutes after court resumed, she returned and sat next to Caitlin on the outside. "The handsome, well-dressed man is, indeed, Scott Seager," Anita whispered. "As I said, he's a private investigator, but works exclusively for insurance companies, insurance fraud. That sort of thing. He's excruciatingly thorough."

"Too bad he's on their side," Caitlin replied. She rubbed her fingers across her brow.

"It's not all bad news," Anita said.

"What do you mean?"

"Get a verdict of not guilty and Martin will have Laura's life insurance check in less than a week. Too bad you're not working on contingency. Your third would be a half million." Anita grinned.

Caitlin and Wollman came to terms on a jury about eleven-thirty Tuesday morning, earlier than she had expected. They ended up with twelve jurors – seven women, two black; and five men, none black. Everyone else was white, even the two standby jurors. She was pleased to have the two black jurors, figuring it might help her with Sgt. Clemens's testimony.

"Trials are pretty tedious," Caitlin explained to Martin. "There are moments of high drama, though. Kind of like baseball, only slower."

After opening statements, the prosecution began pretty much as it had at the preliminary examination. Wollman brought the fire chief, the state fire marshal, and Ed Cooper, the firefighter who discovered Laura's body, to the stand.

During cross examination of the Johnson County Medical Examiner, Caitlin asked if there had been a determination of blood alcohol.

"Yes," he said, "she registered point one seven percent alcohol."

"Is that medically an indication of inebriation?"

"Yes, point oh eight is considered under the influence for drivers in this state and most states."

She asked if the doctor had found any disease.

The medical examiner said that he had detected some liver damage. Following his testimony the court adjourned.

The next day all of the detectives testified, except Steinert. During cross-examination of Sgt. Willie Clemens, Caitlin declined to bring up the evidence tampering issue. She planned to save it for later and had informed Clemens of her strategy before the trial, that she would recall him and Steinert to the stand.

Prosecution resumed the next day with Wollman devoting more detail to motives. Philip Wain and other former partners from the medical practice testified on the sale of the practice and the amount being paid Dr. Morley. Several of the partners testified about Laura, her drinking and her strained relationship with Martin.

The trial continued with Wollman always returning to money and Laura's drinking and their marital problems. He had painted a convincing picture of greed as motive. The inheritance was considerable: there was life insurance, insurance on the house, the sale of his share of the practice, and their investments, which over the years had amounted to a substantial sum. With Laura dead, Martin stood to receive more than sixteen million dollars from the remains of her father's estate, plus another three million dollars in insurance reimbursements, both life and property damage. Divorced he probably would have received none of her share of her father's estate and only half of the value of the investments he had accrued over the years of their marriage. "In total," Wollman said, "it's a poke in excess of twenty million dollars in cash. Yes, cash."

As the trial adjourned for the weekend, Caitlin figured that the state did not lack a motive. But motive alone was not enough.

As the trial resumed on Monday, investigators testified that Martin had been registered at Western Alps Ski Resort, which they said was only a ninety-minute drive from his home. Clemens testified that none of the employees interviewed at the ski resort could recall seeing Dr. Morley with anyone.

Wollman brought the manager of Western Alps Ski Resort to the stand.

Wollman: Was Dr. Morley registered as a double or single?

Manager: There is no extra charge for double occupancy, only if we have to provide an extra bed. So I don't know if he was alone or not.

Wollman: Did you see Dr. Morley with a companion?

Manager: I don't remember. I mean, we have well over a hundred rooms and cabins. It's a resort, not a bed and breakfast, and it was New Year's, a lot of partying and beautiful people.

Wollman also brought Martin's children to the stand – Carlton and Cathy. Both testified about their father driving them to the airport. Wollman also asked them if they had ever seen the two-gallon gasoline can that had been entered as evidence. In separate testimony, both said they had never seen it, that they had only seen two five-gallon plastic fuel cans.

Under cross-examination:

Caitlin: Do you live at home?

Cathy: No, I'm about to start my second year of medical school at Cornell in New York City.

Caitlin: Could that metal gas can have been in your garage and you were unaware of it?

Cathy: I suppose so.

Caitlin: On the drive to the airport what if anything did you discuss with your father?

Cathy: We talked about Mom. He said he planned to file for divorce the first full week in January. And he said how Mom was an alcoholic, how he had tried to help her with treatment at St. Alban's Rehabilitation Center.

Caitlin: Do you know if your mother was an alcoholic?

Cathy: I'm only a second-year medical student and I've never seen any blood test results, but I thought she was an alcoholic. For the past few years when I was at home, she drank excessively, more than three or four large, strong drinks a night. She seemed not to be in total control of herself.

Carlton's testimony in both direct and cross-examination mirrored his sister's.

Neither had smiled as they passed their father on their returns from the witness stand. Their relationship with him at best had been strained since his arrest.

Wollman, despite objections from Caitlin, introduced a portion of the transcript from Dr. Morley's interview with police in which he said he owned no metal gas can.

By Tuesday afternoon a heat wave had enveloped the region, temperatures hitting in the high 90s, but the courtroom participants were unaffected until they adjourned for the evening. Then they walked from a cooled courtroom only to be greeted by high heat and oppressive humidity.

The prosecution's case continued at a slow pace. Before the prosecution rested at mid-morning Thursday, Wollman called Steinert to the stand. He testified much as he had during the preliminary examination. He was a key witness and practiced at delivering testimony for the prosecution.

During cross-examination Caitlin asked him: "Are you sure you found Dr. Morley's prints on the gas can handle, that you're not making this up?"

Wollman immediately objected. Caitlin, however, said: "Your Honor, I have reason to doubt the veracity of the witness, and I want his testimony to be perfectly clear." The judge directed the witness to respond, but cautioned Caitlin about language suggesting that police were tampering with evidence.

"I found Dr. Morley's fingerprints on the gas can handle," Steinert said, a slight smile twisting the corner of his mouth.

She ended her cross-examination.

During lunch break Caitlin went to her office where she received a call from Erik on her cell phone. "I've got some great news for you," Erik said. "That Steinert fellow told our recruiter during interviews that he had doped fingerprints on a number of cases to make sure the guilty went to prison. He apparently bragged about fixing some doctor. I presume it's Dr. Morley. They've got it all on video tape – "

"When can I get it?" she interrupted.

"There's a hitch. There are two tapes. One went with a memo to someone in the Justice Department. I don't know who. It's probably on a circuitous route to nowhere. And, I don't know where the other tape is. The only person who can help us is in the Adirondack Mountains in Upstate New York on a hiking expedition with his teenage daughter and son. They aren't due back until Wednesday. And his administrative assistant said she did not know where the tape is. We've looked everywhere for that tape."

"Damn. I need him, Erik."

"I can probably find out from his wife where he went in the mountains. Apparently, they do this every year."

"You locate him and I'll hire a guide and we'll get him out in time to testify."

Anita Zombrowska was sitting in the office during the conversation. "Sounds interesting," she said.

"I don't know if I can get an early adjournment, especially without tipping my hand. What I really need is the whole damn day tomorrow. Can you locate a guide to take us into the Adirondacks? You up to mountain climbing?"

"I do anything for money."

Caitlin returned to the trial without Anita.

Before court resumed, she explained the good fortune to Martin. "I'd like to go along," he said. "I couldn't stand the suspense waiting around here."

"I suppose you can go. I hate to reveal the deep dark secrets of lawyering, though."

He laughed.

"You know, there's no assurance that this will all pan out."

"I'm prepared for that, but I figure we're going to win anyway." He grinned.

When court resumed, Caitlin began simply enough with character witnesses. She had lined up enough respected witnesses to paint a picture of a gifted physician, stalwart of the community. Among those witnesses were the executive director of the Comfort House, the Chairman of the Board and the president of Community General Hospital, and even Pat Nordstrom from the Johnson County Mobile Clinic where Martin had volunteered before the trial. She called Cathy,

Martin's daughter, back to the stand. She had Cathy recount the discussion she had with her father about the divorce.

Caitlin submitted as evidence the papers that were to be filed in Family Court to initiate divorce proceedings. "You will note that this is dated December 11 last year, indicating that Dr. Morley had every intention to file for divorce during the first full week of January of this year."

She called Pete Rant to the stand and had him testify about seeing Angela and Martin in the room together, pointing to the defendant and identifying Angela by the picture in her brochure. He said that he had seen them each day around five o'clock in the morning.

During cross-examination, Wollman asked Pete how he could be certain.

"I seen them naked one morning," he replied. "You just don't forget a woman like that, naked and everything."

The courtroom audience laughed.

Late in the afternoon, she called Angela Wain to the stand. After initial inquiries, Caitlin directed Angela to her affair with Martin at Western Alps Ski Resort.

Caitlin: Ms. Wain where were you from the late afternoon of December 29 until January one?

Angela:I was with Dr. Morley at Western Alps Ski Resort.

Caitlin:For what purpose?

Angela:We skied and had a love affair.

The courtroom audience emitted a soft collective sigh.

Caitlin: Could you describe what you did from the moment you met Dr. Morley on the twenty-ninth until mid-morning of December thirty-one?

The courtroom hushed in anticipation.

Angela provided an expansive description, but without the most intimate of details. Her husband was not in the audience.

On cross-examination:

Wollman: Let's go back to the evening of the thirtieth. After skiing all day, were you tired?

Angela: I don't remember being tired. We were having a great time. I really like the outdoors, skiing and everything.

Wollman: You were outdoors for six hours or so and you weren't tired?

Angela: Later I was, but not in the early evening. I am not a stranger to vigorous exercise. I need the exercise to maintain my appearance for my modeling business.

Wollman: Well, what happened at dinner? Could you recount it again? Did you have wine, or mixed drinks?

Angela: We drank white wine. Dr. Morley had one glass and I had two.

Wollman: Then you went back and made love?

Angela: We had a glass of champagne first then made love.

Wollman: That's when you finally fell asleep?

Angela: Yes. I can't remember when I last slept that well.

Wollman: The net result was that just before midnight you fell asleep and didn't see Dr. Morley until eight the next morning?

Angela: That's right.

Wollman: But you have no idea for certain whether Dr. Morley was there the whole night through?

Angela: I don't know for certain. I slept solid.

Caitlin questioned her again when Wollman finished, then called James Crane to the stand, her last witness of the day. He testified to having had an affair with Laura Morley.

Caitlin: Did Mrs. Morley give you any money?

Crane: Yes.

Caitlin: How much?

Crane: Five hundred thousand dollars.

Caitlin: When did you receive the money?

Crane: I received half in October and the other half on December 30.

Caitlin: Why did she give you five hundred thousand dollars?

Crane: It was a gift. We were in love. I needed some

cash. Most of my assets were not very liquid and I needed a quick fix for my business.

Caitlin: But this was not a business loan?

Crane: No. We had talked about her filing for divorce early this year. We were going to marry each other, so she figured a loan wasn't necessary.

Caitlin pursued the line of questioning further. She introduced the bank statements and cancelled checks as evidence. She declined to enter the photographs Anita had taken of Crane and Laura, figuring the prosecution might suggest they were another motive for Martin. She asked Crane if police investigators had interviewed him.

"Yes, a Sgt. Clemens came by one day and asked a few questions."

"Is that all?"

"Yes."

"You were never a suspect?"

"I guess not." He shrugged.

Caitlin figured she could call Crane back and later bring Julie to the stand if necessary.

Wollman began cross-examination, keeping it to a few simple questions. He ended his cross-examination by asking: "So, Mr. Crane, Laura Morley, who just inherited sixteen million dollars, gave you a meager six and a quarter percent of it to bolster your public relations business, to tide you over?"

"Yes, sir."

"When did you and Mrs. Morley fall in love?"

"Last year, July the fourteenth. I remember it very well. It was Bastille Day. We had already started an affair, but it was at that time that I told her I loved her. In French and then in English."

"That's very romantic, Mr. Crane." Wollman shook his head,

smiled at the jury and said, "That'll be all."

On re-direct, Caitlin asked Crane if he had ever been to Laura Morley's home.

Crane: Yes, twice.

Caitlin: Were you there the afternoon or evening of the thirtieth and the early morning of the thirty-first?

Crane: No.

Caitlin: You testified that you received two hundred and fifty thousand dollars from Mrs. Morley on December thirtieth. When did she give it to you?

Crane: I received it in the mail with a short note, a love note.

Caitlin: Do you still have the note?

Crane: No.

Caitlin: You testified that you were Mrs. Morley's lover. Police said that they found two glasses with the remnants of scotch in them after the fire. One glass had Mrs. Morley's fingerprints, the other, police said, had none. Did the police ever request your fingerprints?

Crane: No.

Caitlin: Are they on record anywhere?

Crane: No.

Caitlin: You were simply then never much of a suspect?

Crane: I guess they had no reason to suspect me.

Caitlin: Until now.

Wollman immediately objected, and Judge Grossman concurred.

Caitlin was about to counter, then decided to ask for a recess. "Your honor, the defense needs tomorrow to gather some additional evidence that will completely exonerate. . . ."

Judge Grossman granted the recess.

CHAPTER FORTY

When Caitlin returned to her office she found Anita sitting at her desk, spent cigarette butts piled in the soil of a potted plant the private investigator had moved to Caitlin's desk. Caitlin's son had given her the snake plant for Mother's Day.

"Boss, good news," Anita said and inhaled deeply on her cigarette, blowing a long stream straight up.

"What's that?"

"Your friend Erik called. He knows where this CIA Langton fellow is, or roughly where he is. Somewhere up in the High Peaks of the Adirondacks. I've got it written down here," she lifted a notepad with her notes, "including the trail he's taking. I've hired a guide in your name. We're meeting at the Hotel Saranac in Saranac Lake tomorrow night. It's a long drive, but I figure we'll get out of court early tomorrow and make it by nightfall. Erik's going to meet us there."

"I don't think we'll get out any earlier than five o'clock."

"Sure we will, we'll find a way."

Caitlin paced around her desk once. "I've camped in the Adirondacks a couple of times with my son. I should have a map over in the bookcase." Caitlin pointed in the general direction.

"I already found it, right in between the Green Mountains of Vermont map and the map of New Hampshire." Anita rose and walked over to a small table and opened the map laying there. "Here's where they are." She pointed to a location on the map.

Caitlin followed and looked at the map with Anita. The High Peaks Wilderness Area was just a little south of the city of Saranac Lake. "It looks pretty close, we can start off from there," Anita said. "Do you have gear for this?"

"Yeah, I've got everything I need. Martin wants to come along. Said he'd buy some stuff tonight. What about you?"

"About fifteen years ago the guy who's now my ex-husband – The Sonofabitch – and I went on a ten-day fishing expedition in Alaska during mosquito mating season. I am prepared for all things – bugs, bears and grizzled guides."

Anita left shortly, saying, "I gotta take care of some business."

When Caitlin walked out of her office door at seven o'clock it was like walking into a wall of heat. By the time the air conditioner in her car was pumping cold air she was sweating. At home she jacked up the air conditioning and waited for relief. She pulled her camping gear out of storage and made sure she had everything she would need for a one-night trip in the mountains. At ten o'clock Erik called with more details. "I talked with Langton's administrative assistant again. She just doesn't know where the tape is, only Langton knows. Apparently Steinert admitted on tape about fixing Dr. Morley's fingerprints. He was bragging about it as though he thought it would help him get a job with us. She's pretty sure of all this."

"If we can track him down, we'll win this," Caitlin said. "I'll talk with the park rangers first thing in the morning and see if they can help us. Do you know Langton?"

"I met him once, but we really don't know each other. He'll be cooperative."

"I'm not worried about that. It's finding him."

* * *

Shortly before midnight, Anita sat in her car next to the courthouse annex. She was wearing shorts and a t-shirt and the car was running with the air-conditioner at full throttle. She slipped into a pair of black sweat pants and a black sweatshirt and pulled on a navy blue baseball cap, her short fair hair sticking out from under the cap. She slid out of the car.

The annex, a four-story building, housed the Sheriff's Department, Social Services Department and a few other offices. It was connected to the older courthouse at the second floor by a skywalk. She waited at a side door where deputies exited at shift change. As one was coming out she boldly walked to the door, grabbed it as the deputy let go, stating, "Another fucking, lousy hot night, isn't it," and walked into the building as though she owned it.

She quickly found the service stairway and climbed it to the second floor, eventually winding her way to the skywalk and into the courthouse. She went to the top floor and found the service stairway to the roof. As she suspected, the air conditioner was the original York. Anita yanked a pair of latex gloves from a pocket and put them on. She was ready for surgery. From another pocket she pulled a plastic-handled screwdriver and opened the door to the electric panel. She pulled out a small flashlight and looked at the wiring. She knew sparks would fly as she laid the screw driver across some wires to short out the system, but the sparks startled her anyway. The county would have to replace the panel. It would take them awhile to find a panel for a 1964 York and install it. She figured it was a sound investment the taxpayers would be making toward a better justice system, at least a cooler one.

Slowly during the night, heat seeped into the building in quiet search of cool spots.

CHAPTER FORTY-ONE

The courtroom was uncomfortably warm when the trial resumed at 9 a.m. Friday, although the heat hadn't compacted and built intensity yet. But as the morning wore on the people in the courtroom began to feel uncomfortable. The insurance investigator today was wearing a blue and white striped seersucker suit with a white shirt and bow tie. As usual, he carried a large black leather notebook in which he seemed to take few notes.

Caitlin produced three witnesses, defense attorneys who had questioned the authenticity of fingerprints discovered by State Police. She called it "miracle evidence, fingerprints that suddenly appeared out of nowhere." Cross-examination fairly well negated the testimony. But she hoped she had begun to plant an element of doubt in the minds of jurors.

At eleven o'clock, the judge called a recess. He placed an inquiry with the building maintenance department. The manager told Judge Grossman about the malfunctioning, antiquated air-conditioning system, adding that he was trying to locate a replacement part. "If we can't find one in town, we'll have it shipped in by air tomorrow and we'll be cool by Monday," the manager promised.

The trial resumed ten minutes later. Judge Grossman didn't like to waste time. He cautioned the state and the defense that the trial might have to be delayed if the air conditioning were not repaired before noon.

By eleven thirty jurors were sweating, the judge was hot under his black robe and tempers had frayed. He rapped the gavel after both sides had finished with the last of Caitlin's attorney witnesses. "The air conditioner is out of order," the judge declared. "I am going to adjourn this trial until nine o'clock Monday morning and hope that the system is repaired by then. If not, we will find another location to continue the trial. Court adjourned."

Caitlin looked at Martin and smiled happily. "What a piece of luck, Martin."

Anita and Martin met at Caitlin's office at one o'clock with their gear. Anita brought a sleeping bag and backpack. Martin also brought a sleeping bag along with a foam rubber mat, and a large backpack stuffed with supplies. He was wearing an expensive safari jacket, khaki shorts and new hiking boots.

"Looks like you walked out of an Orvis catalog, Martin," Caitlin observed.

He grinned and admitted, "I bought everything at one of their stores last night."

Caitlin had stowed her gear in her car: a small backpack, a two-person nylon tent and a bedroll. She and Anita were going to share the tent, and Martin was going to sleep in Erik's tent. It was a hell of an expedition, Caitlin thought.

They packed their gear in her SUV, and she was glad she didn't buy the sedan.

As they left town, Caitlin with Martin next to her said, laughing, "I can't believe our luck. The damn air conditioner goes out. We must be living right. Can you believe that?" She took a deep breath. "I can feel acquittal just around the corner."

Caitlin looked in the rear view mirror and noticed a smug smile on Anita's face.

Caitlin suddenly slapped the steering wheel and shouted, "Anita, you threw a goddamn monkey wrench into the air conditioner, didn't you? Shorted the thing out."

"Let's just say that I assisted its demise. It was sick anyway. Damn thing had a death wish. Think of it as a mercy killing."

"Christ, what if they figure it out?"

"No chance. The Sonofabitch taught me how to do this. It was a perfect malfunction of a 1964 HVAC system. Besides, the county's been talking about it dying for years. They were just too cheap to buy a new one. Serves 'em right, waiting 'till the last minute."

Martin was laughing then Caitlin started. They were all laughing.

They arrived in Saranac Lake at seven o'clock. Caitlin found the old brick hotel without any difficulty. As they walked from the parking lot Anita said, "This place is owned by a local college. A lot of the students work here. Someone told me it's a neat old place. In fact, he promised no roaches and no bedbugs."

When they checked in Caitlin inquired about Erik, who had planned to arrive a little earlier. He had flown into Albany and taken a small plane to Saranac Lake. A half-hour later they gathered in the restaurant with Erik. The restaurant was rather modern looking for an old hotel. They sat around a round table, drinking a pitcher of beer and waiting for the food they had ordered. "I talked with our guide," Erik said. "I met with him at an outfitter not far from here. He'll be here at five o'clock tomorrow morning with coffee and rolls. We'll eat in his van as we head to the High Peaks. His name's Raquette LaFabre."

A waitress brought appetizers: huge mounds of fried onion rings, Buffalo wings and baked potato skins.

"Raquette?" Caitlin said as she slid an onion ring into her mouth, "that's a strange name. Isn't there a lake by that name around here?"

"Could be, but it's French for snowshoe," Erik explained. "His parents and he were from Quebec. He moved here forty years ago and looks it."

"Is he fit? Do you think he can hike and climb and find Langton?" Martin asked.

"The Rangers say he's pretty good," Erik said. "All he has to do is find the trail and head us in the direction of Langton who'll be hiking toward us."

Erik poured a round of beer from the pitcher.

"Sorry, Erik, for sounding so distrusting. I can't help it," Martin said.

"Don't worry," Erik said, swooping his hand toward Caitlin. "She'll get you off the hook, Martin. You should see some of the scuzzballs Caitlin's saved. Yours is easy."

"The only difference is, I'm innocent."

"So were they," Caitlin interjected.

"This'll be much easier," Erik said, disregarding Caitlin's claim. "Just think how difficult this would be if you were guilty. We'd be in the Himalayas instead of these little baby Adirondack Mountains."

"It won't be bad," Martin said. "They call them the High Peaks, but a kid at the desk says they're only 4,000 feet or so."

"Don't be too cocky," Caitlin warned.

CHAPTER FORTY-TWO

They assembled in the lobby before morning sun had broken. At precisely five o'clock a short wiry man with a full gray-black beard strode into the hotel. He had soiled green trousers, worn leather boots and a wrinkled, frayed khaki, long-sleeved shirt with a faded olive drab t-shirt peeking out at the throat. He shook hands with Erik, who in turn introduced him to everyone else. Caitlin took him aside and gave him three hundred dollars. "Here's half now. You get the rest when we return – alive."

"That's good Miss Schroeder," he said. Raquette chuckled and tucked the money into a pocket. They turned and began walking back to the others.

"Call me Caitlin."

"Call me LaFabre."

They shook hands.

"You guys got it all straightened out?" Anita asked.

"Yeah," Caitlin said, "I told him I'm the one carrying the cash so he better not lose me on the trail. The rest of you don't matter."

They headed for the parking lot where they found a twenty-three-year-old Chevrolet van, gray and rusted with an aging Adirondack guide boat tethered to the top. LaFabre opened the side and front passenger doors. He directed Caitlin to sit next to him and said to the others, "There are no seats in the back, so you have to sit on the floor. There are some cushions." They piled in. Erik and Martin leaned their backs against the sidewalls and Anita found a spot toward the rear, resting against her pack. LaFabre handed a Thermos and some paper cups to Martin and pulled out a bag of doughnuts. Martin poured and Erik served doughnuts.

They pulled out of the parking lot and LaFabre said, "I talked with the rangers, they found Langton's point of entry, where he and his kids signed in. I calculated how far they must have come. One of the rangers had spotted them the day before yesterday. The way I figure it, we'll hit the trail between where they are and where they had intended to exit."

"I can call the ranger post to see if they've seen him more recently," Caitlin offered.

"Cell phones don't work real well up here," LaFabre said

"How far a hike is it?" Martin asked.

"Just a couple miles, depends."

"That isn't bad," Martin said.

"It's not sidewalk and a lot of it is up," LaFabre cautioned.

"Rough terrain?" Erik asked.

"Some places."

Anita, sitting in the back, rolled her eyes.

Erik looked out a van window, but the mountains didn't seem perilous or even difficult.

They headed into the wilderness area and onto a dirt road. "My son and I have camped a few times in the Adirondacks," Caitlin said. "But I don't know the mountains. I'm a flatlander. The others are probably less experienced than I am."

"It's not that bad," the guide said. "No rock climbing and no repelling." From her side of the car Caitlin could tell he was grinning because his beard rose and the creases around his eyes deepened.

"We'll spend the night up there," LaFabre said and grinned at everyone. "I brought freeze dried food."

They all smiled back.

LaFabre drove to an obscure spot, an opening along side the road with a brown sign whose yellow letters said, "Trail Head." LaFabre parked his van. Forest surrounded them. Green mountains stood above the treetops, some with rock-like cliffs exposed, bedrock laid bare by the ancient upward heave of the mountains and slow erosion. But the mountains didn't seem ominous. They didn't look as though they would be difficult. Everyone except LaFabre and Caitlin joked about the climb.

LaFabre opened the back door of his van. "Fill your canteens here. It will be hot today."

Caitlin pulled off her boots and removed her long pants. Underneath she wore olive-drab hiking shorts. She put her boots back on. She pulled her hair into a ponytail and fastened it with a rubber band. Out of her back pocket she retrieved a faded blue bandanna with white polka dots with the Oshkosh B'Gosh ligature and the words "Union Made." She rolled it up and tied it around her forehead.

"That a sweat band?" Erik asked. It was a little cool this early in the morning.

"It's going to get hot. I hike. I sweat."

"Umm," Anita said. "Our tent's going to have a nice, ripe aroma tonight."

A hiker's logbook was stored in a wooden box attached to a post in the ground at the trail's entry. LaFabre opened the hinged door and signed in, noting the members of the team. He had already alerted the rangers.

The trail began easily enough. It was just a straight path into a darkly wooded area. There was no climbing at this point. They walked briskly about two hundred yards before beginning a small incline. Their pace slowed slightly. LaFabre led the way. Caitlin, Martin, and Erik followed him in single file with Anita bringing up the rear. LaFabre didn't say anything. He had a substantial pack on his back, carrying the food and utensils they would use. The others talked at first, but conversation diminished as the trail narrowed and gravity began to have its effect. The trail slowly became rockier and the hikers began to pick their way more carefully. LaFabre slowed his pace to accommodate the others.

The forest was mostly aspen, birch and maple, but would turn into conifers higher up. They came to a slight opening, an opening only because large boulders stood in the way of trees and the climbers. The way the boulders were lodged, like giant stepping stones, they created a narrow, steep ledge that wound its way to the top of the configuration of boulders. They were able to follow that. It was slow exhausting work, even though it only covered a distance of fifty feet, had they been going in a straight, flat linear fashion. When they reached the top of the rocks, a little plateau formed. LaFabre called a break.

After a short rest they returned to the trail. By ten o'clock everyone's shirts were soaked with sweat, their faces moist from exertion, and their chests heaving for air. They took another break. Erik pulled five oranges from his backpack and handed one to everyone. As they peeled their oranges a woman in a dark green shirt and shorts, pack on her back and a canvas sack of tools in her hand, hiked by in long, strong strides. "Good morning! Great day for a hike," she said and kept going. LaFabre gave her a casual two-finger salute. She was walking much faster than they had been. Everyone, except LaFabre, watched her. The muscles in the backs of her legs rolled upward like powerful waves.

"Now, that's one strong woman," Erik said, shaking his head in amazement.

"Who is she?" Martin asked.

"Park ranger," LaFabre said.

"How big is this park?" Martin asked.

"About as big as Massachusetts," LaFabre explained. "About half is state-owned. What the state owns stays forever wild."

"What do you mean?"

"Whenever the state gets more private land, that land goes back to nature. The forest takes over. You can't build on it. What buildings are on it get eaten by Mother Nature."

"I was here once a few years ago in Lake Placid skiing," Martin said. "I never realized the immensity."

"You don't 'till you're in it, and climb it," LaFabre said. He pulled a rock back and asked everyone to put their orange peels in the rock's hollow. He returned the rock to its place.

They resumed hiking. At noon they reached a high, fairly level section of trail. LaFabre had a sack of roast beef sandwiches and two bags of nuts and dried fruit. "After this we eat freeze-dried meals," he said.

There was more climbing in store for them, most of it harder than the morning's portion of the hike. About three o'clock they passed a small waterfall that landed in a small pool. They stopped to splash the cool water on their faces. About four in the afternoon on a stretch of flat terrain they spotted three people in the distance across a meadow. "Is that Langton?" Martin asked Erik.

"Too far for me to see."

As they hiked closer, Erik said he thought it was Langton. At a quickened pace Caitlin moved ahead of the group and pushed toward the trio. She could see now that it was a man and two teenagers. They waved and said hello. She approached them, offered her hand and said, "Mr. Langton, I presume."

"Yes, but how – ?"

At that point Erik ran up, offered his hand and said, "Erik Wanzer from legal affairs." He displayed his CIA identification.

Everyone gathered, dropping their packs to the ground. Erik began to explain the reason for being there.

William Langton listened, nodding. He hadn't shaved in nearly a week and looked like a man who really had been out in the wilderness.

After Erik finished his story, Langton shook his head and said, "Steinert at first seemed like a pretty good find. But during our last interview a couple of months ago we were talking and suddenly he began to recount how he had engineered all this evidence, fingerprints mostly. He talked about Dr. Morley here. He thought it was pretty funny. I thought he was demented, but soon it became apparent that he was bragging, trying to impress us with his dirty tricks, his capabilities. I don't think he was lying about the tampering. He did enough lying on the polygraph tests. On the fingerprints, though, he just provided too many details on how he had done it. It was more than just the Dr. Morley case. There may have been dozens. Steinert kept saying he was doing it to assure society that the real criminals went to prison, to safeguard society." Langton shook his head, "But you know. That's not what it was all about. It was self-aggrandizement. He wanted to look important in the eyes of others, especially if he considered the others to be important. And he also was doing it for his own personal gain."

Langton agreed to return to Washington, bring back a copy of the videotape and testify. "I think the kids were getting bored with the hike," he said smiling at his son and daughter.

"It just got pretty interesting," his son said.

LaFabre recommended they camp that night by the pool they had passed a little while ago. They headed back and in less than an hour they were at the site. They erected their tents, forming a crude semi circle. Erik offered to cook.

"What?" Caitlin asked.

"Basmati rice, a little dahl, some bread that I brought."

"You've been carrying all that food for all these hours?"

"It wasn't that bad. It's all dry. I just have to add water, spices, a little onion, garlic and cook it. There's no more than seven or eight pounds."

"I'm going down to the pond, see if I can wash up," Caitlin said. She walked to her tent and retrieved a small towel and a small plastic box with hand soap. She headed around an outcropping of rocks and trees to a secluded area of the pond where a stream emptied into it. She took off her boots and top and athletic bra, checking over her shoulder to make sure no one was near. Her shorts were a quick drying synthetic fabric that she thought she could leave on. Caitlin waded into the water. It was cold and startling. It was colder than the Minnesota lakes she had been accustomed to. She eventually dunked her head and pulled the soap from her pocket to wash. With her hair lathered, she turned her head over her shoulder and saw Martin about thirty feet away. He was watching her. She didn't know for how long. He mumbled an apology, turned and walked away. She dunked her head to rinse the lather out. She was embarrassed, angry and curiously titillated.

When she returned to the fire she saw Erik starting to work on his meal.

Anita asked, "Well how about cocktails?"

Everyone laughed.

"You men are so crude," Anita said. "Guys might like roughing it, but I, quite frankly, enjoy a little civilization." She pulled a plastic liter bottle of one hundred fifty-one-proof vodka and a jar of powdered orange drink from her backpack. With everyone's eyes following her, she walked to the pool, reached down and pulled out a plastic bottle of water she had stored there to cool before they had put up the tents.

Anita handed Morley the bottle. He looked at the label. "A hundred fifty-one-proof? You trying to kill us?"

"Don't worry, I'll dilute it a little," she explained. "With a hundred fifty-one-proof I only have to carry one bottle. Travel light is my motto." She collected cups, made a plain orange drink for Langton's children, then made cocktails while Erik sliced onions and minced garlic. She brought the first drink to Langton and said, "I call this cocktail a Trail Blazer."

They toasted the mountains and the CIA.

Martin had slipped off his hiking boots and socks. After the toast, Anita looked at one of Martin's feet and pointed, "You've got a blister, Doc."

"Yeah," he admitted sheepishly. "They're new boots."

"We'll have a couple of drinks and then I'll operate," Anita declared. "I do my best work under the influence of rot-gut."

Later she went to Martin with a safety pin. "Now Doc, this, I promise, is going to hurt." She laughed. "You like my bedside manner?" She nudged him in the ribs.

"This is not necessary, Anita, I can do it myself."

Everyone stood around the two as though they were in an

old nineteenth century auditorium for viewing surgical procedures.

"Doc, you know what they say? The man who operates on himself has a fool for a surgeon." She sat down, pulling him with her, picked up his foot, and placed it on her lap. She had a bottle cap full of vodka, and stirred the pin in it, then pierced Martin's blister. "Does it hurt?" she asked. Martin said no. "I'll see if I can do better." She jabbed a couple more times and pressed fluid out of the blister with her thumb. Then she poured the vodka onto the blister. His leg stiffened. "I'm purifying your wound," she explained. "Is that good enough?"

"I think so."

"I can always go to the fire for an ember to cauterize the damn thing."

"I think the vodka killed the bacteria."

When the blister finished drying she bound the wound with a Band-aid.

They sat around the fire where Erik was cooking. The aroma of garlic and onions in cumin, turmeric, and other spices intensified everyone's deep hunger. "I've never had Indian food before," Langton's son said.

"Me, either," his sister added.

"I think they've been perfecting this cuisine for five thousand years," Erik said.

"The only Indian food I ever ate was native American," LaFabre said. "I've eaten just about everything in these mountains, some things you wouldn't care to hear about."

"There ought to be a lot of game and stuff," Martin said.

"Yeah, that's what you'd think," LaFabre answered. "But, there's not much up here to eat. Some deer. Moose were gone, but a few are coming back. Lots of coyotes. Maybe we'll hear them tonight. Legend says Adirondack is Indian for 'Barkeaters,' and that's what they called the few Indians who lived in these parts. Smart ones lived down in the Mohawk Valley. Only people who lived here in the rough full-time in the last hundred fifty years have been hermits and guys like me." He scratched his scruffy head.

Caitlin helped Erik with the food, squatting on her haunches and stirring his dahl while he made the rice. She kept a distance from him because the wind seemed to shift, blowing smoke in his face every time he moved. Finally the meal was completed and Caitlin served everyone while Erik pulled out pita bread, apologizing because it wasn't Indian-style naan.

"Well, Erik," Martin said. "This is going to be the most memorable meal of my life. It's my ticket to freedom, and I've never tasted anything better. Thank you for the food and thank you for locating Mr. Langton."

They swapped stories for a while. LaFabre described winters in the Adirondacks. Everyone except LaFabre eased closer to the dwindling fire.

Later, as night had fallen, they headed toward their tents. Erik and Martin crawled inside theirs. They undressed to their underwear and scooted into their sleeping bags. The night would be cool in the mountains. Erik turned off a little battery-powered light he had brought with him. Except for dark amorphous forms, they couldn't see much of each other.

"Erik," Martin said, "would you mind if I ask you something about Caitlin?"

"No, go ahead." He was lying on his back staring at the nearly invisible ceiling of the darkened tent.

"I was wondering if you and she are. . . are, dating?"

Erik laughed slightly, almost a snort. "You mean you want to know if we're lovers?"

"I suppose that's the precise way of putting it."

"No. We're just friends," Erik seemed to sigh. "At one time I sort of harbored a notion that we might become more than good friends, but it never evolved."

"Umm," Martin replied, rolling onto his back.

"Why? Are you thinking about – ?"

"It crossed my mind, but I should wait until my legal affairs are settled."

"Good idea," Erik muttered. He rolled over.

Two tents down from theirs Caitlin and Anita crawled into their sleeping bags.

"You tired, Anita?" Caitlin asked.

"I am fucking dead."

Caitlin chuckled.

"The only reason I'm not really dead is the money. It keeps me alive. What about you, Caitlin, you tired?"

Caitlin responded with a soft snore.

CHAPTER FORTY-THREE

Adams County Courthouse maintenance workers repaired the air conditioner over the weekend. The trial resumed at nine on Monday as the heat wave finally broke.

Caitlin's first witness was another attorney who described what Caitlin was still calling "miracle evidence." Steinert sat toward the back of the courtroom, holding the hand of a pretty blonde woman who he had once described to Caitlin as his "Significant Other' – the woman who had recorded the detective's appearances on television newscasts and helped collect news clippings for his scrapbook. She seemed nervous, and should be, Caitlin thought as she envisioned the outcome of the trial.

Wollman was able to blow holes in the testimony of Caitlin's most recent witness. Finally, Wollman was more than annoyed with her tactics. "Your Honor," he said. "This court and the jury have been subjected to a number of witnesses who have testified to the most amazing phenomenon of our times – defense attorneys who admit that they were surprised to learn that their clients' fingerprints were found at the scene of the crime they were charged with committing." Courtroom spectators laughed. "Is Ms. Schroeder going to continue this *ad infinitum?*" Wollman asked.

"Ms. Schroeder," the judge stated, "you are beginning to repeat yourself with little to suggest that you are going to come to any substantive conclusion."

"Your Honor, the defense has been trying to establish a pattern of questionable practices on the part of the Criminal Investigation Division of the Enola State Police Post. Our next witness will elevate further doubt and incriminate certain detectives.

News reporters, who had been lulled, suddenly stiffened to attention.

"It better be good, Ms. Schroeder," the judge cautioned.

It was only mid morning and Caitlin needed to make it until noon recess. Langton and Erik were expected to arrive at eleven at the airport.

She called Sgt. Willie Clemens to the stand. The sergeant described his position with the Enola Post and his involvement in the investigation of Laura Morley's murder.

Eventually the sergeant testified as he and Caitlin had discussed that night in Sarah's Restaurant and later at a second meeting. "I'm convinced," he said, "that several of our investigators have been tampering with evidence for at least the past four years."

The courtroom stilled abruptly to just the sound of pens scratching across reporters' notepads.

Sgt. Clemens named the investigators he thought were involved, citing Steinert as the detective who seemed to have engineered most of the tampering. The detectives in the courtroom stared sternly at Clemens during his testimony. The sergeant tried to avoid their eyes.

Caitlin: Sergeant, could you recall for the court what you witnessed, if anything, in the handling of material evidence at the scene of the investigation of Laura Morley's murder, specifically the gas can that is now tagged as state's evidence?

Clemens: I had gone back to my car to retrieve some more latex gloves we use to avoid contaminating evidence. It was about ten o'clock in the morning of December 31. Investigator Steinert was in the little woods just on the left side of the driveway facing the garage. He was stooping to look at a gas can. He picked it up by the handle. His fingers were bare, no latex gloves. This was not standard operating procedure. I remember walking back to the victim's house thinking we were getting a little sloppy in our investigative work. Frankly, after picking up the can by the handle I don't know how he could have gotten clear prints of anyone, or at least convince a jury that the evidence had not been contaminated.

Wollman quickly objected, but Caitlin responded saying Sgt. Clemens was an expert witness whose testimony bears relevance. Judge Grossman concurred with Caitlin.

During cross-examination, Clemens admitted that Steinert's one finger may not have touched or disturbed any fingerprints on the can.

On Clemens's testimony regarding evidence tampering, Wollman asked, "Do you have any proof, any hard facts?"

Clemens: No, sir. I've testified to what I have heard and what I have experienced. They just come up with evidence whenever they need it, and their work gets sloppier. To me, as a police detective, it is at the very least, suspicious.

Wollman: But you have no proof of any of this? And you have never witnessed any direct tampering? This is just casual observation. Is this correct?

Clemens: Not quite. I have not been a witness to anyone actually tampering with evidence. But it is wrong to say that it is just casual observation. I've been a detective for twelve years and I observe things with intent and purpose.

Wollman: Has anyone from the investigative unit

said to you that they have been fabricating evidence?

Clemens: No, sir.

Wollman: Have you overheard any conversations regarding fabrication of evidence?

Clemens: No, sir, just innuendo.

Wollman: You testified that this so-called tampering has been going on for four years. Why has it taken you so long to come forward?

Clemens: I don't know. Afraid, I guess.

Wollman: You're a strong looking man. What's to be afraid of?

Clemens: It's not that kind of fear. It's the fear that comes from within.

Wollman turned to the jury smiling and nodding knowingly. He decided to pursue a different tack now.

Wollman:You testified that you've been an investigator and Sergeant for more than ten years, have you ever been passed up for promotion?

Caitlin objected, but the judge overruled.

Clemens: Yes, three times.

Wollman: Why?

Clemens: I'm not sure. I think it was because I'm black.

Wollman: Could it be for lack of competence?

Clemens: No, sir. I've received citations for good work.

When the witness eventually stepped down, Caitlin asked to approach the bench. It was 11:40. "Your Honor, I have one more witness, a crucial witness from the Central Intelligence Agency, one who will corroborate Sgt. Clemens's testimony and provide hard evidence. He's arriving on an eleven o'clock flight from Washington. Could we recess until one-thirty?"

Wollman started to object, but the judge stopped him and ordered a recess for lunch. "Let me caution you, Ms. Schroeder," the judge warned, "this better be substantive."

An hour later Langton and Erik arrived at the courthouse, escorted by Anita who had met them at the airport. Langton carried the video disc. Caitlin had ordered a video screen and computer for the jury to view the recording. She previewed the disc with Langton and Erik, cueing it for the segment she wanted the judge and jury to see.

When the trial resumed, she called Langton to the stand.

Caitlin: Would you state your occupation, Mr. Langton?

Langton: I'm in the Human Resources Department of the U.S. Central Intelligence Agency. I'm a personnel recruiter and background investigator.

Caitlin: Have you ever met Detective Steinert?

Langton: Yes, I interviewed him for a position with the CIA on May eighteen and again on June one.

Caitlin: Could you describe the interviews for the jury?

Langton described the interviews just as he had done in the Adirondacks. As soon as he mentioned the evidence tampering and Dr. Morley, the audience stirred loudly. The judge called the courtroom to order and Langton resumed his testimony.

Caitlin glanced over her shoulder and saw Steinert. She wasn't sure if he was squirming, but his face had paled

Wollman asked for a recess. Caitlin said she would like to introduce one more piece of evidence and complete Langton's testimony before recessing.

Steinert suddenly rose and headed toward the back door of the courtroom. As his hand reached the doorknob he paused then returned to his seat.

Caitlin introduced the videotape. Langton identified it and she played it. On television and before the entire courtroom, Steinert talked about how he had falsified evidence to assure a conviction of someone he knew was guilty. He discussed the Dr. Morley case specifically. "Mr. Langton, all of us knew Dr. Morley murdered his wife," Steinert said on the tape. He smiled. "All we had to do was prove it. Unlike terrorists captured by the CIA in the Middle East, we couldn't torture Morley." He offered a conspiratorial wink. "Know what I mean?" Langton said nothing on the tape at this point. "We had his fingerprints, so it was a piece of cake. Slam, bam, guilty ma'am. He's behind bars for the rest of his slimy life. . . ."

Steinert, who was still in the courtroom, slid down in his seat and didn't say a word, his arms folded across his chest. There were tears in the eyes of the pretty blonde Significant Other. With her right hand she reached for Steinert's left hand. And with her left hand she wiped a tear with a pair of bare fingers.

Sitting next to the couple was the man in the pinstripes. This time he was wearing a navy blue suit with dark red stripes. He seemed to pay no attention to Steinert.

Judge Grossman recessed the court. In his chambers,

Wollman said that in light of the evidence, the state was willing to drop the charges against Dr. Morley. "There's no use continuing. There isn't a person on that jury who won't vote for acquittal. "

"What are you going to do about Steinert and others involved in this ongoing obstruction of justice?" Judge Grossman asked.

"As soon as court ends I'm calling the state's attorney general."

"Good." The judge turned to Caitlin and said, "Ms. Schroeder?"

"Your Honor," Caitlin said, "I'd like to proceed with the trial. Mr. Langton was my last witness. Let it go to jury and have the whole thing finalized. Dr. Morley needs to have this put to rest, have his name vindicated. He deserves a finding of not guilty. I want him absolved, totally absolved." Everyone knew she was seeking protection from double jeopardy that with a verdict of not guilty, her client couldn't be tried again for the same crime.

Judge Grossman concurred.

They returned to the courtroom. Both Wollman and Caitlin made their summations. Wollman's was brief. The jury then left to deliberate. They returned in less than an hour and the foreman read a verdict of "Not Guilty" on all counts.

The courtroom erupted into a loud roar. Martin's daughter ran to her father and hugged him while Carlton stood back, observing. Martin turned and hugged Caitlin. Erik came forth and shook hands with Martin. Erik touched Caitlin's shoulder, smiled then shook his head with a big grin. The television cameras rolled.

One of Martin's former partners came up and congratulated him, saying, "I always knew you were innocent."

Pat Nordstrom and two nurses from the Johnson County Mobile Clinic approached Martin and smiled, saying, "I guess you were on your best behavior all along."

From the corner of the courtroom, Sgt. Clemens walked over hesitantly. His wife followed a few paces behind. She was a husky woman, blacker than the sergeant, with a huge smile on her face. The sergeant approached Caitlin and said, "Thank you for proving me right."

Caitlin leaned toward his right ear and whispered, "Thanks for being the toughest man in town. You kept this girl from drowning." She kissed him lightly on the cheek, raised his hand and announced, "My hero."

Clemens then walked off. He knew the tough part would be returning to work in Enola, still alone.

Martin put his arm around Caitlin's shoulder and raised his right hand forming a victory signal for the television stations. He offered his most ingratiating smile.

Out of the corner of her eye Caitlin could see the private investigator in the pinstripes talking with Wollman, the prosecutor shaking his head, part disgust, part consternation, total disappointment. The investigator was wagging his finger in front of Wollman's face. Caitlin wanted to know what he was telling the prosecutor.

Later, Channel Nine television led off the six p.m. news:

"State Police have begun an extensive investigation into evidence tampering by its Criminal Investigation Division at the Enola Post. This was the immediate reaction after a State Police sergeant and CIA agent testified today in the murder trial of Dr. Martin Morley that State Police had falsified fingerprint evidence to gain a conviction of Dr. Morley and perhaps dozens of others over the past five years. . . ."

Martin had declined to be interviewed by any of the reporters, saying he'd rather let his attorney speak for him.

After conferring with Martin, Caitlin made a brief statement to the media, which all of the stations carried on their six p.m.

newscasts: "While Dr. Morley certainly has been wronged, he holds no rancor and hopes that his ordeal will result in a stronger and improved criminal justice system."

Later in the evening at the airport, she sat with Erik and Langton waiting for their return flight to start boarding.

"They just got too sloppy," Erik was saying.

"The only other person who could have done it was Jim Crane," she said. "He's getting a free ride on this."

"What do you mean?" Erik asked.

"The state police post is in turmoil. The whole damn homicide unit and maybe others, except Willie, will probably be suspended until they can straighten things out. No jury is going to believe a damn thing those guys turn up, at least for a while. Meanwhile, everything gets colder and colder. Laura's murderer is going to go free – shy of a confession."

"What about all the other cases those guys investigated?" Langton asked. "What will happen to them?"

"The attorney general's office is going to have to appoint a special investigative team and prosecutor," Erik said. "Every defense counsel in a five-county area is now checking his files to see if he's got a possible case. It's going to be at least a year, probably more. A lot of guys are going to walk out of prison – finally."

Boarding time for the Washington flight was fast approaching and Langton and Erik rose. Caitlin walked them to the terminal checkpoint. She shook Langton's hand and kissed Erik on the cheek. "Thank you, Erik, for everything. We would not have won without you." She brushed back a few strands of his hair that had fallen over his forehead. "I'll call you Sunday when things have calmed down."

CHAPTER FORTY-FOUR

On Monday two weeks after the trial ended, Caitlin sat at her desk in the early afternoon, waiting for Martin to arrive. He had called, asking to stop by. She also needed to see him to put the finishing touches on her work for him.

The Morley case was the best thing that had ever happened to her, she figured. She received more clients, notoriety, and, of course, her finances improved dramatically.

She became a local hero for a short time. Caitlin had never seen the media go so crazy over an attorney before. She attributed it largely to being a woman. They wouldn't have gone this crazy over a man, but she enjoyed it anyway, recognizing that it was good for business.

By the middle of the second week when *Times Plus*, a weekly alternative feature tabloid, carried her photo on the cover, the story of her and the Martin Morley case had peaked, although the investigation into the State Patrol would continue for some time. Michael had begun keeping a scrapbook of his mother. He clipped news stories and pasted them on loose-leaf paper in a three-ring binder. He used the cover photo from *Times Plus* as the opening page of his scrapbook.

Now, after two weeks, she had become old news and life returned to normal. And as the media shifted its attention away from her and renewed interest in the investigation of the Enola State Patrol Post, as well as other news events, Caitlin began to wonder who really did kill Laura Morley. She began to think that Wollman might have a chance of gaining a conviction against James Crane. Julie, his employee with whom he had been having an affair while with Laura, would provide some damning testimony to contradict his plans to marry Laura. Whatever happened, Wollman would have his work cut out for him. Authorities would have to bring in a whole new investigative team to work with stale evidence. But worse, the public would have little trust in anything the State Police did for the next few months. Wollman's only chance was a change of venue to the other side of the state where the news had not been constantly on the public's mind. She was relieved, though, that Dr. Morley's matters were at conclusion.

Martin arrived carrying a thin, brown leather portfolio. He wore a medium gray suit, blue shirt with a silk necktie with a pastel floral design. He crossed his legs upon sitting. His shoes were expensive medium brown Italian slip-ons. Martin placed the portfolio on his lap and folded his hands on it. "Well, Caitlin, we both wanted this meeting. You go first."

"Okay, Martin. There are a couple of things we should discuss. One, as you know, you were wronged by the state and I believe you are entitled to compensation. I think you can recover considerable damages and become an even wealthier man. You certainly have the right to recover damages."

"Are you suggesting that I sue the bastards?" He grinned.

"I am suggesting that you may sue the bastards and I'd be glad to represent you." She, too, was laughing lightly.

Martin shook his head negatively. "I hate to disappoint you, but I don't want to sue."

Caitlin shrugged. "That's your prerogative." She actually felt relieved.

"I want all of this behind me. I want no more grief, no more publicity, nothing. And frankly," he paused, "I'm thinking about leaving the country for a while."

Caitlin raised an eyebrow.

"Not right away, but maybe next spring." Martin stopped for a moment then resumed, "You said you had a couple of things to talk about. What's number two?"

She pulled the center drawer of her desk out and removed several checks. "Money. First, we have a check from the life insurance company that held the policy on Laura. You'll note that it contains some accrued interest. We also have checks from the insurance companies for the two cars that were ruined by smoke, and for the contents of your house. And we have a check from my bank that covers the difference between what the insurance company paid on your home and the balance of your mortgage, which has been paid." She then handed him the checks and various papers, some of which had to be signed. "That tidies up everything that I'm responsible for."

He signed the papers with his Mont Blanc fountain pen, looked up, smiled and said, "Good. Now, I wanted to see you in order to take care of the invoice you sent me. Is it final?"

"Yes. No more bills unless you ask us to do more work."

"Good." He pulled a check out of his portfolio and handed it to her. "I do want to thank you for doing such an excellent job." He rose to shake her hand. "I am most grateful." Then he sat down again. "Will you deposit this today?"

"If you need me to wait until you make a transfer of funds, I can do that."

"No. No. Deposit today. It'll probably clear by Wednesday or Thursday."

"Why is that important?"

"At that point I will no longer be your client, right?"

"That's a way of looking at it," she said and furrowed her brow.

"And I'm no longer your physician, right?"

"I have a new physician and you're no longer in practice."

He pulled a letter from his suit coat pocket and handed it to her, saying, "This is my letter to you officially ending our professional relationship, relieving you as my attorney." She seemed taken aback, and he quickly said, "I may retain you again some day." He paused for a moment then asked, "Remember when I first retained you, when we had a drink at the Country Club, and I mentioned that I had been a bit of a philanderer?" He watched her nod. "I told you I never fooled around with patients and you said the same thing about clients.

Now we have no professional relationship and I can ask you if you'd like to go out to dinner with me Saturday night? I was thinking of flying to New York, getting a couple of rooms at the Waldorf and flying back Monday, Labor Day. What do you say?"

Caitlin shook her head in amazement over his elaborate planning then asked, "Are you asking me for a date?"

Martin cocked his head slightly, smiled and said, "Yes. Does it surprise you?"

"Yes." She didn't know what to make of it.

"Well?"

She looked at him, cocking her head slightly, too. "I don't think so, Martin. I've been representing you for a year." She shook her head negatively. "Besides, I have to be in New York Thursday through Saturday for a lawyer conference."

"Where are you staying?"

"Some hotel in back of the Waldorf, as a matter of fact, on Lexington – Loew's Summit, I think."

"Nice place. What's the conference?"

"It's a two- and a half-day seminar for trial lawyers."

"I'll tell you what. What if I picked you up Saturday afternoon, we'll take the ferry to the Statue of Liberty. I just want to celebrate my newfound liberty there. Afterwards we can have dinner. Does that sound harmless enough?"

"Sure, Martin, that's harmless enough."

***

Caitlin participated in the conference enthusiastically, but awaited Saturday with some trepidation. It didn't seem quite ethical, going out with a former client, but then it wasn't really a date. What about Laura Morley, though? Who in the hell did kill her? He could have hired someone to kill her. She shook her head as if to dispel the notion. Caitlin had to admit that Martin had some appeal, even if he was a scoundrel with women. And he is an arrogant ass. But then, there was some sort of inexplicable appeal. She figured it was Eros and Evil in a squeeze play.

Early Saturday morning Martin called Caitlin at her hotel room and said he'd be waiting for her in the lobby about one p.m.

It was a clear day and a little hot for late summer. Caitlin wondered whether she was up to climbing 354 steps to Liberty's crown.

Later, as they returned to Manhattan, Caitlin said it had been many years since she was last in New York. "But, you know, I can feel an emptiness with the absence of the original World Trade Center. Maybe it's my imagination."

"Probably. We've all been inundated for years with stories on the event." Martin paused a moment. "I suppose that sounds a bit calloused."

After the trip to the statue they took a walk in Central Park, toured the Fifth Avenue store windows then had dinner. Near midnight they went back to the hotel. Martin explained that he had taken a room at the same hotel. "Would you like a nightcap? I have an excellent port."

Caitlin declined.

"I have some important things I want to discuss." He offered his most earnest look.

She finally relented, but was a bit nervous as they walked to his room. As they entered his room he went to a table where he pulled two elegant crystal glasses.

"Did you bring these especially for tonight?" Caitlin asked.

He smiled wickedly. "Yes."

"You plan your attacks very well," she said with an amused, but cautious tone.

They took a sip. He set his glass down and then kissed Caitlin – what seemed to her like a kiss that would last forever. He pulled back and said, "I've been wanting to do that for a long, long time."

"You control your passions well." She offered a puzzled smile, wishing she weren't there, but unable to walk out.

He began to unbutton her blouse. She put her hand on his to push it away.

"I've had to control my passions for so long." Martin said, pulling the blouse from the waistband of her skirt. She moved back slightly. He ran his hands around her bare midriff to her back and kissed her on the side of her face. "I've been so tight for the past year, for more than a year, very careful not to let an unguarded thought escape."

"What do you mean?" Caitlin asked, suddenly fearful, his tone alarming her. She pulled back another inch.

"Given the situation I was in, the slightest slip of tongue could have meant that we wouldn't be here today."

They were both silent for a moment. "Are you trying to tell me, Martin, that you actually did kill Laura?" She stepped back a pace, hands on her hips.

"You mean you didn't suspect that all along?" he asked with a tone of incredulity.

"No," she said, stepping back farther. "I believed you were innocent all along. I mean I had moments of doubt. In the very beginning and when they found the fingerprints. But I always had this suspicion of innocence."

"Amazing." He scratched the side of his head lightly. "I didn't think I was that convincing."

"You were so convincing on the park bench outside Enola when you told me about the fingerprints. And I remember it well as you said, 'Absolutely impossible.' There was such passion in your voice, as though it truly were impossible."

"It was absolutely impossible. I was exceptionally careful about everything. I cleaned and oiled the gun wearing surgical gloves, never touching it with bare hands. I wore gloves when I bought the gas can and never touched it with bare hands. At the house, I wore surgical gloves throughout the whole procedure. I took the right glove off once, but never touched anything except Laura. My fingerprints could not have been on that gas can or the gun. It really *was* impossible."

"Why did you do that?"

"What?"

"Take your glove off for Laura?"

"I tied her to the bed with my good silk neckties. What a waste. She thought I was Jim Crane. I ripped her nightgown off her. She was becoming sexually aroused, so I took the glove off my right hand and played with her clitoris until she had an orgasm. And then I shot her with my gloved left hand."

Caitlin jumped, as though she had just heard the pistol shot. "Oh, my God, this is awful. You're awful." She put her hand to her forehead, suddenly realizing she was alone in a room with a killer.

"Don't think of it that way, Caitlin. You might try to think of it more as a medical procedure. She was a diabetic, an alcoholic. The medical examiner even testified that her liver showed early signs of cirrhosis. She clearly longed to die."

Caitlin was pacing. "She didn't ask to die. She didn't call for Dr. Death. You just killed her because it was convenient and rewarding."

"With her drinking she obviously had a death wish. I just helped fulfill her desire."

"But she wanted it on her own terms, not yours." She put the back of her hand on her forehead momentarily. "I bet you set the house on fire to throw police off the trail, too."

"Partly," Martin admitted, "but there was more to it than just that. I knew I never could get the full value of the house on the open market, but the insurance company would certainly pay the right price based on their appraisal several years before, when the market was at its peak." He seemed almost gleeful.

"This is callous, absolutely premeditated."

Martin sat on the bed cross-legged. "Yes, it was." He uncrossed his legs and leaned forward slightly. "I mean, that's why I retained you in the first place. My regular lawyer could have handled the sale of the practice and those divorce papers, but he's not a criminal lawyer. And I needed a good one. You." He pointed right at her. "I didn't want a flashy law firm. It might have made me appear guilty. And it would have cost too much."

"You expected to be arrested?"

"No, but I thought it could happen. Who knows? I had planned this for several months before retaining you. As you said, I am thorough if anything. If I were to be arrested I wanted a good lawyer who knew his way around the criminal courts. It was you – a former prosecutor, and a defender of some of the worst scuzz. I knew you'd break your back defending me. And it turns out better than I ever expected. I was found not guilty and can't be tried again." He rubbed his hands together. "I mean, I had every little detail planned. I gave Angela a sedative so she wouldn't wake up while I was gone. I took an amphetamine to keep me alert and moving. Intimidating Laura so she would stay at home. I decided on this method rather than fixing her medication. That was too much like a physician. No, a gun seemed like the perfect choice. No detail was overlooked." He shook his head. "Except that the police were crooked." He shook his head again to emphasize his incredulity.

She picked up her glass of port, was about to take a swallow, looked at the glass and quickly set it down. "I feel deceived and betrayed."

"Why, because we were about to make love?"

"That has nothing to do with it. It's just that I had believed in you."

"Without that belief I wouldn't have gotten such a superb and impassioned defense. I needed the passion of your conviction as well as your legal skills."

"Thanks a hell of a lot." She shook her head. "Look, I'm going back to my room." She thought for a moment then asked,

"Why did you relieve me as your attorney? Is it because you're afraid if you sue the state over false arrest, the truth might come out?"

"Not at all. I wanted to make love with you and figured you wouldn't if we still had a professional relationship."

"I guess you lose."

"I haven't lost at anything in a long time. I'll have to savor this rare moment." He raised his port glass toward her then took a small sip.

She shuddered slightly. "You know, Martin, I could have handled the deception part. I mean, no client likes to say, 'Yeah, I did that dirty deed.' But I let my guard down. I knew better." She shook her head, more disappointed with herself than the revelation.

"Well, you wouldn't have learned the truth."

"Jesus, Martin," Caitlin was shaking her head again. She buttoned her blouse, tucked it in and realized again that she was in the room alone with a murderer. Caitlin reached for her purse and added, "You'd have found a way to tell me, or someone, to bolster your ego. Hell, Martin, you have no moral values."

"Of course I do, Caitlin. They're just different than yours. Anyway, you're taking this all wrong. You should have just let yourself go." Martin rubbed a finger on his temple for a moment. "You would have enjoyed it – a lot."

She walked out, closing the door softly behind her.

CHAPTER FORTY-FIVE

For the next month, Caitlin was morose, not to the point where it affected her work, but enough so that her son noticed. She knew it was stupid. She had performed her job, providing Martin the best possible defense. That's what lawyering is all about, she reasoned.

And she didn't know what to do with the information she now had. Martin Morley had admitted killing his wife to Caitlin after ending their client-attorney relationship. He couldn't be tried again. Not for murder, but there was always insurance fraud. It was a true dilemma – he had been a client and to turn him in for fraud would seem inappropriate even if she were no longer his attorney; and to do nothing smacked of being an accomplice, or at least turning an eye to a major felony.

It was early October, Saturday morning, and Caitlin was making breakfast for Michael. It was just a bowl of cereal and a glass of orange juice. She made the same thing for herself. They sat at the table quietly, Michael reading the back of the cereal box. He had a soccer match in an hour and a half.

"Mom," he looked up, sliding the box aside, "why don't you take a vacation?"

"What do you mean?"

"We didn't go camping this summer. You were too busy. I think that Dr. Morley trial wore you out."

"You're in school. We can't take a vacation." She tried to change the subject.

"Not me. I mean you. You seem down in the dumps ever since you went to New York. I thought you were going there for fun, but it looks like you lost a trial. So that was hardly a vacation. You're just different. You don't even bring pizza home anymore."

Caitlin smiled and laughed a little at that. "Where would I go?"

"Just a little vacation." He suddenly became animated and excited. "Next weekend is Columbus Day weekend. Three days. Courts are closed. Dad could take care of me. Visit your friend, Erik, in Washington. Or that other friend in Philadelphia. I can't remember her name."

"Celia Walters."

"Yeah, well, why don't you do it? You need a break. I need a break. I'm sick of eating frozen health food dinners – no fat, no calories, no taste."

Caitlin laughed. "I suppose the dinner table has been a little dreary lately. I find it hard to believe, though, that we haven't had pizza in over a month." Sudden inspiration struck her. "After your soccer match let's have your teammates over for a pizza tasting. We'll get pizzas from different restaurants and we'll have the official Michael Brownell Pizza Taste-Off. We'll make it an annual event. Get me that list of your teammates and I'll call their parents to make arrangements."

She called the parents, apologized for a last minute idea, and invited their soccer players. All but one of the parents were able to let their children attend. She searched the Yellow Pages of her phone directory and selected six pizza parlors.

After the game, her home was inundated with boys in black nylon shorts, dirty white shinguards and bright blue shirts with black numbers. At twelve-thirty the delivery cars arrived, almost as a caravan. Inside, she had set up a chart, listing the restaurants. Across the top she had written judging points: taste, crust, stringiness of cheese, topping, and design.

She cut the pizza into slices small enough for everyone to taste every pizza. Then she had them rate each pizza on a score of one to five for each category.

After everyone had left, Michael said, picking at the topping of one of the remaining slices of pizza, "That was a pretty good gimmick to get your mind off taking a mini vacation."

"Ploy, Michael, not gimmick. That was a ploy and it worked."

He smirked, swiped at his mouth with a wrist and said, "Good pizza, though."

"Tell you what. I'll call my friend Erik and see if he isn't busy. If he is, I'll call Celia, and if she is, I'll just fly to Minneapolis and goof around there. How about that?"

She called Erik later and said, "My son told me to get out of town for a few days. I was

wondering if you might be able to take an old friend around Washington next weekend?"

He was thrilled. He wouldn't let her stay at a hotel, insisting she stay in his spare bedroom.

"On one condition," she said. "I buy dinner and you choose the place."

"Any other requests?"

"Friday, when I get in, meet me at the Vietnam War Memorial. I want to see that before I do anything else."

Caitlin had never been to Washington for fun, just business. A few days before she left for the capital, she wrote a list of places she wanted to see in addition to the Vietnam War Memorial: Washington Monument, White House, the Capitol, Lincoln Memorial, the Holocaust Museum and others. She decided to be a first-rate tourist. She bought a guidebook and street map, and figured out how to find the Vietnam War Memorial.

On Friday afternoon she arrived at the Mall, parking her car across from the Department of the Interior and slowly walked along Constitution Avenue to 21st Street. She couldn't tell if she was in the right place. She could see the Lincoln Memorial in the reflecting pond. And to her left at the other end of the Mall was the Washington Monument. She followed a sidewalk into the Mall. She noticed a stand with a directory of those who had died in Vietnam and had their names carved in the marble. It was a little after four o'clock. She continued on the sidewalk to the Memorial. Carrying her car keys in her hand, playing with the old dog tag her brother had given her so many years ago, she walked beside the long, ominous black wall of thousands of dead men's names. She supposed there were women on that wall, too, but it's really dead boys. She rubbed her right hand across some of the names on one of the marble panels, and kept playing with the dog tag with her left, rubbing her thumb over the embossed name of her dead brother. Klaus and Kathleen, her parents, were never able to bring themselves to visit the Memorial. They just didn't want to refresh their sorrow.

She examined the panels abutting landscaped embankments. She couldn't understand the order of the placement of names. Caitlin walked the length of the wall to the west toward the Lincoln Memorial, pausing from time to time to see up close the thousands and thousands of names engraved in the black marble. She ran her hand over some of them again, feeling the chiseled letters. She lingered for a long time toward the center at one panel that seemed to rise a foot or two above her head. At the base were flowers and little gifts and mementoes left by visitors. At the west end were more stands with catalogs. She looked at one and figured out how the names were placed. She found her brother in the thick book. She went back to the wall and located the panel, finding his name nestled between a Runyon and a Schwartz. Caitlin traced the outline of each letter of his name with her fingernail.

"Pretty powerful, isn't it?" a voice from behind said.

She turned, startled by Erik. Tears had filled her eyes.

"Sorry, Caitlin." He pulled a handkerchief from his pocket and handed it to her. "I come here once in a while. It saddens me, too. I come for a sense of futility."

She kissed him on the cheek.

"Whose name were you looking at?" He went to the spot where she had been touching. "Schroeder. Your brother?"

"Yes."

He rubbed his hand over the name and shuddered. "Sean S. What's the S for?"

"Seamus."

"Sean Seamus Schroeder. Ah, those *S*s slide so smoothly, so sibilantly."

"Mom, with our German surnames, wanted to make sure we didn't lose track of our Irishness."

"What's your middle name, the *M*?"

"Mary."

He pulled two sheets of blank white paper and a pencil from his attaché case. He stooped, pressed one of the sheets against her brother's name and rubbed the pencil's lead sideways, back and forth over the surface, tracing the name. He repeated it with the second sheet of paper. He stood up, handed them to Caitlin and said, "I've seen people do this here."

A friend from the agency had dropped Erik off at the monument. They walked to Caitlin's car. She tossed him the keys. "You drive." She paused. "I was just a tiny kid when he died at the end of the war. I didn't even know what it was all about. I still don't." She paused and added, "Sean Seamus, I hardly knew ya."

Erik looked at the dog tag on the key ring and then at Caitlin. He unlocked the door for her. As they drove toward his apartment, he said, "I've got a pretty nice brownstone. Renting it for a song. It's a nice price for living on the edge of an urban war zone."

"You know what happened Erik?"

"What?"

"He killed her. Damn Martin did it."

Erik shook his head. "I didn't like the guy, but I thought he was innocent, especially after you proved evidence tampering. How did you find out?" He looked at her. "Oh."

"What's that supposed to mean?"

"Nothing."

"Well, you're almost right, if you're thinking what I think you're thinking," she said. "But I didn't go to bed with him."

"Well, that's a relief."

"Erik!"

"I was a little jealous, I suppose. Up in the mountains when we lay down to sleep, he asked me if you and I were lovers. Of course, I told him we weren't. He said that after the trial he wanted to court you."

"Erik, you were jealous?"

"Yeah. I mean if I wasn't going to be your lover, I certainly didn't want that sonofabitch to be your lover."

"Well, isn't that something?"

"Men are nuts," he admitted.

"Yeah," she agreed then told him what happened. She had finished the story by the time they reached his apartment.

They walked up two flights of stairs, the aroma of East Indian food cooking in a first-floor apartment followed them. Inside his apartment she used her cell phone to call the office. Maggie was still there. "Dr. Morley called," the receptionist told her. "He wanted an appointment to see you. I set it up for Wednesday at ten a.m."

Caitlin sighed wearily and asked if there was anything else.

"Yes, Ms. Schroeder, a Scott Seager, a private insurance investigator, also wants an appointment with you. I set him up for two p.m. Wednesday."

Caitlin finished talking with her and immediately told Erik.

"So what are you going to do?" he asked.

"Meet with Martin." She shook her head. "I was kind of hoping all of this would just go away. Maggie also made an appointment for Scott Seager, a private insurance investigator who sat through the preliminary, every court appearance, and the trial."

Erik escorted her to the spare bedroom his daughters used when in town. She was wearing a pair of khaki slacks and a blue Oxford cloth blouse open at the throat. Erik suggested she not change into anything else. She slipped on a brown blazer with a gold weave. She didn't like what she saw in the mirror. She pulled her dark hair back on either side and inserted a pair of brown tortoise clips. She unbuttoned two buttons of the blouse. Now she thought she looked like a harlot in men's clothes. She re-fastened the second button. The look wasn't right. She peered into the small case of jewelry she had brought with her and fished out a gold necklace. It was a simple chain. Then she removed her earrings, switching to a pair of gold shells. She looked in the mirror then lifted her wrist up: a button was missing from the jacket's sleeve. There was nothing she could do; she would never look right.

Returning to the living room, Caitlin said, "Are you sure I'm dressed okay."

"Caitlin, you're absolutely beautiful."

He meant it, and Caitlin could tell.

"You're dressed perfectly. It's just an Indian restaurant we're going to. Nothing fancy, but the food is exquisite. And khaki," he said pointing at her slacks. "What could be more Indian than that?" He began to leave the living room. She followed him. "Now to do this right," he said, "we need a gin and tonic for starters. Dinner's not 'till nine."

In the kitchen a bottle of blue Bombay gin with its black ink drawing of Queen Victoria stood on the counter next to quinine water and lime wedges. He quickly made a pair of drinks.

"So now you're an Anglophile? Or is that at Rajophile?" Caitlin asked.

"Something like that. I've given up on the French. No more French cuisine unless I have to, and no more French phrases, unless, unless it's the . . . ." Erik couldn't think of the phrase.

"*Le mot juste,*" Caitlin suggested. "Did some woman tell you all that French stuff was phony, and then refuse to go out with you?" She was leaning her buttocks on the kitchen counter, holding the drink in her right hand.

Erik looked a little sheepish for just a moment. "You're close. The reason for the Indian food, however, is the couple down stairs. Their kitchen aromas were too inviting."

They finished their drinks. Erik walked to her and took her

glass. He set it and his on the counter just behind her. He put his hands up to her left ear and began unfastening the earring. "Pretty earring," he said. "Prettier ear."

"What are you doing?"

"Unfastening your earring."

"Why?" She stood perfectly still.

"I want to nibble on your ear."

"Are you trying to seduce me?"

"Yes."

They kissed and became lovers. It was a bit awkward, but with great desire and passion. And they laughed afterwards, not about the lovemaking but about things that amused them.

It was still early in the evening, nearing eight o'clock. "This is a good time for making love," Caitlin said. She still had the gold chain on and one earring, but nothing else. "We can still go out to dinner, come back and do it again."

"And then, as midnight approaches," Erik was drawing circles around her navel, "we could do it one more time."

"You know, I often wake up at three in the morning."

"That's the best hour for making love," Erik said. He was now drawing lines from her hipbone to her knee.

"And dawn. It's October. Dawn must be about seven. A perfect time for love." She giggled and said, "That tickles."

"I didn't know you giggled."

"Very girlish, isn't it?" She rolled over and scratched his eyebrows lightly. "I have a very important question, Erik, being here naked and in a state of rapture."

"Rapture?"

"Yes, rapture. Do you remember when you taught me how to tie a necktie?"

"Yes, in the men's room at the office. A perfect studio."

"Now, go back to your Francophile ways for a moment. You said back then that the French had a phrase for women's breasts. I'd like to know what it is, especially since you have developed such a fondness for mine."

"I'm sure the French have many phrases."

"I think it regarded smallish breasts."

He couldn't see the twinkle in her eyes, but he sensed it. "But yours aren't small."

"But what's the phrase?"

"Oh, it's something a young university man might say."

"Like an American just out of college and touring France for a year."

He laughed. "Yes."

"Well?"

"Elle a assez pour le creux de la main d'un brave homme."

"My French isn't good enough for that," she said.

"Elle a. She has. *Assez.* Enough." He took her finger and put it on the center of his palm. *"Pour le creux.* For the hollow. *De la main d'un brave homme.* Of a brave man's hand."

"Indeed you were." She stared at his face for a moment and said, "That's one heck of a triumphant grin you have there."

"Can you blame me?"

They laughed and a few moments later finally left for the restaurant. It was only a mile away on the second floor of a two-story building, just above a karate studio. "It's a touch tacky. It's where east meets east," Erik explained.

The host seated them at a table large enough for four, and Erik ordered two Kingfisher beers. Recorded sitar music played softly in the background. Hanging on the walls were what looked like velvet paintings of scenes from the Kama Sutra. "Very appropriate art for tonight," Caitlin observed. A broad grin enlivened her face. The room was nearly filled with diners. Despite the velvet art, the restaurant was on the verge of being discovered.

"On Monday or Tuesday nights it's not nearly as crowded or as loud," Erik said. "You can hear an occasional thunk below as karate students throw one another. But the food's good."

"That was a marvelous Indian meal you cooked in the mountains. Imagine Basmati rice and dahl at the top of the

Adirondacks."

"It was Anita's hundred fifty-one-proof vodka that made that night," Erik replied. He paused for a moment then said, "You're still bothered by the Dr. Morley business, aren't you?"

"I suppose so, but not as badly as before. You have a nice quieting effect on me."

"I'm going to give you some advice. One, you did a hell of a job defending him, just what you were supposed to do – nobody else could have done it as well. Two, you're taking all this too seriously. Three, why not see what's up the insurance investigator's sleeve, but play your cards close to the vest. The prosecution only charged Morley with insurance fraud for the life insurance on his wife, never for insurance fraud for torching the house and cars."

"I wondered about that in the beginning, but just figured Wollman didn't want to complicate matters. Who knows."

He took a swallow of beer and said, "Your problem is that you were a reporter and a prosecutor and now you're a defense attorney. The result is constant conflict: you want to give your clients the best representation that they're entitled to, and at the same time you still want justice. Maybe you'll get both."

She laughed and asked, "And the reporter part?"

"It's a good story."

She laughed and asked, "Any more advice?"

"There is a fourth thing: So you slipped and almost slept with Martin, so what? Hell, I actually slept with him."

"Really?" Caitlin asked as her right eyebrow rose.

"Yeah, we shared my pup tent up in the Adirondacks. Remember? We didn't do anything, of course. But we did sleep together, which is more than I can say for you."

Caitlin was smiling and twirling her beer glass. "You always make me feel good, Erik. When I was a reporter I always needed a strong editor, someone to make me think straight and help me write clearly. I wish you were back in the office."

Just then, before she could become maudlin, food began

arriving, altering the mood at the table. Erik had ordered ahead. Crispy, seasoned papadum came first, quickly followed by dahl and *pouri*. Then a mound of rice with peas and cumin seed arrived, followed by a platter of assorted foods. There were also three chutneys and a bowl of cucumbers in yoghurt, and little bowls of coconut and peanuts. Soon there was no room on the table. "I may have over ordered," Erik finally admitted.

They dug into the food with gusto. Erik talked about his own job, admitting that it was rather boring, but the city was exciting. When they finished their meal both of them looked like they couldn't move. Erik suggested they take dessert home with them. "I'm mixing cuisines, but I'll make some Turkish coffee to go with *golub jaman* and *kheer.*"

Caitlin didn't know what those things were, but she agreed. "I bet it never comes to that," Caitlin said.

"What?"

"We'll never eat dessert. We're going to end up in bed."

"That's where you're half right and half wrong." Erik was making precise gestures. "First." His hands had long, strong fingers. "First we make love." He waved his hand slightly. "It'll be midnight. Imagine making love at midnight. Then," he held his finger up as though he were about to say something very important, "we go into the living room for dessert and coffee. Just think how good it will taste. And then." He put both of his hands on hers. "Do you know what time that is?" He watched her head shake no. "Three o'clock, the best time for love."

Caitlin had been watching his hands as he talked. The hands were fascinating, even if what he was saying was delightful nonsense.

The smile suddenly dropped from his face and in a serious tone, Erik said, "You know, Caitlin, I greatly admire you. I've never known a woman like you."

"Hell, Erik, I'm no different than any other woman. I put my pantyhose on just like everyone else – one leg at a time."

Erik laughed, then stopped and watched her for a long time. She seemed to struggle for an idea.

"Are you at a loss for words, Caitlin?"

"Yes, for a change."

"Looking for *le mot juste*?"

She smiled slightly, put her hand on his and said, "Erik, *je t'adore."*

CHAPTER FORTY-SIX

By Wednesday Caitlin was still basking in the afterglow of her weekend with Erik. She hadn't felt this good in a long time. But thoughts of Martin Morley's pending visit interrupted the lingering pleasures.

Martin strode into Caitlin's office all smile, cocky and bold. He extended his hand and she shook it firmly. Suddenly, she remembered Wollman quoting Emerson: "There is an optical illusion about every person we meet." Maybe Martin was like a chunk of glass; every time you turn it the light shines differently on it, creating a different image.

The doctor settled into his usual chair across the desk from Caitlin and said as if the weekend in New York had never occurred: "Caitlin, I'm ready to take your advice."

She cocked her head and asked, "What's that?"

"I'm prepared to sue the bastards. I've given it careful consideration, and I feel they – the state police and the prosecutor – have caused me egregious harm. And I would like to retain you as my attorney. I figure it's worth several million. You can probably handle it out of court, a negotiated settlement. You work on contingency in these matters, don't you?"

She nodded without enthusiasm.

"Well then. Suppose we settle for three million dollars. After all, I'm a doctor with a besmirched reputation. Your third's a cool million dollars."

Caitlin shook her head as if she couldn't believe what she was hearing. "Martin, you have relieved me as your counselor. I prefer to keep it that way. You told me just a few weeks ago that you did, indeed, murder your wife. You gave me all of the details. With that kind of information I would be hard pressed to give you the kind of legal representation that you would require. You should look for another attorney."

"You're turning me and a million dollars down?" His voice rose what seemed like an octave, as if this were impossible for him to comprehend.

"Yes. I do recommend that you contact another law firm, however. May I suggest Durstin Barton Bidwell. Contact William Thornton. He's very good. In fact I'll put all of this in a letter to you, along with the names of a couple other respectable law firms." She folded her hands on top of her desk and waited for his response.

Martin looked at her quizzically, and then said, "Durstin Barton, that's a big firm, right?"

"Yes, and they'll be able to provide you with every bit of the legal help you will need."

"Pretty expensive, I bet."

"They'll work on contingency, just as I would. With all of their lawyers, they have a lot more artillery to give you the kind of legal firepower you'll need."

"I guess that's a good way of looking at it." He rose as a man who had suddenly realized he was wasting his time. They shook hands and he left.

Caitlin returned to her desk and began writing a letter to Martin, recapitulating their discussion. In addition to Durstin Barton Bidwell, she included three other firms for Martin to consider. She had Maggie send the letter by certified mail.

* * *

At two o'clock Scott Seager entered her office wearing a medium gray pinstripe suit, white shirt and tie. He introduced himself, explaining that he represented several insurance companies with whom Martin Morley had policies.

"First, Ms. Schroeder, that was a wonderful job you did in the defense of Dr. Morley."

She said her thanks.

"Especially since he did kill his wife."

"The jury found him not guilty."

"Sometimes you just wish that we didn't have that constitutional protection against double jeopardy." He paused a moment. "We both know he did it. In fact he confessed to you in his hotel room the Saturday of Labor Day weekend."

Caitlin suddenly pushed her chair back from her desk, saying, "You bugged our rooms, that's a damn invasion of privacy – "

"Hold on, Ms. Schroeder. I bugged only his. Laura Morley's lover, James Crane, told me that you had your private investigator photograph them. Really, what we did is no worse than that – from a personal moral perspective. I want to make it perfectly clear that we did not bug your room. But we did use some rather technologically sophisticated listening devices for Dr. Morley's room, however."

Caitlin shook her head wearily. "Get to the point."

"We plan to push the district attorney to arrest him for insurance fraud. You apparently are no longer his attorney."

"You know that, too?" She watched him nod. "Well, he relieved me of my duties a few days before I went to New York. I was there for a trial lawyer conference and he had asked to meet me there on that Saturday. He wanted to take me to the Statue of Liberty to celebrate his liberty. He originally tried to engineer a date, but I had turned him down."

"We'd like your testimony regarding what he said in his hotel room. I found the assistant manager of an old hardware store where he bought the metal gas can. His ID and testimony will stand up in any court. Had the police done decent, more thorough legwork, they might have been able to get a conviction without resorting to evidence tampering, despite your good work. For example, the doctor purchased gasoline at a Shell station ten miles away about one-thirty the morning of his wife's murder. We have an eyewitness – the attendant – who thought it peculiar that someone would be filling his Lincoln Navigator and gas can at that hour. He couldn't positively identify Morley, but the doctor paid with a Shell credit card." He shook his head in professional disbelief. "You know, no matter how smart these guys are, they just aren't smart enough – amateurs. For the most part he covered his trails very well, but left a couple of openings." Seager shook his head again as if in partial dismay.

Seager pulled out a notebook from his breast pocket, scanned several of the inside pages, pursed his thin lips and continued, "While most of the state police detectives involved in the investigation have been implicated in the scandal you uncovered, Sgt. Willie Clemens, of course, is beyond reproach. And the State Patrol can bring in some investigators from the state capitol. I think prosecutor Wollman has a case, and we're going to push for it. It may not matter what the outcome is. The insurance companies will try to get their money in a civil suit, as well. There are several ways to get some modicum of justice here, Ms. Schroeder."

For the first time that day, Caitlin smiled. She agreed with some reservation to testify to anything that would not compromise her former position as counsel for Martin Morley. She really didn't have much of a choice.

After Seager left, she called Erik.

CHAPTER FORTY-SEVEN

On November 7, Durstin Barton Bidwell filed suit on behalf of their client Martin Morley. They sought fourteen million dollars in damages. It was the big banner headline on the front page of the newspapers in the region.

Four weeks later deputies arrested Martin Morley on three counts of insurance fraud – the house and two cars. He was released on twenty-five thousand dollars bond. That, too, made as big a story on the front pages as did the lawsuit. Dr. Morley retained Durstin Barton Bidwell for defense.

Martin's children did not come home for the holidays. He kept putting money in their checking accounts. And they kept using debit cards and withdrawing cash from automatic teller machines, but they never returned his phone calls. He thought it was collusion, the two of them ganging up on him. He didn't care. They'll come around. He was certain of that.

In early January, a year and a few days after Laura's death, Lacey Larson from the *Daily News* interviewed Martin regarding his litigation and the charges against him. He accepted the interview, despite warnings from his attorney at Durstin Barton Bidwell. It would cost him three hundred and fifty dollars for the advice over the phone that he didn't take. What the hell's the preliminary exam going to cost me, he wondered before Lacey's arrival. Legal fees began to mount, though he still had a great deal of money.

Lacey was working on what the editors called an "in-depth feature." A day later Dr. Philip Wain filed suit against Martin. He bumped into Martin at the Country Club shortly after Martin had been served. Wain was in a lively mood. He seated himself at Martin's table where his former partner sat with an acquaintance. Martin's acquaintance rose, excused himself and said he would return a little later. "Hell, Martin," Wain slammed his hand on the table, forcing the glasses to bounce, "you fuck a guy's wife, that's one thing, but to make a public spectacle of it?" His voice had risen as if he were asking a question. "You know what it's like going to the office every day and everyone looking at you? I know what they're thinking and I know what the hell I'm thinking. And there's malice in my heart."

Wain ordered a drink for himself and Martin. "Hell, I don't want to be exactly anti-social," he explained the reason for buying Martin a drink. Wain's scotch arrived and he finished it in three successive swallows. "Used to be you could punch a guy out for fucking your wife. Now you have to sue the sonofabitch."

"I suppose it's more civil," Martin replied.

Wain walked off. He had also filed for divorce.

* * *

Lawyers were making more money now in Adams County, Caitlin figured, smiling, amused by everything as she talked with her office colleagues. "We were – at least I was – an endangered species before Martin Morley came along." She was scheduled to testify the next day in Martin's preliminary.

The following day she arrived at the courtroom about a half hour before she would be called to testify. She sat toward the back. Martin and his attorneys were unaware of her presence. She imagined Martin came close to a heart attack when he heard her name called.

Wollman asked her several questions about her work for Martin. She refused to answer, invoking the privileges of a client-attorney relationship.

Wollman: Ms. Schroeder, is Dr. Morley still a client?

Caitlin: No, he relieved me of my duties and obligations orally and in writing on September one.

Wollman introduced the letter as evidence. Caitlin looked at the judge who then told Wollman to proceed. He then began to extract testimony regarding Martin's admission of guilt to her.

Caitlin: On the Saturday before Labor Day, I was in New York for an American Bar Association trial lawyer's conference. Dr. Morley met me after the conference. After dinner we went to his hotel room for a glass of port. He had conveniently taken a room at the hotel where I had been staying since that Thursday. He began to make romantic advances toward me. I was distraught by his actions, especially when something he said, or the way he said it, suddenly triggered suspicion about his innocence, and I asked him: "Martin, are you trying to tell me that you actually killed Laura?" He admitted to me that he had killed his wife.

The courtroom erupted. It took several pounds of the gavel and the judge calling for order before everyone settled down. Objections by defense counsel were dismissed and the witness resumed her testimony. She provided all of the details about the murder that Martin had given her. The audience gasped when she described the death scene that Martin had related to her. Then she said: "I asked him if he set the house on fire to throw off the police. He said that was part of the reason. He told me that the real reason was because he could never sell the house for what it was worth, but that the insurance company would give him appropriate compensation."

Martin's face for the first time registered shock. He had forgotten about the letter, the timing – having admitted the murder after Caitlin was no longer his attorney. He broke his pencil in half. His two attorneys to his right glanced at him, but did not speak to him.

During cross-examination defense counsel asked Caitlin what she meant by Martin making "romantic advances."

Caitlin: He kissed me and began to unbutton my blouse.

Defense: What happened then?

Caitlin: I pulled back. Things didn't seem quite right. I was, quite frankly, distressed. Then he said something that triggered the suspicion that I testified to earlier.

Defense: Were you having an affair with Dr. Morley?

Caitlin: No.

Defense: Have you ever had a sexual relationship with Dr. Morley?

Caitlin: No.

Defense: Why were you in New York with him?

Caitlin: After he dismissed me as his attorney, he invited me to dinner in New York to celebrate his freedom. I turned him down. But since I was going to be in New York on business, he asked to see me after the conference I was attending.

Defense: Didn't you find that a bit odd, making a date with a former client?

Caitlin: It wasn't really a date, certainly not a romantic one.

Defense counsel continued in this fashion for a while longer, getting nowhere. Eventually Caitlin stepped down and returned to her place at the back of the courtroom. She stayed there for ten minutes then slipped out to avoid the media.

Wollman did not bring in his big guns – the man who filled the gas can at the Shell station shortly before Laura was killed and the credit card transaction. Nevertheless, the court ruled that Martin would stand trial.

* * *

Reporter Lacey called Caitlin after the preliminary, asking for an interview.

They sat on the sofa in the corner of Caitlin's office and talked. Caitlin mentioned that she had heard that Martin's former practice might sue. Then Lacey said she had interviewed Laura's sisters and brother, saying they would file a wrongful death suit whether Martin wins or loses the trial. "I think his children may join in some kind of suit, too."

Caitlin shook her head, a large smile on her face. "Kind of inevitable, don't you think?" "Do you think we'll see justice?" Lacey asked.

"Has he moved his money off shore?"

Lacey laughed. "No way of telling."

"The state, I suppose, has a chance of winning its case, but the bad cop scene will haunt any verdict," Caitlin said. "Whether it does or not, there will be all kinds of litigants out there: the insurance companies, Laura's family. They're all going to try for a piece of Martin Morley and his money. Even if they don't win, legal fees will eat him alive." Caitlin touched a notepad on the coffee table. She looked up at Lacey, pulled back a wisp of hair and added, "I guess it's another form of capital punishment."

END

BLACK ROSE
writing™

CPSIA information can be obtained at www.ICGtesting.com
Printed in the USA
BVOW04s1241210414

351182BV00004B/15/P

9 781612 963389